EMANUEL CULMAN

8/22/14
For Kay & Neil—
Friends.
Enjoy!
Emanuel

Dreamers:

On Becoming Authentic

Volume One of the *Dreamers Trilogy*

GORDON WOODS PRESS

"Dreamers: On Becoming Authentic"

I deeply appreciate poet Jessica Maness for taking time from her schedule to craft Alabama blues song, **The Seventh Son**, and to make it available for inclusion in this novel. Hi, Issa!

ISBN—978-0-9913842-1-1
1. Contemporary women—Fiction.
2. Visionary and Metaphysical—Fiction. I, Title.
ASIN—B00HOX72V6

Publication date—January 1st, 2014
(Mercury, New Moon and New Year)

Cover photographs/design © Erin Latterell Burk/The Darling Bud

Author contact at: www.DreamersTrilogy.com

Purchase: Code=NGVNZY4D

FOR CHERYL PLANERT

THROUGH THE LOOKING-GLASS

THE STORY

In *Dreamers: On Becoming Authentic*, Volume One in the *Dreamers Trilogy*, estranged and confused NYC bag-lady, Judith Fargoe, conjures up The Trinity to rescue her, thus initiating her extraordinary transformation. Judith's ensuing road trip across America includes a life-changing exposure to Taquinta's wisdom circle where women influence women of influence. Judith's spiritual core is revealed on a native American reservation and Judith embodies her authentic self in rural Corazon. While rallying the townsfolk in defense of the local aquifer, Judith is selected to address U.S. Senators, and, in so doing, becomes brightly conscious of the impact of her power.

The first half of this epic adventure reads like an "every woman's tale" as Judith thrusts herself on a trajectory out of a fog of confusion. As her clarity intensifies, Judith's life steadily builds momentum like Maurice Ravel's, *Bolero.* Readers who are metaphysically attuned will appreciate the story's references as Judith lifts the veil to consciousness, while those who are seeking a joyous ride will find that here.

DEDICATION

I dedicate this book to three important women in my life.

First is my beautiful and incredible wife, Cheryl Planert, who has managed to stay in love with me despite my on-going "affair" with creating *Dreamers: On Becoming Authentic* for the better part of hers and my time together. Second is my mom, Edith Culman, who taught me much that benefited me. Third is Nancy Millage who showed me a view of life I may never have seen without her help and love of the blues.

I also dedicate this book to all women and to men who enjoy their feminine aspect.

I tip my hat to the work and writings of perhaps two of the most effective women in America at defining a pathway to equality and emancipation:

Elizabeth Caty Stanton and Susan B. Anthony

ACKNOWLEDGMENTS

They say it takes a village to raise a child. Well, I think it takes a community to write a book.

Leader of the pack is Cheryl Planert. Enthusiastic supporter just begins to represent her role, and then caretaker, as if she were not doing enough. I am definitely her greatest fan! Hi, Geisha! Hi, Lucy!

For cheering from the sidelines and offering commentary and sage advice, Jay S. Kenoff of Kenoff and Machtinger has become a good buddy through the various iterations of this book's story.

I will be eternally grateful to Life Coach Natalia Reyes for slicing through my Gordian Knot to help me find my writer's voice. Tribute goes to Gideon Culman's astuteness for his introducing me to Natalia.

Add my dad, Emil Culman's impact on my political consciousness and daughter, Hillah Culman, from whom I inherited *my* IT aptitude.

Everybody deserves a fairy godmother. Mine is the late Magda Best who responded graciously and abundantly with a loving heart.

After teaching me shamanic skills, Ariadne Green gave freely of her own writing and publishing knowledge. We are friends forever.

With that inimical laugh, Guru Singh steered my writing and married me the best woman. Sat Nam! Wahe Guru!

I appreciate all my guests and studio personnel for the TV series, *Changes*, and the Institute of Noetic Sciences' (IONS) contacts of my ebullient connection, Tahdi Blackstone.

Writers need powerful teachers. Two of my favorites are Gardner McKay and John Rechy. Inspiration to write came from Irene Bagge.

Kristin and Buzz Kreiger are my First Family. Jan and Bruce Brooks are special, as are my Sisters, Mary Mitchell and ljb.

With creativity and patience, Erin Latterell Burk designed a gem of a book cover capturing the good sides of Liam and Katy.

Much appreciation goes to "comma nutso", Marty Campbell, for her heroic last minute punctuation and James Campbell power computing.

Whenever I need lyrics to a song in future, I know to ask a local poet. This time round I was blessed to be aided by Jessica Maness.

CONTENTS

STORY RESOURCES xv
PROLOGUE xvii

DAY ONE 1

EN_TRANCE 3
WON'T BE FOOLED 6
A_GAIN 12
ESSENTIAL 23
ESS 28
SENSE 40

DAY TWO 49

FRIEND 51
FERVOR 55
FELLOWSHIP 58
FLAMBOYANCE 60
FORTUNE 66
FLIGHT 69
FECUNDITY 71
FELICITY 76

DAY THREE 79

EMPOWERMENT 81
IMPROVEMENTS 91
EASEMENT 102
DIRT CHEAP 105
CLASS SOCIETY 109
TO DIET FOR 117
ONE DOWN 123
FAVORITES 135
PAPER CUT 143
ONE MORE 157
BOOBOO 163
CIRCLES 166
RETURN 173
MARCHE 179
REVELATIONS 188
TAKE A VILLAGE 192
DEPARTURES 196

DAY FOUR 203
SPIRITUS SANCTUS 205
FOXY LADY 213
REFLECTIONS. 223
TRADE SHOW 229
BORDERS 235
BLUE YONDER. 242
PRODIGAL 252
TRANSITION 266
ON THE ROAD.. 273
TURN OVER 279
DAY FIVE 287
VOICE 289
VOICES. 294
SONG'S SONG 303
TIME 308
A_LONE 320
DANCE TO THE MUSIC. 329
THE BENDS 335
RUMBLINGS 343
MAKE PEACE 351
PRELUDE 366
FORGIVENESS 374
YARD WORK 382
ACTION 394
METEOR 408
DAY SIX 419
CAKE WALK 421
HEART TO HART 429
NIGHT OF THE SOUL 435
WHAT'S THE DIFF? 440
SMOKE SIGNALS 459
DAY SEVEN 473
ON THE ROAD AGAIN 475
DAY EIGHT 485
POSTSCRIPT 487
Dreamers Trilogy Volume II -- I AM MIKA: Loss of Innocence
Additional STORY RESOURCES . . . 493

STORY RESOURCES

Over years of researching Dreamers Trilogy, *incredible people provided information for the book. Here are some of the programs adapted in the story:*

from PASSION to PURPOSE

Cheryl Planert's groups support individuals to become more conscious of inner strengths and talents, and, thereby live a more expressed and passionate life of purpose. Cheryl leads **from Passion to Purpose** groups worldwide, utilizing personal stories, vision boards, Authentic Movement, and so much more to find and nurture the creative inner child we may have suppressed.

Visit: **www.dakotalights.net**

KUNDALINI YOGA

Guru Singh was one of the first of Yogi Bhajan's American students to become a Kundalini Yoga instructor. His classes are a mix of philosophy, Kundalini Yoga and pure creativity.

Investigate: **www.gurusingh.com**

SHAMANISM

Ariadne Green is a spiritual instructor. Where she takes her students is cosmic: city Vision Quest; Shamanic Journey; animal spirits; dream interpretation; and much more. Hers is surely a parallel universe.

Learn about her writings and classes at: **www.dreamthread.com**

RAW DIET

Until I followed **Aajonus Vanderplanitz**'s diet, **We Want to Live,** and used his excellent recipe book, I had many health issues. After six months on this diet, I never in my life felt or looked so good.

Check out: **www.wewant2live.com**

YOUR COLOR, YOUR STYLE

You will never feel as good as when you dress in YOUR colors, in clothes that are correctly styled for YOUR body-shape. Imagine a wardrobe where each item works with all the others. Consider making conscious decisions about how people see YOU.

Jennifer Butler is on videos at: **www.jenniferbutlercolor.com**

ESSENTIAL OILS

There are references to *oils* throughout the Dreamers Trilogy. Investigate these all natural, plant derived, health enhancing, therapeutic oils. As a distributor of **Young Living Essential Oils®** network marketed products, purchase these "miracles in a bottle" at wholesale prices. Support Dreamers Trilogy projects - enroll with my wife, **Cheryl Planert, # 119650**, as both Enroller *and* Sponsor.

Go to: **www.YLwebsite.com/CherylPlanert**

See ADDITIONAL STORY RESOURCES at back of the book.

PROLOGUE

It came to me in Dream Time
In dreams, I am all aspects
In dreams, I know my truth
In lucid dreams, **I am all powerful**

Dreamers:

On Becoming Authentic

DAY ONE

EN_TRANCE

"*WAKE UP!*"

><

"What's up, mom?"

"Hi, sleepy head."

"Why'd you wake me?"

"I did!

"I'm connecting to a Telepath, mom. Give me a minute and I'll fill you in."

"Who're you?"

"I'm Judith. I am in the back of a car that was in a head on collision up ahead of you. Make sure they find me, Mica. I'm scared..."

"Relax, Judith. You'll be fine. Hey, you found me. By the way, it's Mika with a "k". Hang in there. Help is on its way."

"Drive along the right shoulder, mom. There's been an accident up ahead. Judith needs my help."

"Promise me you'll be careful."

"Mom?"

"Promise!"

"I promise, mom. Stop here. Oh, this is a bad one. Real bad."

"I'm coming with you, Mika. Some of these lookey loos are spaced out."

><

"Hi!"

"Where'd you pop up from? This is no place for a kid. Ma'am, this your son? Get him the heck out of here."

"Officer, there's a woman named Judith alive in the back of that car."

"I doubt it."

"Please check."

><

"There's someone crushed back here! She's alive! We need all hands on deck."

"Thanks, Mika."

"You're welcome, Judith. We're heading to the hospital so I can be your voice during your surgery."

"That will be great! Can you stay close for a while? I have a story I want to tell people—about a Dreamer."

"My laptop has voice recognition. I can dictate what you tell me."

"You are so clear."

"Considering the circumstances, you are doing amazing yourself."

"Mom, we're making a diversion. We're going to the local ER. I have to assist a surgeon bend a scalpel to convince him to listen to me speak for Judith."

"If you were anyone else's son..."

"Thanks, mom. You have the patience of a saint."

><

"We're here for Judith Fargot. She's headed for emergency surgery as we speak."

"You are...?"

"Betsy and Mika Auchin."

"Relationship to the patient?"

"Mika is in telepathic communication with Judith. He directed the Emergency Responders to find her. He needs to speak with the surgeon in charge."

"Did I miss a memo? Are we having an early full Moon?"

"If I can have you bend that metal spoon while you simply hold it by the handle, will you contact the ER surgeon for me?"

WON'T BE FOOLED

Asleep, I dream that I am sleeping.

I'm riding a subway train in New York City as they approach.

They seek me out as I create them.

I hear their conversation as they arrive.

Understand that I dream lucidly—consciously manipulating my dream while I sleep. There is no part of the dream of which I am not aware. That's how I'm able to create them and I'm able to overhear their conversation.

A woman asks, "What are we doing on this train?"

A man responds, "You have to change someone's life."

She says, "Out here? Michael, it's round about midnight."

"We're cool," Michael says. "We're The Trinity!"

A second woman pipes in, "Tell it to her!"

He stops walking, giving emphasis, gravitas, to his words.

"You need humility, Rachel," he tells her.

"Why is it always me?" Rachel whines.

"Precisely!" he says.

Michael is so—me; a magician with words.

"Relax," he says. "Let go..."

"Let God!" the second woman rounds out his statement.

"I care," Rachel pouts, protesting. "I'm heart based!"

Rachel has to be my dark side.

Yes, even a vile, despicable person like me has both a dark side and a light side. That's basic Jungian.

Michael waxes philosophical.

"There's a disconnect between your heart and your soul," he explains. "Avatars—like the Buddha, Mohammed and Jesus Christ—exemplified what each of us is capable of being. They dedicated their lives to explore their spiritual existence. They likely considered their bodies as so much clothing."

"You're into clothing, Rachel," expounds the second woman, my little culture vulture.

Sometimes, it is difficult for me to accept that what appears in my dreams really comes from me. Take that ditsy woman's response as an example. Do I truly think like that? Perhaps her comment is one of my residual memories from television or a movie.

The Trinity begins to walk again.

Miffed by the second woman's flippancy, Michael reacts.

"I'm serious, Ariel," he tells her. "I believe we are all born humble; but born into dysfunctional families. As children, humility seems to offer little by way of protection, so we discard it."

Ariel interrupts, "Now that we are all grown up..."

"Humility means humbling the ego," he completes. "We are each of us a spiritual being. Collectively, we have incredible power, as in, *When two or more are gathered, I am present.*"

Rachel cuts him off.

"So, how do I go about meeting this—this person?" she asks.

Michael says, "Anyone will do. Take her!"

Sometimes, the license taken by characters in my dreams is downright excessive. I mean, what's a gal to do?

Rachel says, "That—woman? And do what?"

That's neither polite, nor cool. Here's The Trinity encountering their Dreamer and the best they can do is to make fun of me. I need to edit myself better. I really do!

Michael tells her, "Help her regain her sense of self. Put her life to rights. Do all that, tonight!"

Rachel, disbelieving, answers, "Get real! Me? How?"

"Perform an intervention of such life affirming change she can never return to this present self," he says.

He is so the side of me that I like. Why not, considering my present state of affairs?

"Really help her," he continues. "Step into her fantasy and she will allow you to direct her. Give her your best! Become One with her."

I can imagine Rachel's stomach churning at this point. The poor doll has been given the ultimate task of being totally responsible for someone else. When she knows full well, she is barely coping with the purpose for her own existence.

Under less strenuous circumstances, my heart would have gone out to her. Right now, though, I desperately need her to want—to help—ME!

Ariel tells Rachel, "You can do it! I'll support you."

What a sweetie pie.

I admit I am something of an actor. I ham it up.

First, my right eye pops open, then my left eye. I stare, startled, amazed—uncertain if I may be hallucinating.

Even though this is my dream and all the pieces, the scenarios, the settings, the actors, the dialog—all of it—come roaring up from my imagination, I am always amazed at what I get by way of characters to play the various parts. Take these three as an example.

The man is shorter than I expected, although, I should have guessed his height from the angle his voice came in. He is self assured, confident—without being obnoxious—stocky, solid, curly black hair, tending to the Jewish look—Middle Eastern more than the Ashkenazi type. He is well dressed, elegant. He has to be; I need help big time.

I realize they are a lot younger than I expected; in their twenties.

Rachel is African American. That is a shock. Not a trace of Black accent, no inflections—none of it.

I know, I know. My prejudices are showing.

Rachel's hair is stunningly amazing—cornrows ending with dreadlocks! What a combination! What a gorgeous looking woman. Why does she have to whine? That's such a pisser.

The second woman, Ariel, is exactly what I hoped she will be—blonde, immaculate in a flowing, light blue, full length dress. She is skinny as a rail, all Pilates and Yoga, and a fawning personality—sucking up to whoever holds the floor.

Blessed are the moneyed classes, for they believe they are all powerful. Praise be to them!

They stand in front of me, holding onto the overhead hand rail, staring at me like I am a piece of meat, or worse. It's that terrifying moment when the plot dives and the audience wonders whether the director can pull the impending train wreck out from before the crash.

They are looking at me.

I am looking at them.

I alone have the realization that this is my dream. They cannot walk off and leave me. I created them. I look past them to see the reflection of who they are looking at.

Somehow, I hoped the reflected image will be different than it is; that I am no longer a bag lady—that most elegant of terms for someone female, indigent and the capitalist society's version of the untouchable class.

Witch that I am: hair matted and filthy; clothes torn and layered; skin grayed by inches thick dirt; eyes wild; teeth bare—I stare at me. Even I am in shock.

I am that creature. I know it, and, at the same time, I want to deny it. Yet I cannot be anyone else. The time for change has arrived.

So near, but so far away; change the dream. Change it! Change ME—now! Please. Enough of me like this!

Despite all my inner ranting, I remain the same.

For the longest while, as the train races along round bends past empty stations through long straight passages with only an occasional light to disrupt the dark monotony and to prove the train is in motion,

time

stands
still.

I look at The Trinity.

They look at me.

I look at my reflection.

She looks back.

Who sees the real me?

I see it in a dream. Is it real? Am I turned around, or is only my image of me real?

Then a donut appears in my reversed hand. I watch the reflection as my hand jams the donut into my mouth, quickly followed by a Styrofoam coffee cup of cold, sweet coffee to wash my mouth clear. There, I see the source; a box of donuts sits on my lap.

"Ough!" I choke on the sticky dough.

The coffee is of no help.

If not before, now I dream I am wide awake.

The subway lights flicker.

I use the light show to alternate The Trinity's clothing—first evening dress, then, angelic garb. So appropriate; my angels! I change them back and forth.

The process reminds me of paper cutout dolls from my childhood, with different clothes to dress them in. Lay one on, take it away, lay in another; in and out, on, off—evening dress, angelic garb, evening wear, angelic robes.

Sweetie pie, Ariel, breaks the ice.

"We're The Trinity," she tells me.

Michael, with the certainty of testosterone driven confidence, states, "You are the Chosen One!"

Help! I created Holy Rollers. Save me! Spare me from the misery of that conscientious citizenry who go home to their warm beds at night having done a good job of the Lord's work.

Like their Lord, we, the objects of their consciences, never sleep—only dream.

Despite his assuredness, and, my having set this up from the beginning, thus, my overhearing their approaching conversation, Michael's statement lacks excitement, inspiration.

Rachel stammers, "I have to help—YOU!"

Does she have to make it sound like I am stealing her inheritance?

Oh, well, play along with it. It's the best I have going for the evening. I raise my cup and menace them with it. They appear to be unflappable.

It's time for the gruff voice and display of hostility.

I shout hysterically, "Get away from me!"

What? You expected me to roll over, grab the brass ring and make out like a bandit? Pardon me!

Michael asks, "Surely you recognize us?"

Gimme a break!

OK, wait a minute. As Dreamer of my dreams, I need to consider every question asked as if it were being asked by me, and, therefore, I must, at the very least, consider the question, and even answer it.

So where do these folks stem from?

Let me take another bite of that donut while I give this matter thought. I look at their hopeful, expectant, youthful faces. They want something solid.

In a past time, when I first realized I had control of my life through lucid dreaming, except, back then, I did not know the term, "lucid dreaming"—anyway, there was a time...

"Ariel?" I stammer, unsure of the remote possibility. "Michael? This is amaz... You're both still the same age!"

I am having difficulty with Rachel. Then I recall a comic series I loved.

"You!" I snarl, angrily. "You are supposed to be a comic book character?"

A_GAIN

Michael is so smart, so cute. He whispers to them...

Listen up! If they're in my dream, I can hear what they whisper. Right? Right!

He whispers, "We're in. Go along with her story."

Let me give some background of which The Trinity will only receive the briefest glimpse...

I am 12 years old. I go to a party for Jackie, this girl in my class who is really overbearing. The attraction for me is to see how the other half live—let's just say I gave myself a social science project.

Who can tell, maybe I ate too much? Next thing I know, the party girl's parents call my folks. They rush over to pick me up.

To the hospital? To the doctor? Home to bed, to rest? What to do?

My folks know I am essentially as strong as an ox and decide that whatever it may be, it's fleeting. They decide to take me home. Fair enough.

Unfortunately, my condition worsens. I throw up. I suffer loose bowels. I get a temperature. I thrash about in bed.

Next morning, I am in a delirium. Mom calls Doctor Washington across town, Detroit. He will be right over. Can you imagine?

Distressed beyond belief, my dad sits on my bed wiping my fevered brow with cool, moist wash cloths. Every so often I have periods of lucidity and sit up to read.

I am the ultimate reader. My room is a library of classic children's literature. We don't have a lot of money, but, when they are able, my folks sink any extra into buying me books. I read all of them, repeatedly.

I remember them like it was yesterday. They include all 14 L. Frank Baum's *Oz* books, 4 *Alice* books by Lewis Carroll, J. M. Barrie's *Peter Pan* and a huge collection of *Nancy Drew Mysteries.*

My current favorites at that time are, *Ariel, Detective: the Case of the Missing Clue*, and *Professor Michael Explores the Pacific.* I also have an MpowRgirl comic. She does everything any Super Hero can do and then some.

My folks allow me this one comic. My mom says it is rare to have a good female role model, especially in comics. MpowRgirl does everything with the utmost integrity.

At one point, I am floating off into my fever. I see Ariel at her wedding. It is one of those rich people weddings in a cathedral with stained glass windows and the bride's "side" of the church and the groom's "side." The groom is a super handsome son of a manufacturer. The organ plays Felix Mendelssohn's, *Wedding March.* Picture perfect Ariel, escorted by her dad in grey morning tails and hat, steps onto the red carpet of the center aisle, when, CRASH!

Through the vast rose window that had, up until that moment, been casting beams of stained glass colored sunlight down on the assembly, smashes MpowRgirl. Certainly not one of her greatest moments of integrity, but, after all, I am only twelve years old.

She lands next to Ariel who immediately recognizes her.

Look at! If I have to explain everything, this story is going to bog down. They are literary characters meeting in a dream. OK?

MpowRgirl briefly explains that she needs Ariel's assistance to help me.

There is a tense, momentary stand-off.

"Go with you?" Ariel demands. "MpowRgirl, I am about to get married."

MpowRgirl answers insistently, "Ariel, Judith's in trouble. You can always wed later."

Ariel looks down the aisle to her groom. He has actually been in a similar predicament with Ariel one time before in another book, *Ariel, Detective: the Case of the Lost Will.*

The groom graciously shrugs his acceptance of the situation.

All the while, Ariel's dad, his mouth open, is gawking at the cartoon super hero standing before him. I guess the beginnings of my hormones must have been kicking in.

Anyway, MpowRgirl grabs Ariel by the arm and flies off with her back through the hole in the stained glass window.

Pretty soon, comic hero MpowRgirl, holding Ariel in full wedding dress and struggling to keep the veil off her face is flying over a small island in the Southern Pacific Ocean. Using her super vision, MpowRgirl spots Professor Michael doing his Biological Anthropology thing inside a cage belonging to a people practicing Cargo Cult.

As experienced as she is, MpowRgirl has not been in every conceivable situation. She sees bars, she sees Michael inside the cage and she jumps to the conclusion that he is being held against his will.

MpowRgirl dumps Ariel to one side to hide among coconut palms, then marches over to pry open the bars with her bare hands. Being the impetuous type, Ariel has caught up and pushes past into the cage. MpowRgirl follows in hot pursuit.

Despite the ruckus these two make arriving, Michael, overseen by the village leader and a local medicine woman, remains engrossed in healing a sick villager.

He holds his patient by her upper left arm with his left hand absorbing the negative energy of her illness. With his right hand, he holds on to a grounded wood pole, transferring her sickness back into the earth. The patient literally heals right before their eyes.

"Michael?" Ariel calls out. "Are you OK?"

Everyone looks up at the sound of Ariel's question.

Surprised, yet, with the improvisational reflexes of a comedian who is never fazed by circumstance, Michael asks, "MpowRgirl? Ariel?

What's up?"

MpowRgirl does her fists on hips, legs astride pose.

"We need your expertise, Michael," she tells him.

Anxiously, Ariel chimes in, "Judith's in grave danger."

By now, the patient is sitting up looking about, slightly bewildered by having Michael hold her arm, then seeing an African American woman dressed in comic hero primary colored Spandex, and the whitest woman she has ever seen who wears flowing white chiffon from head to toe.

Seeing her leader, the medicine woman and fellow villagers, she realizes she is still of this life. Outside the cage, excited villagers are jumping up and down with joy that their friend and neighbor is well. Her face displaying a look of amazement, the medicine woman checks the patient's vital signs.

The village leader steps around the patient and points over the shoulders of the two new arrivals.

"I am sad to hear of your friend," his voice booms at them. "However, before you leave, please, restore our sacred space."

Dreams are so wonderful like that. Everyone speaks the same language, or, at least, understands the other people.

MpowRgirl checks out where he is pointing. A sheepish look comes over her face. She strides to the opening she made and, with a few deft moves sliding her hands along the bent bars, straightens them to perfection. The villagers, including the leader, the medicine woman and the now well patient, all watch the effortless work with amazement.

That done, MpowRgirl turns back, grabs Ariel by one arm, Michael by one arm, frog marches them both to the entrance of the cage and, as soon as they exit, flies up into the sky.

All the villagers wave them off with cries of, "Good luck!"

Right then, the apartment doorbell rings. Mom answers it. I can hear muffled voices and immediately recognize Doctor Washington's sonorous tones. He hurries past mom into my room, she following with a worried look on her face.

Mom holds professionals in awe. It's embarrassing.

With my dad, it is more that male thing of simple respect. Dad rises to his feet getting out of the way as Doc scrabbles about in his black bag and fishes out a thermometer.

"Hi, Doctor Washington," I say.

"Judith," he says.

He shakes the thermometer well, checks it, and has me receive it under my tongue. He mutters something about keeping my mouth shut and not jiggling the thermometer with my tongue.

He catches his breath, pumps my dad's hand, smiles warmly at mom, nods to me, says something like, "Be a good girl," and with a huge hand on a shoulder of each of my parents, steers them out of the room.

That is good because crashing through my bedroom window comes MpowRgirl with Ariel and Michael. When they land next to my bed, I have to say, I can feel the smile around that thermometer growing so wide, it is about to burst my grinning mouth.

Michael leans across my bed, pulls out the thermometer and places it on the pillow next to me.

At least this doctor speaks to me directly.

"Hi, Judith," he says. "How are you?"

My heart is about to explode with excitement is how I am. This is definitely a new sensation coursing through my veins as I see him so close to me.

"Better now you all are here!" I say as I gaze from one to the next, enthralled.

Michael takes my right wrist and holds three fingers along the inside, smiling at me all the while. After about twenty seconds, he rolls his finger tips about a quarter inch and then "reads" my wrist again for another twenty seconds or so. Then he does the same thing with my left wrist.

I am so excited trying to deflect from this unique flush racing throughout my body; I can hear myself chatter away.

"I went to a birthday party, yesterday," I say, "And maybe I ate too much, 'cos I threw up, and my folks came and got me and I have been in bed since and..."

"Your pulses indicate food poisoning," Michael states matter of factly. "A spoonful of Castor oil will purge you."

The simplicity of the issue and its resolution shock me.

"That's it?" I say with surprise.

A fleeting thought races through my mind about Jackie's parents having loads of money and buying food that causes food poisoning.

I look past Michael at the other two standing by.

"Oh, Ariel," I ask. "Did you interrupt your wedding to be here?"

A doll to the last, she waves it off.

"You're on page 108, Judith," Ariel tells me. "This is par for the course, believe me!"

Feeling overlooked, MpowRgirl presses forward.

"Call me a party pooper," she says, "But, I was relieving a famine in sub Saharan Africa."

"And I really ought to go back to Kings College, Cambridge," Michael adds. "My sabbatical is almost over."

Voices from the adjoining room attract our attention. Doctor Washington is performing his own research.

"Tell me," he asks my folks. "What were the first symptoms you noticed, Mrs. Fargoe?"

Though out of sight, I can see my mom glance to my dad before she answers.

"She threw up and became feverish," she tells Doc. "She has always been so healthy."

His allopathic resolve cleared to land, Doctor Washington declares his intention.

"I'll give her something to lower this fever," he tells them. "And then, I insist you bring Judith in to the clinic so I can complete her immunization shots."

A chill fills the air in my bedroom. The three fictional characters look to each other for a fleeting moment. Michael picks up the slack.

"MpowRgirl," he asks. "What does Doc have in his bag?"

Using her super vision, MpowRgirl sweeps for his bag, spots it on top of my bookshelves, focuses in on it and, applying her X Ray ability, locates a bottle inside.

She reads the label out to the others, "'Antibiotic: Destroys ALL bacteria.'"

Michael leans over me, staring deep into my eyes till I get chills while at the same time my hands begin to sweat. He is so intense and, oh, ever so close.

"Judith, spit it out as soon as you can," he tells me. "He means well but, along with the bacteria, that antibiotic will kill your good intestinal flora!"

No sooner has Michael spoken these prophetic words than in comes Doctor Washington ahead of my folks. Apparently, I am the only one who can see the trio and the broken window since, as soon as Doc spots the thermometer on my pillow, he starts to make a federal case out of it.

"Now why did you do that, Judith?" he blusters.

He leans across me to pick it up. I smell his turgid breath and immediately begin to dry retch.

As he stands up to read the thermometer, my stomach cramps pass.

He shakes his head. He forages in his black bag and pulls out the bottle labeled 'Antibiotic', and then a syringe, loads it, swabs my arm with an alcohol soaked cotton pad and sinks the needle with the casual dexterity of a cowboy dropping a calf and branding it.

Michael's eyes fill with tears as he reaches a disempowered hand out to me.

"Your thoughts can override the shot," he tells me. "Be strong in your heart and mind, Judith. You can overcome the shot's effects."

Ariel is angry. She looks from MpowRgirl to Michael.

"What will protect her good flora?" she demands.

MpowRgirl shrugs her don't look at me ignorance of the topic.

Michael stammers, "She needs live lactobacillus..."

Ariel's temper flares.

"Michael!" she yells. "Enough with the doctor speak!"

"Yoghurt!" he shouts. "She should eat plain yoghurt. Otherwise her immune system will be seriously compromised."

As if he has not done enough damage, Doctor Washington picks up the books and comic from my bed to cursorily inspect them.

He finally locates his calm, bedside manner.

"You need rest, young lady," he tells me. "Perhaps your parents will bring you a television."

"Please, I want my books!" I protest.

My determination causes him to check out the books more carefully.

"These look much too stimulating," he insists.

With that, he closes them up, one after the other.

First Ariel disappears, then Michael. As he shuts the comic with extra gusto, MpowRgirl disappears, too. Suddenly, my bedroom window is not broken anymore.

Despite my folks and the Doc being in my room, to this day, I have never felt so alone.

"May I have some yoghurt, please?" I ask sweetly.

Completely ignoring me, and looking to my parents as if sealing an adult pact, Doc tells them, "Let the antibiotic do its job. She will be just fine tomorrow."

As Doc takes up his bag of tricks to leave, my dad strokes my hand.

"As soon as you get better," he tells me, "We'll all of us go for a drive in the country. Is that a deal?"

My heart leaps with excitement.

"Oh, daddy, yes!" I say.

Like that, all was right with this cockamamie world, once more...

"I am Rachel," Rachel shouts as she leans forward while still holding the overhead rail. "What's your name?"

I stare at her confused. Then I snap alert.

"Judith," I say, like she is supposed to know. "I'm not deaf! I am little Judith Fargoe."

This feels so out of my control. Take charge!

I spit at Rachel and the bolus lands by her feet. She about jumps out of her skin.

Though I don't let it show on my face, I am delighted with having stirred her juices.

I hurl coffee out of my cup at Michael. He simply sidesteps and I miss.

Little Ms. Sweetness and Light tries engaging me.

"I read that 'Judith' means praise," Ariel offers.

I think to myself, she really is anxious to be married. Sounds like she is already checking out the baby naming books.

Rachel whispers to Michael, "She's hallucinating!"

He whispers back, "She is sick, but she has a strong enough spirit to defend herself! Given a chance to change, she will truly become someone."

With the sweetest of smiles he says, "Come with us, Judith."

"Why?" I screech at them. "So you can abandon me again?"

In my memory, though they were shut out by Doctor Washington, I still hold them culpable. They were adults, supposedly conscientious. All they had to do was stand by me, stand up and present a case. They didn't. For whatever their reasoning or the circumstances, I believe they threw me to the wolves.

Ariel reaches out a hand to me. There is something powerful about her innocently good intentions. This blonde naïf intimidates me, even though I created her.

Suddenly fearful, I reach for my plastic bags stacked on the seats to either side of me. I hunch over to protectively envelope my belongings. The donut box starts sliding off my knees. Torn between saving the box versus holding on to all my worldly possessions, I simply watch it fall, to scatter partially eaten and broken donuts all over the car floor.

I can barely hold on to my bags as my integrity falls apart all around me.

What would you do in my situation? It's not like I'm a couple nights homeless because of misfortune. Mine is much of a lifetime spent spiraling down. Sure, I'm conscious and capable of rationalizing. Reality being what it is, I am at rock bottom for city living.

Now, along come saviors; dream or real? I don't know any more than you do.

The question of staying put or going with is on the table.

Split second decision; take it or leave it?

Quickly! Come on. What would you do?

Realize that, though I call it a dream, I am not in the best of mental shape to determine reality from fiction.

Oh, and one final caveat; there are people out there who prey on the likes of me for all sorts of strange reasons of their own.

You confused yet?

To add to my clumsy misery, the train starts braking hard for the station. My center of gravity disappears down the same rabbit hole my pride went years before.

><

I watch my foot cross over the two inch chasm between train and platform as if I am stepping off a cliff into space.

Next thing I know, I am disembarked from the train and following the two women.

Deep in my heart I understand that taking that step is a commitment to a world I am leaving behind. I am entering a new phase, but with such a blank slate as to terrify me—a life affirming change, Michael called it.

If I were not so desperate, I may never have taken that step.

I hear a tiny "tuck" sound followed by "electronic staccato" and a "pop." By now, we are all striding along the platform, stepping out.

Michael issues instructions.

"Meet us at Bleecker Street," he says.

I turn to see what is happening, who he is talking to.

Michael points with his mobile phone, directing me onward.

I take it he wants me to follow his harem. Having come this far, I do as I am told. We break into a run to climb the stairs.

People rush past us going down to the trains.

My plastic bags hang off my hands flapping like wings on a chicken struggling to fly.

I am charged; energized by my youthful companions' enthusiasm.

We hit the street in locked step, closely packed.

Just like in the movies, a black stretch limousine sweeps to the curbside. The driver, in chauffeur uniform and cap, jumps out, strides round the front of the car and throws open a rear passenger door.

He looks off into space, ignoring The Trinity and me.

ESSENTIAL

Rachel dives in through the open car door. I hesitate.

As if she anticipated me, Ariel offers to help me with an outstretched hand and there I am—inside. Ariel follows me in and sits on the same side as Rachel, their backs to the engine. Michael confers briefly with the chauffeur and then joins us as the door closes.

Abducted? I don't believe so. Petrified? You bet.

I was alone on the train. Now I am alone with three strangers and a chauffeur.

The cabin has a muffled silence, as if our ears have had the sound sucked out of them. I swallow the way I would if I ascended to an altitude where my ears may pop. No "pop" effect occurs and the space feels even quieter.

An eerie glow from a small orange light in the ceiling illuminates the interior with its plush, purple upholstery. The windows are dark tinted causing lights outside to reduce to wispy blurs. Any sidewalks may as well be empty if they even exist from our perspective inside this capsule.

I become super conscious of my condition in proximity to The Trinity. The women settle back comfortably, facing us. Michael is square in his seat, legs crossed in my favor. I perch nervously on the edge of my seat, clutching my bags tightly to me. The car swoops along, arcing through the night in soft undulations. We're in the Mother Ship.

Ariel reaches back beside her and fiddles with something. A fine hiss of mist emerges filling the car instantly with a rich, foreign odor. The smell alerts me.

"What's that smell?" I scream. "Is it a drug?"

Ariel reaches a hand out toward me making a patting motion, air caressing me.

"It's essential oil from Frankincense trees of Oman," she says. "Diffused like this, it helps clear brain fog."

Maybe she put it on for Rachel who, to my mind, definitely thinks in mysterious ways.

I feel myself cheer up.

"So, Ariel... did you ever marry?" I ask.

She smiles at me and, not missing a beat, responds, "Thanks for asking. I..."

My anxieties and racing thoughts eased, I feel safe hitting stride and, doing so, unintentionally cut her off.

"I stopped reading," I say. "Everything... got... messed up."

Ariel offers a sweet smile of support.

"I'm sorry," she says.

I say, "That's OK."

I turn to look at Michael.

"So, Michael, how's your research coming?" I ask.

"Good," he says. "I am based here now; offices down from Wall Street."

"Really?" I say, aware that we are talking at cross purposes. "I often think about those Cargo Cults. They were amazing!"

"Were they ever!" he flips back. "And you?"

Though to be expected, the effect this has on me even surprises me. Probably unintentionally, he opens a core issue.

"My folks both passed," I explain as if he and I are old friends reconnecting after an extended separation. "I am on my own. I'm still struggling to recover."

Seeking a means to displace my sudden upwelling rage brought on by discussing my folks' passing, I realize that Rachel is not participating. I glare at her.

"You have got such an attitude," I burst out. "How can you be MpowRgirl!"

That wakes her up.

"Who?" she yelps. "What a bunch of nonsense!"

The donut sugar is still messing with my system. The coffee charges my nerves like steel needles and this bitch needs a wakeup call a whole lot more than I do.

Bags sent flying, I vault off my seat to slip my hands about Rachel's throat and squeeze hard enough to make her choke. She tries to pull away, terrified by the ferocity of my attack. Next thing I know, Michael has interceded and has loosed my grip and is steering me back to my seat. I pick up my bags onto my lap to wall myself off.

As she nurses her throat and neck, Rachel looks at me as if I belong in a zoo.

"Relax, Judith!" Michael tells me gently. "Rachel is teasing you. When she needs to, she changes back into her super character."

I make them sweat the difference.

"Did MpowRgirl have an ego character?" I ask.

As if capturing the moment psychologically, he offers the perfect answer.

"Her nemesis was closing in on her," he says. "She changed her name to Rachel to be safe. Besides, try and imagine MpowRgirl living a normal life. Impossible. Right?"

Dang, the guy is good! I let it go. I am almost ready to slide all the way back into my seat, but I am not that comfortable yet.

I look at the three of them as if we are at a reunion. After all, who brought everyone together? These are my children gathered to send mom off on a trip. I focus on the stream of Frankincense. I lean into it to smell it and fill myself with its essence.

Half closing my eyes to relax, I watch them exchange glances, those looks of, "She has hope after all."

I smile to myself as I think; *We are none of us home yet.* Stay prepared.

After driving for a long time with everyone involved in their own thoughts, the limousine stops.

The same passenger door opens and this time a uniformed door attendant appears prepared to welcome us. Everyone wears uniform in this world, even my hosts, as I suppose I must do too.

Rachel vaults out of the car. Ariel follows more gracefully.

I hear Rachel whine, "This is nuts! She's dangerous!"

The door attendant pretends to hear nothing.

"Good evening, ladies!" he says with practiced, bright refrain.

I see this as a turning point. I hesitate while I reflect on myriad details, cramming them down my psychological throat so I will be free to devour the next course. Clearly, I hesitate too long.

Michael grasps me by my upper right arm with his left hand, probably meaning to be kind and helpful.

Wild eyed hysterical, staring and rolling my eyes, I'm about to tell him in a screechy voice, "Let me go! D'you think I am your patient?"

"RAPE!" might have carried a similar response.

All of a sudden, I realize I am alone in the backseat of a car with the man who, despite his faults, is my childhood dreamboat. My tween girl reserve takes over.

"Thank you, Dr. Kaliban," I tell him. "I can manage."

He lets go instantly, smiling at me—as relaxed as he was on the Cargo Cult island when he looked up to see Ariel and MpowRgirl standing before him.

Right then, Ariel pops her face in the doorway, her hand reaching towards me.

"May I help you, Judith?" she asks.

I shake my head, no. Clutching my bags, I edge off the seat and, crouch walking, inch past Michael. It is as if he is ignoring me completely. He sits there scribbling on a note pad, rips off a sheet, folds it twice and then hands it to Ariel.

That is when I realize he is out of the picture. I see I did not plan this well. In fact, I do not have a game plan. I am letting this unfold without focused lucidity. It is time to get back in charge.

The door attendant greets me, "Good evening, Ma'am!"

What a jumped up kangaroo this one truly is! As I step clear of the car, he closes the door and the limousine hisses off into the night, taking the man of my dreams away from me, perhaps forever and with not even a farewell.

1

ESS

Left alone for the briefest of moments, I am once more separate and distinct, standing holding bulging plastic bags as I stare at the doorway to the apartment building. A taut green canvas canopy extends from the curb and envelopes the space right above my head. It leads to an entrance with neo classical pillars on either side of a clear glass door. An acorn cluster garnishes the top of each pillar. Beyond the door, filling the interior space, recessed lights cast soft enticing illumination expecting that those who enter there know they are wanted in this shadow less world. Above the door is an arched transom with the number '5' etched into the glass.

My attention begins to wander. I note a similar pathway canopy half a block distant. It would be easy for me to simply start walking down the street as if nothing had happened. Sinking deeper into my daydream, I analyze my situation. Though this type of building typically has the trash pickup inside, there must be restaurants nearby with dumpsters out back able to serve up meals fit for a king or a queen.

I determine it is time to have the girls take charge!

At great personal cost, Rachel grasps me by my right elbow as Ariel takes my left elbow. They steer me toward the softly lit doorway. I begin to resist. As if coordinated, they press gently, but a little more firmly in the direction they are steering me.

Their grip is not so tight that I couldn't break free and walk or run. I look down the street. It's another anonymous street, like I am anonymous.

Michael instructed Rachel, "You have to change someone's life."

Like on the schoolyard, I'm IT.

Yet again, like on the train, it's decision time.

The door inches closer. My feet on the red carpet runner are complying with my elbows being pressed forward. If I create a scene now, their obedient, uniformed serf will admit that from the moment he first laid eyes on me, he expected something like this all along. The girls will be off the hook. They could tell Michael I got too wild. I'd be free.

Free? Free to do what? Die in the streets when the cold winds win the battle to push my elbows where they want?

Here is my "other half" pushing the social discard that I am into their life!

I am ignored by their serf... He would be a witness! They are in public.

He's someone who has seen me enter the building so that if I don't leave, he will raise a hue and cry. Or would he? Would they pay him off with something extra for the holidays?

"Here, take the little lady out for a treat..."

He's no witness for me. He'll be more party to their plan than they are.

Then, it's too late. As we approach the door, their unquestioningly complicit, obedient servant spryly runs around us to grab the handle and swing the door open so we may enter without breaking stride.

There is no sound. The shift in air pressure is all I have to tell me the door has closed behind us; behind me!

I don't care. Yes, I am glad. On many levels, whatever happens now, I submit.

We cross deep pile carpeting as we head for an elevator directly ahead. On either side of us, we pass two huge, stuffed chairs in each of which sits a man, identical in every way, mimicking each other as they operate their own electronic gismo, laughing alternately with being earnestly engrossed. They're twins!

Apart from the men's outbursts of laughter, the lobby is silent, but in a more uplifting way than the limousine—hushed. I note the ceiling is high up. That spacious feeling is gratifying. I relent to my captors with each lessening of my paranoia.

Rachel presses a button by the elevator and the ornate door slides noiselessly open. We enter. They release me and we turn and face the doors. I retreat one step to the back of the elevator, ever conscious of my olfactory presence.

Ariel passes the note from Michael across me to Rachel.

"I have something for you," she says.

Rachel expresses her surprise as she takes it.

"My marching orders?" she asks.

Ariel winks at me and I feel forced to grin back self consciously. Having had the decency not to read it before hand, Ariel clearly still expects to be included.

"Well?" she demands.

Dropping the hand holding the note to her side, Rachel stares off into space.

"It's his compensation plan," she states dismally. "So, why do I feel set up?"

Ariel looks at her with short tempered disgust.

"Try humility, Rach." she says.

A smile creeps across Ariel's face.

Her voice takes on a mischievous tone as she announces, "Then, again, think shopping—such a life!"

I am wondering to myself if it is within the realm of possibility for me to even conceive of people who live like this; when the elevator stops. I check the numbers. As the doors open, a soft, green numeral tells me we are at the seventh floor. We step into further realms of silence. Rachel steers our ensemble along the corridor to the entrance to suite 727. On either side of the pale orange door are bas relief versions of the pillars on either side of the front door; continuous identity, how sweet.

Ever since I was a child, I have added combinations of numbers together. With no exceptions, I determined that any number added to nine equates to that number. I reflexively work with the suite numerals, 7+2 equals 9. Therefore, 7+9 equals 7 (actually 16, where the 1 plus 6 adds up to 7). In addition, 7 is a combination of 3 and 4, where three is the Holy Trinity stacked on 4, perfect balance. I can't recall from where that information stems. Touching base with my childhood considerably stills my uncertainty.

Rachel keys in to a security pad and the door swings open. Finally, I know I have arrived in Heaven. No more do I have to toy with imagining The Trinity in angelic garb with or without wings. Stepping through the portal, everything, but everything, is... white!

Definitively in her lair, Rachel transforms. She moves off, pulling at books on a shelf outside her all white kitchen. I glimpse one title, 'Healing with Food'. I turn to a completely nonplussed Ariel clearly waiting for my attention. As soon as our eyes make contact, she brightens up, steering me with the lightest of touches on my elbow toward an all white bathroom. We girls are going to play. Her energy is alive at the prospect.

She quietly closes the door. All I see is white and mirrors—huge, floor to ceiling, wide mirrors across wall space adjacent to a shower stall big enough to wash an elephant, a commode with next to it a second... a bidet, a counter with lights around the mirror back of two sinks, a pool sized sunken bathtub, and cupboards. The room is large enough for a family of ten. OK, not ten; but several people could live comfortably here, or at least perform various ablutions while remaining distinctly unaware of the others' presence.

"Let's get you cleaned up while Rachel organizes food for us," Ariel calls to me as she opens cupboards from which she extracts plush, white towels and a voluminous, white bathrobe before heading towards the gigantic shower stall.

I struggle with the notion of disrobing in front of a figment of my imagination. My concerns mount when I realize I will be doing it many times over before every mirror facing into the room. I struggle to recall when was the last time I took off all my clothes, never mind with someone else present.

Ariel breezes over to me as if she does this sort of thing every day.

"Let's get those clothes off you," she says.

She stands next to me. The mirrors replicate the two of us countless times around the room. She is wearing sheer blue silk. I am wearing layer upon layer of rags, their colors merged into the darkest possible brown short of black. The contrast is unbearable.

I want to descend into the earth to disappear. In these surroundings, I appear to have risen out of the ground, bringing much of the soil with me. Tears form in my eyes. I am no crybaby. I have survived much that is unspeakable. However, the clash of my presence to these surroundings becomes too much for me to bear. I feel a hand gently stroke my left arm. I turn to see Ariel, on the edge of tears herself, watching me.

Speaking with the softest of voices, she says, "I know. It has been a long time. Everything is about to change for the better, Judith. You'll see."

Entering the shower and washing my body, and my hair, repeatedly—able to have endless amounts of water, turn it warmer and cooler, increase and decrease the pressure—is close to inhabiting paradise. There is an assortment of cleansers and conditioners. I extend my hair ahead of my face. I am a redhead. It's like seeing a sibling for the first time after spending years apart. See, I said you do have red hair. I remembered correctly.

With Ariel not speaking and no limitations put on me, I shower and shower. I sit on the floor under the spray. I lie down and roll in and out of the spray. I stand. In my excitement, I even consider attempting a handstand, but lose courage that I may slip. All I hear is the water splashing on me and on the floor of the shower.

Have they abandoned me?

I stick my wet head out the shower door. As the gust of steam clears, I rub my eyes to see Ariel, far across the room at a massage table—all white, naturally—organizing little bottles on a tray. I look to the floor where I put down my bags, took off my clothes.

It's completely clear.

I look around in case I am mistaken. No, there is nothing of mine in sight. I slam off the shower controls and, out of some primitive sense of modesty, grab for the bathrobe hanging by the shower door and throw it on me. Hardly covered, I careen out. Mad as a charging rhinoceros, I pad wet footedly across the white marble floor.

On the top of my voice, I interrogate her as I approach.

"Where are my bags?" I demand to know. "My clothes? All my... things?"

She barely looks up from her bottles.

"I threw them away," she says matter of factly.

I stop still, stunned. I experience my arms performing random rotations off to the sides, my hair curling as it speed dries from the heat of my anger.

I scream, "What! Why did you do that?"

The door flies open and Rachel walks in with a glass of green drink in one hand and her other hand holds a soup spoon filled with what resembles cream. She seems a whole lot calmer compared to me who is bouncing off the walls.

"When did you last have any bodywork done?" she inquires.

I am losing my patience with these two. With Michael's stabilizing influence gone, they feel loose, out of control.

Who gave them control? That's beside the....

Rachel walks up to me and stuffs the spoonful of—it is cream—into my gaping mouth. She feeds me like I'm a child. The fattiness tastes good. I clamp down and suck as much cream off the spoon as possible as she withdraws it. Guiding me to the massage table, she hands me the drink. I am still seething, but putting food in my mouth calms me. This sweet, vegetable drink, which is all I can describe it to be, is delicious and settling. I climb on the table, removing the robe as I slide under a white sheet, and lay on my back.

Ariel begins with my feet, rubbing oil on the undersides, and then just laying her hands against them. All my anger subsides into irrelevance. Ariel holds the sheet while I, instructed by her, turn to lay face down. She splashes me from her bottle collection onto my exposed back. Up and down my spine, then distributing each oil using finger rotations, sometimes digging her finger tips lightly and rubs with the heels of her hands. The smells are magnificent. I feel my mind float across the massage table to drip down and form warm puddles on the floor.

That is one dream I do not recall.

Again, I am laying on my back and Ariel finishes by oiling between my toes, flexing each foot in rotation at the ankle while I drift in and out of consciousness on a cloud of rich and subtle smells piled one on top of the other.

If there is such a thing as a rainbow of smells, I am a double... no, a triple rainbow.

Ariel helps me into a fresh bathrobe, then, off of the table and into a pair of slip on, white slippers. She escorts the perfumed cloud I have become out of the bathroom, along the hall and into the dining room.

On a glass table the size of a small football field, Rachel has set up a meal. There are three settings, each with a square, white dinner plate, white handled silverware, and, ahead of them, a series of white bowls with food in them. The place settings are huddled at one corner of the glass expanse.

Rachel has us perform a small ceremony before we start eating. We hold hands, bow our heads, and close our eyes.

I am fully expecting Ariel to break into a rendition of, 'Dear Lord Jesus, be our guest, and, unto us this food be blessed'.

Rachel simply has us observe a moment of silence. I find that to be different, refreshing. Nothing like a church shelter, that's for sure.

They begin passing bowls back and forth. Frankly, I have eaten out and eaten well—I have had my glory days—but I never ate like this. First, everybody takes a chunk of strong smelling—not a bad smell like the one my body gave off before I took my shower—cheese, about a tablespoon full. We eat that with about an equal amount of butter. I look for something to drink. There is nothing in sight. I determine to wait and watch.

They begin a light banter about how relaxed I am and teasing me about how proud I am. I see a bowl of meat in the middle of the table and I am ready to devour it all. Then I look for vegetables, bread, potatoes or rice. None is visible. Nor is there steam rising from the meat.

After about ten minutes of chatter, they pass the meat around. Each person takes a couple big spoonfuls onto their plate. The meat is thinly sliced and cut into narrow strips. It looks way under cooked. There is an extremely oily, green sauce on it. Rachel tells me that's avocado oil. I guess for garnishing, there are capers that have been soaked in water to deplete them of salt to the point that they are tasteless. That is it!

When I gather we will not eat anything else, I make no bones about it and pull the meat bowl over to me. Neither of them seems to care, so I load up my plate. Head down, I devour that serving in record time. I look up. They are calmly watching me, almost as if they expected this performance. I gesture that I am willing to share, but they demurely hold up their hands to indicate I go for it. I push my plate aside, pull the bowl to me and dig right in. It is delicious!

I am barely chewing. I have not had good protein in so long; I literally shovel it into my gorge and swallow. As I near the end of the meat, I am slowing down, though still with an inch or two of room left in my stomach. That is when Rachel comments about never seeing anyone like steak tartar as much as I appear to. I look up.

"The meat is uncooked?" I say. "Raw? It tastes great!"

I was so hungry; so, so hungry. I can barely contain myself. Energetic enthusiasm comes bubbling up instead of the usual loud emission of gas that I typically have with any meal.

"And I just love how I smell from those oils!" I exclaim. "I feel incredible! My mind is clear! It is as if I am reborn! Thanks, guys!"

Ariel, smiling generously, tells me, "You are very welcome."

After another bite of cheese and butter, Rachel wipes her mouth with her white napkin and stands.

"This raw protein diet is especially for you," she says. "Excuse me."

I start to rise until Ariel waves me down. She gestures for me to eat. I am stuffed.

She explains, "Rachel is preparing the next step."

"There's more?" I ask.

Ariel laughs and says, "You were going to leave in a robe?"

I am perplexed. I had sought a change in my life, but I did not define it to be any more than pulling me up a couple of notches. This is a jump from photographing the family with a point and shoot to bringing in a Hollywood movie crew to do it better. I am getting the full treatment.

I ask, simplistically, "Why are you doing this?"

Again, Ariel laughs.

"You focus on being conscious," she says. "OK?"

That is an insult.

However, I am so calm; I cannot rise to the occasion more than to comment, "You are weird. I am so conscious!"

Once more, she laughs as if she has the inside track over me. She takes another chunk of cheese and more butter, passes the bowls to me to do the same then stands to leave. I take a spoonful each of the cheese and butter. This time, though, I have to force it down. Reluctantly, I stand up and follow her. I look back at the table longingly in case this may be the last meal I will ever eat.

Ariel moves quickly through a maze of rooms and hallways making me feel like Alice chasing after the White Rabbit. She leads me to a bedroom fit for a queen. We step around rolling layers of a bed that resembles something from a showroom. There before me is a walk in closet the size of a warehouse with rack upon rack of clothing. Rachel is marching up and down the rows assessing what she is looking for as I gawk in amazement from the doorway.

"These are all your clothes?" I ask naively.

"*Be careful what you pray for*," repeats in my head.

Then I stare at Rachel carefully. Something about her—despite making a wonderful meal and playing host—leads me to believe my presence antagonizes her. She's still holding a grudge.

If only out of gratitude, I resolve to look for a way to make peace. Meanwhile, she scours a wall of shelves, pulling unopened packages of underwear from drawers. She hands me a small stack.

"Try these on," she says. "In the bathroom."

It does not take me more than a glance to see this is all silks and lace. I wonder to myself; if these are her cast offs, what is she wearing?

I take a wrong turn out of the closet and there is a huge mirror. This woman must dance through the house. It is like being in a studio.

I open my robe and start trying on the various bras and panties.

My ears prick up as, inside, I hear Rachel shuffling the clothes on the racks and Ariel attempting to soothe her.

"You are doing great!" Ariel tells her. "She seems OK. Why the raw meat meal?"

Rachel speaks with calm resolve, "Based on her zero to sixty temper, Michael thinks she is hypoglycemic. We may stabilize her temporarily. But, after us, she's on her own, again."

I walk back in pretending to be oblivious to the overheard conversation. Holding open the sides of the robe, I make a little flourish to demonstrate how snugly the underwear fits. I suddenly realize how disheveled my hair is, and my enthusiasm to show off dissipates.

Ariel beams back her joy for me. Rachel smiles wanly and beckons me to her. Turning into a dynamo, Rachel starts pulling select items off the racks and holding them up to my face, looking carefully at my eyes, hair and facial coloring. Following along after her, I stroke the textiles of the clothes as I pass, my excitement mounting by the second as I realize, they are playing dress up and I am their doll—except, this is for real.

Armed with a huge stack of selected blouses, skirts, jackets and pants, she steers me to the bedroom saying, "Let's see how these work for you."

This is the real test for her. I change in and out of the clothes that she offers me. Those that Rachel determines are right for me form a small stack on the bed. Those that are not join heaps on the floor. I periodically look to the one huge mirror but, each time my head begins to swivel, Rachel catches my chin and gently steers me to look straight at her. Clearly, my opinion is not wanted.

To add to my confusion, I am stunned that I, who tend to be full figured, even fit into this tall belle's wardrobe. I have not the first idea how she makes it work. All I know is it looks like I am coming out of this with a sizable collection of high end clothing.

We finish with clothing and move onto shoes. I have petite feet and here, again, we are almost identical in size. Rachel embarrassedly tells me she is only giving me shoes she wore once, twice at most.

As Rachel finishes up accoutering me with belts and scarves, Ariel, standing by a cupboard where Rachel keeps most of her jewelry, is clearly looking for something specific. Rachel ignores her, until Ariel spins round with a flourish and demonstrates her choice. It is a simple gold band with a stunningly huge, oval, dark blue sapphire stone.

Before Rachel is fully aware of what is happening, Ariel presents the ring to me, saying, "Judith, wear this in good health. May it be your eternal guardian."

As I slip the ring on to my left hand middle finger for a perfect fit, Rachel steps over to confirm her worst suspicions. She is clearly about to explode.

She hisses at Ariel, "That is my favorite ring!"

Ariel levels her with a joyful, "Give it up, girl. Only when you can let it all go..."

For one brief moment, I believe I can see sparks emanating from Rachel's ears as she squirms and grinds her teeth.

I cannot believe the transaction is complete. I fully expect an outraged Rachel to pull the band right off my finger. Instead, she turns to focus on folding and organizing my new clothes collection into a small, elegant suitcase.

As Ariel moves in right by me, I look her in the eye and appreciate her out loud.

"Thanks, Ariel," I say. "I shall treasure this."

I go to Rachel, who is surprisingly calm. I touch her shoulder. She stands and turns to face me, her eyes searching for my crazy state.

I give it to her straight.

"Rachel, I so appreciate you doing all this; it's a miracle!" I tell her.

Ariel calls over her shoulder as she heads out of the room, "How right you are! How right you are."

Rachel slips deeper into hustle mode. She quickly pins up my hair, lays a coat over my arm, and passes me the suitcase by the handle for me to pull. She gestures to the door. Ducks in motion, out we go to the elevator.

We ride in silence, each checking the others. They are assessing how I am dressed. I decide not to be a complete wuss and thank them any more than I already have.

We stride into the lobby area and, as we approach the front door, the attendant whips open the door. I hope for a hushed, 'Wow!' or a whistle, or some reaction.

He is the same bright light, not going to give himself away by expressing an opinion about someone upon whom his career may depend. I find him obsequious for doing that.

Me? I'm above that.

Outside, the limousine arrives in perfect time with our walk along the runner under the canopy to the curb.

We're going out on the town... at three in the morning?

SENSE

We are driving, driving. The girls are silent.

Once, I catch Rachel glancing at my ring. Ariel also sees and cautions her with a comic, metronomic finger; no, no, no, no, no! Rachel recoils, looking embarrassed when she sees me searching her face for a reaction. Ariel laughs aloud which breaks the tension. Even Rachel joins in. Again, I am left pondering my place in the scheme of things.

The gentle sway of motion ceases. Rachel instructs me to leave my coat and suitcase in the car. We step out onto the sidewalk in a skuzzy, commercial area. I feel surges of comfort being back in my kind of hood. Not surprisingly, all the shops are closed for the night, except where we are, out front of Zayin's Beauty Salon. Ariel charges ahead, leaving Rachel to encourage me to enter.

For one brief moment, my mistrust returns. Then, I pluck up my courage to go with them wearing my confidence as well as I wear this exquisitely draped haute couture. While I am taking in the décor of a 3 D jungle, Ariel hugs two people farther into the store. They release her and approach Rachel and me. As these Goth monsters embrace Rachel before taking an interest in me, I use the extra few moments to compose myself and push down my fast mounting anxieties.

Rachel introduces the duo as TRiXi and Jeri. They swarm me like a pair of locusts. Chunky TRiXi wears her hair as a spiky black cap arrived from a recent tornado raging through the neighborhood. She wears no make-up but has metal rings implanted along the edges of her ears, in her nose, her lips, and her nipples that she seems more interested in promoting than hiding. There are metal spikes in her eyebrows, her tongue, the side of her nose, her exposed belly button, and, I count my blessings, she is wearing corduroy pants. Her bare feet show off rings on her toes, and what looks like a bolt going through her right ankle. She extends her hands to me like a matron greeting the family arriving for a wedding. I feel my Charlie Brown smile coming on and I do not bother to stop it.

Bubbly Jeri is the salesperson of the two of them. As she turns to face me, I see a crew cut on top of her head transition to long curly tresses from Little Bo Peep around the sides. The thought crosses my mind, fleetingly, that this is where Rachel got the idea for cornrows above dreadlocks.

Jeri slides the sleeves of her leather jacket up to her elbows exposing elaborate, colorful tattoos on her forearms. Snakes embrace daggers while pink roses and green leaves create a verdant backdrop. Jeri flexes her muscles. The snakes appear to crawl down her arms. She grins at my shocked response, seemingly the reason for her tattoos.

"Fix you up with some great tats?" she laughs manically.

I wonder if I can trust Ariel and Rachel any further. This is the dream heading off the edge of a cliff. It may be time to seek some alternate activity.

"Jeri and TRiXi are totally the best hairdresser and makeup artist in town," Ariel beams at me.

This is serious. She is serious; she truly admires them.

Ariel turns to them with arms out, offering an air embrace.

"Thank you for working late, ladies" she says.

Yes, thank you. Can we go now?

I do not intend to let these two psycho, fashion freaks anywhere near me.

I briefly lose track of TRiXi, when her arm wraps around my waist and, with strength beyond her size, she propels me to an old fashioned barber chair, seats me and slaps two straps around me to hold me in. She swivels the chair, and, with her heel, kicks a pedal to flip the chair back. I scream, more at the thought that I am powerless in the hands of two demonstrably, questionable people. On the street, I was able to choose most situations and work my way out of bad ones. Here, I realize, I am a prisoner.

Abducted? For sure. Petrified? I am terrified!

Up and back of my head, I hear water running and occasional splashes land on my hair. TRiXi lets my hair fall free with a couple of deft gropes about my head, dropping out the clips that Rachel had applied. She caresses my head in a dreamy, faraway fashion, and then snaps to business, wetting my hair in preparation for shampoo. Her hands and fingers are strong as they press into my scalp. She leans over me so that the metal in her nipples brush up against my chin through her sheer blouse. She slides back and forth putting her face within an inch of mine as if we are about to kiss. Her total presence is oppressive and dominating at the same time.

My hair washed and damp dried, the chair spins through a 180 and TRiXi disappears from view.

As if I am trapped in a perpetual nightmare, Jeri appears at my knees slinking onto the chair to straddle me. She crawls up my body sniffing me, intrigued, until we are eye to eye, her curls forming curtains to either side of us.

She whispers to my mouth, "You smell sweet enough to eat!"

She watches my horrified look and smiles, sinking into a fake French accent.

"Ne t'inquiet pas, ma precious," she tells me. "Ah cut ze best. Ah makes you ador*a*b*le*."

I blink my eyes shut twice, hoping that she interprets the action as, Yes, whatever!

She smiles. We have a contract!

I roll my head sideways to see what Ariel and Rachel are doing since I can hear them singing. The two of them are in separate, adjoining barber chairs taking turns spinning each other in opposite directions, screaming hysterically as they harmonize rounds of, "Pop! Goes the Weasel."

'Round and 'round the cobbler's bench
The monkey chased the weasel,
The monkey thought 'twas all in fun
Pop! Goes the weasel.

A penny for a spool of thread
A penny for a needle,
That's the way the money goes,
Pop! Goes the weasel.

A half a pound of tupenny rice,
A half a pound of treacle.
Mix it up and make it nice,
Pop! Goes the weasel.

Up and down the London road,
In and out of the Eagle,
That's the way the money goes,
Pop! Goes the weasel.

I've no time to plead and pine,
I've no time to wheedle,
Kiss me quick and then I'm gone
Pop! Goes the weasel.

As they sing, I struggle with a paranoid delusion that it is really a meaningful song. I try to appoint rationale to the words—another elusive dream that only briefly keeps my mind off my scissors wielding assailant.

Jeri takes swipes at my hair, sliding in and out, making cuts in a blur of speed. I shut my eyes, wincing out of sync to the scissors' clicks.

The clicks stop, and I slowly breathe a sigh of relief. An industrial sized hair dryer takes up the sound space as Jeri styles my hair. That, too, finally stops. All the while, I am searching for a visual connection to my head. With mirrors everywhere, my chair's position is such as to keep me blind to my progress. Judging from the cuts and what hair I can see about me, I am more likely to resemble Jeri than Rachel. Perish the thought!

Next act into the circus ring is TRiXi with a rolling, make up tray. She works deftly, plying my skin as if it were plastic, applying colors according to Rachel's strict oversight. I relax. Having Rachel's eye on the job is amazingly reassuring to me.

I am aware of how awake I am. Energized!

The work seems endless, yet, I am conscious the whole while, following most of the details of what happens. Beginning to relax, I start to slip into a comfortable state similar to when Ariel applied oils all over me.

The thought comes to me that it was my old self that was scared of these two, definitely strange women, Jeri and TRiXi. But hadn't Rachel given freely of her time and energy to prepare an incredible meal and used her skills and clothes to make me look impressive? Didn't Ariel do the same with the oil treatment and give me a stunning ring even if it was not hers to give? And, in Rachel's and Ariel's company, Jeri and TRiXi treated me at the very least as an equal if not better.

Something happened. I can't put my finger on it. I am different, noticeably so.

For no apparent reason, the chair flies upright. If I were not strapped in, the motion may have thrown me clear out of the chair. As it is, the straps restrain me, momentarily digging into my flesh.

The four women crowd around me, picking at my hair with well intentioned fingers, almost touching the make-up job until Ariel has her hand slapped by TRiXi for coming too close, making everyone remain respectfully distant.

They compliment themselves, each other, "Looking good!"

"Wow!"

"Pure artistry!"

TRiXi releases the straps and spins the chair for me to look in a mirror. Before I set eyes on my reflection, she is in my face.

"You cry one tear, girl...!" she warns. "And keep your hands away from my artwork."

She slips away to allow me to look. I am stunned. After all these years I am finally a swan!

Ariel, unceremoniously, holds up one of my hands.

"Well?" she asks Jeri.

Jeri takes my hand and, while inspecting the creases of ingrained dirt on my skin, the cracked, broken and ridged nails, she squeezes my hand tenderly between her first finger and thumb. The nature of the squeeze catches my attention. I look at Jeri with a revised attitude for making my hair stunning. In the momentary glance she gives me, I feel my heart stop and then start with an extra strong beat.

"You know me," Jeri says. "I love a challenge. Feet, too?"

"One price," Rachel tells her. "The whole package."

In my life, I have never been as confused as by the attention lavished on me by Jeri. Though, in essence, all she is doing is giving me a manicure and pedicure, the intimacy she manages to evoke is overwhelming.

I play it straight and let her "do" me the way she knows best. I admit to myself that I've come a long way since walking in that shop doorway, being terrified of their appearance, only to realize that Jeri and TRiXi are probably without equal in their respective trades. I give myself over to them with a level of trust that was completely foreign to the old me. The results are truly impressive.

When it is time to go, I receive an abundance of air kisses in contrast to the physicality of our arrival, presumably, not to damage the goods.

The limousine drives more slowly than before. Opening her window to allow in the encroaching dawn, Rachel mutters low under her breath.

"But Soft!" she quotes. "What light through yonder window

breaks?"

Ariel responds passionately, "Parting is such sweet sorrow, that I shall say good night till it be morrow."

They look to each other with an intensity I had not seen previously. They turn to look at me, smiling like proud parents at their daughter's graduation. I feel special.

The limousine stops and our door opens. We exit the car while the chauffeur takes out my suitcase and raincoat. Though I did not see her leave, Rachel returns with a ticket. I look around and recognize that we're at a bus terminal.

The night is over. It's time for Rachel to be graded.

As for me? I guess it's the highway.

I take the offered ticket.

"Oklahoma City?" I read aloud, fearfully. "Oklahoma?"

Rachel smiles the sweetest smile I have seen from her yet. She holds my right hand with both of hers.

"It's not Oz, but that's OK."

I mull her words and realize that she just cracked some kind of joke. She looks into my searching eyes and gives me a neutral stare. I tell myself, this is one cool person.

"To choose a place to live," she tells me, earnestly, "Stay only where you are effective."

As a rule of thumb, that sounds logical. How do I judge what is effective?

Rachel becomes more serious.

"Realize you likely are hypoglycemic," she tells me. "Avoid eating sugar foods, grains and processed foods."

I nod agreement less from understanding and more to appease her. She hands me her clutch, which elicits a gasp of surprise from Ariel.

"Here's some cash to hold you for a while," Rachel says. "And, here's a food parcel."

The chauffeur hands Rachel a silver colored, soft sided box with shoulder strap which she passes to me. It is a cutely fashioned, portable icebox.

I give Rachel a hug. Initially, she is reticent, then, she sinks into my arms as if all is forgiven. Now it is she who is grateful to me. That makes it my turn to recoil in surprise at her willingness to release.

I stagger to Ariel who squeezes me with playful joy.

I stand back looking at them both.

"You are my Super Heroes," I tell them. "Thank you!"

Ariel smiles her standard smile, joy and light filled with well meaning, as she tells me, "I love you!"

This is becoming embarrassing. I run for the bus. It's all I can do not to cry because I know that if I do, I will set them off. In the back of my head is my instruction from TRiXi. I refuse to be dictated to. I will cry when I am good and ready. This is just not that time.

I find a seat on the right side of the bus in the middle so I can watch them from the window. I hang up my coat, put the suitcase on the overhead luggage net, and drop the ice chest at my feet. I place the clutch behind me at my back as I sit. I turn to face them. Ariel slaps a big, friendly arm about Rachel's shoulders, pulling her in close. They look straight ahead at me as they talk.

Ariel proudly tells Rachel, "You changed someone's life."

Rachel responds seriously, "I do feel more comfortable with her now that she looks like one of us."

Ariel squeezes her for emphasis.

"Or, she appears different now you have accepted humility," she says.

There is a long moment's quiet while Rachel digests that statement. As if to punctuate the silence, two tears slowly form in the corners of her eyes and genteelly make their way down her cheeks leaving glistening tracks in the early morning light.

DAY TWO

FRIEND

I keep my eyes closed as I experience the bus roll along city streets, turn corners and then rumble for an extended period. For a short while it slows, compressed air releases and then we climb entering a new flat phase with constant low level hissing noises. I open my eyes to see almost horizontal rain lashing the large windows of melancholic, morning grey light as we pass a sign welcoming us to New Jersey.

Outside the window, I faintly see someone and refocus my eyes. I am stunned to see the swan I am become looking quizzically back at me through the inclemency displayed on the screen. I feel a strong twinge of joy—it is possible to look pretty!

As my tired eyes close, faint shades of blue eyeliner meld into sleep.

I open my eyes periodically. The day has turned to night and I have not eaten since Rachel's place. That's OK. I am practiced at running on empty. Besides, I decide to maximize how long I keep the food Rachael gave me. I open the icebox, remove the top sandwich bag—peeled avocado slices and cheese cubes—and zip the icebox closed before putting it back on the floor.

I try to eat slowly remembering some edict from years past. No use. I am ravenous. I scarf it down. The limit I imposed on myself is all that prevents me from wiping out the entire contents of the food box.

Racing beside us at our speed, be that fast or slow, is a wonderful sliver, barely two days after the New Moon. Ever present, the sliver plays a game of hide and go seek ducking behind clouds, puffy little things and the occasional large ominous one, to emerge, satiating me in the joyousness of its reappearance.

On the ground, passing by, are one field after another, many of them badly maintained, visibly desolate in the wan light of that skinny moon. The screen I look at shows derelict factory towns, shattered, as if some maniac with a Gatlin gun sat out in the back lot and swept layer by layer shooting out warehouse windows. Occasionally, street lights accentuate the desolation, the isolation, the ghostliness of it all.

Vast shadows reflect my existence, the true emptiness I am beneath this patina of woman made beauteous. If someone fixed the windows, painted the building exteriors, filled in all the potholes and repaired all the street lights, these places will look a lot like me, a construct of acceptability covering the same old, empty, useless structure.

After a while, I change the scenery to endless sunlit fields of rolling green pastureland with animals. I am amazed how few animals I see in a land with so many people and such a constant need for food. I glance nervously at my fellow passengers. They all appear to be utterly engrossed with eating non-stop. Where does all this food come from?

A huge, arcing form reaches up into the sky marking the confluence of the two great rivers of America. I am in St. Louis, Missouri. The sound of saying that, even inside my head, is one of wonderment. Little Judith Fargoe from Detroit has been in two major cities, including New York and now St. Louis.

That mysterious, silent woman sitting beside me eyes me carefully, likely as in judgment of me as I am of her; perhaps looking for flaws, chinks in my armor. Beside the perfect make up job, impeccable manicure—and I most surely did test Jeri's consummate skills—I realize how exactly appropriate is the neckline of my blouse. It is not only right where it needs to be, it perfectly mirrors my chin, thereby, accentuating the structure of my face. The jacket top permits only enough blouse to show to do its job focusing in on my chin. Rachel has created the perfect me. My concern now is how long can I make it last.

I have finally found myself a goal beyond survival; staying perfect.

I slide a hand back of me and pull out the clutch book. I am certain there will be a compact in there along with my color of lipstick. There is something ineffably glorious about being able to anticipate their every move after such a brief encounter. I click open the clutch and, as I anticipated, there is a round, gold colored compact, a lipstick and a wad of bills. That is so bizarre for me to have money.

I cannot remember when I last had money. As I wandered the streets, sure, people gave me change, the occasional dollar bill, even a five once in a while. Mostly, I handed what I had to other people who asked for it to remedy some pressing emergency. Money. What a strange concept? People never have enough. It's what people talk about all the time; money, the weather and relationships. I have lived without money for so long, having it is completely anathema to how I survive.

Performing a sort of miracle, Ariel and Rachel have orchestrated my life so I blend in. Reflecting on the few times on this bus that I went to the bathroom, many people tried not to stare at me but others endeavored to catch my gaze, giving me a smile and brief greeting. They apparently do not know that I am a wretched creature feeding my face from a box of donuts found on a park bench. This veneer is just that; a veneer. Princess for a day or two does not change who I am.

However, some niggling thought says to play with the money now that I am this false incarnation of civilization. When it's gone, I will survive. I have this far. My silent friend smiles concurrence. How nice is that? She and I are in total agreement.

I release the issue and focus on my make-up. The compact is exactly right for me and all that I need to resurrect the complete picture is to apply more lipstick. Once my face is good, my hair only takes a brief tweezing to bring it back to shape. I replace the compact and lipstick, being careful not to disturb the money. Somehow, I am convinced it does not belong to me so I know to take extra good care of it.

I reach out my hand and stroke my coat.

After the bus pulls into a terminal, the couple sitting across the aisle gets up and leaves. Many people leave, many others get on the bus. I look up at my suitcase as if it might have disappeared en route. Over the years, so many of my possessions have simply vanished the way my plastic bags and clothes did from Rachel's bathroom.

Yet, there sits my suitcase, patiently waiting for my next demand. I pick up the silvery ice chest and take out the next layer, a plastic bag containing slices of raw meat alternating with slices of butter. This diet is so strange; everything is eaten in combination with something else. I nibble as I watch a mother and her young daughter sit down in the seats vacated by the couple.

I am used to people ignoring me, so watching peoples' each and every action has become second nature to me.

"It's rude to stare at people!" only if they are aware of you.

The girl has a gentle disposition and goes to lengths to appease her mother's finicky ways. The child takes out a bag of candies and, one at a time, begins popping them into her mouth. Mother looks out her window, misery etched onto her face as if she tries to forget what she is condemned to remember. The girl looks about until she and I lock eyes. She gives me a smile of appeasement. Playfully, I bare my teeth, forgetting they may hold strands of raw meat. Not the least intimidated, she laughs silently, clearly aware of her mother next to her.

I imagine her to be Alice, sitting with her sister out in the flower speckled green meadow. I gesture to her to give me one of her candies. She unflinchingly leans towards me offering her bag. I am about to lean out when mother's arm extends out and around, reflexively hooking her daughter back into the bosom of her paranoia. With the irate glare of someone who would enjoy the benefits of an enema, the woman casts a brief look at me as she bears down on her generous innocent. Like the Queen of Spades, she spits out her thoughts.

"Do we talk to strangers, Susie?" her mother rebukes her.

The child crumbles into uncertain personhood.

Mother retreats to her unrelenting pain.

All is in pieces with the world.

FERVOR

In keeping with Rachel's instructions to me only to stay where I am effective, clearly, this is not a row for me to sit in. I stand and stretch. Oh, that feels good.

I look about. As I perceived before, everyone on the bus is eating. It is a veritable mobile orgy of eating. Many children and adults are pushing lollipops in and out of their mouths in innocent gestures. I see candy bars at various stages of consumption. White bread sandwiches proliferate, as do sodas, boxes of fruit juices with their bent straws, bubble gum and chewing gum mastication, chocolate bars as profuse as at Wonka's factory, and that strangest of condiment candies, the vine licorice.

Taking down my suitcase, laying the coat over my arm, I pick up the icebox by the strap and grab hold of my purse. I move to an empty pair of seats two up from Susie and her mother, ahead of a pimply faced youth barely able to wear the clothes draped over his skinny frame. Placing the pocketbook back of me, I sit in the window seat.

Along a quiet stretch of road, for his own amusement, the driver steers the bus to straddle the center line. Whether or not his road manners take his charges, we passengers, into consideration seems irrelevant. I pray a cop is hiding off to the side somewhere and will rescue us from this crazed man in charge of our lives racing along a decidedly isolated stretch of highway.

My prayers are promptly answered. From behind us, a car horn beeps indignantly. I crane my head round trying to see who can be cutting up so. It is not a cop, but another sentient life form using the interstate hereabouts. I glimpse a red sports car with the top down driven by what I take to be a young woman.

"It's Nancy Drew!" I tell myself.

Better than a cop; she will solve our woes. I am in love with this woman already.

The bus driver is unfazed. Now with a purpose—to prevent this woman from overtaking him—he hogs the center lane.

He is a chauvinist; I can tell by the air of grandeur with which he pursues his mission. How dare he prevent Nancy Drew from passing? Who knows, there may be a terrible accident ahead or behind us as she desperately endeavors to reach a hospital? I feel compelled to assist her!

I lean across the adjacent aisle seat to get a view of the driver. As I start my lean, a man walks by me on the aisle from back of my row. We catch each other's eyes. I recognize him, but cannot place him. He wears a shabby raincoat, and he shuffles. He looks old for his years. He is stocky, short, has black curly hair. No matter, I tell myself. I must return to my mission, immediately.

"Let her pass!" I shout out down the aisle at the driver.

The driver raises a hand and waves the back of it at me. Obviously, he is a multiple offending chauvinist since he now includes me in his list of offended women.

From behind the bus, the horn beeps insistently. That is enough for the bored passengers to find cause to rally. This is no longer La Donna Quixote tilting at buses; this is a fully fledged peasant revolt akin to the Tale of Two Cities.

With one voice, the cry goes up, "Let her pass!"

I am impressed. Many people took time out from eating to do this. That is cause for celebration. The driver, heeding the democratic opinion of his community, steers the bus to the right side once more. As he does so, the man in the raincoat returns and gives me a big, congratulatory smile. From where do we know each other, I wonder?

Now is not the time to ponder strange men. The red sports car easily begins to overtake us. The license plate reads, "FOHAT." I have no idea what it means. I sense I have a spirit connection with this remarkable charging machine. The car's driver is a slip of a woman in a cowboy outfit, her cropped, blonde hair untrammeled by the wind.

The youth behind me mutters excitedly in the hope that his mutterings have meaning for others, and, best of all, that someone hears him and can offer praise at his defining the car.

"Wow!" he says. "It's a Lotus Elise in Ardent Red, 6 speed, button ignition. Those are so rare. Wow!"

Feverish clicking tells me he is sharing his joy with his electronic universe.

As the car pulls alongside me, the driver turns and looks straight at me. I realize she is looking at me because I am waving frantically to my hero. Driving with one hand holding the wheel and pressing the car horn with her forearm, she makes a finger gun with her other hand and shoots at me. Each shot goes straight to my heart. I explode.

As quickly as she arrives, she is gone.

My waving hand sinks to my lap. Not gloomy as in past such incidents, I tremble with joy. My heart was opened by the make believe gunshots, or was it the experience of expressing myself

A quest reveals itself. I must track down this dynamic woman.

FELLOWSHIP

The mini palace revolt leaves its mark. The red sports car, long since vanished along our future road to travel, has stimulated all manner of conversation. The library quietness of much of the prior journey has transformed into a veritable hubbub.

By switching on the public address system, the driver endeavors to regain authority over his passengers. His voice booms his statement of intent throughout the bus.

"Ladies and gents," he opines cynically. "We're approaching a bathroom break. The next stop is two hours on. If you are not here when the bus leaves..." he pauses, the way a sadist holds off hurting his victim, knowing the anticipation is a more intense sensation than any inflicted pain.

He intones an off key interpretation of, "Happy Trails To You!"

The revolting passengers revert back to memories of summers at camp, and, following the bus driver's lead, begin to sing a stumbling chorus of "Happy Trails." The familiar looking man in a raincoat moves to station himself next to the driver, facing his chorale and mouthing the words, conducts his fellow passengers. People hold hands and sway, side to side, as they open their throats to give rousing voice to an old standard.

A few minutes pass and the singing bus slows before veering off the road into the vast parking lot of a diner.

In one final act of desperation to resume command, the bus driver bellows over the intercom, "Ten minutes, people, ten minutes; starting now!"

Passengers politely help one another and extend courtesies such as waiting for slow ones to go ahead. Compared to the isolates that got on the bus, this is a remarkably convivial bunch that disembarks.

The size of the diner's overall structure represents what it is possible to build with endless resources and limitless fantasies. The building runs two stories high; presumably with sleeping quarters upstairs. There are so many light sources attached to corners and protuberances, the entire building has the potential for acting as a beacon. Fortunately, it is daytime, and all that is visible is a surrounding zoo of parked vehicles. Fleets of trucks fill one section, and cars, to the horizon, fill another. In front, parked obliquely to everyone else, is a red sports car, hood down, driver missing. That raises my spirits, and, at the same time, I feel trepidation.

I take my pocketbook and follow the shuffling hordes off the bus. Our present and future peasant revolt becomes sedition reduced to sedation by the need to go potty.

By the time I enter the massive building, the lines for the restrooms are over flowing spilling out into the hall.

Taking pride of place, the cornerstone, the central attraction of the diner, are glittering, pie display cases—all glass and chrome protecting brightly colored, sugar stuffed jewels in glorious pastry settings lit by vibrating fluorescent tube strips. Following my magnetic attraction, knowing in my stomach from smells in the air that sugar lay just ahead, I set a course for the chrome trimmed counter that arcs off in two directions in an endless curve to oblivion each way.

Momma's coming, sugar!

FLAMBOYANCE

Straight ahead, seated at the counter on a round, red leather on chrome, cantilevered barstool is my cowgirl. I approach her with the eagerness of a puppy whose human companion is returned home after a day's absence.

The man in the raincoat from the back of the bus, the same man who conducted enthusiastic choruses of the song, "Happy Trails," walks across my path and we almost collide. His refusal to stop forces me to hesitate. Close up, I realize it's Michael! Is that possible? He is so out of context. I cannot begin to imagine what Michael is doing riding a bus, especially looking so shabbily dressed. Impossible! Yet, I feel my heart skip a beat.

I look around for him. He's gone; lost in the people circus of this gigantic place.

My eyes return to my original target.

The possibility of meeting Nancy Drew, the lure of the pies, the smells of cooking food all fill my head scrambling my brains like those of a lovesick teen.

The typically shy, introvert me is now fearless. I walk right over and sit down next to her. I stare at her as she picks with boredom at a plate of apple pie a la mode. I speak before I realize I have spoken.

"That looks good!" I say loudly, shocking myself.

She turns, her bored face lighting up with a welcoming smile at the same time as she disinterestedly pushes away her plate of pie to a place obliquely in front of me.

As I have said before, I amaze myself with what I am capable of creating. This time, I am in awe of the dialect that emanates from this cutest of self confident young women. Her accent, I guess to be from somewhere mid Atlantic, sweeps me off my feet with its over the top lyricism.

"Hi! I saw yer wavin' ter me from the bus wi' that big ol' purty smile," she poets.

I am enraptured!

I tell her my name.

She tells me she is Betsy Auchin, "...of the Winston Salem Auchins, yer know."

With the joie de vivre of a beauty queen contestant, she asks, "Did yer know Winston Salem tied with Lexington, Kentucky; Osaka, Japan; Pittsburgh; and Seattle as the 46th best city in the world ter live?"

Out of the corner of my eye, I notice a waitress behind the counter making a beeline for the barely eaten food. I grab the plate and pull it toward me. Without stopping the motion in play, I use Betsy Auchin's fork to resume where she left off, fulfilling my deep seated craving for sugar and gluten. Beaten to the punch, the waitress makes a swift recovery, beginning to grab for my wrist and then thinking better of it. I pull the pie plate closer to me just as the waitress points to her new focus of interest, my ring.

"That is one exquisite stone!" she gasps, staring at it and then with embarrassment at me. She has a similar look on her face to that of those people on the bus. It's as if she is seeking my approval.

I relax, switch hands holding the fork, and offer to let her ogle the ring close up.

"I am sure it's a fake," I tell her.

I mean, who gives away a valuable stone? The answer is: someone who gives away a pocketbook filled with cash. I realize this part of my dream is deeply symbolic.

Before I can become hung up on analyzing my dream, Betsy glances at my ring and proceeds to back off her stool to stand up, and, with not a hint of doubt, raises her hands to heave her breasts as she declares, “About as fake as these, honey!”

I choke on the pie in my mouth, spitting out chunks of pastry crust onto the counter. The waitress adeptly sweeps with her cloth so that, a second later, there is no trace of my regurgitated food. I look at Betsy and watch the fantasy of Nancy Drew evaporate right in front of my eyes.

“Have you no shame?” I whisper, embarrassed for me more than for her.

Clearly challenged by my embarrassment, she slams her personal bravado into overdrive. This sweet child transforms into a flaming monster.

“Gimme some cash,” she states loudly, attracting attention throughout the restaurant, “An’ I’ll show yer. One dollar, five, one hundred, a thousand. Hey, Jude, it’s all of it only change. Even a million.”

My mind is spinning. This is not a jester; this is the anima unleashed full force. I am facing my death by a thousand cuts as she pushes button after button. Then it dawns on me, she is not testing me, she is testing her. I am merely a means to an end. My role is to protect her, to save her from public embarrassment. Everyone at or near the counter is watching the showdown. The waitress seems to believe Betsy and I are together. I am the only one who is protesting. I turn aside slightly so no one can look into my pocketbook—mine now—and grab the first bill that comes to hand. Raising the stakes, I offer the money to Betsy.

I check the denomination as I pass it over, gulping when I realize what I am giving her.

“Here is a hundred.” I say. “But I need it back!”

She smiles a look of relief that I played along.

She takes my financial offering with gentility, shouting loudly,

"Watch! I learned this in Paris."

This beauty queen turned diva transforms into a clumsy, innocent Dorothy from Oz. That's when I realize she had been checking for her victim from the moment she arrived. Unwittingly, I became her shill. Having watched this sort of action go down along the busy pedestrian sidewalks of Manhattan, I am exhilarated to finally be a player.

This woman is nothing less than thrilling to be around.

Feigning awkwardness, she heads through an archway to the next room where two burly truckers are drinking coffee and passing the time of day shooting a friendly game of pool. She fumbles picking up a cue and edges ever closer to them until they stop what they are doing and give her their undivided attention.

"Hey, boys!" she calls to the two men, each old enough to be her father. "Either of yer gamblers?"

The men smile to each other clearly wishing for their libidos to be gratified. The smaller of the two—my guess is he weighs in around 230 pounds—towers over her. She steps closer, as if relishing his size.

"What are you willing to bet?" he asks, realizing she already has the upper hand.

I press the pocketbook to my body using the elbow connected to my hand holding the pie plate. With my free hand, I wield the fork as I step closer, curious to observe how this drama will play out. I lean against a wall, trying to be inconspicuous.

Pulling my bill from her back pocket in a calculatedly salacious gesture, Betsy waves it under the trucker's nose.

"A hundred bill," she tells him. "Winner takes all."

He looks at his buddy. The buddy grins back that male look of; How bad can it get; she's a chick! He indicates his willingness to join in by pulling out his wallet and selecting a one hundred dollar bill. Betsy slaps hers on top of the pool table cushion, and both truckers lay theirs on top of hers.

All the while staying in character, her confidence rising by the minute, she asks, "If yer'll permit, I'll set us up."

They nod agreement, digging each other in the ribs as they watch this nymphet walk round the table selecting balls out of table pockets. She assembles three of them at the far end. A brown and a red she sets touching each other up against the cushion. Then, she delicately balances a black ball on the cushion to rest on the brown and red balls.

The second trucker, I guess weighs 290 pounds and is fit and nimble, nods towards me.

“Is your friend in?” he asks.

He is either assessing if Betsy is alone, or, what I now realize, is that, by the time I reached the counter, most everybody saw something coming without knowing the play in detail.

For one terrifying moment, I wonder if this is a set up to steal my money instead of theirs. I release my fear by telling myself the pocket book of money isn’t really mine to begin with.

Fishing out the white ball from a pocket and setting it on the start spot, Betsy includes me in, telling them, “She’s seein’ everyone plays fair.”

“Oh, we play fair,” says the first trucker with a smile. “Real fair.”

These two can barely contain where their fantasies see this bet leading. Betsy pretends she is straight up with them. Her innocence is overwhelming. She holds the cue pointed at them, not turning it away until she finishes her explanation of the rules.

“This is like me, boys,” she informs them as if MC-ing a boxing match, “Simple. All yer got to do is hit the black wi’out touchin’ other two balls an’ the money’s yern.”

The first trucker takes his cue, and walks over to look at how the three balls are set up. He returns to the white and without a further thought, strikes with the cue sending the white ball crashing into the red and brown ones.

Betsy looks chagrined; like she wanted him to win and now he lost. She collects the three colored balls and sets them up as the second trucker moves into place. Betsy sends the white hard and it shakes him to catch it. She breaks his confidence right there.

I feel like I am watching a complete pro the way she works these two. Any residual paranoia dissolves as the game progresses.

The second trucker lines up his shot, talking to the table, but addressing his buddy, "What this little lady likes is the gentle touch."

Betsy twitches her butt just enough to catch his eye as she looks at me instead of him.

He has to receive confirmation.

"That right?" he inquires.

"Shot's impossible, if you ask me," his buddy responds.

Betsy turns to study the three balls as if psyching herself up for her own shot. The second trucker realizes Betsy is not attending to him and hits the white gently enough to send it down the table but not enough to hit the target. He was trying to impress on Betsy that he was the one for her, not his partner. The effort falls flat.

Without comment either physical or spoken, Betsy steps to the foot of the table, clutching her cue in the dorkiest of poses. The first trucker retrieves the white ball. He holds it out to her on a flat upturned hand.

"Let's see how you make your money," he spits at her.

Clearly, she should win the bet, but the game itself has miles to go yet. Right this minute, everyone is watching the game, not the bet.

Still playing the fumbling cutesy, Betsy lamely sets up the white, hits it gently down the table to stop three inches short of the triumvirate.

"Oops!" she says, pathetically.

The first trucker is elated. He swings on her as if she is the reason his whole life has been the way it is.

"See," he says, stabbing a finger at her. "There's no way to make that shot!"

Betsy looks at him with shock, as if, all this time, it is she who has been misled. She has that soft look of a woman let down, about to cry. The move catches the truckers off guard.

Pointing the tip at the ceiling, she lifts the cue above the table. The guys are heading toward her to retrieve their money.

Startling everyone with the ferocity of her action, Betsy slams the handle end of the cue down hard on the three one hundred dollar bills pinning them under her cue and to the rim of the table.

FORTUNE

The second trucker is reaching out for the money when his pal catches him by the arm and points to the far end of the table. Under pressure from the black, the jolt to the table by the cue hitting the money has vibrated the two colored balls apart. The black ball drops to the table, rolls forward and, ever so lightly, kisses the white.

The two men are stunned.

I am stunned.

This is better than *Deus ex machina.*

Everybody appears stuck in freeze frame. Everybody, that is, except Betsy who calmly picks up the cash and stuffs it into a tight, jeans back pocket.

As the projector reconnects with the sprocket holes, the film jerks forward and everyone returns to normal speed. Betsy smiles her sweet, friendly smile at the truckers.

"Boys," she tells them, "It sure has been a business doin' pleasure wi' y'all."

She is so pleased with herself, she moves too slowly. For all his size, the second trucker is on her in a flash, grabbing her by the shirt with one hand clenched about her collar and lifting her clear off the floor. He begins walking her towards the door.

He snarls at her, "Now, missy, you are gonna earn my money."

From my viewpoint, Betsy does not struggle, she does not resist. She goes limp.

The trucker is angry mad, but uncertain what he will do with the dead weight rag doll he is holding. His stride drops in tempo as he looks to his buddy.

The first trucker picks up his pool cue and points it at me as he works his way around the table to approach me.

His voice takes on a low, hard delivery.

"You be a good girl and come along, real quiet," he orders me. "You hear?"

This is when dreams spin out of control. This is when I call on my super powers to scale walls and fences. This is when doors will not open. Danger is visible and I feel everything, but pain. I am terrified. The plate in my sweating hand loses weight. First goes the fork to the floor and then the plate. The fork bounces. The plate smashes.

The noise brings in the waitress who sizes up the situation in a flash. Blessed are the service industry workers, for they know both sides of each story.

"Everybody—separate—NOW!" she barks.

She can get down and dirty when she needs to, and she needs to, now.

"Or do I call the Sheriff?" she asks. "He's enjoying his break, one room over."

She gestures with a thumb over her shoulder in a vague implication. Maybe she is raising the stakes and has a bad hand. These truckers are aware of how public the situation is. This is one of those times when it is best to play by the rules.

Maybe the truckers are simply attempting to intimidate us so they can recover their foolish bets. Maybe they are still planning on some entertainment that has not been offered.

They stand still. My self-appointed dance partner drops his cue onto the pool table and half turns away to signal he is becoming non combative. When Betsy's feet touch back down on terra firma, she springs to life, stepping back as her own partner laughs a choked rumble that implies embarrassment, but has stall written all over it.

Under the protective cover offered by the waitress, I step over to Betsy and, grabbing her left arm, steer her out the emergency door.

Imitating her little show off speech from earlier, I tell her, "I learned this on the streets. RUN!"

FLIGHT

Outside the door, our run to freedom rapidly disintegrates when we prepare to separate toward our individual exit strategies.

The bus I rode in on is in motion, slowly heading out a distant exit.

I stop dead in my tracks, utterly confused as to what choices are left me.

Betsy looks back to the door and sees two huge figures emerging to pursue us. She grabs my arm and drags and pulls me in the direction of her car. Conflicted, I twist away from her to watch after the departing bus.

"We in worse trouble 'n missin' a bus," she yells in a panicked voice. "Move! Go!"

Behind me now, she pushes with all her might. I am automatically in motion. To resist her forward propulsion, I dig my heels in to the gravel making my body lean backwards. My mind attempts to piece together a way to get on the now disappeared bus. I am being of no help to Betsy.

Using totally sheer, panicked will power, Betsy propels me to her car. She opens the tiny passenger door and shoves me in, my feet lifting and going forward inside as she clambers over me into the driver's seat, presses the ignition button, and engine roaring to life, fishtails dust into the air behind us causing the forward motion to slam my door shut as we now head for the exit.

Through fear-induced haze, energetic activity and finally relaxing into the control of a woman of immense power and drive, I see two huge wood trunks of trees on either side holding up a wood beam framing our exit. Beyond, on a billboard advertising bungee jumping, a man is suspended upside down by his feet.

Slipping into our past, two outraged men scream incoherent epithets after us.

FECUNDITY

Out on the open road, Betsy gives her car full throttle and the vehicle literally sinks down toward the road as trees on either side of the highway become a blur. The wind destroys any hair styling I had left as I engage in a dream come true, my exhilaration of riding with Nancy Drew as she and I escape one danger and our lives entwine as we head into a future—together.

Betsy checks her rear view mirror, as if a truck has any hope of catching this firebird. Holding the wheel with one hand, she stands fully upright in the car, pumping the air with her free fist yelling a full bloodied, "WEE HA!"

She pulls the money from her back pocket and sits. She hands me two crushed, one hundred dollar bills.

"Here!" she yells into the wind. "Like I promised yer."

I refuse to take them.

"I only gave you one hundred," I tell her.

She sits up in her seat with arms rigid straight like a race car driver, concentrating on the road ahead, chattering as she goes.

"My dad says," she tells me, "'If there's an element of risk, use other peoples' money.' I get one; yer get one, plus yer stake. We're even. Yer earned it."

It's that simple to her. The two hundred on top of my one hundred was profit. We split the profit since we are equal partners in the action. I have never been in a real financial gain situation. This was utterly scary to me.

I take the money she offers, turning from her as I stash it away in my pocketbook, all the while thinking through the circumstances.

Though I told her I wanted my financial stake back, if she had lost the bet, by giving her the money, I was completely prepared to lose one hundred dollars. In fact, I gave it up; I released it the moment I handed it to her. I was not lending it to her. I was not financing a risk investment. I gave it to her for a bunch of wrong reasons. I wanted her to like me. I was hoping to buy her friendship. I had her on a pedestal, which meant I was beneath her; this young woman who must be half my age. What a moron I am.

"Would you have paid me back the hundred if you had lost?" I ask nervously.

Without looking at me she laughs.

"If I was gonna lose," she says, "Then the risk outweighed makin' the bet."

"But," I argue, "You just got through saying you used my money because there was a risk."

"Listen up, smarty pants," she grins at me briefly. "My assessment of the risk outweighed losin'. What yer really askin' is, would I have paid yer back if I had lost? Answer's the same; if the risk is too high what's the point in makin' the bet."

My brain has turned to taffy; she is like a money machine. She clearly lives in a world dominated by money conversation. How different we are.

I am deep into negative thought when Betsy calls me out of my self-degradation reverie.

"What d'yer think 'bout changin' my name to Lucy?" she asks.

I look at her. The little girl has returned. After everything I have just seen her go through, she is concerned about receiving my approval of her. As I ruminate on what exactly to say, I recall how Rachel got her name.

"MpowRgirl changed to Rachel," I mutter out loud.

"What?" she says.

My remark has no meaning for her so she focuses on her driving waiting for a more definitive answer. Right then, we round a bend and almost drive into the back of my bus.

Panic stations!

I roar into conflict mode again. I need to get back on the bus because I have a ticket to use up. Conversely, I do not want to separate from my first possible friend in many years.

Am I being a leech? Obviously, I am being self centered; thinking of what may be good for me, not for her. We have not yet talked future, she and I.

An image of my seat on the bus floods my brain. There's my coat hanging by the window. On the floor is my food parcel. Up above is my suitcase with my customized wardrobe. If I don't get on the bus, it'll probably go to waste. Who else can wear those clothes? Anybody, I guess. But no one but me and my doppelganger will look "good" in them.

As Betsy moves the car to the left of the bus into a position intended to pass up the bus, I hear my voice scream, "My coat and suitcase are on the bus!"

We are now parallel to the bus and speeding past. Betsy turns to me as if we are safely driving the open road with not a care to consider.

"Buy some new!" she laughs merrily. "It's only money!"

She infuriates me with her rich mind set. Her statement about her dad's financial philosophy resonates in my mind.

"Someone else's money, Lucy?" I ask, not realizing until I had spoken that I had answered her question at the cost of my possessions.

Her right foot goes flat to the floor and the car's rear end drops down noticeably as we race ahead sending the bus into the distant past.

"Hey, Jude," she screams with joy. "Lucy it is! I love it. Yer think on yer feet—smashin' that plate was priceless!"

There she goes again with the money thing. At the same time, we have not only cemented our friendship, we move it to the next phase, immediately.

"Come wi' me ter..." she pauses while she mulls the sound in her own head first, "Taquinta!"

I have not the least idea what she is referring to. My eyes are closing. I struggle to force them open. Life is blurring as the excitement level tapers off. My energy level sinks into the floor.

Up ahead, sitting on the hood of the car, I see a figure. It resembles Ariel. She is gently rocking a baby. I have no idea where this thought comes from but, as seems my wont these days, I speak first and listen later.

"The three of us?" I ask.

Even as I slide into oblivion, I can feel Lucy's stunned expression as she turns to stare at me, my head falling back, mouth probably open, gone, asleep, instantly dreaming.

I lay on my back on a hospital gurney covered with a huge white cloth draped over it. The gurney is rolling down one of those straight highways they have out west, eternally long, no bends, just the gradual rise and fall to accommodate an occasional hill.

I lie in state, dressed in white robes, silk, flowing, loose fitting. On my stomach is the largest imaginable apple pie, at least two apples high and wide enough to cover my entire stomach. My hands would be in prayer mode except the pie separates one hand from the other. A half gallon of ice cream is on top, melting, dripping down the sides.

The two truckers from the diner are in charge of keeping me mobile, on each side, one in front and one to the rear. Lucy, dressed as Peter Pan, attacks them, flourishing her sword in a threatening manner, though all she accomplishes is to slice the apple pie into eight precisely equal sections.

The truckers have left me. My gurney is beginning to roll down a grassy hill. Steep. I'm not in Kansas anymore.

I catch a glimpse of two other gurneys. My parents are each on their own blood stained gurneys. One trucker pushes my dad; the other trucker pushes my mom. They head up hill. The hill grows steeper with every step. My folks appear lifeless.

I scream, "MOM! DAD!"

Nothing. My voice is gone. I panic. My gurney moves faster the more I panic. I have no choice. Peter Pan flies alongside me pointing with his sword. I try to sit up. Pieces of ice cream drenched apple pie break away and fly into my mouth. Lucy laughs gleefully as we go faster down the hill. Being Peter Pan she can fly. I realize I am strapped to the gurney. I start passing mirrors reflecting me. Soon there are so many mirrors that they blur together and I can see myself screaming silently, my hair matting with ice cream and apple pie. The wind tears the white robes off of me exposing me to be wearing the clothes I left on the floor in Rachel's bathroom. Books fly by me. I try to see the titles. The books open. I begin to calm as I read occasional lines. These are new books I have never read before. The gurney slows. Lucy Peter Pan turns away and chases after butterflies. The mirrors disappear as the hill levels out. The more I read the more calm I become. It grows dark; warm, peaceful sleep.

From behind and overhead, a screeching hawk sails through the air, as if guiding us all to our future. No noise can wake me now.

The fantasy disappears as I open my eyes. Lucy is quietly, determinedly, driving us along one of those straight highways they have out west, eternally long, no bends, just the occasional gradual rise and fall with the surrounding desert terrain. Where was I for the longest time? Clearly, not paying attention.

I realize we like each other, Lucy and I. When we talk and when we are silent, we're comfortable together, at peace, each of us, in our own skin. She drives, I fantasize.

We arrive in the tiny town of Casper, New Mexico, to gas up at the only store there is. I stumble out of the car as if I am drunk. I stagger along, propping myself up with my right hand on the car as I make my way over to the store. Though I have never been here before, I know in my heart what I will find inside, to a greater or lesser degree. With my profits burning to leave my hand, I am going shopping.

FELICITY

There they are, arranged as so many glistening, brightly colored, regimented, candy bar friends. Since money is no object, I load the counter up. It may be a long way from this ghostly town to the next stop. I do not want to run out. I start in right away. I can feel the bar smearing my face, but I don't care.

Toot, toot, goes Lucy's car horn.

"Toot, toot, yourself," I say. "I could give a hoot."

I like Lucy. I like Lucy a whole lot more than Betsy. There was something stuck up about Betsy. Lucy is a free spirit; a little, pregnant angel. Oops!

I feel my energy coming back in a cloying kind of way. I walk out in a rolling motion and head to where Lucy finishes gassing up the car. I hold out my bag of goodies to her as she stashes the nozzle back on the pump. She looks at the bag with curiosity, then at me.

"Candy?" I ask.

She pats her flat stomach as she tells me, "I'm off that stuff now."

I stare at her for a long moment deciphering the coded message. Oh, the baby, sugar and other stuff—pregnancy. Right! I say to myself, I get it. Truth be told, I don't.

She points to the side of the general store where a wooden sign hangs crookedly on one nail, the words, 'Women/Men', are faintly legible.

"We need to clean up fer visitin'," she tells me.

I nod concurrence though I have no idea without—my suitcase, my hairbrush, my clothes—how am I going to do all this. Whatever!

The bathroom walls are corrugated sheets of metal standing on end and tacked together. A slight wind, warm as it is, blows through holes where nails had been.

Though our color palates are completely different, Lucy makes a valiant effort to turn me into a presentable person again. She brushes my hair straight losing any remaining flexibility it had. She insists on using her own lipstick. It's far too bright scarlet red for my complexion, and the powder she uses, though it smells nice, is again the wrong shade. Applying mascara to my eyelids is an over statement. As I watch in the busted mirror, I see a cracked version of my recent former self. That's OK. I have no idea who I am anyway. It thrills me that all these strangers feel they should control my appearance.

Then she turns to herself, and a real transformation takes place. Lucy, the mom to be cowgirl waif, becomes like a million dollars. All of this change is done with swift, conscious strokes. She is practiced in the arts of deception. As she finishes, she turns with a flourish, flaring her pink, knee length dress out and then down, as if pointing to her matching leather pumps, and she gives me the sweetest lecture, waving her open lipstick at me for emphasis. On her left hand middle finger is an intense, green rock, symmetrically bezel cut that makes my ring look cheap and small.

"Somethin' I learned in Tokyo," Lucy informs me. "Fudge the details. Yer my aunt to supervise me through the delivery. That's all they need to know."

I realize that wherever we are headed, these folks will eventually ask for, or hear through accident, more than those two simple facts.

"OK?" she asks for finality.

I'm with you, Booboo.

"I guess," I say.

We drive a short ways and stop at a rise. Once Lucy shuts off the engine, the quiet is deafening. Then a cricket, or cicada, or some ratchety insect, starts up followed by another and then another. In no time at all, there is no more silence as the hot air throbs with insect chatter.

I sit eating candy while Lucy gets out. She stares at something, her eyes growing big and melancholic. In the 0distance, a rhythmic sound lays a bass line to the higher pitched insect noises. This sound is more human in its regularity and insistence. A drum beat, metal on rock?

When I sit up straight and look out, I can just catch a glimpse of what Lucy is looking at. In the valley below us, what resembles an Easter Egg Hunt collection of colored igloos, scattered about on the local red dirt with an occasional bushy Pinon tree. Some building with a large, thatched, round roof sits at one end. In the middle there is an open area with a huge round building adjoining it. The layout of the buildings resembles a Dragonfly, the colored domes picking up the theme of iridescent colors. No, it's a human being sketched abstractly. Then, again, it's igloos and large buildings. My mind is playing funny tricks on me.

Whatever it is we are looking at, it makes my tough as nails cowgirl tear up. I guess this is where we are going. It must be exciting because we are dressed to party.

DAY THREE

EMPOWERMENT

Though to my addled brain there appears to be no access road, Lucy quickly finds a way in. There is no signage that I can see, implying, to me that these folks really do not invite visitors. We pass one sign telling us we are now on a private road, emphasized by there being no road at all just a dirt path with ruts where vehicles have driven in the wet. Lucy's low riding sports car does great on highways. Here it is like being in a basket tossed by the elements. She slows way down. I assume for the sake of the car as much as for our comfort.

The "road" is straight. Still, we gradually lose altitude in a slow descent.

Out of nowhere, two enormous women dressed identically in one piece blue jean coveralls step into the roadway brandishing shovels. As we stop, I see they truly are identical and, probably, twins.

Lucy is excited. Talking over the windshield, she half rises out of her seat prompting the Amazons to take a more aggressive posture with their yard tools.

"Hi, ladies!" Lucy chortles with glee. "This Taquinta?"

They say nothing, but, with adept gestures, indicate the car stays right where it is. They lead off, intending for us to follow. Lucy jumps out of the car as if back at boarding school after a long summer home.

I want more confirmation from these two behemoths. "Yes" or "No" will suit me fine. The stoic people of the world always feel passive aggressive to me. They scare me because I'm always waiting for the other shoe to drop. Both of mine do; we walk.

The place we head for is close to a mile down the dirt road. All I can see from the road is more road leading to a mud red valley with green fields. The valley is deceptive. The road runs between two shallow slopes so it takes until we are almost in the valley and make the slightest turn to the right for the community to appear. Anyone on the road not knowing where they were going will be hard pushed to imagine there is a place up ahead where... women—all I see are women—live!

In New York I walked all the time, though not in alligator skin pumps, especially alligator skin pumps on dirt road. By now, I am stumbling along. In our hurry to comply with the demands of the two guardians who escort us in, I have left my bag of candy bars in the car. I do take the pocketbook. Though, looking about, there is not even a tourist shop. Ahead of me, Lucy strides along in elegant cowboy boots that are perfect for this terrain.

Our two escorts pass us to other women outfitted in what is clearly the local uniform of blue jean coveralls. That's when I realize they are both mute. I feel embarrassed by my hostile reactions. They walk off without batting an eye in my direction, so any bad feelings I have, the embarrassment and anxiety, are all mine.

Lucy and I are immediately separated. I am led to an igloo painted bright yellow. Close up, the igloos are hemispherical domes resting on the ground. They have doorways, little triangular windows and side pods that, I quickly learn, are attached "rooms." Entering through the door, it is surprisingly spacious inside. Maybe, because there are no corners, there is less waste of space.

The igloo I am in has one other occupant, a woman, who introduces herself as Lea. She offers for me to sit on a simple, wooden, dining room chair in the middle of the glazed Saltillo tile floor while she paces around the space barefoot. Her pacing is more like strutting;

the stalking of a tall bird wading in water seeking fish. I think of her as being an aristocratic stork; her eyeglasses perched far along on her nose accentuating her skinniness and definitely her striving to be intellectual.

Through a triangular window, I see Lucy chatting with two women and gazing about with sublime joy at being here, clearly feeling blessed to be wherever here is.

"Tell me about you," the stork, Lea, asks, "So I may represent you to the Elders."

Elders? Elders! Is she nuts? Where are we? Is this some primitive society where drums accompany bizarre rituals? I have no idea where I am other than somewhere in New Mexico. Duh! More fool me for not asking some simple questions, but Lucy has me agreed to a plan. Now, as a result, I am being prepared for presentation to the Elders!

I take a notion to play at being Alice and see where that will get me. I use a baby like voice.

"*There is no use trying,*" I quote from *Through the Looking Glass*. "*One can't believe impossible things.*"

Without batting an eye, Lea responds in a deeply majestic voice, "*"I dare say you haven't had much practice," answered the Queen.*"

Touché!

Lea smiles confidently at me.

I feel my face assume a Cheshire Cat grin.

What fascinates me is that, sitting in the center of this dome, my voice comes back at me from all around. It is the strangest feeling. It causes me to be doubly aware of what I say.

I make a point of adhering to what Lucy told me she learned in Tokyo and so I fudge, mumble and look dumb; at doing all of which I am well practiced.

Lea finally relents and holds the door open for me. On reflection, I realize she has asked many of the same questions in different ways so that I am unable to recall how I answered what. She has snookered me. I hope that Lucy can talk our way out of this.

Then I wonder to myself, why am I trying so hard? I have no idea what this Taquinta place is and why I am here, other than that Lucy felt it will be a good idea for me to string along. Playing her aunt is foolish, but I said I will, and I will do the best I can, having not been an aunt before.

We are on the move. Lucy apparently had her own entry interview. We meet up with her as she leaves a blue dome. She looks like the cat that swallowed the canary. She slips an arm about my waist and gives me a big hug as we walk with Lea.

Out of nowhere the Amazons take over escorting us. Lea strides off at a speed which boggles my mind to watch.

We are by the round central building. Being in proximity to it, I see how huge it is, as is the open area next to it. Off to one side of the big building, I spot a couple of dumpsters filled to the brim with food scraps. I realize it is hours since I ate anything, except for candy. I make a beeline for the dumpsters.

There is some good food in there. From years of eating out of dumpsters, I know the routine. If it looks edible, eat it. Unless it smells bad or has insects crawling on it, eat it. Then, again, some insects are good to eat, too; more protein.

I forget about Lucy and the Twins as I dig down and consume a couple mouthfuls. Lucy's hand lands firmly on my shoulder, spinning me round.

"Jude?" she screeches, shocked.

"It is such a waste," I tell her pointing to all the food in the dumpsters, appalled that people will throw out good food.

'It's trash..." she trails off.

Clearly, she does not comprehend my point of view as she steers me away, wiping my mouth clean with her hand, then wiping her hand clean on one of the Amazon's coveralls. The woman looks at her with a grin, looks over to me and grins even more. What's so damned funny? I wonder.

We walk past countless colored domes to what must be the head of this place. There is the round, thatched structure I saw from the hilltop. It is slightly elevated giving it a 360 degrees view of the entire valley.

We come to a stop at the beginning of a pathway leading to the thatched building. I look closely and see people, women, of course, squatting in a circle on a clay floor under the thatch. In fact, there is insufficient vertical space to do anything other than sit, since the thatch comes low to the clay base, raised above the surrounding terrain. The entire thing is circular with wooden posts every few feet. The top of each post splits into a short Y shape on which rest horizontal posts. The horizontal posts support the three feet thickness of thatch that looks like it may be corn stalks bound together.

Inside the structure, the women are having a heated conversation. Their words do not carry to us since those doing most of the talking have their backs to us. Then I spot Lea. She is facing us. When she speaks, her voice is barely audible.

"Lucy, born Betsy, daughter of trustee Babs Auchin," Lea tells her colleagues, presumably the Elders, "Brought her eccentric aunt, Judith Fargoe, with her to Taquinta, to oversee her child's birth."

Eccentric? Oversee the childbirth? Wait one minute here! Not Lea.

She continues.

"Judith studied classical children's literature," she says. "She is a patient of Harley Street physician, Dr. Michael Kaliban, a professor at King's College, Cambridge, treating her for hypoglycemia."

Wow! Did I ever unravel? I guess stuff from my book reading got mixed in with my recent past and Lea made her own construct of it all. I sound impressive. I can feel myself gloat when Lucy digs me in the ribs, sharply. I wince as I look at her. She casts her eyes down, indicating, I guess, for me not to react.

Lea is still presenting.

"In considering their application," she says, "I keep coming back to staying on the right side of Babs."

Lucy jabs me in the ribs again, this time more gently. I feel anger mounting as I look at her. She secretively gives me the thumbs up. Oh, I get it! Her mom finances this place in whole or in part. No wonder we're getting the royal treatment. Least, I assume that's what is happening. Judging by her presentation, Lea, for one, is a great believer in sucking up.

Sitting to Lea's left, a zaftig woman I later learn is called Serena, snidely rounds on Lea's last remarks.

She states about Babs Auchin, "...Who guiltily underwrites us with her hubby's blood money earnings."

An Earth mother type, Petrina, across from Lea with her back to us cuts off Serena by asking loudly, "What about Judith is eccentric?"

"She arrived here without luggage, no documents or credit cards, but over ten thousand dollars in cash," Lea states in a shocked voice. "And, of course, Judith wears the Auchin emblematic Texas Piggy."

I instinctively feel the ring on my finger and reflect on the glorious rock Lucy is sporting. Texas Piggy? Not exactly a term of admiration.

Lea ends, by stating about me, "The only Judith Fargoe online presence I found is a tween. All told, Judith seems to be quite bright, when you cut through the brain fog."

Chrystal, a woman with a thick braid of silver hair down her back, explains, "Brain fog can be a symptom of hypoglycemia."

Serena jumps in again.

"I say, let them stay till the baby is born and make a final decision then," she announces. "We Elders will monitor them."

That sends chills up my spine. This place is definitely Sci-Fi territory—all women, Elders, everything done in circles, monitoring people. We may have arrived in a version of John Wyndham's Zealand with a bunch of female Midwich Cuckoos.

One woman, who has not previously spoken, appears to be in charge. Maisha, an African American, calls for a vote. I strain to see what they do. My vision becomes powerful like MpowRgirl's and I zoom in and see the women give a collective thumbs up sign.

I am so focused on watching the proceedings, I am unaware I am blocking the path. A short, stocky woman pushes past to get in front of us. She edges me out of her way and stands squarely on the path, rolls her head back and lets out a sound which shakes me to my core. She has a beautiful voice. Incredibly, the sound is so loud; it reverberates off the walls of the valley.

Lucy whispers to me, "Aroha is Maori. This is a song of the

Goddess woman. She is announcing guests arriving at the host's home."

By the time Aroha finishes, Maisha has arrived at the base of the short steps leading into the thatched structure. She responds with a rich and powerful voice, but she's no match for Aroha.

I study Maisha. She must be in her early fifties. She is slim and with the darkest color skin I have ever seen. Her jet black hair is pulled back. Her slender face and delicate long fingers remind me of pictures of Miles Davis. This is most assuredly the head priestess. Her heart is in the right place. She has a head on her shoulders and power in her belly. I relax and enjoy the show.

The singing ends. Aroha smiles as she strides forward leading Lucy and me along the path toward the Elders. The Amazons stay back. Women begin arriving from all over the place. Something of significance must be happening.

By the time we finish the short walk along the path; all the Elders have stepped out of the structure and are lined up. Lucy is positively vibrating with excitement. Obviously, she knows all about these activities and is enjoying each moment as if reliving a memory.

The Elders have formed a greeting line. Aroha steps aside and invites Lucy forward, as guest of honor. Lucy and Maisha grasp each other by the shoulders, and, without more than a brief glance into each other's eyes, close their eyes and lean toward each other so they are touching foreheads and nose bridges. It is most moving.

I wait, realizing my turn is next. The two of them keep hugging. I can feel my own impatience rising. OK, Lucy, I think, enough hogging the African Queen.

They hug like that for at least one and a half minutes. Lucy moves to Serena who gives her a short, ill tempered glance. I make a mental note to watch out for that one. Then, there I am in front of this majestic woman towering over me. She must be six feet tall and perfectly proportioned. I immediately understand, I too will meet and greet the same way as Lucy is now doing with Serena.

I follow Maisha's lead and lay my hands on her shoulders. I cannot believe the feeling of pure muscle and sinew. Maisha must have the lowest body fat of anyone I have ever touched. She leans her head towards mine, her eyes searching deep within me for my soul. I give it up to her. How can I do anything else with someone so potent?

She and I hold each other in this strangely peaceful place. Images race through my mind, images utterly foreign to me. I see worlds crossing back and forth between us. It is the most clean and simple transfer of ideas I have participated in with another person. By the time we eventually separate, I feel she and I go back lifetimes. Our ancestral paths, our DNA, have intertwined and our future, too, now locks into a closely knit path. She gives me one final look into my eyes, and I know right then, Maisha and I will go head to head one of these days—perhaps, in a power struggle for the control of this community. I see in her eyes, not only that she, too, recognizes this possibility, but, also, that she relishes the battle to come. She invites it!

Shaken, I move to face Serena. Lucy is already two more people on. I see this does not have to take the same amount of time with each person. Serena stays true to her attitude. Though gracious and sharing, beneath any invitation stands a warrior at the gate. In our mental exchange, I interpret that she will be an obstacle to my ever being at ease here. She despises what Lucy represents, and, by association, I assume she despises me.

All twelve Elders greet Lucy and me in this remarkable manner, another gift, I later learn, from the Maoris. No wonder I keep reflecting so much on Wyndham's last remaining territory, Zealand.

The Elders parade back inside the thatched structure taking Lucy and me with them. We crawl to places designated by Maisha. I sit in the North at 12 o'clock. Lucy is to my right at 3 o'clock with her back to the entrance. Directly across from Lucy sits Maisha, and to her right sits Serena. Lea sits to my left, and I face the Elder, Chrystal.

It is surprisingly cozy in here. The circular structure implies, like the knights at the Round Table, that there are no leaders; all are equal and everyone's strength is appreciated for its special significance.

These women, also, wear the uniform coveralls, except their bibs are distinguished by a large white circle. A couple of them, like Chrystal, have sewn embroidered patches for their circle. Characters, with personalities overflowing, are welcome at Taquinta—they're expected!

I look past Chrystal's shoulder to see that many women have gathered on the slopes around this place. They sprawl and sit, generally at ease with the excitement of the moment. As I look about, I can see out in every direction. Women surround us, women of all ages, races, colors. This is the melting pot, feminized!

"We meet in this Togu Na, our House of Words," declares Maisha in a voice as majestic as her demeanor. "What is spoken here is binding for all time."

This close up to her, I am riveted by her presence.

She looks at Lucy, then, at me, as she offers a warm invitation with a sweep of her extended hand.

"We embrace you both," she tells us.

Focusing on Lucy, she says, "Lucy, you shall strive for a healthy birth of your baby."

Lucy does not hold back her tears. This is the invitation she was anticipating when we stopped at the top of the hill. She bet all her chips on this move. It paid off.

Maisha turns to me. She studies me long and hard before she addresses me.

"Judith, you honor us with your desire to live at Taquinta," she says. "You are invited, as our guest, to be our equal, our peer, to share in our lifestyle till the birth of Lucy's baby."

As spokesperson for this community, Maisha is inviting me to stay. I have not been invited to stay anywhere, ever, in my life. My parents cared for me. When they passed, I was alone. Life has been one long struggle, and for whatever reason, I never learned the real know how, the reality, that most people grow up learning. I have book knowledge. That is exactly what it is, fiction. I learned the hard way; there is fiction, and, there is non-fiction. People have fantasies, but, typically, they set those aside as they endeavor to fit into a world of non-fiction.

I have fantasies born of fiction and I live in a fictitious world. No wonder it is always a struggle. If I had not created the Trinity, I may still be wandering the New York City streets.

I cry like a baby, TRiXi be damned. The whole world be damned.

My mothers have called me home and I accept!

"Our goals," Maisha instructs us new members, "Are to keep fit and to learn, so we may increase our levels of consciousness."

That is a decidedly different mission statement.

I reflect briefly on the conversation with Ariel and how she had laughed when I said I was conscious. Was she anticipating my coming to Taquinta? I may never know.

"That said," concludes Maisha. "Welcome!"

My eyelids, wet with tears, flicker to clear my vision. I look over at Lucy. Cocky with excitement, she accepts greetings from the women to either side of her. I already feel so entwined in this community, and yet, as the Dreamer, I also sense how alone I am. I have never felt both sensations quite as strongly as I do right this minute.

I receive brief, warm, tenderly welcoming hugs from the Elders on either side of me.

The Elders sing out in chorus, "WELCOME!"

The word itself, the sound they make, reverberates through each cell in my body. Every part of me has been accepted—the good and the bad, the flesh and the bone, the spirit of me and the concept of me. Considering, three days ago, I was still...

"WELCOME!"

It is a rolling wave. All the women outside the Togu Na, this house of words, resonate the same feeling to us. I am in community. I am part of a family. I am one of many; such a delicious sensation that is.

As I look about this sea of warm greeting, I wonder to myself, How long will all this last? Will they break from me or will I break from them? It's a fine thread that weaves us together.

At this moment in time, I feel deeply conscious of exactly how strong that thread will need to be.

IMPROVEMENTS

As an almost immediate reaction to Lucy's and my initiation into the welcoming bosom of Taquinta, I feel an intense desire to explore, to escape—to be alone. I realize how much I have been in the company of others almost non-stop for days. This is so unlike me to have companionship. I'm a loner. I deeply relish hearing only my own head thinking.

The street, if such a vaguely appearing thoroughfare may be called that, leading from the Togu Na to the Commissary, is sign posted, Lysis Strada. Someone has a sense of humor.

Is that what this place is? A runaway hideout for women tired of war? Is this a desert Never-Never Land where women can remain celibate until their men make peace? I'll have to ask.

Lea catches up with me and requests, "May I walk with you?"

It seems inconsequential. She makes it appear as if she is keeping me company to explain about life in Taquinta. Clearly, I have a lot to learn. However, we walk in silence.

At an open space below the Togu Na as the "head" of the community, Lea starts to drag her foot as if marking out some territory. She begins to talk about books she has read as she draws me into comparing notes from some of my readings. All the while, she is forming a wide circle about herself in the red dirt using the toe of her shoe.

All this is a precursor to her and me talking about Lucy and her to be born baby.

Lea asks me, "Are you familiar with the story of what occurs when the Archangel Gabriel arrives just prior to when a baby is about to be born?"

I plead ignorance.

Her story says that the baby spends the nine months of gestation in the womb studying with angels about all aspects of Life. Right at the very moment of birth, the Archangel Gabriel arrives to see what the baby has learned. Gabriel strikes the baby on the upper lip, hard enough to cause the cleft beneath the nose. The baby is so shocked by the force of the blow that all the knowledge learned is instantly forgotten, lost forever.

Like an empty vessel, knowing it is a vessel but not what it is meant to hold, upon being born, the baby arrives in the world to spend the rest of her days seeking the knowledge of her purpose that was "stolen" from right under her nose, just as she was about to be born.

Camaraderie forming, we both of us laugh at this story. Her circle finished, she stops and looks at me with a twinkle in her eyes.

"Did you know," she inquires of me, "That there is a contemporary version of this same concept?"

"Tell me," I say, enjoying being told folk tales.

"This one is attributed to Yogi Bhajan, who recently passed over," Lea says. "He was a principle teacher in America of Kundalini Yoga which is the morning exercise of choice here in Taquinta. The Siri Singh Sahib believed that we each of us know everything that we need to know."

That fits well with my understanding of Dream Time.

"To substantiate the knowledge we have, when we choose a book to read," Lea continues, "Each of us chooses specific books that confirm what we already know."

"How," I ask, "Do we know which books to choose?"

Lea laughs.

"It is an existential concept," she says. "We pick the books to read that confirm what we know. Those are the only books we read. If a book contains knowledge unfamiliar to what we know, we let it go, unfinished."

I stop her while I ponder that. Yes, that works with Dream Time, too. For example, Lea is only here because I am dreaming her. If she were a book, or even a character in a book, she will only be here in the book if I read the book; in other words, if I dream her up.

Wow! If everyone here is able to push the envelope like this, no wonder people come here to open their consciousness. I sense that being here may be fraught with problems for me, but living at Taquinta is going to raise my awareness to much that I already know! I assume there is some reason she is telling me all these stories.

I look around. Lea is gone, vanished into thin air. I look down to see the circle she drew in the ground. It, too, is gone. All I see is a short, vague scratch mark in the baked soil next to my own left foot.

I continue to walk "into town," wending my way between the many colored domes, aiming for the Commissary, searching for Lucy. She comes looking for me and waves me over.

"It's time to trade in our civilian clothes fer the local uniform, an' learn some basics of livin' here," she says. "Where were yer?"

"I went exploring," I say.

Right then, Lea comes out of the Commissary with a plate of food.

She smiles a greeting, and asks, "How are you doing?"

Standing in the Piazza, as they refer to the large open space, I drag my foot across the baked dirt trying to inscribe a circle.

Lea looks down at what I am doing and asks, as if I had initiated a game of Charades, "Foot dragging?"

I see she is serious and appears to have no memory of our being together just now.

"We gotta go get dressed," Lucy tells Lea by way of changing the topic.

Lucy takes my hand and leads me inside the Commissary to an

office where we trade in our civilian clothes for new uniforms. We're one of the guys, now, alright!

It certainly is a way to blend in. We receive a set of coveralls to wear, including heavy work boots, socks and standard issue underwear. We also receive an identical set for change.

Lucy asks the woman assisting us, "What do we wear at night? Evening dress?"

The woman grins as she tells Lucy, pulling up her coveralls, "You're wearing it."

The face Lucy makes is worth a thousand words. I am receiving the first inklings that I am not the only one who is unprepared for life in the community they call Taquinta.

As we turn away and head past the chow line, I bump into a woman who resembles a popular television show host. Lucy sees my double take, and, digs me in the ribs as she confirms what happened.

"Yep," Lucy says. "If they look like someone yer recognize, that's who they is."

She looks about the crowded room and points out people to me. Most names are unfamiliar to me. Lucy is like a Who's Who of Who's Who. It appears to me, from Lucy's color commentary, that ten percent of the Taquinta population are women from the "outside" world taking a few days of refuge.

Some present papers to the community, others just take advantage of the "anonymity" to unwind, to escape and to be among people striving to improve themselves. Taquinta is a women's resort for the intellect of the aware.

While I had wandered off into my imagination, Lucy was guiding me to a chartreuse dome on the east side of the community.

"This is our temporary lodging," she explains.

"Why is it temporary?" I ask.

"Yer'll know, by mornin'?" is her enigmatic response. She opens the door and we take the three steps down into our dome home, our womb.

This is one of several guest lodges. It seems we are located in the guest quadrant.

When I look out one of the triangular windows, I am amazed at who is walking by that Lucy pointed out to me earlier. I call her to the window. Again, the names have little meaning for me, but they are clearly people who impress Lucy with their achievements and station in life.

As we ready our beds, in each of two pod additions to our dome, Lucy tells me about Maisha as my bedtime story.

About the time she was a candidate for the 2nd Circuit Court of Appeals, Maisha was offered the possibility of developing and implementing Taquinta. Being recently divorced, with grown children, it was an option to explore infinite knowledge. She is a powerhouse for developing funding by bringing in paying visitors. Less a feminist than an activist for women's rights, she saw an opportunity and took it. Barely five years into existence, Taquinta is already well known among certain circles, thanks to Maisha's leadership. Maisha and her peers have consciously created a place intended for women to influence women of influence.

"So, why am I here?" I ask.

Snoring lightly is Lucy's reply.

Other than a secret, unspoken desire to influence and be powerful, why is Lucy here? Surely, having a baby is something a woman of means can do just about anywhere. If that is the case, why did this recent child choose this less than nature friendly place? Having sworn me to secrecy, this is something that may or may not ever reveal itself.

The evening sunset in the southwest comes fast and glorious. While Lucy sleeps, I step outside to watch the line of orange and red recede into dark blue and become a night sky lit bright by a cast of stars the like of which I never saw before. I am tempted to sleep outside, but recall that, this being desert, I am not familiar with the native nightlife. Mice, rats and the occasional stray cat or dog of the big city are one thing; the creepy crawlies of the desert are novelties I will study first.

I turn in and sleep as I have never slept before, dreaming bright Technicolor dreams, which I allow to flow unimpeded, so I may have the pleasure of watching the influence of the locale on myself.

Morning comes all too soon and, with it, another equally dazzling light show. We make it to the late shift for breakfast. The choices are stunning. I load up with orange juice, scrambled eggs, bear claws and scads of butter and a big cup of coffee. Lucy eats like a bird.

We sit outside on benches at picnic tables at the edge of the Piazza. Women in uniform scurry about like ants. There seems little rhyme or reason to each journey but no one wastes time.

Petrina joins us to discuss our objectives. Lucy knows this place from discussions with her mom. I apologize for having to ask questions and, thus, for appearing slow and stupid.

Petrina immediately supports me.

"We are all here to learn," she informs me.

Lucy nods agreement.

Two women come over and join us. Petrina introduces them and explains that they will guide us to build our home. Lael is originally from Los Angeles, a housewife and homemaker. She has elegance written all over her. The other is Zichrini, a muscularly built woman from Israel. She is introduced as the local expert on Kibbutz life.

The possibility of building our home excites Lucy. I am terrified when I understand that everyone is serious. I have never done anything particularly physical in my whole life. Opening closed dumpster lids is my best recollection of heavy lifting.

As soon as we finish eating and buss our plates, Petrina leaves us in the capable hands of Lael and Zichrini. For all her gentility, Lael is a worker. She revels in the joys of digging. Zichrini, who is built like an ox, and likely can outwork anyone in the place, assumes the role of supervisor and instructor. Her thick accent is difficult for me to understand. She knows what she is saying, and, for her, that is all that matters.

The unlikely couple march us to an outside door of the office in the Commissary. There we pick up two shovels, a plastic tarp, a huge bag of fiberglass tubing and a role of barbed wire. I cannot begin to imagine what we are about to do. If it is to build one of these dome houses, I have not the least idea how they are constructed. I know little enough about construction, and these round shape houses, despite their apparent simplicity, confound me as to how they are created. There is not one in progress to give a clue. Thus, then, what are we doing with a tarp, two shovels, a coil of barbed wire and a bag of fiberglass tubing?

When we arrive at the site of our future home, it is loosely cleared dirt. Zichrini pulls a skinny chain out of a coverall's pocket and a small metal stake. She slips one end of the chain onto the stake and with seemingly no particular spot in mind, drives the stake into the ground with the heel of her boot. About ten feet along the chain is a nail. She grasps the nail and starts to score a circle on the ground. She waves me over. I hand the shovel I am leaning on to Lucy who steps out of the way, allowing it to fall to the ground.

Zichrini has me complete the circle. Every time I let the chain go the slightest bit slack, she lets forth with a stream of invective in a language I have never heard before.

"What are you saying?" I ask.

With a grin on her face, Lael tells me, "Zichrini's first language is Ivrit also called Hebrew, but it has few good curse words. She's cursing you out in Arabic."

"Why Arabic?" I ask.

"Beckhose iz ze language forr telling perrzon yourr zoughts... ebout zem, zeirr femily, zeirr encestorrs, end zeirr unborrn generrations zu follow," Zichrini explains.

Lael adds, "I doubt you will appreciate the translation. I suggest you avoid asking."

"In other words," I tell Zichrini, "You want me to keep the chain taut all the time during the scoring."

"Execkly!" she replies.

Constructing the house may turn out to be easier than being taught how to build it.

Then it is Lucy's turn. She receives a separate, shorter chain for marking off four semi circles, each centered equidistant on the circle I made, each center being on my score line and outside the large circle I made. There, before us, scribed into the dirt, is the blueprint for a house, our future home. I am easily impressed.

Zichrini tells us, "Wherre I em frrom, zerre iz two weyz we do zings. One iz easy way. Zat iz correct. Ze other way... I chas no idea what zat iz."

I have never heard logic like this. I resolve to keep my eyes and ears open around this strange woman.

Zichrini finds a shady spot cast by a Pinon tree in which to sit leaning her back against the tree's trunk, and goes to sleep.

Lael has me help her open the tarp and lay it on the ground close by our markings in the dirt. Grabbing Lucy's shovel from her to demonstrate, Lael takes over. She starts digging around the inside edge of my circle. She jabs the shovel into the dirt and with her right foot strikes the top of the blade to drive it deep into the soil. With a twist of her wrists, hands spaced well apart on the handle, she lifts the dirt out.

After the one shovelful, she stands, looking at us expectantly. We look back uncertainly. She nods in the direction of the tarp. She sticks the shovel into the loosened dirt and walks off, disappearing from sight. These women depend a lot on gesture to convey meaning. I pick up my shovel and head to the main circle.

"My guess," I tell Lucy, "Is we dig the circle out and chuck the dirt onto the tarp."

"Show me," she says.

"Lucy!" I yell at her loud enough to cause Zichrini to squint at us through one eye. "This isn't other peoples' money. This is our home. Leastways it will be. We both work. Right?"

"Keep yer shirt on, Jude," she tells me. "Also, remember, I'm pregnant."

"You should have worked that out before you got pregnant," I say.

I am miffed.

Right then Lael returns pushing a wheel barrow carrying two bags of cement.

Seeing no progress she asks us, "What have you been doing since I left?"

"Chevving femily squabble," Zichrini pronounces without opening her eyes.

"Dig in, ladies," Lael tells us. "You want to be done here before we rent out where you're currently living."

Lucy steps across me to get to her shovel intentionally treading down the dirt in front of me that Lael had already loosened during her demonstration. Lael observes the move.

"Lucy," she calls her. "Take Judith's shovel and let Judith take yours. You might prefer it."

"They look the same to me," Lucy answers.

"What do you think, Judith?" Lael asks me. "Do they look the same to you?"

"It's hard to know," I tell her as I head over and grab Lucy's shovel. "But I'll take your word for it."

Lucy realizes she's been caught at one of her games. She takes hold of my shovel and begins digging into the soil where she had trodden it down.

"Wow!" she exclaims. "An' they look so similar. Thanks, Lael."

The two of us buckle down and after an hour of digging and shoveling the dirt onto the tarp we have a small pile of dirt on the wide expanse of tarp and the circle is barely dug into, and that, only around the perimeter. My hands are sore and at least one spot looks like a blister forming. That's when I realize, even though we are rank amateurs at digging; Lucy is waiting for me to stop so she can. Neither of us is willing to be first to quit.

As I move around the circle looking for loose dirt to shovel, I check out what Lael and Zichrini are doing. Lael sits facing Zichrini, her legs outstretched in the opposite direction alongside Zichrini's outstretched legs. They are chattering away in a foreign language and totally ignoring us. I calculate that Zichrini is watching us on peripheral vision without having to look directly in our direction.

"I am about ready to take a break," I tell Lucy. "How're you doing?"

"I'm good," she says.

That tells me nothing.

"Lael, Zichrini," I call out. "Is it OK if we take a breather break?"

I catch just the briefest flicker of a smile cross Lael's lips as they continue chattering, ignoring me.

"Looks like up ter us," Lucy says.

"Count of three," I tell her. "One, two... "

Lael calls over to us, "Take a break anytime you feel like it."

"I feel like a headache comin' on," Lucy declares.

Sounds to me, she is prepping the scenario to get out of work.

"Are you regularly drinking water, both of you?" asks Lael. "This is desert, you know? Dehydration is an issue here; big time. You need to make sure you always have an adequate supply of water with you. If you can be quick about it, head over to the Commissary and get a flask for each of you."

We look to each other and can't wait to make a break for it.

When we return only a few minutes later, Zichrini is backing up a pickup with a huge plastic tank on its bed. As we walk up, Zichrini jumps out of the truck and begins to release water into the small indentation we have created around the circle. Shutting off the spigot when she decides she has released enough water, she gets back in the pickup and drives off.

Lael checks us out as we walk up.

"Amazing what a little water can do," she says. "You both look refreshed. By tomorrow, the water Zichrini poured into your circle will have soaked down and ought to make digging easier."

"Why didn't yer wet the ground, yesterday, so it would be ready fer us?" asks Lucy.

"Three reasons," Lael answers my cranky niece with good humor. "First, you got here in the afternoon and we had to be certain you will be staying. Second, it's best to learn from experience."

Lael leaves a long pause.

"Yer said three reasons," Lucy insists. "What's the third?"

Zichrini walks back to our little group bearing an enormous pound cake, silverware, napkins and plates.

"If I known you come cherre, I beck a keck," she sings with a birdlike voice.

That takes the sting out of Lucy who totally melts at the thought that people she doesn't know feel like celebrating her.

"Gals?!" is the best she can come up with.

"When do we find out what all this other stuff is for?" I ask indicating the barbed wire, fiberglass tubing and cement.

"After cake," Lael tells me. "It's a little known and greatly overlooked fact that cake preceded the creation of the Universe. In these parts, anyway, everything, but everything stops for a cake by Zichrini."

If I was uncertain of it before, Lael has just confirmed it for me; the Mad Hatter was a woman.

EASEMENT

With only the hint of lemon, a mere flavoring of sugar—"Xylitol," Zichrini corrects my description—and a lightness belied by its height, this is a cake my mom would have been proud of the way it dissolves on the tongue.

OK, so we do hard labor; look at the perks!

My little bird, Lucy, helps herself to three portions. Zichrini glows with delight that we appreciate her baking.

Handing the remaining cake on its platter to Lucy, she tells her, "In kess one ov you err chung-gerry in ze night."

Lucy does not need telling twice. She grabs the platter and takes the cake home for safe keeping.

Lael makes short shrift of clearing the dishes and takes them away. Zichrini points to the fiberglass tube.

"Tie epp one end," she tells me, now and forever, her most obedient servant.

I tear open the containing bag and the compressed tube spills out and begins to unravel. With the speed of a predator hunting dinner, Zichrini is on her feet and by my side catching the hoops of cloth before they became uncontrollable. She is totally non critical, no cursing in Arabic, just a helpful soul giving a needed hand.

"I will chold while you will tie," she tells me.

Frankly, I can't see why it's so important but I do as I am asked.

"Meck tight," she says.

I make a simple bow knot out of this unnatural-to-work-with textile. Zichrini gestures with her arms, elbows bent, put some muscle into it. I do.

"Verry good," she tells me. "Tekk shovel ov dirt end drop in cheerr."

She holds the other end of the tube open for me and I tip the shovelful of dirt into the opening. Well, some of it goes in and most of it goes all over the place else. I look up embarrassed at my awkwardness.

She looks at me, again non judgmentally.

"Zis is ze ferrst time you werrk wiz a shovel?" she asks. "Rright? Tomorrrow you err expert."

With that she shook what dirt I got into the opening down to the knot I had tied, and then carefully laid the bunched up tube on top.

"You chev begun zu meck walls off ze chouse," she says. "Enough forr one day."

Zichrini picks up one of the bags of cement and tosses it to cover the fiberglass tubing. At that moment Lael and Lucy return from different directions.

Zichrini beckons Lucy and me over.

"Show me yourr chends," she tells us.

We hold out our raw, tender skin for her. She barely looks at them.

"Tonight," she says, "when you pizz, wash yourr 'ends wiz ze pizz. Leave to dry. Wash off beforre bed."

Something tells me she is not joking. I see Lucy eyeing me.

"What?" I ask her.

"Yer face," she says.

"I was thinking what Jeri would say," I tell her. "She gave me my last manicure."

"Course yer were," she answers.

She picks up her shovel and heads for the wet ring of dirt.

Lael calls out to her, "We're done here for today."

"That's it?" Lucy asks, surprised.

"Take a walk, explore, relax," Lael tells us. "You're on Taquinta schedule now. Too much of anything takes the fun out of it. Clean your tools. Make sure nothing can blow away or hurt anyone walking by here and you are free to go."

Lucy and I look at each other as if we're both at a loss for what to do for fun.

Lael catches the look.

"You are here for you," she tells us. "Once you get out of your own way, the true you will catch up with you. You'll know it when it happens. The true you is someone you have known all your life and kept telling to take a back seat while you satisfied everyone else. Here in Taquinta, only the authentic you counts."

As Rachel said to me in the limousine, but I do not voice out loud here, "You're talking gibberish!"

DIRT CHEAP

What is fun? I do not rightly know or care. I park myself inside the Commissary and make multiple trips to the cases of food. Apparently the place is open 24/7. Most of the time, they set out basic snacking food. They roll out the big meals at breakfast, lunch and dinner.

Lucy sits with me for a short while to keep me company. When she realizes I am a serious eater and am here for the long haul, she goes back to our dome to sleep.

Some kind soul steers me, in the dark, to our dome. It's amazing how complex navigation becomes when the landmarks all look the same.

Gone midnight, Lucy is passed out in her bed when I come in burping something fierce but fed till I can barely breathe.

A loud fart wakes me. The sun has been up for hours. I look for Lucy. Her pod is vacant and there are few places to hide in a dome. I clean myself up and put on my work clothes. I race to the Commissary where they have cleaned up from breakfast and are setting out snacks. For the first time in forever, I am not hungry. I make a beeline for the construction site. All the while, people I pass greet me. I mumble back at them but I feel out of sorts.

Lucy is merrily digging away all by her lonesome. Lael and Zichrini are by the tree sitting on the ground chattering. They all become aware of my arrival at the same time. Lucy digs her shovel into the ground and releases the handle so she can applaud me. The others join in hooting and whistling.

I stop, feeling my face flush with embarrassment.

"You should have waked me, Lucy?" I whisper.

"I tried," she says. "Yer were dead to the world, auntie."

She hangs on the name. I take it as some kind of hint. It means nothing to me.

"Some niece you've turned out to be," I retort. "Letting me sleep so you can look good for our supervisors."

"OK, OK, you two," Lael yells at us.

She bounds to her feet and joins us. Zichrini stays seated but briefly throws me the sweetest smile.

"Now you are both here," Lael says, "We can start to fill the tube."

Feeling as if I owe something to everybody, I step around the sizable excavation Lucy has achieved all by herself. I bend down to pick up the cement bag Zichrini tossed on top of the tube. I can barely lift it enough to get a grip.

"Bend your knees and lift with your legs," Lael instructs me. "The way you were going at it you can put your back out. That is a painful state that can last for days. Believe me."

With Lael coaching me I struggle to shift the bag off the tubing, the same bag Zichrini tossed like a bean bag pillow.

Lael has us half fill the wheelbarrow with dirt from the pile on the tarp. We add a half shovel full of cement and mix it all up. The mixture is then shoveled into a plastic 5 gallon container. Aided by its swivel handle, the container is used to fill the open end of the tubing. Periodically, we tamp the dirt tight inside the tubing. After a while of doing that, we return to digging out the "hole." Variety is the spice of life here.

As we work I talk to Lael about Zichrini.

"Why was she swearing and carrying on and then is gentle as a lamb, later on?" I ask.

"Zichrini has two passions in life," Lael tells us, "Construction and baking. She's a perfectionist at both. Her cakes are like a badge of honor to her. By cursing you out, she was preparing for you to dislike her cake. Then she saw you could tell how good her cake is. That's it."

"Thanks, Lael," I say as I turn to Lucy. "Where did you put the rest of the cake? I looked for it this morning."

"Someone musta et it," she says with a poker face.

"Yeah, right," I snarl. "Someone sure better have enjoyed it then."

"Someone did," Lucy says. "Besides, after all I ate, last night, there was only a small piece left this mornin'."

I check out Zichrini asleep under her tree. She has a big smile wrapping her closed eyes and mouth.

Lucy and I dig a little while longer. Lael calls time as we are beginning to make headway.

"That way," she says, "There will be some anticipation for coming to work the next day, like the cliff hanger at the end of a chapter in a novel."

Chrystal, she of the long silver braid, stops by to inspect our progress and to utter words of encouragement about how we are doing. She accompanies us to lunch so she can tell us about morning groups we may be interested in attending.

"If you are inclined," Chrystal says, "There is a meditation group that meets before dawn. The infrared bands that encircle the Earth before sunrise are able to take all pure thoughts and transmit them around the globe."

"At that time, my thoughts are dreams," I tell Chrystal. "I lack any desire to share those with anyone. Lucy for sure sleeps through the night."

Lucy nods agreement. She likes it when I offer her protective cover.

"When the morning light breaks," Chrystal pursues her recounting of the daily schedule, "We work out on pads, inside the Commissary on cold days and outside on the Piazza on warm ones, doing Kundalini Yoga, following Yogi Bhajan teachings."

Yogi Bhajan? Yeah. His name had surfaced during my questionable conversation with Lea. He seems to be some big influence around here.

"Serena calls KY 'human technology'," Chrystal explains. "It's control of the breath while exercising and meditating. Serena is the main instructor."

The mention of her name clinches KY for me; strike that off the list of morning activities. Lucy expresses a cautious interest.

"If I ever wake up that early," she says, "I'll give it a try."

"The other choice of exercise in the early morning," Chrystal tells us, with complete patience for our rebelliousness, "Has various names – Combat Conditioning, Chinese Prison Workout and Hindu Health. Led by Elder Yen Lu, this is body weight resistance exercising. It is strenuous, but an excellent way to gain overall body strength in a short amount of time."

"I guess that's me, then," I say reluctantly.

"Remember," Chrystal points out more or less what Lael has already told us, "Here at Taquinta, life is to be enjoyed to the full. Going to bed at all kinds of time can get boring if you want to fight imagined controls. When your body's natural clock settles in, unopposed by you, your Circadian Rhythms become more resonant. Rising, before the sun breaks on the horizon, becomes both easier and more meaningful. Exercising the body will appear to be essential for good health. You will begin to feel these needs come on as a natural consequence of receiving enough sleep. I am simply offering directions for where to go when you experience the desire."

"Thanks, Chrystal," Lucy and I harmonize, like two little girls from school.

"Enjoy your lunch," she says as she breaks away from us, just as the Commissary comes into full view.

"Are you really going to do yoga?" I ask Lucy.

"Yer betcha!" she says. "As soon as I see yer doin' the Hindu thin'."

Whatever did I do to raise this competition? It is new. We did not bring it with us.

CLASS SOCIETY

I realize how hungry I am as we approach the Commissary. Having gorged myself the previous day, and then panicked about allowing Lucy to go to work without me, I am aware I am returned to my old ways of feast or famine.

As she and I pass a table, I grab a coffee cake someone left on a plate. As I gulp it down, Lucy gives me a disapproving glance, but leaves it at that. At the service counter, annoyed with monitoring myself about what I eat, I load up on corn bread, fresh fruit and a milk shake.

"Chrystal mentioned you are here," Petrina's voice breaks into my reverie.

I am cheek down in a pile of fruit juice soaked crumbs on my plate. I lift my head up and accept the napkin Lucy offers me to wipe my face clean. Petrina is looking at me closely, gauging my responses.

"Taking a quick nap," I tell her.

"Judith, you have serious dietary issues," Petrina tells me.

"Issues?" I say. "Serious?"

"You told the Elders you were being treated for hypoglycemia," Petrina says. "Basically, you are allergic to sugar. Judging by what you wiped off your face, that whole meal you just ate was all sugars."

"Huh?" I say.

"How did you physician treat you?" Petrina asks.

What did I tell these people? That was what? ...two days ago. Physician? Er... she means Michael. They are attributing me with airs and graces by my association with young moneybags here. I guess if I'm playing her aunt, I'm tarred with the same brush.

How was Dr. Michael treating me?

"Let me remember," I say to stall while I recollect what I ate with Ariel and Rachel. "There was cream, some green drink, uncooked meat, cheese and butter—stuff like that."

"Raw protein diet," Petrina says. "That is one unusual physician."

"Yes, he is that," I agree, dreamily.

"How long were you on the diet?" Petrina asks.

"I was just getting started when I met... up with... Lucy asked me to..." I tell her. "And we came here."

"OK," Petrina says. "I will plan your meals with the kitchen staff. From here on out, you come and pick up your food at the far end of the counter, down there. It will be labeled with your name. Leave all other foods alone. You eat every two hours while you are awake. You will wake up every four hours and eat a raw egg while you sleep. Can you remember all that?"

"I'll try," I say.

Lucy's eyes are bugging out again.

"Raw?" she asks.

"Her entire diet will be uncooked, unpasteurized, organic..." Petrina replies. "Your aunt is massively unhealthy, Lucy. It's good you brought her here. Most places are ill equipped to handle such special needs. What about you? Are you eating for two yet?"

"She's barely eating for one," I opine.

Lucy flashes me an eyes narrowed look before turning her sweet, innocent smile to Petrina.

"You're our first pregnancy," Petrina says. "We have several doctors here. I will research who has the most pre natal background."

As Petrina rises to leave, Serena walks up. It feels like an orchestrated plan. What can we do? They're our hosts. Living here costs us nothing, at least, directly. When I see Lucy glow with all the attention, I begin to wonder if my objection is just me wanting to be left alone. I reluctantly go along with the agenda because I feel obligated to do so.

Serena has an idea that we want to know about available classes, too. I guess if you're obsessed with knowledge acquisition that makes sense.

As well as leading the morning group in Kundalini Yoga, Serena also teaches Emotional Freedom Technique.

"EFT is the use of pressure points," Serena explains pointing at her eye brows, below the eyes and the upper lip section, where Archangel Gabriel left his mark. "While mentally focusing on an issue for clearing, such as giving up smoking, or anger at parents, we tap with our fingers in a prescribed fashion on the pressure points."

For her, there appears to be no antagonism between us. However, I am not so quick to let my guard down. I sit back on the bench paying attention but not looking overly interested. Serena picks up on that and focuses on Lucy with the obvious intent to draw me in. Not this go round, I tell myself.

Serena abruptly changes course and begins telling us about Maisha's two classes.

"Her Long Stride Walking is a must take," she says. "She begins at 1 o'clock. You can make that with ease."

Lucy wrinkles her nose.

Serena adds, "Walking is the best exercise for everybody. I know you will enjoy it, Lucy. Maisha's other class is all about money. She leads that whenever she can gather four or more people together. Now that you and Judith are here she will have enough people to start a class. That will surely be fun for both of you."

"Sure!" Lucy says with a sneer.

"Maisha is important to you," Serena admonishes Lucy.

I don't fully understand that remark but I pick up a sense of resigned acceptance from Lucy. And auntie goes, too.

Serena talks of other possibilities; including Lea's Brazilian Ju-Jitsu self defense class.

"Do either of you play any musical instruments?" Serena asks.

"I play a little piano," says Lucy.

My mind flashes on Lucy sitting on the floor with a toy grand piano in front of her.

"Do you read music?" Serena asks.

"Some," Lucy replies.

"There are all kinds of groups playing different music almost every night after dinner," Serena explains. "As with the classes, check the notice board as you enter the Commissary in the morning before breakfast and at night before dinner. It is constantly changing. See, over there. Maisha's group is forming. You can make it."

Discharged by mother, we are free to go do as she says. I buss our dishes to give myself a few moments of own time. Rest and relax, find yourself, that's what I recall from Lael. Hardly are we relaxed, then along come Chrystal, Petrina and Serena with lists of activities to make sure we have no down time. Something needs clarifying here.

Maisha is delighted to see us amble towards her group. Once we are there, she explains the basics of taking longer strides at a slightly slower pace than a brisk walk with the intention of going further faster—like Lea did when the Amazon Twins took over escorting Lucy and me to the Togu Na.

The nearest I can come to describing it is footage from television of East German soldiers goose stepping. Maisha's foot does not make the full height of that cartoon like step and, at the same time, where the soldiers have bolt upright straight backs, she is relaxed and leaning into the step so it carries her forward. For the longest time, her foot seems to hover in space, giving up the vertical for a forward lunge to gain as much ground as possible. That foot has barely touched down when the other foot propels forward and up.

Compared to a goose step Maisha's foot never reaches being level with the hips in part because she is leaning her weight forward. Also, I notice, the knee is firm but not rigid to allow for the impact with the ground on the descent. She really is quite graceful as she does it.

I am glad I said that because neither Lucy's nor my legs are inclined to emulate Maisha's movements. For me, it is as if my hips are locked up tight and such a movement is opposed to what my body parts are willing to do. Lucy folds into a ball of uncontrollable laughter which is contagious. Even Maisha joins in.

"Thank you, Lucy," Maisha tells her. "We needed to break the tension. After all, this is supposed to be a relaxed exercise."

Maisha marshals her group to stride round the immediate outskirts of the town, community, or whatever it is we are. I feel Lucy is being intentionally disruptive as she and Maisha work something out. Maisha's willingness to give ground to Lucy tells me she is still in charge and Lucy's glory days are numbered.

That walk exhausts me. I head off to the dome to nap. When I arrive, Lucy is right behind me.

"You can take a nap, Jude," she tells me as she lies on her own bed.

"I know," I answer, with more edge to my voice than I intend.

"Sleep tight, auntie."

This kid is lonely. She took me under her wing to protect me. She knows who and what I am. Wait a minute, though. How can she? Even Rachel said I look the part. I have jewelry, money. I'm confused. I guess we both have our secrets.

We wake at the same moment. Night has fallen. We slept through dinner. I am hungry. As I swing myself out of bed, I can make out Lucy propped up on one elbow.

"If yer see somethin' that looks good," she asks in the dark, "Please brin' me some back, Jude. Thanks."

"OK," I answer.

Looking through a window, I see off in the distance over the tops of neighboring domes the lights of the Commissary are still on, so getting there will be simple. Coming home will be another matter. I decide to cross that bridge when I get to it. Right now, my objective is to eat. I am already fixating on all the possibilities.

The moment I open the door, my ears are assailed by the sweetest of music. It fills the air. It resonates across the valley. Our dome is sound proof in and out. They all are. Aiming for the lights of the Commissary, I pass many domes with lights on. They are soundless, mute homes.

Heading towards the light, I can hear the music more clearly the closer I come. There is definitely a violin supported by a cello, maybe. The energy is tantalizing; reeling me in like a fish on the line.

It's a warm night. I left without shoes and socks and feel the hard dirt underfoot. That, too, is exhilarating. I have never been so alive. Where is this charge of energy coming from?

A large crowd of women, mostly seated with a few standing, are gathered to attend four seated women bowing orangey brown instruments. It looks like three violins and a cello. One of the violins is bigger than the other two. Each musician alternates from reading the music in front of them to watching the other three. There is a fury to their effort only exceeded by the beauty of the collaborative sounds they create. I feel light as a feather, buoyed by the music. The audience is enraptured.

A small group, forming their own quartet, knits while they listen. Some others are equally furiously writing in books. A few are reading; that astounds me. How, with such vibrant music, can anyone concentrate on anything but simply listening? Everyone else is driving the engine with their focused attention. What a place this Taquinta is!

A sharp, hunger pain reminds me of why I am here. I decide to test Petrina and walk past everything to the far end. Lo and behold, there is a glass of green drink with a paper cover held on by a rubber band. The glass sits on a small orange plastic tray with my name on it. There's the cream and a couple of cubes of cheese with an equal cube of butter on each. A small glass bowl has three eggs in their shells. Seeing my name printed out, JUDITH FARGOE, next to that food reminds me of how I began this adventure being fed cream by Rachel. Add in music, plus, bare feet resting on dirt, I am elevated, ecstatic.

I grab the cream and lick it out of the little bowl it's in, leaving not a trace. Instantaneously, a sensation of satisfaction courses through my body. Reading the hand written note on the flip side of my name card, I realize I am supposed to eat one of the cubes of cheese and butter first. I look around. No one cares what I am about. They are totally involved in the concert. I eat the cheese and butter. There is both a sense of satisfaction and a craving for more at the same time. I ignore both feelings and chug down the green drink. My body literally uncoils as I relax.

I didn't know I was tense. I was hungry, yes, but tense? Whatever it was in me that relaxed, I was not aware of it before. Now, according to my brief note of instructions, I get to eat the remaining piece of cheese and butter, except I am supposed to wait ten minutes between the cheese plus butter and anything else.

Interestingly, I'm not sated, but the hunger edge is completely gone. I nibble on the last piece of cheese and butter as I turn to watch the musicians. Nothing in my past life compares with that feeling of joy, to be eating good food and listening to fine music with my bare feet on the dirt. Heaven has some stiff competition.

My mom taught me to spin eggs in their shell to determine if they were cooked or not; an uncooked egg jerks to a quick stop. I test the eggs by spinning them on the tray. They are all three of them uncooked, raw, as Lucy called it. My instructional note tells me to eat one egg every four hours during the night by cracking the egg into the cream bowl and swallow it down, without chewing. I'm not squeamish about food; dumpsters teach a person how to be non judgmentally open to eat most anything. I can just imagine Lucy's face if she wakes while I am throwing down a raw egg. Wee ha! Indeed.

Talking Lucy, I am supposed to pick up something for her. I walk along the line of food and nothing appeals to me now that I am appeased. I reflect on what I have seen her eat and nothing stands out. That girl needs to go hungry for a day or two to learn the purpose of food. Meanwhile, what to bring home?

A cheese sandwich with lettuce and tomato sticking out looks passable. I take it, and, giving one final look to the quartet, all fired up and probably charging down the final straight, I head for home with my cache of foods.

Finding the dome is a cinch. Lucy is waiting in the open doorway calling out to me as I trip along.

"Jude?" she calls. "Over here."

That was easy.

Lucy is hungry. She barely has the sandwich unwrapped before she tears into it. She waits till she finishes eating before she says another word.

"Thanks, Jude," she says. "Good choice. Did yer eat?"

"Yes," I tell her with some amazement. "Petrina was good to her word. It was all laid out, with instructions."

"How was it?"

"Perfect."

"We make a good team, Jude."

"We do," I say.

For a couple of lonely hearts, we back each other up fine.

"Were there people listenin' to that Mozart strin' quartet?"

"Place was packed."

"I hope yer like it here, Jude," she says.

"I do, Lucy," I say. "Meeting you has been quite the adventure."

"We're jes' getting' started," she says, crawling into her bed.

"OK," I reply.

I better recognize it soon; Lucy is an above average adventure seeker. She has found an audience cum player in me and, as she has shown me once already, she is prepared to rise to any occasion.

I put the eggs beside my bed along with the cream bowl. Climbing back into bed, feeling sleep come on winged feet, I wonder, How will I know when four hours have passed?

TO DIET FOR

Up until now, I was always grateful to have food to eat. There was no selectivity involved; it was simply a question of eating enough. Now, I feel like I am a horse being fed to race. My attitude, even my thought process, has changed. It's perfectly noticeable. Not only am I eating enough, I am eating the correct food, for me. I am food secure.

The change manifests itself more or less the way Chrystal predicted. Going to bed at about 9:30 soon becomes routine.

The nights following my excursion to forage for food, the principal quartet, as I think of them, embark on an odyssey to play the entire catalog of Beethoven's string quartets sequentially, about one or two nights apart between each. My Lucy is knowledgeable about music and explains enough to make listening more meaningful. Better still is when we find out that on the nights the quartet will play, for about half an hour before hand, one or other of the musicians gives an introduction to basic themes and melodies as well as some historical background about Beethoven's life and times.

A natural time flow results from waking early in the mornings and feeling energized to join an exercise program. I determine to continue avoiding Serena based on my initial reaction to her. That makes yoga a non starter for me. Seeing Zichrini in the Combat Conditioning, I make a beeline for that group. That is a good decision for me. After the initial experience leaves me wheezing and choking, lying down heaving as I try to catch my breath within minutes of starting, I am encouraged to progress at my own speed, to stretch where and when I decide.

Zichrini is not showing off when she free forms a head stand and begins doing what seem like an endless series of pushups going into full arm straight, all the while keeping her balance. Even with a wall to work off of, I am eventually able to go into a head stand, but totally unable to push enough for my head to leave the ground.

True to her word, when Lucy sees me attend exercise class regularly, she takes up yoga. She says she is glad she did.

My determination increases daily and I can see the change reflected in our house.

Lucy and I dig down three feet on the main inner circle. That's a lot of dirt stacked up nearby and by now our hands are toughened up. In the wheelbarrow, we make a mix in a ratio of nine shovelfuls of dirt to one shovelful of cement, mix it well and empty into the five gallon plastic bucket. We empty the bucket into the fiberglass tubing and pack the mixture in. We lay the tubing around the perimeter of the "floor" of the hole. When one layer is installed, we lay two roughly parallel strands of barbed wire on top to hold the next layer of tubing on top of that.

When the first round of tubing is installed and packed tight, the chain attached to the stake in the center of the floor is given a new marker—the inside of the first ring of tubing. That gives us the distance at any point for the inner wall as we lay in each subsequent layer of tubing. We are creating a hemisphere where all points on the wall are equidistant from the stake.

Where the four semicircles that Lucy scored are marked, we build walls for them in exactly the same way except for the east facing unit that is the doorway.

I learn something with every activity. Why choose east for the doorway? Because it is good Feng Shui. What is Feng Shui? Essentially, as I understand it, it is the "right" way to place things—in a house, office, garden, room, even on a desk. There are rules that can be learned and then there are some people who just "know," instinctively, where things belong. So, doorways are best facing east. It will mean that, until someone builds in front of us, we shall have a clear view out our doorway of the rising sun.

I mention this to Lael, who refers me to Zichrini. She smiles at the question and walks me to the foothills, about one hundred yards from where we are working. She has me look back at the layout of the houses. From this vantage point, I can see every house and every doorway. She pats me on the head as one may do with a child.

"See," I hear her say in my head, "No need to worry; everyone gets a view."

As our house construction comes along, I feel more able to integrate into classes. About the time we cut spaces for the windows and the air vents, I begin to learn American Sign Language from Elder Sophia. I am thrilled with the earliest few words I put together. I run out to the field by the road where we came in. I have learned this is in and around where Didi and Dada, the Amazon twins, work daily, seven days a week.

I approach them as they are cutting dead sunflower plants in preparation for using the field in a few months. I am stunned when I realize that the two of them do most of the field work to support the entire village of about one hundred people. They seem to anticipate my arrival as they stop work the moment I come into view. I wave and they wave back. I smile and they smile back.

Though out of breath from racing to see them, I realize something amazing about ASL; I can chatter away signing even though I am out of breath. By contrast, I would be unable to make audible words connect without a breath between each word if I spoke.

Dada and Didi break into grunts of laughter. Apparently, I am blundering all over the place and saying, I have no idea what. They slow me down and make me pace myself. Gradually, the signs come together and we are having a very simple conversation. I am talking and making sense in another language. I am thrilled. They share my excitement by giving me hugs that I think are going to crack my ribs. When they let me go, I admit I am much relieved to find I am still whole.

Back at the dome site, Lael and Zichrini both spend more and more time sleeping under the tree as Lucy and I sweat our way through the construction. Basically, they determined that all they are there for is to be our instructors and, apart from checking in at the beginning of a work spell and reviewing us at the end, they do nothing else but talk to each other, eat and sleep. I guess when no one gets paid for doing anything, what you do and how you do it is entirely up to you. I notice that no one apart from Lucy and I comment on their behavior which is visible to anyone who passes through the area.

Imagine Lucy's and my embarrassment to learn that Zichrini and Lael are the patrol for Taquinta keeping us secure and safe all night long.

One day, Lea stops by the house site as we are attempting to install the door into the roughed in framed entrance to our house.

"You are making excellent progress," she says.

"Then why is the door goin' in crooked?" Lucy asks.

We've been working this problem for almost an hour now, trying to do one piece of the puzzle without having to ask our instructors.

"May I help?" Lea asks.

Lucy and I slip into what are the beginnings of a comic routine. We give each other studious looks as if deliberating a serious issue.

"I guess," Lucy says, finally.

Using the back of her heel, with a few deft kicks to the bottom of the hinge side and then striking high up by the lintel with the heel of her fist, Lea slides in the door without either Lucy's or my help. She lets us secure it.

She sits on a half finished pod wall.

"Take a few minutes break," she says.

We grab our water flasks and sit inside the pod on its wall. We're already having guests over.

"I waited for you to get established," Lea tells us, "Hoping you would come on your own."

"Where?" Lucy asks.

"My classes," Lea says. "Jiu-Jitsu. Brazilian Jiu-Jitsu."

"Why would we want to?" I ask.

"Every woman deserves to know self defense," Lea says seriously. "So she may be more trouble than it's worth."

"What can happen here?" Lucy asks.

"You should ask?" Lea tells her.

"Meanin'?" Lucy bristles.

Lea hit a nerve.

"With all the traveling you do," Lea answers, "You are better off being able to take care of yourself."

"Yer right," Lucy says, throwing an anxious glance at me.

I play dumb.

"Lea has a good point there, Lucy," I say.

Lucy looks down at her modest belly well hidden by the looseness of the coveralls. I gather I am expected to create another auntie to the rescue moment.

"Maybe once the house is done," I suggest.

Lea gives me a disdainful look before turning her attention to Lucy. Lucy bounces Lea's look to me, adding a shake of her head, no.

"When I improve at the Chinese Prison Workout?" I ask.

Lea looks at me askance.

"I understand you managed a headstand pushup, this morning," she says.

I look at Lucy who is shaking her head, no.

Starting to feel pressured, I begin grasping at straws.

"I guess I can stop going to Maisha's Long Stride walking."

"Do you see it as one or another?" Lea asks.

Lucy grins a big wide smile as she shakes her head, no.

"OK, OK," I submit. "One class… trial basis."

Lea stands up preparing to leave.

"Tomorrow, two thirty," she tells me. "Make sure to eat an early lunch and bring your coach."

"Who?" I ask her. "I have to find someone to coach me?"

Lea gestures a thumb in Lucy's direction.

"Those who can, do," Lea tells us.

"Thems as have an excuse," Lucy says, her head nodding a vigorous yes, "Coach."

Yet again, an Elder approaches us with a class recommendation right before an afternoon with some free time. They have to be plotting these approaches. There are too many parallels for these to be coincidental.

ONE DOWN

To help me appreciate what is Brazilian Jiu-Jitsu, Lea demonstrates with a woman opponent three times her size. The two grasp each other's belted jackets at the collars and pull each other around, for a moment or two. The next thing I see is the heavy set woman lying on her back with skinny Lea's hands in a grip around the woman's throat and the woman banging the floor with her hand for release. It's that easy.

For my benefit, Lea demonstrates the whole process in slow motion. To my untrained eye, the woman sparring with Lea ought to have just stood her ground and simply used her weight advantage.

Then it is my turn. I am matched with Agnes, a sweet, older woman who graciously insists on shaking my hand before pulling me in close for a big, soft hug. She is all smiles. One blow to her face with my fist and her smile will be receiving dental work. Wow! I didn't realize how much of my mental life lives in a violent noir world.

Lea guides my grip on Agnes' collar as Agnes grasps my collar. Lea arranges how to fill my fist with cloth so there is a solid grip. She also adjusts how I position my feet and asks Agnes to move slowly enough so that I can feel the movement of our weight, allowing me to adjust my feet appropriately. This is so easy.

Lea calls out for us to go a little faster. We start dancing with each other. Agnes pulls on me, I pull on her; this is comfortable.

Lea asks, "Do you remember how I explained for you to take a fall?"

"Yes," I tell her.

"Good," Lea remarks, "Because Agnes is going to drop you now."

To my mind, it is Agnes who is in a tiger's grip and it is she who is about to...

I am lying on my back, all the wind knocked out of me. Sweet, dear Agnes is astride me with one hand holding my collar across my chest, my arms pinned by her knees so I can barely raise one hand off the mat. Agnes' other hand is poised, with knuckles prominent, for a punch aimed at my throat.

I gasp through my closed throat to Agnes, "This is the one and only time you will ever do this to me."

Lea claps her hands and Agnes stands, pulling me by my collar to my feet as if I were flypaper. I am not amused.

That session lasts one hour. Agnes decks me seven more times and I deck Agnes in my dreams.

"That," I tell Lea, at the end of class, "Is the reason this is the one time I am taking your class."

Lea smiles.

"That," she says, "Is the reason you will be taking my class six days a week before going to work on the house."

"Why before?" I ask her.

"Because you will benefit from pushing your anger into building the house," she tells me. "It will speed up construction."

We are scheduled to finish in four weeks. We do it in three.

I am mad as hell with Agnes and I want revenge! Not once do I receive it. Agnes is able to drop and pin me time and time again. However, I am occasionally able to drop other adversaries.

I do not care how old and how sweet that woman is; my goal, my focus, my target for revenge is Agnes. I am going to put her in a life threatening position from which only I can release her. All Agnes does is grow older and sweeter. Five years of constant training has made her lethal. I know. I spend more time getting up from falls than I do gripping her collar. The smoother I become, the faster I go down. It just is not fair.

For her part, Lucy is my biggest fan. She has contrived herself a rationale that, by being my supporter, my manager, my trainer, my coach and my shoulder to cry on, she is attending Lea's class, Just not getting whupped on the way I am.

Our house's central dome structure plus the four pods are done. The layer upon layer of tubing resembles the Michelin Man, or, leastways, what his house might look like. Inside, we have roughed in shelving for the kitchen and living areas. We have created two bedrooms and a bathroom. With Zichrini's help we have the plumbing and sewer piping in place as well as the electrical. The hookups are almost ready to connect us to the Taquinta sustainable electricity generator, water main and septic field.

Once Zichrini sees how we work the electrical according to her directions, she becomes more trusting, and lets us do things that, Lael is quick to point out, she cannot recall seeing Zichrini allow anyone else to do unsupervised at our level of experience.

One morning in class, I mention to Lea with great pride the episode of being allowed to install the electrical lines by myself, as if even Lucy did not help. Lea laughs. That class feels as if she instructed Agnes to take the gloves off.

I become a furious child's rag doll on the receiving end of someone who performs from an earnest perception that she has been deeply wronged and obsesses on one defenseless target to vent her spleen. If pride comes before a fall, let's just say I fall more times than usual today. By contrast, everything subsequent to that class is sweet relief.

That afternoon, Lucy and I make up a group of four students to begin Maisha's Money Course. For this first class, we sit at a picnic table shaded by the Commissary.

Maisha tells us, "As we start this class, I ask you to do two things: firstly, be patient as I explain some possibly new ideas. Listen closely from beginning to end—most ideas are simple once you hear the whole story. Secondly, be gentle with yourself. It's perfectly normal that it takes time for you to "get" it. New ideas often require time and repetition before they make sense. Like riding a bike for the first time; you probably will fall off once or twice. Stick with it and even money may begin to make sense."

Lucy yawns.

I determine no more falls for me. I'll keep my pride under wraps from here out.

Maisha points to a one dollar bill and a glass of water on the table.

She asks the class, "Which is more valuable, the money or the water?"

To me the answer is obvious. After watching the lengths people go to obtain money, I see money has an intrinsic value that a glass of water can't have. I say nothing.

Maisha asks each of us in turn to tell the class their choice and their reasoning for it. The others choose the dollar because it has so many ways to purchase something. They see the water as only having a couple of uses. Lucy is emphatically in the money camp, claiming the answer is obvious to anyone with a lick of sense.

With the patience of a saint, Maisha asks me, "Do you agree, Judith?"

"I choose the water," I say.

Lucy laughs.

"Yer kiddin', right?" she asks.

"Explain your reasoning, Judith," Maisha asks me.

Without going into detail, I talk about having been dehydrated and desperate for water in the middle of town.

"Water nourishes the soil to grow plants," I tell them. "Water can become ice or steam, turn into clouds. It recycles itself. Comparatively, money has few uses. Thus, for me water is the more valuable."

By this point, Lucy's eyes are bugging out.

"There is no right or wrong answer when it comes to expressing an opinion," Maisha says. "In this case, I would agree with Judith. Water is a function of life; tangible. By comparison, money is a belief system. It is worth what people can be convinced is its "value" by central bank postings, stock market trades—courtesy of the high priests of mammon. Also, water, though there is a lot of it, is finite; there is only so much of it, never more nor less. Yet, at any time, of all the water on Earth, only three percent is drinkable. Conversely, the quantity of money is relatively flexible; the amounts available can be manipulated. A country in debt can print enough money to pay its way out of debt.

"In 1914, when WWI broke out, a loaf of bread in Germany cost maybe one deutschmark. Germany lost the war, people lost faith in the government and there was high unemployment, such that, by 1922, eight years later, a suitcase filled to over flowing with tens of thousands of deutschmarks was barely enough to buy a loaf of bread."

"People should've emigrated to reduce the population," Lucy pronounces. "Take the pressure off the society; create demand."

"People tend to do what people do and governments manipulate the society by controlling the money flow," Maisha explained. "That's why I call it a belief system. When people finally perceive that money may be a golden calf, a false god, an agreement to create a substitute for goods simply to expedite an otherwise crude system of barter, then we humans can shift into becoming a higher, more sophisticated culture. Let me give you the simplest of analogies. Take this one dollar and go up into the Appalachians. It is like a small fortune compared to what that same dollar will buy in, say, Chicago. Why?"

"Cos land prices, therefore cost of doin' business, is higher in Chicago," Lucy fires back.

"Why?" asks Maisha.

"'Because there are more people in Chicago," Louise joins in. "More people means greater demand."

"Why?" Maisha asks with a smile.

"There's competition?" offers Kathy.

"Why?" asks Maisha.

"OK, OK," Lucy Jumps in. "This is goin' round in circles."

"You think?" says Maisha. "You're right that it's a numbers game.

The more people there are, the lower the need to negotiate a sale. If Sheila refuses to pay my price, I'll sell it to Joanne. The fewer people, buyers, there are, as in the Appalachians, the lower the prices people are willing to pay for locally produced goods. Take Taquinta. What do we use for money here?"

Lucy is momentarily dumb founded by the question.

"Everythin' here is paid fer by donation, mostly by benefactors," she states.

"Only till we become self sufficient," Maisha argues.

"As I hear it, that's been a long time comin'," Lucy says derisively.

"We're completely energy independent," stated Maisha. "Especially after we pay off the equipment. We're closing in on food independence. When that is in place, we will want for little. Then we can even consider expanding to additional sites."

"So?" Lucy says, growing impatient. "What'll that prove?"

"That applying the concepts of Quantum Physics to need is more effective than money," Maisha replies.

"My dad loved this when he heard it," Lucy laughs. "He called it, "Now yer see it, now yer see somethin' else." I'd love to hear yer current version, Maisha."

"We're working with the money modality only as long as we have to," Maisha says. "Before I give Lucy a response, I want to set the stage with an anecdote. You decide if there is truth to this story. OK?

"A stranger arrives in a town and talks to the manager of a motel. *"I need a room for the night,"* says the traveler. *"Here's one hundred dollars while I go check out the room.*" The stranger puts the cash on the desk, takes the key from the manager and leaves to inspect the room.

"The manager grabs the hundred dollars and races down the street. His destination is the laundry to pay off his debt for washing the motel sheets. As soon as the motel manager leaves, the laundry owner takes the hundred dollars around the corner and pays off his debt at the liquor store. The liquor store owner pays a deposit to the painter to fix up the liquor store. The painter goes to the lumber yard and buys materials for fixing up the liquor store. The lumber yard owner pays the printer for his outstanding bill for printing promotional flyers. The printer stops over at the motel to pay for the night he and his wife spent there recently, away from the kids. As the printer is leaving the motel, the stranger returns to the front desk and asks for his hundred dollars back.

""*Is there something wrong with the room?"* asks the motel manager.

""*The room is fine,"* the stranger replies. *"I checked the time and realized I can still drive a couple more hours in daylight."*

"What can we learn from this story?" Maisha asks us.

Lucy is chomping at the bit.

"If yer have somethin' to sell, avoid this town like the plague," she tells us. "Everyone extends credit. Despite all the dollar turns, those businesses need educatin' how to earn money."

She sits back on her chair, folds her arms and presents a smug look that does not become her; probably imitating her dad.

"Anyone else?" Maisha asks.

"It's how I've always seen money," I venture to say. "Where does it come from? All it seems to do is go round and round. Then, where does it go? I mean its sheets of pretty paper with different denominations printed on it."

"Along with pictures of old men," Kathy says with a laugh.

"What about the truckers?" Lucy asks earnestly. "We made a profit. Din't we?"

"I suppose," I mumble. "Was it right what we did?"

"Sure it was," Lucy replies. "They was grown men able to make decisions."

"But did we earn their money?" I asked her. "Or was it a trick? Look how angry they got."

"Would they've tried what they did if we was men?" Lucy snorted.

"If we had been men pulling that, probably a fight would have broken out," I tell her.

"They bet," Lucy says emphatically. "They played an' lost. So they paid."

"You're discussing gambling?" Maisha asks.

"Pool hall game," Lucy proudly announces to everyone.

"Did you need the money?" Maisha asks us.

"I bought gas fer the car," Lucy says. "Jude, here bought candy."

"I was hungry," I say.

"Gettin' defensive agin?" Lucy asks.

"You're saying you spent the money, or some of it, anyway?" Maisha asks. "You're making an argument to Justify obtaining the money. It's a similar argument a wife might present her husband. *'There is not enough money for food, fuel, rent, clothes and help in the house. Go earn some money to change that situation.'*

"The man and woman may own or rent a piece of land they work to raise crops, animal livestock. In a good year, they live well. In a bad year, they may not have enough to eat or even to trade so they sell off an animal or a portion of land, or they work for someone else. Another possibility is that they barter for what someone else is willing to share. They may barter their labor; a day's work for so much food stuffs, or an animal, some land, clothes, salt, honey, medical services of a local midwife or the man with leeches to draw blood.

"Money is called currency. It "runs" between people. If you work my land for a day to earn salt, but my salt supply is down, instead of you having to work for the person with salt to trade, I pay you money. You take the money to any person with salt to sell and buy what you need. The salt seller takes the money to the barber and buys a haircut. The barber goes to a bar and buys a drink before going to the general store to buy his wife the dress she wants. The store keeper buys a replacement dress and some candles to build up his stock. The candle maker has more candles than he can sell so he begins to lower his prices to clear the stock. A traveler passing through town buys all the extra candles because, two days earlier, he passed through a town that was desperate for candles. He goes back to that town with his stock of candles and sells them at a profit.

"He now has more money than he can spend on his own needs. Then, he remembers a friend of his who uses money to make money."

"Other peoples' money!" Lucy shouts gleefully.

Maisha continues, "The friend turns out to be a smart gambler. By keeping an eye on the weather, he can guess if this is going to be a good or a bad year for farmers growing certain crops. He takes the traveler's extra money and fixes a price he is willing to pay farmers for their crops. The farmer gambles that the weather will provide enough crops at the fixed price to sign over his yet to be harvested crop. The friend, meanwhile, sells his future interest in the crop to another man who trades paper, deals written and paid for but whose outcome is yet to be realized. Gradually a chain of people form who buy and sell paper. That is all they do. They make a living profiting from the difference they make from each sale.

"The weather is perfect. The farmer sets up all his laborers to harvest. One man takes to his bed sick. Another gets kicked by a mule and refuses to work near animals ever again. All the women who were going to stack the carts take an offer from a man who needs seamstresses and allows babies in the workplace. So the farmer, who has been focused on his crops, comes up short on labor at the peak of harvest. He has some workers in the field but not enough when the weather turns and begins to ruin his crops. He offers more money to anyone who can help.

"The traveler's friend hears about the problems and buys back the paper he sold but he will only pay a discounted price hoping the results are not as bad as he told people they were looking to be. Again, there is more buying and selling of paper on the way down and, of course, more profit taking.

"When many farmers or manufacturers or stores or fishermen have dismal years, the prices they charge in the market impacts how much workers are paid which impacts how much money those workers have to spend.

"Add into the mix the government taxing income, purchases, profit taking and many other aspects of commerce, and there is a complex industry simply called money.

"Central to this industry are banks, exchanges where people and businesses go to buy or sell money. People buy Certificates of Deposit,

CDs. Banks sell bonds to raise capital for communities.

"If you plan to travel in a foreign country, you will need some of the local currency. When you go to the bank to exchange your currency for money to use overseas, the bank evaluates the going rate, adds in a margin of profit and sells you the foreign currency.

"We believe that money has value, albeit a fluctuating value. In 1970, a gallon of gas cost 30 cents. Forty years later, a gallon of gas cost $3. It's the identical amount of gas, but it requires ten times as much money to buy it. Why?"

"Inflation," Lucy tells her.

"Inflation reflects a weakening belief in the value of the dollar," Maisha says. "It's how we accommodate price increases. Like buying a house with a 30 year mortgage loan; the loan allows someone to buy something expensive on a modest income. If the house sale price increases in value, did the value of the house increase, say by demand, or did the value of the currency decrease by the country printing more money?"

"How does someone end up underwater?" asks Louise.

"Usually that happens when someone buys a house when values are going up," Maisha explains. "The belief is that the market is going to keep rising. When it tops out and belief in the value of the dollar drops enough, the loan ends up being for more than the market believes the house is worth. This is further impacted by other conditions like rising costs of living and uncertain job security."

"That's a pretty dark picture you're painting," Kathy comments.

"Yes, it is," Maisha says sadly. "Now, let's look at the glass of water as an alternative to money."

"Here yer see money," Lucy says. "Now yer see water."

"You are a skeptic, Lucy," Maisha says. "I'm not trying to convince you. All I'm doing is offering you a way to see things from a different perspective. It's healthy to play the field. If we refuse to see alternative options we limit our choices. We become stuck. For example, it requires two people to make money work. Water only needs one."

With that she nonchalantly picks up the glass and throws the contents at Lucy. Lucy vaults out of her seat, staring with disbelief.

"What're yer doin'?" she screams.

"Oh, Lucy," Maisha says. "I meant to throw the money at you and accidentally picked up the glass of water instead. Please excuse me."

Lucy glares about with disbelief. Then she hears Kathy desperately stifle a giggle. She glares at her, then at Louise who is smirking. Lucy looks to me.

I can't resist.

"Yep, and me, too, Bruta," I tell her.

Maisha calmly says to Lucy, "Looks to me like you're underwater."

Lucy huffs and puffs as the rest of us break into cackles of laughter. Just like Rachel, Lucy gets the joke, or something, because the corners of her mouth turn slowly upwards as she starts to unwind. She steps over to where Maisha sits on a bench. Grabbing the soaking bib of her own coveralls, Lucy shakes some of the droplets on to Maisha making her Jump.

"I felt like sharin' wi' yer, Maisha," Lucy says.

"Very good, Lucy," Maisha says. "So which is the more valuable, the money or the water?"

"Clearly the money," Lucy says as she vainly dabs at Maisha's wet arm with the dollar bill mocking an attempt to dry her.

What I begin to take away is Maisha's idea that human beings have the ability to choose what will be, be it black or white, male or female, zero or one. That last she calls the Binary System.

Maisha parallels her description of choice of water or money as an example of Quantum Physics where the smallest particle also has two forms—matter or energy. This particle is in constant motion, disappearing then reappearing, continuously, in a sine wave type cycle. However, what determines whether the particle appears as energy or matter depends on the observer. Basically, what the observer wants, of the two choices, the particle becomes—matter or energy, water or money.

Maisha postulates that contemporary society has the ability to work with or without money. If you will, it is the observer's choice. Her goal for Taquinta is to become money free, both internally and in its workings with the outer world.

Being someone who has lived most of my life in an absence of money, I feel comfortable with the idea of no money, in principle.

Only, I don't fully understand the logic of Maisha's argument, especially when she closes with statements like, "In primitive matriarchal societies, people traded for goods and services and war was almost unheard of."

As Lucy and I walk back to our dome, she asks, "Did yer agree with what Maisha said?"

"I think so," I say.

"Then yer a dreamer... Just like her," Lucy states.

"The best ideas are first sowed in dreams, Lucy," I tell her.

"Yer wanna bet?" she asks with a twinkle in her eye.

"That's it!" I say. "You prefer to gamble. You are always seeking a way to increase the odds in your favor."

"What's wrong with that?" Lucy asks.

I have to laugh. "Here? In a moneyless society?"

"Only to yer mind," she tells me. "I'm backin' my mom. She's pretty much underwritin' this entire operation. I'm bettin' with her."

That catches me off guard. Coming, as she does, from deep left field, I have no argument for her. Time will tell.

I only hope I dream long enough to learn the answer, if there is one.

FAVORITES

What amazes me is Lucy's love of music. She takes classes in piano and soon masters the basics. As her hands lose blisters and the calluses moderate from constructing our home, she takes up the violin and is excellent.

I am beginning to feel like I have a brain made of cheese, cottage cheese, soft and malleable, unable to absorb one more thing. However, I do enjoy listening to music. As if monitoring my niece's progress, I visit her class at each week's end. Week after week, I am duly impressed by how she is advancing.

The principal string quartet is finishing up playing Beethoven's early quartets. It is as if I am growing older and wiser listening to each of B's quartets in a progression of nightly performances. I go to sleep these nights and have the sweetest of dreams. I am ever so definitely dreaming my dreams now.

While Lucy attends music instruction with Chrystal, I participate in Lea's Social Studies Class. Attendees form a circle and, after her introductory remarks each time, we discuss in Socratic form, i.e., we are all equal, and comments may fly so long as they have bearing on the topic at hand and add to the issues on the table.

Sometimes, Lea divides the class randomly in half and has each side debate the other. For such classes, she brings out her "Robert's Rules of Order" and lays it on the table for all to see and reference.

I admit debates are one place where my internal tension is provoked. With focused concentration, I manage to harness the tension and, thereby, allow it to find an appropriate application.

However, if I did not stop myself from believing it to be so, I can easily imagine that some of these classes are specifically aimed at training me more than anyone else. How egotistical of me? Then again, how amazing to me that I have uncovered an arena in which I endeavor to excel above my classmates?

On her favorite topic, "Voting, what is it good for and how it is (ab)used?" I believe I am Lea's most ardent student. Lea will offer up a statement as our Jumping off point for discussion, such as: "Typical voting patterns show the largest percentage of turnout are homeowners, though they are the smaller percentage of the eligible to vote population. Those with the most to gain—renters—tend not to vote, or, if they do vote, are often convinced to vote against their own self interest."

Having never voted, mine is, as in the Money Course, a view apart. I feel as though my opinions are tolerated but not appreciated other than as a contribution to be beyond Just being different and, often, contrary.

There is one class, in fact, a series of classes the Elders request everyone take—Math, Applied Math, and Physics. These are the only course where there is absolutely only right or wrong. It's almost a relief to have unequivocally definitive answers. Lucy laughingly refers to these classes as Madness, Apple Madness, and Physicality.

I have no recollection of school math beyond multiplication tables and some division. Lucy and I begin at what Lucy refers to as remedial classes; in other words, starting at the beginning. As usual, Lucy elects herself the class comedian, seeking ways to ignore the topic at hand, to be noticed, and endeavoring to distract everyone else. I am amazed by how much latitude she is given. Can it be a policy to allow her to reach everyone's limit of endurance? It is becoming intolerable to me. I feel as if Lucy is constantly itching for a fight and she will provoke away until someone takes her on. As her "aunt," I suppose that may fall to me, but I have designated Agnes to be my nemesis. She alone occupies my every waking thought of revenge.

By not participating in BJJ, I believe Lucy avoids finding a safe outlet to bring her rage to focus and this causes her to cast it out onto a wider and mostly disinterested audience. Our Math instructor, Elder Gupra Kuar, amazes me with how she tolerates Lucy's antics. Most everyone ends up attending to Lucy except for me.

In a class on Trigonometry, lights go off in my head. Using the dome Lucy and I are engaged in constructing as an example, Sophia, a gentle, older Elder from Russia, with a thick accent but the sharpest of minds, demonstrates on the white board why the chain from the stake to the base fiberglass tube creates identical length wherever it is applied inside the dome. To me it is a reverse rationality, but it rings true. Applications to practical matters have always assisted me to learn. Sophia strikes the perfect chord.

I must have made some noise of recognition because Sophia turns to look at me over her pince-nez spectacles, her demure appearance breaking into the slightest of smiles that someone in the room was making sense of what was being said, when Lucy interrupts making some wisecrack about being chained into our house on a short leash. No one laughs but her. At class end, Sophia suggests to me that I consider moving to a higher grade. She admits it may be tough on me but I will learn more applications to construction. I am actually beginning to enjoy some Math. Will wonders ever cease?

Yet another separation from me seems to weaken Lucy's constant efforts to lead the class in humor. Daily, Lucy becomes quieter and more sullen. Working on the house becomes function, not pleasure. That I am growing without her seems to be a big issue. I am so engrossed with taking in as much as I can; I am only peripherally aware of the division which that separation by class is creating. If it were not for her music, I worry that she will become a lost soul. I don't believe it is Just competitiveness.

Zichrini and Lael push for us to finish the house. The windows are installed, as is the door. We install an adjustable wind funnel over an opening left in the roof. Now the house is ready for the application of adobe. This is where Lucy comes into her own. She is a humdinger at applying mud by hand and creating a smooth finish. Maybe she gets off on the plasticity. I do well, but Lucy does way better.

We have the first skein on the exterior of the house within a couple of days. With the bulk of the tubing obscured by packing the mud into the gaps, the dome crudely takes on a resemblance to other igloo houses nearby. What a relief, we are doing this right!

While the exterior dries, we work on the inside, repeating the process of adobe application. The thinnest of skeins makes all the difference to change from looking like a construction zone to potentially being a home. From being a clunky looking object, floating on the landscape of nicely finished buildings, our house rapidly transforms into resembling the beginnings of a house.

A day later, we apply a finish coat to the outside and smooth out the rough spots. As a special treat, Lael arrives with colors for us to create a palette for our home. Again, Lucy's energy picks right up. A different person emerges as Lucy chooses how the house will look, outside and inside. She generously allows that if I wish to have a different color for my bedroom pod that is my choice. I demure, encouraging her to decide for both of us. I am comfortable with her choices, even for my sleeping pod. Lucy is elated.

Satisfied with her decisions, Lucy celebrates by attending ecumenical Sunday services in the Commissary. I take great joy in her doing that. Meanwhile I do my own celebrating by sleeping in. Religion has never appealed to me. Lucy returns from services smiling and happy Just as I wake. It was a good decision all around.

Sunday evening is a rare treat in this mostly minimal media community. A few people listen to the radio, and those few mostly listen to talk radio, though not the talk shows where the host rides an agenda and the audience either cheers or is damned to wherever for as long as the host declares them damned. This is talk radio where mostly people talk, as in giving lectures, discussing with or interviewing guests on various topics about a variety of persuasions. Thanks to bud earphones, the sound is typically muffled or inaudible to non participants and that's it. There is no television at all. I have an aversion to television, so that is fine with me. However, movie night is fun, especially at Taquinta.

Tonight's show is the film adaptation of Jerzy Kosinski's book, *Being There*. It's the story of a middle aged man who is mentally challenged and spends his life caring for the garden of a powerful broker in the community. Closed in by a high wall, he receives all his input about an outside world from the maid, the owner and by watching television. When the owner dies, his family takes possession of the house. Having no use for Chance, the gardener character's name—played in the movie by Peter Sellers—they cut him loose. Dressed in the cast off fine clothing of his deceased employer, Chance is sent out into the streets to fend for himself.

Basically, being inexperienced in the ways of the world, having been protected from real life by his employer, Chance is at great risk. Chance's only ability to converse is as someone who views life through the cycles of plants. What happens to him is remarkable, and, in some ways, I identify with him.

The fun thing to know about movies at Taquinta is that the women use the occasion to vent their opinions on everything the screen has to offer in a wildly, public display. Sometimes it descends into seeing who can make the most lewd remark. Most often, there are public declarations critiquing the way life is portrayed on the screen. The absurdity of plot aggravates many of them. The way women are portrayed angers them the most. Sex scenes, certainly their manipulation, receive the greatest commentary, mostly derisive. Going to the movies at the Commissary is not something anyone does for the opportunity to listen to dialog, other than that of a lot of women who let their hair down in the dark and carry on like banshees.

I sit there aware of what is going on, observing. The higher the energy level, the quieter I am. Lucy, on the other hand, is, not surprisingly, one of the loudest participants. It is as if these events are occasion for the young women especially, though there are only a few of them, to release their pent up libidos, at least, vocally. Every once in a while, I sense that I have a libido, but it is a fleeting feeling and not one I activate intentionally.

In "Being There," through a series of coincidences, Chance winds up advising the President of the United States on how to run the country. Though in that respect the plot becomes absurd, Judging by what has happened to me, I can vaguely see it as plausible.

The day after the dome is declared completed by Zichrini and Lael there is a full blown Taquinta celebration. Apparently, this day is special. Though no one ever dresses differently from one day to the next, other than for yoga and BJJ, today the Elders appear stronger, different. Starting at the Togu Na, they form a procession replete with noise making instruments such as hand drums, triangles and tambourines to generate a vibrant atmosphere. All women stop whatever they are doing to participate.

Lucy and I are instructed by Lael to stand by our Lavender colored home to wait for the procession to reach us. It is unclear whether we will, or even how we are to participate. There appears to be no rush. This is no quickie ceremony.

Maisha leads the Elders and all the women in a dance wending their way between the houses, touching each one with their left hand as they pass, then touching that same hand to their hearts. Sometimes, they reach out with their right hand and gently touch the person ahead of them. Ever so slowly, the procession arrives at the house we constructed.

Lael and Zichrini come over and stand on either side of Lucy and me. Maisha stops the parade in front of us. When Maisha thrusts a hand into the air, the music abruptly ceases.

In the stalled silence, Maisha asks, "What is the condition of the new house?"

Lael and Zichrini respond together, "It is done!"

As if echoing their words, Maisha calls out, "It is done!"

The procession picks up the phrase, loudly shouting, "It is done!"

over and over.

With banging of drums, ringing of triangles, rattling of tambourines, all of it growing in crescendo, the procession presses forward to surround the house.

Lael and Zichrini step away from us, removing any protection. Overwhelmed by the intensity of the surge towards the house, I stand with my back pushed against the dome.

Lucy takes the opportunity to scale the house and stand on the roof with her arms wide open, reaching to the sky, screaming as loudly as she is able, "It is done!"

The energy exerted to acknowledge our home is incredible. Yet, again, the women of Taquinta embrace us, invite us in, and wrap us in the warmth of caring, feeling people. I stand with tears streaming down my face, hugged by Zichrini as she tells me what a great job I did on the house, then by Lael. They are like proud parents at graduation, recognizing that, though they helped, it is Lucy and I who did the work. They are not shy about releasing that concept to us. My heart feels ready to burst.

Chrystal invites Lucy to join us for one last ceremony. After Lucy Jumps down and stands beside me with one arm wrapped around my waist, Chrystal holds out a gigantic piece of rough hewn, pink crystal about one cubic foot in volume.

"According to the ways of the Ancient Ones," Chrystal tells everyone, "Rose quartz tunes people's heart to a gentle and loving wave length. Placed by the front door to your home, this stone will ensure that all who enter there will do so with only good intentions in their heart. You may now go home."

Lucy accepts the rock and places it by the front door. That's when I realize every dome has a different rock by its front door. I was looking for landmarks to find my way around. They were there all the time; I Just didn't see them. Duh!

As if on cue, the assembled women scream over and over, with all the force their voices will permit, "GO HOME! GO HOME! GO HOME!"

Going inside and closing the door behind us is the only way to shut them up.

Once inside, though Lucy and I worked on this place from start to finish; now it feels different. Our dome has transformed from a construction site to be our home. The difference is palpable.

"We did this," Lucy tells me with quiet amazement in her voice.

"You and I did all of this," I reply.

"We are incredible," she says.

"We are powerful," I answer.

"We can do anything," she says.

That gives me pause. Lucy steps over and gives me a long hug.

She whispers emphatically, "We can do anything."

To stop from tearing up, I look out a window. The crowd has dispersed.

"Let's start by moving everything from the rental over here," I tell her.

That is the first night Lucy and I inhabit our own home. The tile on the floor is barely installed and grouted and we are moved in. I can't believe it's less than two months since we drove up. Though I do not tell Lucy, I reflect once again how my life has changed.

As we cover ourselves up to go to sleep, Lucy calls over, "Did yer notice wi' all the people who celebrated wi' us, we were the only ones to enter the house?"

"Yes," I answer. "Now you mention it. Why do you think that is?"

I see her smile in the fast arriving darkness.

"Because this is our home," she states. "An' people only enter when invited. We will invite everyone in. This is the home where my baby is to be born."

As she mumbles into a sleep of the exhausted, I stare into the dark that is home.

PAPER CUT

At breakfast, the next day, the air is clear, more clear than usual.

It feels as if a huge load has been cast off and left behind. For Lucy that is definitely the case. She is so glad the house is complete. She is proud of the work she did constructing it, but happy that the effort required is now behind her.

I feel that I have done something remarkable. I am not myself, leastways that self who arrived—confused, and very ill at ease. My eyes have been opened. I have seen possibilities. As difficult as surviving is here, and it is not easy, especially being among so many bright and talented women, there is an air of expectation that Taquinta is not a retreat, or an escape, but a place filled with the promise of future unknowns, exhilarating, an enormous expansion beyond what has, until the present, been assumed to be possible.

At the Commissary, I pick up my tray and walk back past the buffet line. The entire way, I receive compliments on the house. I know full well that most compliments are from women who have likely built their own house.

I marvel again that there are people of notable social stature among us. A nationally known radio host is in the line arguing the toss with an Academy Award winning actor on social activism and the media. I know who they are now because Ms. Who's Who whispers in my ear, along with a brief explanation, so they are no longer simply names but people of meaning, substantial, real.

I stroll back to Lucy at a bench where she reads a magazine on green living. She is seeking ways to decorate our home. I have a sinking feeling that our relative simplicity is about to be accoutered off the charts with Lucy objects.

She sees something of that thought in my eyes and laughs, "I'm preparin' fer a baby, buildin' my nest."

I cannot imagine why having just built a whole house is not enough. Next comes decorating, with a vengeance.

While she reads, I eat. Yesterday, we celebrated completing the dome. Today, I reason, must be a day of rest. No one has said a word to the contrary.

"Judith?" Chrystal calls me out of my reverie. "The house looks great. We have a new construction job for you."

Lucy checks my response. She knows I was looking forward to time off.

Brushing my tray to one side, Chrystal drops a rough sketch in front of me. I can't make heads or tails of what I am looking at. Lucy edges round the table and looks over my shoulder. As soon as she understands what it is she is looking at, I feel her retreat emotionally. I turn to Chrystal with a puzzled look on my face.

She spares me any more doubt, saying triumphantly, "We are finally going to build our library!"

Lucy stands up holding her belly, though she is not beginning to show.

Shaking her head to emphasize her attitude, she declares, "Count me out, Jude. Buildin' our house was enough. Yer go, gal!"

The rest of the day is completely relaxed. No one speaks to us beyond social greetings. Lucy lies down on the picnic table bench and sleeps, soaking up the sun's rays. I go back to the house and lay down for a nap before I attend tonight's concert of a Beethoven quartet.

It is pitch dark when I wake. I stumble out of my bed, bang my head lightly on the edge of my pod as I stand. Through a window, there is faint light from the moon streaming into the room and reflecting dully off the glazed floor tiles.

As I collect my senses, I realize I have missed my concert. Lucy is fast asleep in her pod. I search for her tiny travel clock and locate it by its tiny blue LED. I pick it up. The time is 3:42. I have slept for over fourteen hours!

I am wide awake. This is the first time I have been up this early since we got here. I feel an urge to step outside into the balmy night air. I scan the ground for creepy crawlies. It appears that I am alone.

All the houses reflect an eerie glow, shades of gray against the dark background of dirt beneath a star speckled sky. Lit by the moon, I feel the houses comprise some sort of science fiction lunarscape of their own. Far off is the Commissary, a black looming structure with a reflective roof. To the north, I locate the Togu Na. Its hand rubbed wooden posts reflect light in the moonlight while the clay and the thatch are dark. It is as if I am seeing a skeleton while, at the same time, seeing the whole being.

A tiny light, reminiscent of Tinker Bell, floats between the houses. It takes an arbitrary path and wanders at about the speed of a human. Then it disappears. I wait, watching, eyes straining in the half light.

I am becoming used to strange happenings here; I harbor neither fear nor expectation. On the one hand, this place is primitive after a fashion. The houses are an example of rude living, simple, but effective. The Togu Na is definitely primitive, from some other continent. Then again, there are electronics such as the movie projection that are top of the line. The little health care I have seen is immaculate. They have a first rate clinic capable of minor surgeries. The "pharmacy" is for all manner of holistic care from essential oils to energy healing. These folk cover the bases.

I receive a light tap on the shoulder causing me to about jump out of my skin. Thinking, as I turn, it must be Lucy, a smile rises to my mouth. I jump back a step at an all dark figure with a tiny spelunker light on her head. She turns on a small flashlight and points it to her face. This reminds me of when I was a kid using flashlights to play ghosts with friends. The flashlight weaves about until I recognize Sophia. She does not sleep many hours a night, and, to be helpful, she does night patrol a few times each week. It was her I saw twinkling in the distance moving between buildings. She is my June bug. We hug briefly before I retreat back into my cave.

Amazingly, sleep comes easily and I wake an hour later. This time, as I move about, Lucy stirs.

She pulls back the covers from her face for a moment and mutters in a sleepy voice, "Have fun, Jude."

She rolls over and covers herself. She can be so sweet and homely when she has nothing to prove. I lower the blind in the bathroom and turn the light on low. I slip out of my jammies and take a long hot shower. People here tell us to turn it to cold to finish. I am not ready for that. I dry off, dress, and head for the door.

As I step outside into the breaking dawn's soft light distinguishing the sky above the surrounding dark hills, four women approach. They have a jauntiness about them. They've come to collect me. These are my teammates for building the library. Zichrini sticks out her hand and is clearly impressed I am on the team. The same goes for Lael. Overnight, I have moved into the big leagues. Thank goodness I slept.

The other two women are equally friendly. Lael introduces Hazar who is extraordinarily tall. She shakes my hand with a deeply serious look on her face. She has the sweetest voice as we exchange names. Zichrini tells me Hazar is the word for Nightingale in Arabic. Hazar smiles at Zichrini, almost shy, but confident. It is a fascinating exchange.

The last woman introduces herself in an abrupt and forthright manner.

"My name is Yen Lu originally from Tien Sien in China—where the rugs come from," she says out of desperation as if no one knows her country. It dawns on me that I have been a regular in her Combat Conditioning class, but we've never been introduced.

Yen Lu has incredible posture. She is definitely a dancer. How did she end up among this band of bricklayers?

The camaraderie expands as we approach the Commissary. We each pick up our mats from the pigeonhole complex inside the entrance and return outside. Yen Lu leads off and we do fifty Hindu Push-ups, followed by 100 Hindu Squats. I do what I can and stop when my heart is pounding so hard I cannot even think. Completing the triad, we all bend backwards until the bridge of the nose and forehead rest on the ground, (a Maori greeting with Mother Earth?), as do the feet and hands. With a slight push each of us projects our stomach upwards, releases the hands to fold across the chest and holds the posture.

I'm good for about one minute before the beginnings of nausea flood my breathing tract. My hands grab the dirt and push up my shoulders to free up my nose.

The others kick into headstands and begin doing pushups. I go to the nearest wall and invert. I have never seen anyone work out like this. Hazar starts to sing, in Arabic I guess. What a voice, and she is singing, upside down. She sings and sings and everyone holds position, rhythmically rising and lowering together. After a couple of weak presses, I quit, though I remain upside down along with the others.

As if an eternity has passed, they end and we stand up and hug each other in turn. Yen Lu confidently tells me I will be equal to them very soon. I laugh at what looks like an impossibility. She takes my hand and playfully slaps my wrist.

"Be positive," she instructs me. "Life is hard enough without each of us adding to our misery."

We put away our mats and head to the kitchen. As Lael opens one of the huge refrigerators and searches for packages, I walk over to my corner of the service counter. For the first time, there is nothing prepared for me. Dejected, I go back into the kitchen.

Lael has been pulling out food for each person; each of them is on a special diet. I edge closer and Lael sees me coming. She slams the door shut as she tells me there is obviously no food for me. She looks at me and I can only imagine how crestfallen a look I have on my face. She laughs as do the others. She opens the door of another refrigerator, grabs the package nearest to her and thrusts it into my hands.

"Raw Meat," she says with a laugh. "This must be yours."

The others laugh with her. This is definitely a bunch of extrovert athletes. I am going to have to work hard to keep up.

After our breakfast, we head out. I follow along mostly listening to a constant stream of chatter on many different topics. We walk across the Piazza and down between houses. We emerge at an open space about half way between the Togu Na and the Commissary. This is precisely where I had my imaginary conversation with Lea. At least, I tell myself it was imaginary.

Yen Lu pulls out an architectural blueprint, a series of drawings much more detailed than the sketch Chrystal showed me. I can barely comprehend the details, but the concept is clear; a roundhouse with a slanting roof. That much I get.

This is yet another one of those times I feel like the outsider. The four of them zip off this way and that, coordinated, aware, chattering the whole time. I am left standing like the village loon.

One by one they have me help here, do this and fetch that, until, bit by bit, I am as much a part of the process as anyone. Each of them periodically refers to the sheets of drawings pinned down with a rock at each corner, set side by side off at a distance from the work area.

As if out of nowhere, Zichrini plants a stake in the determined center, and, Just as with our house, except this time on a huge scale, a circle is marked out on the ground.

It is almost identical to what I saw Lea design with her foot but this circle is so many times larger.

Reflecting on that, I must have turned pale for a moment in the encroaching sunlight because Zichrini, passing by me, stops to make sure I am alright. Probably I was feeling overwhelmed by the company and the scale of the project.

I tell her I am fine. She hands me a shovel and a pair of work gloves as she points to a spot on the marked out circle on the ground.

"Ziss iz yourrs," she tells me.

I take up my position and the others take up theirs. Lael begins a chain gang song and each of us starts to dig. We dig and dig and dig. The dirt goes outside. We each dig a trench up to where the next person around the circle has begun theirs, preparing for the footings.

Scared I will not be able to keep up with these dynamos, I work off rhythm.

Yen Lu, who is behind, "chasing" me, calls out, "Dig with the song. We all arrive together."

She is right.

Over the next three months, I do very little else but build, eat and sleep. We pour concrete into the trench's wood sided forms, criss-crossed with rebar. We attach a wide wood base to the elevated foundation. We bolt two inch pipe with universal joints to the wood base and install 16 feet high wooden 8x8 posts every ten feet around the structure. We create the wall out of square straw bales, and tie them off at the top with another wood board system crimping down using the pipes with the universal joints. We cut in the windows and install double glazed units. We install an exquisitely made, wood double door entrance, and a functional exit across from it. The roof comprises steel beams fanning out from a central post to the wood top of the wall. Across the beams we tie on concrete sheets and then install solar panels to cover the entire roof.

By the time we finish coating the outside and inside walls with three coats of gunnite concrete mix to seal the walls, I am a changed woman. Between the raw food diet, which, I can hardly believe, grows tastier by the day, the exercises in the morning where I am able to easily keep up with everyone else, constructing a library from nothing and sleeping deep and long every night, much has altered.

One big change is that Lucy and I are like ships passing on an ocean of sleep. The only time we spend together is at night saying goodnight and in the morning my leaving as quietly as possible. We have so little time left to talk; I am beginning to wonder what there is to say to each other. As seems to be the Elders' plan, we begin to drift apart.

Serena still seems to watch me out of the corners of her eyes. Maisha is so busy we rarely do more than greet in passing. Petrina checks in on me, once a week, mostly to see that I am on the right track with the diet and balancing out my needs. She calls it stabilizing. She is assiduous about keeping me away from sugar foods. I can feel the difference in so many ways. I no longer pass out after meals. As long as I stick close to the eating schedule, which is an effort in itself, my energy level is high and consistent.

The others on the crew have made every possible allowance for me and they even check in to make sure I am on schedule. Then again, at night, I sleep like a log. The only struggle is to wake every four hours and eat a small amount of protein. I do not even have to get up, just swill the raw egg down and go back to sleep. This, Petrina tells me, is to prevent my red blood cells cannibalizing my body which they will start to do after five hours without protein. No cannibals in me!

Probably what I miss most are the lectures by the visiting guests and the concerts. About the time we finished our house, I began making a point to read the notice board by the Commissary entrance. Because there is so little planning, it's a catch as catch can situation.

I did hear a Fresno farmer talk about Biodynamic farming theories. Since the farm supporting the community is run along pure Biodynamic theory, there is a lot of basic knowledge at hand. However, she went into details that people rarely discuss at Taquinta and she was very provocative judging by the heated discussion that ensued. I was barely able to follow the issues, but I liked her and her presentation.

Another presentation was by an elegant lady from Los Angeles who had converted an old house and its garden into a total ecological living organism. She is another live wire.

Finally, one I participated in the Saturday before starting the library was an artist who spent a luxurious day teaching us to make paintings with natural, found objects dipped in watercolor paints, rubbed, pressed or stuck directly on paper. She had us cut out quotes and paste them into our paintings. She gave away already cut mattes and we created little finished "found" paintings in one day. Such a quiet person, she was steady energy that I truly appreciated. She never said a critical word to anyone but was always encouraging, seeing something beautiful in each individual's work. Lucy was delighted that I brought my own piece of artwork to decorate our dome.

The other missing part of my time is Lea. I wonder to myself a lot whether it is her or her teaching I long for. Probably, it is both.

How quickly I find myself attaching to different people such as with the library construction crew. We work six long days every week, rain or shine and mostly it is shine. We finish the roof and first coat on the exterior before the rains start, and the full exterior before the first snow.

The thought of Lea made me wonder how I will be in BJJ. In my mind's eye I can see Agnes gripping my collar, my gripping hers and the pull and push beginning. I cannot wait to engage that woman and show her some new mastery of my own.

At lunch break, Hazar invariably sits off to one side and serenades us with songs from her country of Yemen. Sometimes, if they are particularly poignant, she translates. To sit and hear her sing is a treat and makes up for not attending concerts in the evening.

Whenever possible, if we engage in some group function involving repetitive motion, Lael finds a song in her repertoire. One day she catches us all off guard by breaking into what she describes afterwards as a sea shanty for raising anchor on a sailing ship. The lyrics are immensely stirring with the ship leaving port and loved ones behind with the uncertain knowledge of ever returning.

That sets both Zichrini and Hazar into fountains of tears until Yen Lu points out that she has left her country and is not crying. When Hazar accuses her of having no heart, I think we are going to have a fight on our hands. But after posturing and sinking into some extremely unpleasant swearing, similar to Zichrini on her first days building our house, they both laugh and hug and that is the end of it.

I talk to Lael about that because I am so struck by the way the anger resolves. She tells me about Non Violent Communication. She deconstructs the discussion and what each person said about the other. She demonstrates how they switched from abusive accusations to constructive compliments that, at the time, all sound the same since I thought there is a tone of invective I could hear underlying everything.

Lael explains the intention of each statement and how it was responded to. No wonder they ended up hugging each other. Each declared needs to be met by the other and they had praised each other so highly in the end; it is the easiest way to conclude.

She adds that when Zichrini was laying in to Lucy and me during the construction of our house, she was inviting both of us to respond so that there will be resolution. When neither of us responded, she did so herself, first telling herself how wonderfully rude she was when she swore and how well she had confused us with her swearing. Apparently, Lael had also studied Arabic and that's how she was able to follow along. As I say, none of these is your average bricklayer.

In no time at all, the Library is complete. This time the celebrating is extensive. Lanterns are strung from building to building until the whole community is lit and resembling a fairy tale village. Everyone participates in the parade until the event merrily disintegrates into wildly ecstatic singing and dancing.

I enjoy the celebrating of my colleagues and me.

At some point, I realize people are disappearing into their houses and returning with boxes, stacks and handfuls of books. People are giving up their own collections to form the Library. It is like an arrow to my heart. I who had one of the finest collections of books, albeit children's literature, have nothing to give to the very Library I helped build.

Watching people walk in to the Library with books brings back so many dark memories. I feel myself cringe, sinking deeper and deeper with each memory, retreating further into the shadows, both literally and metaphorically.

I am wrapped in my own dismal cloud of misery, haunting the shadow cast by the Commissary environs when I hear Lucy shout, "Hey, Jude!"

That cheerful voice breaks into the depths of my depression like a stone into a lake of still water. Warm ripples swim after each other, cycling to the edge.

I enjoy my depressions and yet, when Lucy bursts in on me having one, I am unable to contain them. She pops my depressions like a pencil into a floating soap bubble.

At first, the bubble wraps around the pencil as if to suck it in, only to succumb in a dazzling display of tiny fragments that, when they too disappear, leave a momentarily bright, fresh space where the bubble used to be.

"Sidney's an ol' friend from Mexico City visitin' here," Lucy speaks in raptures.

My space, our space, is to include a third party. I am not speaking of Lucy's baby.

As they approach, Sidney sparkles. In her early twenties, about the same height as Lucy, I immediately notice the difference; if Lucy is energetic, Sidney makes her look like a wall flower. Sidney's every movement seems to want attention from whoever surrounds her. Sidney is a dance to life, to freedom, to the celebration of every last moment in time. It is no surprise these two hitched themselves to the same star.

Sidney wears clothes that accentuate her lithe body. She dances when she walks. There is flow and life to her all at the same time. Sidney is dressed in silks, layered and cutaways, multiple colors, yet short to accentuate her long skinny legs attached to flaming spangles for shoes which wrap her feet, leaving the impression that her entirety is bouncing toward me.

Sidney wears make up as if going to a wild party; heavy on the blush, brilliant red lipstick with a thick band of navy blue lip liner. Blues and purples line her eyes including tiny sparkles. Shoulder length black hair, in ringlets, bounces in perfect time with this concert of motion.

In the midst of all this, Sidney is two enormous brown eyes; glistening and glimmering, shooting every which way to take in what is happening, while, at the same time, knife focused fixed on me, the target of her attention.

I am dazzled. I know I am meant to be. Yet again, Lucy has dipped into her magician's hat of international wonderment to surprise me.

Like Diana returning from the hunt presenting her catch, Sidney bears a wooden bowl filled with exotic fruits. She stops a breath's distance from me. Her large, round, brown eyes soften as she looks into my eyes; a child searching for my soul, yet, naively unaware that that is her objective.

"Hola! Usted es infeliz, Judee?" she asks.

Sidney came to take charge. She does it with one brief greeting in a question as to whether I am unhappy.

"All my books are gone," I tell her simply. "I'm unable to contribute."

I cannot see Lucy. Sidney is so close and demanding of attention with her bouffant hair filling out into my peripheral vision.

Sidney realizes what Just occurred.

"Usted habla espanol!" she manages, almost screeching at me.

"I learned poquito in Nueve Yorque," I explain.

I am proud to say I can manage a few words in many languages. It is a point of honor for me. Something that amused my parents immensely and secretly made them very proud.

To me, English is not the be all and end all of the spoken word. In fact, I wish I spoke other languages so I could express the nuances which often do not translate into English, despite its magnificent potential for complexity. Shakespeare reportedly knew 80,000 words in English. Imagine having a sit down chat with the great bard!

My mind takes off on a tangent influenced no doubt by the myriad flavors of subtle perfumes which swim deliciously around this pretty child. She wants to hug me, get physically close, but she obstructs herself with the fruit bowl. Lucy calls out from beyond the flow of ringlets of hair.

"Break out the fruit, Sidney," she says.

Sidney steps back, and I momentarily flash on TRiXi washing my hair. Sidney is an angel by comparison; light and airy, free flowing, attractive.

Then I wake to the fact that the fruit is for me to share. My alarm bells start ringing. I zip from my mire of depression, to ecstasy at the sights and smells that are Sidney. I soar on the ebullience of the Spanish language, to crash with fear, almost terror, that I will have a sugar reaction.

"Fruit?" I shout at Lucy spinning to seek her out, indignant that she is willing to break a convention. "You know that's off my diet!"

Lucy somehow moves Sidney sideways in a subtle operation that I perceive but do not comprehend. Lucy is back in charge for the moment. She looks at me with her warm, gentle eyes that are probably what won me over back at the diner.

"Relax, Jude," she comments with gentle pride. "We're celebratin' yer!"

I am flattered, though I do not immediately make the connection to the library. To me that is simply a job well done, a joy, a way to pass the time, a place to learn and share camaraderie. I did not anticipate there will be a celebration for its completion.

The Library is a needed function for the community; period. Filling it with books; now that, to me, is celebrating, even though I can't contribute.

To my mind, Lucy is going overboard importing this luscious flower and having her transport a bowl of exotic fruit.

Lucy. studies my mental wanderings as best as she is able from outside my mind.

"Once'll be OK," she concludes, not willing to have her idea of a celebration aborted by my health condition or any protestations. She nods to Sidney.

Sidney slips a hand inside the layers of clothing and pulls out a hunting knife; truly Diana in disguise. In a continuous flow of motion, she sticks a kiwi fruit with the point of the six inch blade, puts the bowl down on a table, and slices the fruit more or less in three. She sticks one slice with the knife and offers it to me. I hesitate.

She takes the fruit off the knife, puts down the knife, and eyes sparkling, demonstrates a slow, lascivious lick of her tongue along the length of the fruit's white pulpy center all the while looking up at me with open eyed innocence.

"Celebre con mi," she invites me. "Como!"

And she does the lick again, in case I missed her the first time.

She sticks another piece and holds it out to me, taunting me. Lucy stares, watching closely to see how I react. Reluctantly, I accept the fruit offering, and, half heartedly, awkwardly, endeavor to imitate Sidney's performance. Sidney laughs.

Her light laugh is not a condemnation of my effort. It is the laugh of someone with every reason to enjoy life. Lucy laughs too. This is the first time I hear Lucy laugh for no good reason other than joy. Lucy accepts the last piece of fruit and stuffs it whole into her mouth and chews, grinning with delight at her three way marriage.

Sidney points to the bowl with her knife and looks to me questioningly. It's the international language of mime. She's good at it.

Curious as to what it may be, I point to a dark pink, wrinkly, small fruit. Sidney skins it with a flourish, slices it and ejects two smoothly round, shiny brown pits from the Juicy, succulent, white meat. It's a lychee.

I feel myself sliding into a place I have not been in a long time. I relax and laugh with them. The Library's existence, the celebration, fades quickly. My opposition to sugar fades even more easily. It is time to get high, sugar high; that perceptible condition of giddiness and effusive energy which people call, "having a good time."

My body rejoicing resembles flexing a muscle that has lain dormant for a long time.

It is as if I hear Pan's pipes calling me to the Dance, a dance with Dionysius himself, "Glorious abandonment, take me on gossamer wings deep into your succulently fetid woods... to dance the night away."

I am girded up and protected by the demi-gods of pleasure. I am beyond harm. I am liberated from the bizarre constraints of pure, raw health.

Once more, I am free to be me, the real me.

ONE MORE

Out of thin air, Sidney, leaning sideways, produces a square shaped bottle of amber liquid with something floating in the bottom. She unscrews the top and takes a swig. She wipes her mouth with the back of her hand and passes the bottle to Lucy.

My eyes track the wiping hand with its newly acquired swath of red and navy blue.

Lucy turns Sidney down. Party pooper!

She points to her protruding belly; again, the baby. Everything she doesn't want to do, for any reason, is converted to being in defense of her unborn child. How bad can it be?

Not showing rejection, Sidney takes another long, deep swig, wipes her mouth with the back of her hand again, and passes the bottle to me. I take it, guessing it must be alcohol of some sort.

I am already so high on fructose, I do not care anymore. I turn the bottle around to read the label. It is some private stock of Mescal. I smell the opening. I receive a deeply satisfying smell of mildly sweet alcohol. I hold the bottle up to look at what is floating in the bottom. I almost drop the bottle with shock.

Curled up with eyes wide open is a small rattlesnake suspended in the Mescal. I hold the bottle out to Lucy and she shakes her head no. I offer the bottle to Sidney who smiles sweetly. She puts a hand beneath mine on the bottle and presses the bottle to me. I indicate my refusal. She seductively bats her eyes and presses my hand with her hand, her index finger brushing across the back of my hand. Maybe it was unintentional; maybe not. I look into her eyes and behind the bright effervescent smile is a hint of sadness at my refusal to play.

It is almost as if I can hear the sugar rush say to me, "What the heck?"

I go for it. That liquor goes down so smoothly, with barely a hint of heat. This is good stuff. I pass the bottle to Lucy who defrays from drinking and gives the bottle to Sidney. Both she and Sidney are in heaven. I have no barriers left to break.

We sink to sitting on the benches, the girls on one side, giddily ecstatic, me on the other. It is a friendly competition, an agreement unspoken, that this bottle must be killed right here, right now. Lucy is in her element, cheering both Sidney and me along. She is an impartial fan of us both. It makes the game more intriguing as to what Lucy will do when there truly is a winner and a loser. How will she divide her loyalties then?

Sidney and I have long since passed the euphoria that may occur when drinking alcohol. As smooth as this alcohol is, it is strong. The bottle is passed back and forth in noisy slides across the table. We both slouch, our faces drooping closer and closer to the tabletop. Irrespective, we are determined to put an end to John Barleycorn, tonight.

The realization comes to me in waves.

The light bite of the warm alcohol surrounds my tongue. A bump as I gulp warns of an alien object. My reactions are greatly reduced to halting slurs so I presume it is the opening of the bottle with which I am doing battle. I suck down one more swig and there is almost no liquid to drink when something round, firm and solid strikes against my tongue. I pull the bottle away from my mouth and strive to focus on the opening.

I am staring straight into the cold, bright eyes of a rattlesnake, its mouth open enough to show top and bottom rows of teeth as it bares its fangs.

I cannot throw the bottle away from me fast enough or hard enough. The exertion exhausts me. I can feel my eyes roll downwards as my head lolls forward. An escalating cackling noise fills my ears. I struggle to raise my head to search for the source. I can vaguely distinguish Lucy falling about, laughing hysterically. At one point she stops, as if in pain, grabbing her belly with both hands.

Across from me a drunken clown with smears of color around her raw mouth is laughing.

I think to myself, "If you think I'm funny, wait'll you look in a mirror."

With great effort, I pull myself into sitting up straight, though parts of me try desperately to submit to downwards. I tell myself, if I can do free form head stands and pushups. I certainly can hold myself together. I'm strong. My head is up, occasionally weaving here and there. I'll show you who can hold her liquor.

It helps to have my elbows on the table and my hands supporting my jaw. That steadies me. I look directly at the clown face. My eyelids are trying to close. The clown face leans toward me, her lips puckering up. Her head twists to a slight angle. I feel her fleshy lips touch mine, in ever so light a kiss. Then it's lights out; the warm darkness of oblivion.

I must be eight years old, out taking a rare walk in the country. The grass is lush; the leaves are fully formed on deciduous trees. Spring abounds. High above me a hawk rides a thermal current, languidly circling, letting the wind stroke its feathers. With the slightest of motions, the hawk turns downward in a decisive move toward some trees. Clouds race past as the hawk gathers speed on its targeted descent.

Like two scrambling fighter planes, a pair of crows, cawing menacingly at the hawk, lifts off from tree tops. Forced off target but dropping too fast to pull up, the hawk veers sideways to evade its attackers. One crow gets in a nip that clearly hurts the hawk. The hawk cartwheels out of control. Feathers mussed, it tumbles towards the ground with the crows taking advantage to peck at it. With one major effort, the hawk strokes deeply with both wings lifting it out of range of the crows that cannot follow such a power filled maneuver.

I am 12 years old out for a precious family drive with my folks. I ride in back. In three part harmony, we sing, "I Love to Go A wandering." Still recovering from being sick, I sing flat. Mom wants me to sing a half note high and dad says to drop down, that'll be easier on my voice. I am the only one singing as they argue back and forth which will be easier for me. The volume of loud voices in the car is growing oppressive.

"Let's go out into the country," my dad offers.

"Can we afford to joy ride, George?" mom asks.

Dad winks at me in his rear view mirror.

"Sure we can, Ethel," he assures mom.

"Is this our on ramp?" mom asks.

Without hesitation, dad swings the wheel and we are racing toward the expressway. Ahead of us, a hawk rides on the hot air updraft from the blacktop, low to the two lane highway.

A metallic bulldog comes at us as it rounds a bend in the road. Snapping his square jaw, the dog roars at the hawk. The dog comes at us since we are in the left lane. Dad steers us into the right lane and the hawk also veers right to avoid the snapping dog. Another bulldog appears in our lane, passing up the first dog, aiming straight for the hawk and us. The hawk attempts to lift off while at the same time baring her claws to scare the second bulldog. As if in slow motion, not the least bit intimidated, the second bulldog jumps at the hawk, snapping ferociously.

Truck air horns blare. Performing out of control cartwheels, the hawk whirls over the car. I turn in my seat to watch out the rear window as the hawk smashes to the road. I turn forward and, in that one split second, feel my breath totally sucked out of my lungs.

Eyes closed, I gasp for air. I choke for a moment. My eyes flutter open to see Lucy leaning over me. I lay on my back on the dirt.

Surrounded by other women, Lucy looks mightily concerned. My gasping for air continues for a minute. Lucy holds my shoulders, but I can feel that she has no idea what to do to assist me.

Petrina arrives and quickly takes charge, moving the gathered women and Lucy back out of the way.

Petrina lifts me by my arms into a sitting position. That helps my breathing to ease and my eyes to focus as I blink to make out who all is gathered around. Gently, Petrina helps me to my feet as Serena arrives, pressing through the crowd and instructing the assembly.

"OK, everyone," she says. "The worst is over. Go back to your celebrating. Everything's fine."

Though I hear her through a fog, I wonder, based on what makes everything fine? Wasn't it fine before? Why is it that, now Serena has arrived, everything is suddenly fine?

I am aware that I am standing, Petrina has let go of me and a much stronger grip has hold of my right upper arm. I look down to the hand wrapped around my arm with a tight grip as if preparing to direct me forcibly. I look from the hand along its arm to see it belongs to Serena. I struggle to free myself.

"Take your hands off me!" I bellow at her.

People, who were moving away, hesitate at the sound of my outburst. I make as if I am falling. Since she still has hold of my arm, Serena starts to go with me. I roll slightly to the side causing Serena to completely lose her balance and have to put out both hands to protect herself as we fall. Rolling as I drop, I make a swift sideways sweep of my right foot, obliging Serena to move her hands further apart forcing her face down to the ground. I continue my fall and now I am atop of her. It takes me no effort to kneel astride her and spin her face up, trapping her legs with my feet, and throwing my hands about her throat in a lock intended to strangle, and quickly disable her.

At this moment, I am fully conscious. Accumulated anger, from way back, assembles to be driven home on one target—Serena. She feels the full intensity of my rage. Left to my own devises, I am sure I would have killed her.

With deft, sure moves Petrina slips her left hand under my right armpit to create a torque intended to throw me off balance. I am forced to release my hand grip on Serena so as to defend myself against my attacker. Having loosed my right arm, Petrina twists it sharply behind my back and leans hard into my torso. The move is fast. She pitches me forward and sideways to hit the ground next to Serena, my arm behind my back rendering me powerless.

As she struggles to her feet, I see Serena wave over Lucy and, hiding behind her, Sidney.

"Take her home and put her to bed," Serena stammers imperatively. "There'll be a hearing tomorrow..."

As Lucy approaches, followed by a giggling Sidney, Petrina rises, maintaining her hold on my right arm, forcing me to stand also. She shoves me at my companions in an unceremoniously abrupt push. I stumble into their arms. They grab a hold of one of my hands each. They have such light grips; it's as if they never had to assist anyone before. Instead of them helping me, I head for the house dragging them after me hanging on to one of their arms each. I feel my rage transfer to Sidney.

Lucy is too juvenile, but Sidney feels worldly aware, as if she ought to know better. Something about her touches a nerve. I feel anger rise, but this is cooler, more vicious, aimed at her. She ignores me and continually seeks eye contact with Lucy. Every time their eyes meet they both burst into paroxysms of laughter and giggles.

I am tempted to pull them off the ground by swinging my arms together and smashing their heads into each other.

BOOBOO

I awake on Library construction time. It is pitch black. I have no recollection of going to bed. A rhythm, set by my heart beat for every pulse of blood, slams a sledgehammer against my head. It takes an uphill battle to gain each inch of movement as I struggle to sit up and look about. I feel an urge to get out of bed. I lean out of my pod, head first. My stomach convulses and I throw up. That's when I recall the expression, "to hurl."

The violent noise wakes Lucy.

I believe I see her disengage from a tousle of black hair as she slips out of her bed. She goes into the bathroom, turns on the light and rinses a washcloth wet. As she emerges, the light glares into my eyes making them develop a counter rhythm to the sledgehammer. I wave one hand toward her but it drops uselessly into wet slime on the tiled floor. I convulse again, this time just a dry heave.

"Yer OK, Jude?" Lucy asks.

"Sure, honey lamb," I want to tell her. "I'm peachy."

Instead, between heaves, I say, "The... light..."

Lucy turns, opens the bathroom door once more to blind me with light so my eyes scream with pain. Then, she switches off the light. My hand on the floor slides away from me and I tip head first onto the floor, dry retching as I slither about.

Lucy is unflappable. With the same calmness that she used to steer me away from the dumpster, she wipes me down, cleans me up and takes care of the floor. She points out the egg she brought me from the Commissary. She doesn't bat an eyelid when I crack it into the jar and slurp it down. Maybe she did bat an eyelid. I'm in no shape to notice much of anything. Amazingly, not only does the egg stay down, it seems to stop the retching.

Lucy maneuvers me to sit on one of our two chairs. I watch her bustle about in the shadows. She insists on removing my nightshirt. That's when I find out I have it on backwards. We start to laugh, except my head cannot handle such activity. I have to still myself way down to stop the sledgehammer from beating my head to a pulp. After removing the nightshirt, Lucy bird bathes me with a fresh washcloth then slips a clean t shirt on me.

"I'm in big trouble, Lucy," I tell her.

"We got yer covered," she tells me.

"You and... who?" I ask. "Sidney?"

If I think I am in trouble now, wait till they see my primary witness.

"Her family can buy out mine wi' their pocket change," she says to reassure me.

"Money can only do so much, Lucy," I explain.

It may be a while since I took one of Maisha's classes but the principles remain the same. The goal is to make Taquinta self supporting. Throwing money around, especially to resolve my episode with Serena, of all people, seems about as logical as throwing gasoline to douse a fire.

"If Sidney joins," Lucy answers, "Their income here is set. We're here forever."

Yes, there it is again, her belief in parents paying the way for their child to succeed.

"You live in a fantasy, Lucy," I snarl.

Of course, it takes one to know one. When it comes to living inside dreams and fantasies, I am the Queen. Perhaps that and the money thing are really the glue that holds us together.

"You know Serena wants us out of here," I plead.

I can feel myself becoming stern and adult. What I am really hoping for is to gather some background details so I can piece together what all happened, last night. Not that I cannot remember, but I know from similar such events in the past; I may not know all the details.

Lucy stands, feeling put upon. She swings on me.

"Yer all work an' no play," she spits out. "I thought maybe a live wire chickey like Sidney'll be fun for yer."

Somehow we got off on the wrong foot. There is some darkness between us, some unspoken aspect of our relationship which leads us astray when, as now, we are forced to face reality.

I feel it when I ask, "Are you lesbian?"

Lucy stares at me with a non comprehending look of, what is all that about? I try to cover my statement, but, too late.

"I thought with the pregnancy..." I stammer.

Lucy looks away. This is a topic we never raised. Is this our issue?

"Yer understandin' of sexuality is primitive, Jude," she says turning on me. "We all got some of everythin' in each of us. Any point in time, some part of us shows. Yer repress yern most all the time."

Looking over to Lucy's pod where Sidney rummages deeper under the covers, I comment, "She is bizarre!"

"She's herself," Lucy says. "Flat out, all the time, herself. Somethin' yer... an' me ... still have to find."

I pray we have glissando-ed over my egregious comments. I weakly go back to my greatest fear.

"They'll wise up to me soon," I tell her.

With deep mothering instincts she rubs calming circles into my back as she tells me, "Yer sleep. Let me handle thin's."

CIRCLES

"Last night was bad, Judith," Maisha tells me.

I sit across from her inside the Togu Na with the Elders assembled in full force. I am in big trouble. I look at Maisha with as straight a gaze as I can muster, desperately attempting not to show even a flicker of emotion. I am challenging her point by refusing to respond to it.

Inside, I can feel after effects of the sugar drawing down. My body is exhausted from supporting the sudden surges of energy used when I fought with Serena and Petrina. Now craving more sugar, I am plain angry, unable to do more than snarl and snap like a caged wild beast.

As I look around the circle from one face to the next, I catch momentary glimpses of Lucy, prowling like a mad she-cat a distance off from the Togu Na. She is mulling over and forming her thoughts in proximity. She is preparing to pounce, though how she will enter this formal enclave is beyond my imagination.

"Did anyone research Biological Anthropologist Michael Kaliban of Kings College, Cambridge?" Serena asks pointedly.

She drips sarcasm as she adds, "The Harley Street physician!"

My heart sinks. I knew Lucy and her Tokyo experience was a crock. Why did I go along with her? I know I can't stick to a simple story. Now Serena, in her desire to find fault with us, has done the inevitable.

The other Elders clearly have no agenda with Lucy and me. They are working the rules. That is all.

"Who?" "Where?" "Is that in England?" are some of the responses.

Serena looks about with rising glee. The target of her dislike is in sight; if not yet to the other Elders, it is to her. She stares me in the eye. I find my gaze forced to wander knowing that, in the pending denouement, it is now her turn to have me by the throat and she is in a position of power. The fateful end is nigh. The end of the world...

Puffing herself up at the responses of ignorance about who is Dr. Michael, Serena lays it out.

"He's a fiction," she tells the assembly, looking from face to face, always reverting back to me with the cold look akin to that of the baby rattlesnake.

"As in *Professor Michael explores the Pacific*, also, *South America* and *Africa*," blood rushing to her face, flushing her with excitement as she closes for the kill, Serena lists off some of my favorite travel books.

"We have here," she pauses for effect, "Jerzy Kosinki's *Chance*."

And with that she stares straight at me, seeing that I know of whom she speaks.

My ally, Lea, is completely baffled by the tactics taken by Serena. She looks directly at Serena as if they have a deeply complex philosophical puzzle to unravel. Lea is short many of the pieces.

"What?" she asks confused. "Who?"

Serena gloats, "The book and movie, *Being There*."

"I am here, now!" I yell out. "You're talking about me as if I'm a child or absent."

Fortunately for me, Serena's argument was sufficiently complex for those of the Elders not familiar with her references, that my outburst is what everyone needs for the conversation to revert to the topic at hand. Maisha grounds us all.

"You were taught Brazilian Jiu-Jitsu for self defense," Maisha reprimands me. "You used it to attack Serena."

Unable to stop the residual sugar spike, I blurt out, "Serena has had it in for me from the moment she first set eyes on me."

Somehow, my antagonist and I have reduced a discussion of community principles to a school room spat. Serena struggles to stand, outraged by my accusation. Gurgling sounds rise in her throat. Maisha waves her down.

"Judith," Maisha begins as she takes charge. "You have worked hard, learned a lot, and been a good team player."

I can hear the twist in the set up. At this point, I realize I am at fault, if not with my desire to do away with Serena, for once and for all, but for breaking house rules. From here on out, it will be a matter of the severity of judgment of how I am to be dealt with.

"You were all Brownie points... until, last night," Maisha states. "Based on your potential for violence..."

"One time?!" I protest.

Even I can hear the resonance in my statement which tells of countless prior outbursts, just none of them here at Taquinta. Rage is my uncontrollable issue which, amazingly, has lain hidden and sequestered from sight for a long time here at Taquinta.

Maisha lectures me, "Violence one time means it is possible again. I am obliged to ask you to leave."

The declaration is abrupt, cold, and direct. I am stunned. I suspect others of the Elders are equally surprised by the toughness of a decision which is made independently of a vote. Looking especially pregnant, Lucy appears, her head sticking through the entrance behind Maisha.

"Promise 'em yer'll work hard, Jude," she shrieks at me. "I want yer to stay."

The plaintive quality of her voice, and her demands of me, cut into everyone's soul. Reduced by circumstances beyond her control, Lucy reverts to being the little girl she is at heart.

"Lucy," Maisha turns her head slightly and speaks over her shoulder with a calmly quiet voice, "We're in council. You had the right to attend. You opted to stay out. Please leave so we may finish."

Feeling victimized, Lucy snaps; the dark side of her little girl roars into place.

"When I tell my mom what went down," she argues back, "This whole place is done."

It's a specious argument when I think about it. Here is a facility, supported extensively by her parents, which permits Lucy the opportunity to be under the wing of her parents without living in, or near, their home. And she is going to destroy the subsistence of Taquinta and thereby her refuge? I think not. And I can see by looking around the circle, most Elders silently see the fault in her argument. Lucy backs off as if a shroud is falling about her. She sits on a nearby grassy slope , regrouping her thoughts.

"Did you eat sugar food, last night?" Chrystal asks me.

Having thought the decision was made and the discussion essentially closed off, I am surprised by the tactic.

"Why?" I demand back.

"Please answer me," Chrystal requests.

I find myself mulling over possibilities. I become immersed to the point of not remembering what set my thinking off and how to pull the various arguments to coherence.

"YES!" I blurt out, bitterly. "OK? Everybody happy?"

"You are hypoglycemic, Judith," Chrystal points out, sympathetically. "Eating sugar foods makes you unpredictable, temperamental. Knowing that, why did you eat sugar?"

I give it up simply.

"I wanted so badly to donate to the library," I say. "I made a poor choice of masking my hurt. I own that much."

The effect is unexpected. I went from being challenged and seen as a malcontent to pulling sympathy for my desire to contribute.

"I move," Lea jumps right in, "That Judith remain—under supervision—till Lucy's baby is born and we decide then."

"Oh, please," Serena wails. "The Twinkie Defense? Really?"

"Any opposition?" Maisha asks, checking the faces of her colleagues. "OK, vote."

I think it is the speed of decisiveness that endears me more than anything to these women and their ideals for Taquinta. After all, it is merely a place with a bunch of odd looking buildings and a society totally on another set of scales, unbalanced by the absence of men. And, yet, it is as if that very absence makes decision making, from the smallest to the largest issue, simple and easy to perform.

I watch the earnestness with which all give the thumbs up sign; all, that is, but Serena who declines to vote. In itself, that is a vote and Maisha calls her on it.

"That was a majority," Maisha says to the assembly as she turns to face Serena, sitting by her side. "Will you abide by their decision?"

Serena turns her gaze away from Maisha and looks across the space to me. The look is of pure cold determination. The energy she puts into the look brings her into tight and close focus, as if she were a foot from my face instead of fifteen feet distant. There is no malice in her look. In fact, I have no experience interpreting such a look.

"I accept," she says.

"Until then, Judith," Maisha intones solemnly, "You work the fields. However, one more incident and you are out! Take it or leave."

"Deal," I respond, without further thought. It is an excellent deal. It is so much better than I expected. It feels like a total reprieve.

"The words are spoken," Maisha concludes. "So be it."

The assembled Elders seal the decision along with Maisha.

They intone, "So be it!"

I feel a weight lift off of me.

Lucy's face bursts into my vision through the movement of people exiting the Togu Na. Her face is wreathed in smiles of relief, as if she has achieved her goal.

I clamber out of the ceremonial space as if escaping a chamber of doom. The intensity of energy these women have created by working speech into so much meaning makes the Togu Na a formidable place to be. After such weighty decision making, it is as if they have woven strand upon strand of energy together and, when they physically leave the place, they leave a cloth woven for the future with one end incomplete for the attachment of future decisions. No wonder they refer to it as a House of Words. These are words strung into meanings to last through the ages.

As I reach terra firma, Lucy grabs me and hugs me pushing her pregnant belly against me so that I, too, am holding her baby. That is her goal. From the moment she locked on to me, she has been weaving me into her pregnancy. Now I am twice woven, first by words and now by deed. And it is still early in the morning.

Chrystal comes over and lays one hand on my shoulder and the other on Lucy's, thereby psychically acknowledging our strange union.

"Judith, I want to take you on a Shamanic Journey," she tells me. "It may help you."

A crone has risen; must be the season of the witch.

Taquinta is definitely a place of strange practices and focused energy. Each day unveils possible ways to live that surprise and amaze me. Till this moment, it's as if I have lived my life in darkness and without knowledge. For that to be true is hard for me to believe because I am so well read.

I succumb easily to new experiences because I finally recognize that the path to knowledge resists resistors, while, conversely, it joyously welcomes those who are willing to learn. Enough resistance! Wash me and cleanse me with knowledge. I fear it no more. Look how much freedom it has gifted me already in so short a time.

Chrystal has me lie on a yoga mat on the ground in the shade of the Commissary out on the Piazza. Chrystal works swiftly and answers my questions in brief statements. I am to relax, let her direct me until I am in a light trance. Is that asleep or awake? Wakeful dream state. OK. What are the rocks and crystals? Obsidian is black and goes to the feet to ground me. Citrine, an acid sweet, clear, light yellow rests on my stomach. There are various fluorites of different colors placed about and on me. A beautiful, deep blue lapis lazuli with gold flecks rests on my throat. A resonant, rough, green emerald is placed in the middle of my chest. Moon stone at my forehead and a long, pointed clear crystal rod is above my head. I feel surrounded by charms and good wishes. Occasionally, Chrystal moves a stone, or takes it away, sometimes replacing it with another. She tells me she is weighing the intensity of my etheric body with the different strengths of each stone or crystal. I barely understand this talk.

I remember when Lea, in a moment of exasperation with the general ignorance of the class, suddenly listed off all the major Laws of Physics and Mathematics and explained each one. The second Law of Thermodynamics stuck with me because of her talk about Entropy. I still do not understand what that means, but I feel it applies here.

Chrystal's explanation of the levels of energy fields which surround each one of us, layer by layer, out into the Universe, is reminiscent of entropy. Confusing to my mind is that all the particles that I am, plus the layering of inter meshed etheric bodies, extend until there is nothing and everything.

"Within you without you," Chrystal defines it.

It makes sense up until I reason with it or attempt to analyze it. Then it becomes an exploded soap bubble. I decide to lay back and relish the loving care extended to me.

Chrystal plans to enter into my etheric field with me while we travel back in time to find out why I am sick. That is my intention. She helps me to evolve it as I lay there, face up, my hands at my sides, while she strives for an exacting placement of stones and crystals. She finishes by gently covering me with a blanket so only my head shows.

Lucy stands close by, eyes wide as saucers. I suspect she is impressed more by my willingness to be treated than the process itself. Honey, if it will set me free, bring it on!

Seated by me on a cushion, Chrystal leans forward, slowly brushing the air up and down my entire length, about six inches above me, with a large, beautiful feather. Gently wafting the air, she asks me to close my eyes and hold my intention of learning why I am sick. She invokes energies of the Universe and asks that only good forces participate in this journey. Somewhere on my face a smile begins to slowly creep across me. I am amused at being here and at having this done to me. It is so alien, and yet, soft and loving. What harm can occur?

RETURN

Chrystal has me relax by breathing down into my stomach.

"Take deep breaths in through your nose and release through your mouth," she tells me.

Made conscious of this most natural of functions, I make every breath become an ordeal of mental observation as I strive for perfection.

I am aware of the feather each time it passes over my face in each direction.

Chrystal encourages me to, "Seek a quiet place in the woods or by a stream or the ocean. Find a place where you are alone, at peace, comfortable with your surroundings, and once there, settle down and wait... without expectations."

With no trouble at all, I find a glade of deep greens and dark shadows among trees with wide trunks soaring high into the sky. It is incredibly quiet—no wind, no birds, no animals. Rich, musty smells of the humus swell up and fill my nostrils as I breathe deeply.

Chrystal says, "An animal guide will come and visit you when you are ready."

A new smile on my face startles me. I lose it in an effort to seek out an animal.

"Relax, be patient," Chrystal tells me. "Whatever will come will arrive on its own, independent of you..."

With a high pitched, shrill scream, a hawk drops through the trees and makes a low attacking pass, claws wide open, over my head. I instinctively duck to avoid being hit, and swing around to see where my attacker went.

Off into the trees and climbing. I can barely track its flight as it curves around and heads back preparing to make another approach.

I am ready for it this time. As it comes screeching through the trees, I stand, bracing myself prepared for what is fast approaching—be it a strike, or a miss—my eyes wide open to greet my attacker. I am surprised when the wings spread and the feet drop down, braking to a halt. This exquisite bird does a U-ey in the air in front of me; clearly offering for me to take hold.

I watch as the bird seems to hover in space, not flapping a wing or moving. It ought to just drop to the ground, but it doesn't. It waits for me to get with the program. I reach out gingerly with my right hand and grasp the bird's left leg.

Barely have I got a hold than the bird effortlessly lifts off, with me hanging on. I am like Ariel being transported by MpowRgirl. The hawk rises fast between the trees and up into the sky.

As this happens to me, I tell Chrystal what I am experiencing. She reminds me to maintain my breathing protocol.

She asks where we are flying to. I cannot tell. We're high above the ground, right below a bank of clouds. We are moving tremendously fast and yet there is no oppositional wind. We fly over countryside and small towns until a large city approaches. In moments, we cross over the city center headed towards the suburbs. As if targeting a particular site, the hawk starts a rapid descent racing down towards the specks of buildings below.

I am fearful we are going to crash as we make such a rapid descent. At the last moment, the hawk pulls back and, with a flap of its wings, lets me go. I fly noiselessly through a window to land in a child's bedroom.

It is clearly a child's room Judging by the toys, books and other accoutrements. It's a girl's room. It is my childhood room!

I look to the bed and see myself lying there with a thermometer sticking out of my mouth. I take it out and put it on the pillow next to the Bed Me as Dr. Washington walks in with my parents following meekly behind him. He reprimands the Bed Me for removing the thermometer.

The Visitor Me wants to pop him one for talking so meanly to a sick little girl. He digs in his black bag and with a few deft movements has given the Bed Me a shot of antibiotics. My heart sinks as I watch the condition of my Bed Me's personality change. Literally, right there and then, her energy drains away.

She asks for yoghourt and the doctor makes some remark about letting the medicine do its job first. Now, I really want to pop him. I see the Bed Me slowly close her eyes and sink into a depression. Abandoned by the doctor to this terrible medicine, forsaken by my parents because they are overwhelmed by the superior rank in society of this iceman, the doctor, I can see how my life turned downhill.

Watching this all is so painful I feel a scream welling up inside of me. Out of nowhere the hawk returns to lift me off and out of the room, up into the sky, safe and free from the terrors of that old dream.

Soon I am back in the woods, feet on the ground, the hawk winging its way off through the trees screeching with joy at having assisted me.

A hand on my shoulder is gently rubbing me, rocking me to wakefulness. I look up and see Chrystal leaning over me with large, sad eyes. Beyond her, I see Lucy crying, and other women standing there, empathizing with me.

I stare at this sense of sadness and a huge grin fills my face. The surrounding faces all follow my lead and also switch. People start to laugh. This is my dream after all and I demand we take it seriously, so I laugh. The joy of seeing everyone waiting for my return is exhilarating for me. I pull the blanket off causing the stones and crystals to tumble every which way as I rise to my feet and grab Chrystal for a big hug.

"Welcome back, Judith!" Chrystal shouts into our hug. She pushes me away and holds me by the shoulders as she finishes with her analysis.

"Seems an antibiotic destroyed your internal flora," she explains. "That's probably where your intolerance to sugar began."

I take in her commentary and move to hug my mom to be, wallowing in tears of joy, recognizing what happened the night before and how mistaken it was for me to eat fruit exclusively and especially to drink alcohol. Ours is both a hug of joy and of reconciliation.

I am passed around the small group of women and each one hugs me and makes me feel I am her special friend. This is my first deep experience of community with these folks, probably with anyone, anywhere. I am high as a kite, Just in time for lunch!

That afternoon, Lucy and I are delegated to a beginning Biodynamic farming class out in the fields. I feel we are blessed by having Lea in charge. Whether she knows it or not, I sense a deep affinity with her. Whatever she teaches, I feel like being there to soak up the information.

Lea guides us to a dry section of land and each of us, with shovel in hand, is told to dig a trench two feet long one foot wide and three feet deep. Judging by the trials of previous groups showing up as barely covered over efforts to do the same thing, this is really a joke. The ground is hard as a rock and unwilling to give in to our shovels.

We are soon escorted to a flat section of terrain where a nearby spigot is attached to a post staked into the ground. I am told to hook up a length of hose coiled nearby. I struggle with the connection and finally get the female to fit over the male spigot and screw them together.

Lucy giggles at Lea's graphic sexual explanations as she describes the maneuver with which I struggle. Not being sure that she is laughing at Lea's definitions or at me, and, recognizing unresolved residual anger from last night, and, again, the early morning discussion back at the dome, I point the hose at Lucy as I turn the water on full blast. A few air bubbles splutter out followed by a silver arc which hits Lucy square in the back almost knocking her over.

She spins around and deftly moves out of range of the jet. I try to chase her with the water but she is evasive as she ducks and swerves despite her front loading. She feigns disinterest and I turn the hose away from her. Next thing I know, she sidles up to me, grabs the hose out of my hand, turns the pressure as high it will go and aims the hose at me. I am drenched from head to toe in a matter of seconds. I try to reach out to her to deflect the hose away but she backs up. Also, by now the ground is wet and slippery. Down I go.

Lucy sees me struggle in the wet dirt and sprays me even more, laughing maniacally. She is having the best time. Me, I'm slithering about struggling to get on my feet and having them keep on sliding out from under me. My hands and arms are covered in dirt; my whole outfit is wet and mostly covered in dirt. At one point my face submerges into the wet dirt, and that's when I am struck by the smell.

The smell I picked up while in the woods during my Shamanic Journey was of rotting trees and layer upon layer of leaf mulch. Out here it is just wet dirt. But it is a distinct smell, similarly compelling, something that I want to sink inside of and roll in, become one with, eat, feel, smell, see.

I grab handfuls of wet dirt and rub the slimy earth on my face, all the while inhaling the dark, rich flavors. Lucy has relented with the hose and come over to find out what I am doing. Other women have taken the hint and are slipping and sliding about, pushing each other into the wet dirt and smothering each other with the sweet smell of Mother Nature.

Lea turns the hose so it is washing dirt into the small hollow where we have congregated. She genteelly slides in to join us all splashing about and throwing wet handfuls of mud at each other. Lucy screams with delight at the top of her lungs.

Lea kneels in front of us commanding our attention. She puts her hands together as if to pray. A couple of women, believing she is being deadly serious, imitate her. Lea bows her head as she begins to intone in a deep, stage voice.

"Ashes to ashes, dust to dust..." she recites.

A small handful of mud hits her in the mouth making her stop abruptly to spit it out. She picks up a huge, wet handful of mud and castes about for who was her assailant. A gaggle of hysterical innocents confronts her. She drops her handful and everyone bursts into laughs of relief. The pushing and shoving begins again for a few moments, and then it is time to return to the Commissary and turn in our tools.

Lucy takes charge of the hose as each of us parades past her doing a slow spin to be washed down. I offer to clean her off and she sticks out her belly and tells me to make a good job of washing her baby.

As the sun sets, we take our turns in line for the evening buffet. Still wet and pretty muddy, we are all laughing and carrying on like a bunch of hysterical school girls. As they fill plates with food, I head out to retrieve my tray.

I return and find Lucy eating at a picnic table. She offers up a look of relief. It's been a 24 hour roller coaster ride. I feel released.

Sidney, dressed down in local issue coveralls with one strap hanging loose in flamboyant oppositional posturing, an arm draped about the shoulders of another young woman, comes up and looks at us with utter disbelief. She is truly shocked by our appearance. Lucy humorously flashes her the bird and turns her back on her. Sidney lets forth with a stream of invectives in Spanish, then, giggling with her new found friend, wanders off.

As I am about to start eating, I see that someone has totally transformed my food. It is all the exact same raw foods I have been eating all along, but, now, an artist has been let loose. The vegetables are evenly sliced and layered like an open lotus flower onto the plate. The meat is in strips that lend themselves to easier ingestion. It is as if the food preparer is telling me to enjoy my food compared to how it was before—Here's your food!

For the first time, I realize there is an actual person preparing my meals. I resolve to find out who it is so I may appreciate them properly.

MARCHE

"Please, So'er Maisha, anythin' but the fields," begs So'er Judith, "Don't make me work the fields. I'll do anythin' you ask, but, please, not the fields."

"The fields it is, So'er Judith," So'er Maisha insists. "The fields it is. Yes, indeedy!"

"The fields it is then."

Next morning, work starts in earnest—in the fields.

Under the dual direction of the Amazons, Dada and Didi, I have plenty of opportunity to experiment with my few words in American Sign Language. They are delighted that, when I first began to study ASL, I voluntarily made the effort to visit them. They make time to correct me and to teach me. Within a couple of hours, I adjust to the rhythm and expression of signing and already feel at ease, even though all I have to offer is the vocabulary of a two year old.

What I become aware of, almost immediately, is that, up until my imposed invasion of their world, they had operated as a totally self contained unit. Being identical twins was one thing, being deaf and dumb was another. Add to that their gigantic size, their loving devotion to care for the fields and food provision, their facility to keep going all day, every day, year round, they brought on themselves the intensity of their isolation, their separateness from life at Taquinta. Seemingly, except to talk business, they have the bare minimum interaction with the denizens of Taquinta. Conversely, it is difficult to imagine anywhere else in the world they could be happier.

I have caste in my lot with a rum bunch, to be certain. And they are as happy to have me with them as I am to be here. It's a pact conceived by a mighty hand.

Working with these professionals in the field is similar to working with the crew building the library. I quickly learn good technique for different tools to work the soil, to handle plants and animal life. I cannot believe how much fun I am having. The work is every bit as hard as construction, much more varied, much longer hours even, and considerably more rewarding.

What at first appeared to be endless rows of everything that is grown to feed the community gradually reduces into a surprisingly few compact arenas with specific purposes. Literally within days of starting to work the fields, I become aware of how little land is in production at any one time. By intensively planting multiple varieties of crops to be integrated in close proximity to each other, the land operates to protect plants from most parasites and weeds, and, the shorter, leafy plants offer shade, i.e., soil moisture retention, for the tall, leggy plants which, in turn, cut the intensity of direct, hot sun.

I am working the earth, the soil, the dirt—Mother Nature at her finest. We till, sow, reap and harvest. There are animals to tend—cows and goats—that keep the weeds at bay between the rows of cultivated plants. Their droppings are meticulously picked through by a small flock of fowl such as chickens, geese and guinea hens. They in turn, by separating off seeds and other partially digested plant life, aerate the droppings so they can better promote the microbial life which acts like coral in the ocean, to be the catalysts, the two way directional conveyors of life between the familiar world above ground and that strange, largely unseen world, below ground.

Farming definitely strikes me as being one of those jobs which is never the same from one day to the next, and has no end in sight. Even viewed as being cyclical, it is still barely repetitive as the variables keep us on our toes. Thinking ahead is so much a part of what is truly required of a conscious and successfully productive farmer.

I am, in the true meaning of the word, grounded, and I cannot imagine a happier place for me to be. I have found my métier among the exquisite sounds, smells, sights, feel and taste of Nature. Praise the Lord and pass the plowshares. This is the life!

To retain some of their prior solitude, Dada and Didi quickly evolve a plan that works to everyone's benefit. They insist I maintain some of my classes Just as before so there are breaks in the day when I am away with the vocal crowd. I gather that my energy is sufficiently off key to their highly evolved sensibilities that even a brief class is an appreciated respite for them.

The lift of my energy shows up back at the Institution, as I now refer to Taquinta. My physical strength is so markedly improved that doing the morning Hindu Squats, Hindu Pushups, Head stand Pushups and Back Arches are a cinch. As a chaser, I now join in sprints up the sides of the surrounding hills. That still winds me, it is meant to, but nowhere near the lung bursting extremes when I first ran them. And no more shin splints. The best way to do the hill sprints, I am told, is in short bursts with walking for a minute or so in between. Maybe seven sprints total in a block. I feel invincible.

Maisha's Long Stride walking class is meaningful fun since I walk, sometimes substantial distances in a day tending the fields. My joints have loosened up and sinking low and throwing my feet far out ahead is becoming pleasurable. I am up with Maisha and the leadership now, pace setting for the slow pokes behind us.

Petrina begins a class in aromatherapy which I think is a silly class to take. Then I smell the essential oils and flash back to the treatment Ariel gave me on the table after my shower. Lucy almost falls over with amazement when I push to be among those taking the class. I take Lucy as my client. She tells me how at ease her baby becomes as soon as mommy gets even a whiff of the oils. Baby has become used to my touching mommy's growing tummy. Baby all but demands the oils.

After finishing the Library, I return to Brazilian Jiu-Jitsu. Very soon after that, Agnes went seeking a different adversary. We had met and pulled and struggled with each other. Then I found my concentration. It came to me, almost the way everything else I was practicing and learning, these days, kind of snaps into place.

There we were, she and I, toughing it out on the mats, when, Bam! I stepped into her grip, took charge and down she went. I can't say who of us was the more surprised, Agnes, Lea or me. My subsequent partners tend to be younger and some of them are more difficult opponents. However, I am sufficiently confident now that I willingly take on all comers. Look out, Rocky Balboa! Here comes Judith.

Out in the fields, I coordinate with Lea, Dada and Didi drawing up plans for sowing and harvesting. I am in charge of mixing the Biodynamic Preparations in a 5 gallon bucket. I stir for one minute in one direction, then one minute in the reverse direction. I do this for up to thirty minutes per preparation.

I haul the preparation out to where it is to be applied and with hand switches of straw or sometimes nylon rope splayed at one end, we all dip in the bucket and sprinkle on the compost barrow. About ten feet wide, four feet high in the center and almost one hundred feet long, we work our way meticulously down the length of the barrow making sure to sprinkle as evenly as possible. Talk about the seemingly endless task.

Other times, we add preparations to growing plants. This is all according to an Austrian genius, Rudolf Steiner, from the early Twentieth Century. He worked out the specifics from talking to old time farmers and formulating what the preparations are and when to apply them according to astrological timings.

When I first heard what we were going to do, I snickered along with others of us who are new to this world. We unearth cows' horns. Six months prior, the hollowed out horns, fifty or so of them at a time, were stuffed with a mix of compost and manure, then buried in one big heap about four feet down. The soil above where the horns are is soft and easy to work. Edith, a strapping twenty something, and I are soon tapping the horns with our shovels as we reach the mass. Lea jumps down into the hole to gingerly unearth the horns by hand. She carefully picks them up and passes them, individually, to the rest of the group waiting around the sides of the pit.

Dada and Didi stand by watching approvingly. It is clear they want others to learn what they already know. Letting me and Edith have the experience is just that, a learning experience. Our mistakes are our learning tools. What a concept! This place is beginning to make more sense every day.

The seething microbial contents of the horns are carefully emptied into a 5 gallon bucket until about one quarter full and then water added. What had happened to the stuffing in the horns is that the bacteria in the earth had interacted to make a concentrated living mass of life force. The stuffing, inside each horn, is creeping and crawling—just ablaze with activity.

In the bucket of water, it is diluted down and the liquid is sprayed all over the fields. In the next few days, the changes to plant life receiving the spray is as if each plant were grabbed by its short, protruding, feeder leaves and yanked out of its seed until it stood a foot tall, thick and green, vibrating with health. This is so heartening, I feel moved to tears watching the process work.

Didi sees my sentimental moment as my eyes fog over with tears welling up and I stop to wipe them with the back of my wrist. As I blink my eyes clear, I feel her huge strong arm across my back as she grips me side on and pulls me to her. Then I really lose it. Once I quit bawling, I look at her and she is nodding as if completely agreeing with me.

Somewhere, far from my dense, briar patch, hidden from view from all the So'er Foxes and other wily creatures out to make me pay my dues, beyond the hills and dales of rolling landscape that we work endlessly, there lies a town, a city, a sprawling, expansive mass of humanity with main streets and squares, peopled by a variegated population.

I consider that living at Taquinta is comparable to an open prison, without boundaries and fences, no guards watching over us. An implicit agreement exists among the inmates that there is no venturing forth. It seems most are quite content to operate inside this unspoken agreement.

The Amazons know better. Once each week, we rise especially early to drive to town. I know the day is coming because the whole day prior is spent picking produce and packing it carefully, in anticipation of the next day's market.

When I realize part of my duties working the farm will be to go to town and assist at vending in the open air market, I know Maisha has truly found a penalty with which to torment me. It involves rising early. It means dressing a little more conscientiously, even though we wear our coveralls, making sure they are clean and the shirt underneath is pressed. To be sure, to the townsfolk we must resemble representative jailbirds out on a trip for good behavior.

Having lived almost six months in the Institutional environment of Taquinta, safe and coddled, trusted and trusting, the prospect of re entering the "real" world, even for a day, raises anxiety for me. After spending an extremely long day harvesting and packing boxes, then loading the quaintly antique, International Harvester truck, I return to the dome.

Lucy, looking lonely, is already fast asleep in bed. Thankfully, Sidney was able to snag a dome in the visiting guest quadrant. Word soon spread her dome is a fun place to be, or to steer clear of. Lucy quickly understands that a very pregnant mom has little appeal to the party crowd. Besides, she has to think of her baby!

I sigh deeply as I slump onto a chair. The noise causes Lucy to stir.

"That yer, Jude?" she asks with a sleepy voice.

"Yes," I answer. "I was trying to avoid waking you."

"That's OK," she says. "I hardly ever see yer, these days."

"Are you up for a talk, right now?" I ask.

She adjusts her extra person and struggles through her own entanglement with the bedding to sit upright in her pod.

"What's up?" she asks.

"It seems silly," I tell her, "But I am scared out of my mind about leaving the Institute tomorrow and going into town... mixing with real people."

"Yer know," says my worldly wise sage, "People think everythin' is cool until yer tell 'em otherwise."

That makes sense for all of two seconds before my own tension obliterates the meaning.

"Thanks, Lucy," I tell her. "I need some help."

"Ask Lea," she says.

"It's late," I say.

Lucy slides down into her bed and pulls the covers up high.

"That's the best I got, Jude," she says.

Unlike the old me who dragged her sorry ass into the Institute, I am a renewed, energized and relatively healthy me. The new me makes snap decisions, kind of like the Elders, and follows through. As I arrive at Lea's door, I am shocked that I have not visited her since my first day on site when she did my intake interview.

Her dome is dark. Nervously, I knock on her front door. For the longest time nothing happens. I look around in case someone else is up and about and sees me. The Commissary has only pathway lights on since the concert is long since over. All good people are tucked in their beds asleep. I knock again and a light flashes on almost immediately.

A few moments pass and a bright eyed Lea, dressed in a robe, stands before me in the open doorway.

"Come on in, Judith," she says.

She has me sit on the chair in the middle of the floor and pulls up one for herself. She quietly takes my hands in hers and looks calmly into my eyes.

"So tell me," she says.

Does it have to be this easy?

"Tomorrow is market day," I tell her. 'This will be my first time going off base. I guess I am terrified."

"That is excellent!" she tells me. "We were curious to see how you will handle this."

"And...?" I ask, recognizing my earliest fear that the system is watching me.

"You are completely within range," she answers. "That means you are normal. How may I help you?"

"I need to relax," I explain. "I am exhausted and at the same my system is racing. I was hoping you could manage some kind of intervention."

"You are learning the lingo," she says with a smile. 'OK, this once, because of the lateness of the hour, I am going to do EFT on you. In future, you will attend Serena's class so you can practice on yourself. Understood?"

"Yes," I say.

I need what she has so I am willing to make all manner of promises.

I feel the skin crawl on my lower arms telling me I am consciously cheating, but I convince myself that I will make it up somehow, in the future. That's a white lie.

Lea and I agree on the statement describing my issue as being, "I am anxious about being in public."

On a scale of one to ten with ten being the worst, it feels like eight.

While I repeat the statement three times, Lea pushes her fingers deep into the skin next to my collarbone. Then, she has me say, "anxiety," while she taps vigorously on my forehead above my nose. Then, I say, "public," while she taps under my right eye. Then, it's, "anxiety," while she taps under my nose. Under my lip I say, "public," and so on, back and forth, for the whole set.

Now Lea has me count down from fifty to zero in fives, hum a few bars of, "Happy Birthday to You," and then the whole thing starts again except for the collar bone part.

When she finishes, Lea asks me to rate my anxiety about being in public from one to ten with ten being the worst. It feels like one to me. Not only is my anxiety down, I am looking forward to the expedition with enthusiasm.

Lea looks at me proudly.

"Imagine dealing with every issue in life that way," she says. "Would that be incredible, or what?"

I am sorely tempted to smart answer and tell her, "what," but think better of it since she is doing me a big favor.

"Incredible," I agree.

She rummages through a stash of bottles of essential oils and pulls out an almost empty bottle of Mental Soothing. She gives it to me.

"To be on the safe side, if you feel nervous, tomorrow," she explains. "Drip about three drops of this on your left hand palm, with fingers from your right hand, stir sun wise a few times, then, with fingers on your right hand, dab the oil under your nose, on your chin, the sides of your temples and rub the remainder on the back of your neck. Have a successful day, tomorrow."

"Thank you, Lea," I say.

She steers me out of the dome and, as she bids me goodnight, closes the door. I rush home so I don't fall asleep on the way.

REVELATIONS

As representatives of Taquinta, we, the Amazonians and me, are dearly loved by folks who attend the outdoor market. Dada and Didi have, double handedly, evolved a sizable following over the years. Added to their apparent personal charm for the "natives," Biodynamic produce is so much plumper, better looking, sweeter, and just plain more energetically nutritious, even than organic produce. Conventional food may sometimes look as good but it rarely has the natural bouquet and certainly not the flavors of Biodynamic grown produce. The cost is about the same, and, we have variety equal to that of any other stand. People flock to us, and one hardly need to speak. Business is brisk right up until we sell out. I cannot recall one day we do not sell all of our stock, whether we bring a little or a lot.

Immediately, that first day, I come to understand it is meeting and speaking with a man that is the principle root of my anxiety. After so much time with women, I set men up to be alien beings. Fortunately, most of the men who attend the market and who buy from us tend to be gentle souls. Perhaps it is the climate and location that takes the sharp edge off these men. My re entry into society is a cinch.

On behalf of Taquinta, we always have a box out to receive financial contributions for the Institute. My consoeurs tell me that the donations increase markedly when I am there.

Though it holds little interest for them, Didi and Dada accept my desire to wander the area. In the center of town is a plaza, a huge open square, with a park in the middle with archways made of deer antlers on the corners. Close by, there are big, fancy shops and elegant, colonial period buildings. Along one street is a colonnade of pillars fronting a passage way. Here, Native Americans spread out blankets on the ground. A few of them have small fragile tables. They sell mostly jewelry and trinkets for tourists. The colors are spectacular and, along with finely detailed silverwork, are hard to resist.

My interest is the people. They tend to be short, solidly built. Everyone has black hair and, even the old ones, rarely have grey hair. Their skin is usually a dark nut brown. They dress simply, draping dark colored clothes from the shoulders. Their pants are more like balloons. They tend to look away when I look them in the eye. Rarely will one of them stare back at me. It is embarrassing to me how shy they seem. Dada tells me the American Indians turn their eyes away out of politeness. Underneath their modesty, their care not to offend, there is strength, a fortitude, which stands out. As humble as they appear, they exhibit a latent capacity to spring back and take complete control.

They are careful to correct each other with consideration and politeness. Though their language among themselves is completely foreign to me, I note the facial movements and their distancing from each other when they speak. Such a high degree of respect they show each other.

I had often wondered, what is the point of living in such a rarified atmosphere as Taquinta. By attending this market and walking in the world of the Native Americans, I know that this is Taquinta's gift to me. I feel I have been truly blessed to experience this other world. To know that my world is not exclusively mine, that my dreams can contain the phantasmagoric. Life is lifting the lid of a box of chocolates, to peek inside before taking the lid off entirely, and to indulge in the sweet bliss of the contained assortment.

Day by day, the more physical the work, the more Time takes on a twisting shape. It has strange expansive sections, then, curves round and it becomes like a movie version of time warp where everything flashes past at high speed. A day tends to become structured by the regularity of hunger spasms more than by a clock. It is as if, without meeting the body's specific needs, the day will become an endless, seamless stream of happenings which blend one into the other.

On days expected to be extra hot, we begin our farm work at 6:30 to get a head start on the day. By close to ten o'clock, the sun is beating down mercilessly. Dada and Didi alternate rows. They are so sweet always caring for each other. Watching them makes me wish I had siblings.

Of course, Judging from some people who have siblings, it is like the African proverb, "The two people in life we cannot choose are our neighbor and our brother."

That proverb always makes me wonder if a sister would necessarily be any better than a brother. Again, I recall friends with sisters where it didn't always work out too great.

I stop to wipe my brow. The twins stop immediately as if we are a synchronized operation. They look at me as if doing a summation of my mood, health and emotional well being in one fell sweep. I try being flip.

"It's going to be hot, today, and it's only ten in the morning," I sign as my preamble.

Didi signs back, "How was Lucy when you left?"

"Good," I tell her. "The baby is due any minute."

"How will you know?" Dada signs me.

I pull the petite, thin metal object from a pocket on my right thigh of the coveralls. I have never used a cell phone before, and it took ten minutes for me to learn the basics. As Lucy finally pointed out, she will be calling me, not me her, so I don't need to know how to operate it other than to make sure it is switched on.

As we study the unique appearance of the phone and its screen, a high pitched shriek occurs. I am used to Lucy telegraphing her thoughts. Others are not.

Dada and Didi both drop to the ground in a useless effort to duck below the energy wave. Since this is a telepathic transmission by a mother going into labor, it is completely without modulation and intended to reach me even if I may be in Timbuktu. I stand there momentarily sympathizing with my Amazon twins waiting for them to disengage their hands from uselessly clutching their heads in agony.

When they glance over to me, I sign, "Then, there is telepathy."

They look at me baffled; so much for telephonic communications.

I take off at full speed on the down slope toward the Institute. I thrill at how sure footed I am; how effortlessly I run. It's as if, my whole time I've been at Taquinta, I've been training for this one event.

The thin object starts vibrating as it performs a rendition of the opening bars of Beethoven's Fifth Symphony in clunky, metallic tones; the last note is emphatically off key by a seventh. I wrestle the phone out of my pocket and have to stop to line up the on screen parts.

I hold the phone up to my ear.

"Hello?" I say.

"Hi!" I hear back. "Judeet, this is Naan."

I respond to the sweet voice.

"I guessed as much, Naan," I answer. "I'm on my way in. I suspect the whole valley got the message! I'll be right there!"

I drop the phone back into its pocket and set off to make up time lost on the phone. Talking to Naan always makes me feel like the world is bursting with goodness. It's as if she is permanently on bedside manner. Her task is to comfort all, and she does it consistently with grace and ease.

I wonder if I am running more to be with Naan than to be with Lucy and see the baby arrive. It's close, but, definitely, I'm curious, excited, to see Lucy with her baby.

This impending event has become the approaching point on a horizon of differential calculus; becoming closer and never arriving.

Today is different. Lucy is, according to one wag, about to pop!

TAKE A VILLAGE

On more level ground, I resort to Long Stride walking. By the time I reach our dome, I have caught my breath and am still moving at speed.

Unusual for us, the door is open. I vault down the three steps to encounter a sizable crowd. Sitting in a white, walk in tub with water up to her armpits is Lucy, stark naked and relishing being the center of attention. She is definitely having herself a glory moment.

Prepared for business, long brown hair pinned back with a French clip, Naan towers over Lucy in her tub.

The Elders have turned out in force and are standing by our tiny kitchen tabletop where Zichrini is serving up her cake. Lucy keeps checking to see if there will be some left for her.

Zichrini calls over, "You meck good beby. I brring keck all forr you."

Maisha, Serena, Petrina, Lea, Chrystal, Sophia and Yen Lu eat cake like it's going out of style. For the first time ever, I sense how lonely being responsible for others is for these women. They huddle together, almost as if these are the only friends any of them have.

I think I notice Rachel and Ariel in the shadows. How is that possible? I only have time for a glance before momma, smiling blissfully, grabs my attention.

"Hey, Jude," she yells. "D'yer get my message?"

"Oh, yeah, loud and clear," I answer. "Modulation is OK. How're you doing?"

"Any time now," she says. "This is so sweet."

"Hi, Judeet" Naan says, with her wide, Dutch smile. "We waited for you."

"Sure, you did," I say. "You have control of this... ?"

"Oh, yeah," Naan says. "Watch."

She turns to Lucy the way a conductor of an orchestra may turn to a soloist.

"Ready to invite your baby out?" Naan asks.

"Yeah, let's do this thin'," Lucy yells.

Naan signals to Chrystal who reluctantly puts her plate of cake on the table. She goes out the door and I see her put index finger and thumb to her mouth and give an uncharacteristically unladylike, loud whistle, then, rush back in and grab up her cake.

Within seconds, the worst noise I have ever heard breaks out. Not surprisingly, Aroha is "conducting" this cacophony. Twenty women assemble close to our open door and bang on metal pots, rattle and scrape objects, and generally make the most a rhythmic, off key racket imaginable. It does not take me long to work out that this bedlam is a Maori birthing ritual.

Other women arrive without instruments. They pop their heads around the door, stare in through windows, all of them making rolling, Hakka eyes while their hands perform the dances of ocean waves.

This "happening" is sufficiently discordantly wild enough to make me give birth; and I'm not pregnant.

So loud as to drown out the orchestra and to make sure everyone knows where the center of attention truly is to be focused, Lucy shouts, "Here we go!"

Everyone closes in on the tub.

Naan calmly insists, "Leave me enough room to walk round, ladies."

Lucy, at ease, half stands, slightly squats, watching Naan assist her. Even from several feet away it is possible to see the baby crown.

I look at Lucy. She is smiling as if this is all a perfectly normal, everyday occurrence. She glances down breaking into a grin. By now the baby's head is almost entirely emerged. Naan steps in front of me reaching deep into the tub to assist the baby.

When Naan moves round the tub, Lucy is beaming with tear filled eyes of joy as her baby floats up, smiling, to mom's waiting hands.

Naan guides Lucy to take up her baby to make the first feeding connection of colostrums. Relaxed, Lucy lets all her maternal instincts rise to the fore. There is a perceptible sigh of relief from the surrounding women that their little wild child adapts so easily to motherhood; one less worry for the community.

Outside, the disruptive noise ends abruptly. Unfortunately, it is replaced by profusely loud, dramatic weeping and wailing.

Once Naan has cut the umbilical cord and clipped shut baby's end, she wraps the baby in towels. Lucy is ready to exit the tub. Without a second's thought, Lucy hands the baby to me to hold while she dries off and puts on clothes.

I step forward and gratefully accept the charge. Out of the corner of my eye I sense a movement from the Elders to interfere but nothing happens. I look down at the face of my charge and a beaming smile comes back. Winning me over took all of a split second. I hear cooing sounds and quickly learn they emanate from me. I am gently swaying and musing with my niece's child. As usual, Lucy makes a statement loud and clear.

Pointing to me, Lucy insists, "See? I need Jude to assist wi' raisin' my child."

Naan swiftly drains off the tub and, with Chrystal's help, moves it out of the dome.

Just in time as Dada and Didi arrive with a couple of goats and several fowl to walk through the dome and pay tribute to the new life. The locals refer to this practice as a *posada.* The baby responds immediately seeking out the source of the animal sounds.

Lucy takes him from me and holds him so he may see the animals. He becomes quite studious, almost serious.

Naan takes charge once more.

"I understand you wish to anoint the baby," she says. "May I encourage you to do that briefly and then allow Lucy to rest."

Petrina sets out one of her essential oils bottles on the table where the cake had been. She instructs everyone how to apply Frankincense on the crown of the baby's head.

Lucy holds her baby in his towels and exposes his head.

Each Elder in turn passes by and congratulates Lucy and then greets the baby before lightly massaging in the oil.

When everyone has left, Naan cleans up and does a final check of mother and child.

"Whenever possible sleep when baby sleeps," she tells Lucy. "When your baby cries be prompt without driving yourself crazy. Always check if his diaper needs changing so he always feels clean and dry. Then offer to breast feed him. You will quickly establish a comfortable routine if you listen to your natural inclinations. Avoid letting him cry more than as a signal to you. It's unhealthy for babies to cry themselves to sleep. I will check in with you in one week. I am glad you have arranged to have your aunt here to assist. He is a perfect first child."

"Yer tellin' me to have more?" Lucy says.

"That ease of delivery is unusual," Naan comments.

"Do you think the noise helped any?" I ask.

"Well, it is meant to drive the baby out," Naan says. "So I've heard. This is my first experience of a Maori style delivery. Let's just say we're batting 100 percent right now."

We have a good laugh, hugs all round and off she goes.

I close the door and step into the room when there's a knock on the door.

I open it to Zichrini bearing a freshly baked cake. She hands it to me and hurries away.

Lucy is delighted.

DEPARTURES

In the faint light of morning, I wake to see Lucy is fully adapted to her new lifestyle. Finished up nursing, she walks about the room with baby on her shoulder to burp him then lays the sleeping child in her bed while she takes a shower. I wonder if having me along was simply Lucy's fear of the unknown. She appears to have adapted to her new responsibilities like a duck takes to water.

When she emerges, I take my shower. As I come out of the shower, she is sitting on a chair picking at a small piece of cake.

She asks me, "Yer comin' to celebrate wi' me, this mornin'. Right?"

I am so in a groove working the fields seven days a week, the idea of taking time off for a celebration is antithetical to me. How quickly I have adapted. Of course, there is no way I am going to miss this one. I dress quickly.

"Michael and me are 'spectin' yer there," Lucy tells me.

For one strange moment, I flash on Michael Kaliban. I briefly zone out.

"Why Michael?" I ask.

"That's his dad's name," Lucy reveals.

I shudder at the coincidence. In dreams, all things are possible. The odds of her Michael being Dr. Michael are made all the more feasible because this is my dream.

"That's the only part of his dad's name I'm givin' him," Lucy says with determination. "I can still change his name, yer know?"

I don't know what prompts me, but I take the first two letters of Michael Kaliban's names and put them together.

"What d'you think of Mika?" I ask her.

Lucy goes over to look at her sweetly sleeping baby.

"Yer know, Jude?" she tells me. "Yer right. He is a Mika. I love it. Thanks."

She gives me a full body hug and won't let go. At first it feels like a "thank you" but it goes on and on. I freak at the new level of intimacy she creates. Still she hugs. I finally relent and respond to her needs. Slowly, she releases me and I see she is crying.

Lucy turns away from me without a word and crawls into bed with sleeping Mika. That's when I see the cake crumbs in her bed.

"I am going to the Commissary," I say. "Do you want me to bring you anything?"

"Thanks, auntie," she replies. "We're good. Hey! Today's a good day to wear yer rin'."

The new plural entity is established. The division of roles is defined. I need to learn EFT. Then I can also deal with this sexuality thing that keeps coming up between me and Lucy. As for my ring, long ago Lael had suggested not to wear it doing construction so I don't damage it or compromise my hand if the ring catches on something.

Today is a perfect day for wearing the family colors.

This time, my breakfast tray is more than a work of art; it's stunning. With tray in hand, I go through the swing doors to the preparation area of the kitchen. Edith is there cutting vegetables fast and measured like a chef on television. Someone else is leaving out the far door. In the moment, it felt like Serena but I can't imagine why she will be in the kitchen prep area. I go over to Edith and show her the tray. "Who makes up my tray, Edith?" I ask.

"Is there something wrong?" she answers with a look of concern. "It looks pretty fantastic to me."

"Me, too," I rush to agree. "I want to thank whoever is doing it. She makes me feel like a queen giving me such a presentation."

"If I find out," Edith offers. "I'll pass along your appreciation."

"Thanks," I say as I turn to leave.

There's still a nip in the air so I decide to eat inside the Commissary. Over at the wall where the movies are projected an enormous triptych painting is in progress. It's vaguely based on the Last Supper except, in this painting, all the people are women and the food on the table is desserts. They are not exhibiting much decorum as they reach across each other while stuffing their mouths. The colors, too, are a whole lot brighter, more vibrant than the traditional Leonardo DaVinci interpretation.

I sit next to a notice about the painting. It reads:

JUST DESSERTS

By Ella Bella

Out of consideration to the visiting
Artist, when she is working,
please do not speak to her
unless she speaks to you first.
Thank you. Enjoy!

Courtesy of Galerie Daniel Gouro

The woman in the center looks a lot like me, older and wearing glasses, but I can see a resemblance. Like my work a day me, she wears no jewelry, not even a ring.

It's time for the celebration so I start out for the Togu Na. I join a growing stream of people walking in the same direction.

I find a space on one of the surrounding slopes and I'm about to sit down when Maisha calls out to me from the Togu Na.

"Judith," she says. "Please join our circle."

I want to demure, but eyes are watching me now and Maisha has her hand up waving me in. I pick my way over and enter. Maisha has me sit between Lea and Petrina. I greet them both and acknowledge that I missed speaking to them during the birth.

Petrina is sweet.

"You were busy with all the excitement," she says, nodding her head in Lucy's direction.

Lucy proudly dominates the circle, nonchalantly breast feeding Mika while he and she are gushed over by women on both sides of her. That child is going to live every second front and center in the public eye. He is branded for glory and he's barely twelve hours old.

Lucy waves with her free hand. I wave back and add a smile. Lucy gives me a big wink. I relax. Everything is OK. That's when I see she is wearing her emerald. I glance at my Texas piggy and look up to see Maisha studying me.

Turning her gaze away, Maisha raises one hand for quiet. Everyone mimics her gesture and silence descends across the land to the last woman on the farthest slope.

"Yesterday," Maisha intones, "Was a special first for all of us at Taquinta. Our newest member, Lucy, presented us with our first live birth of a child, an extraordinarily healthy child she named Mika. As if a signal from the Universe, our first child born to this community, which we intentionally designed to be exclusively for women, is a boy child, a male to leaven so many females.

"The Universe makes no mistakes. Every act, every action, from the smallest to the largest, is intentional, intended, and, as such, has far reaching consequences both for our own lives and on into the future in ways too complex for us to understand.

"We, at Taquinta, greet Mika as a messenger. He brings information that was previously absent from our circle. We look forward with eager anticipation to everything he has to share. This is cause for great joy for us, both in our community, and, as it will resonate out into the larger community beyond."

It's a beautiful way of ensuring Mika's future at Taquinta. There isn't a dry eye in sight. Lucy glows with pride at the implication that she may be the initiator of major change at the Institution. As ever, I hear the build up to an alternate scenario. For once, I am dead on accurate.

"This is an emotional occasion," Maisha continues. "As a result of Lucy bringing us a new life, we now bid farewell to someone who has become a pillar holding up the virtual roof of our community. As the posts of this Togu Na support the roof here, she has given freely and generously of her strengths and talents to make Taquinta what it is today.

"There is much many of us can say about her contributions to make our glorious little world a better place. But, just as sharing a photograph absorbs many memories and dominates what would otherwise be an ocean of subtle remembrances, we will each hold our own thoughts of her as she embarks on the next part of her journey."

I am so captivated by the eloquence of her imagery, the poetry of what Maisha is saying; it takes a few moments for the actual meaning to sink in. Basically, she is telling me I had the opportunity to quit. Since I didn't take it, I'm fired!

Judith, doll, babe, you are out of here. You are history; a gonna; over and done with.

I can feel the tears well up as I look disbelievingly around the circle for what is the last time. Clearly, Lucy is not listening to the subtext as she fusses and rocks Mika, who is wide awake. He may even understand what is occurring better than does his momma as she plays doll with him.

It occurs to me that I never once inquired how to join Taquinta. Maybe it is as simple as requesting to join. I don't know. Now, as the pain races up my body with the hurt that I am being cast out, my pride will not permit me to inquire how to join the Institute because it will be seen by some people, most of all me, as begging.

I am crushed, as in steam roller flattened. The process starts at my toes, crushing my feet, ankles, shins, knees, thighs, hips, stomach, left hand, elbows, chest and shoulders. The ring, with its glorious stone, makes my right hand impregnable. They stop at my neck so my head, too, remains intact. They intentionally leave my head whole and untrammeled so that I can feel the unimaginable agony of being crushed right down to every last exquisite detail in the pain center that is my brain.

I can feel my eyes staring, taking in details. I have no voice box with which to express myself; blink once for yes, twice for no. Jeri stares at me strapped in the chair, powerless, I can't see my reflection so I may observe what is being done to me. The me I am disappears down a long tunnel. Everything grows quiet, and distant. I tamp myself into the bottom of tubing, while reality, beyond, outside of the empty tubing, spills away from me, endlessly, farther and farther away. The etheric me has already long since left.

All that remains is for my crushed, useless body to catch up.

DAY FOUR

SPIRITUS SANCTUS

A short, sharp cry from Mika breaks everyone's reverie.

Lucy stops rocking Mika, staring at him to understand what he wants. Then, she looks up and checks the passive faces of the Elders. When she reaches me, she sees a pale, withdrawn facsimile of the tough character I have been playing.

It's as if her brain does an instant replay.

Ping! The coin drops. The Pachinko balls have reached the top and start to rattle and shake their noisy steel impacts to the bottom. No winners or losers this time; just a thick dose of sticky, messy reality to wade through.

Horrified, Lucy attempts to stand, only to hit her head on the low thatch. She is forced to sit.

I am clearly back from my passive aggressive disappearing act. One thing you can say about being in the presence of tough minded, reality seeking, consciousness raising broads, there is no time for feeble cop outs. They want it raw and the rawer the better.

I glare about sullenly, fixating on cool Serena.

"Maisha!" Lucy yells, scaring Mika to a bout of crying. "It was agreed that if Judith works hard she can stay."

"We said until your baby was born," Maisha answers.

She is planning to let Lucy vent. With patience, Lucy will wear out and the decision will stick.

Lucy demands, "What about meeting in council?"

"We did," Maisha answers. "You were there. The decision was unanimous."

"Judith," Petrina says to me. "You are a hard worker, a great asset. However, our decision was based solely on your violent episode."

Oh, that. Didn't we clear that up? Obviously not. Leastways, not enough to make a diff.

I try to turn and face Petrina, but having her sit next to me makes her intensity too much to handle and I find my gaze settling on Serena, again. The Eminence Grise of my demise projects a complete blank. She refuses to give me a handle to grasp hold of.

There seems to be a vacuum in which only Lucy, Mika and I are actively participating. The Elders all appear to have gone into freeze frame, displaying a unanimous, impenetrable, stoic face.

Mika has barely stopped crying when Lucy starts to cry.

Bitterly, I stare round at each of the Elders. Somehow, I know I expected this. I had allowed all manner of fantasy about my living here to override the reality stated at the outset, and restated after the "incident."

"The hell with you!" a voice cries out. I feel my mouth close as I roll over backwards to make my exit out the side. No one attempts to stop me.

Clearly meant for me, Lucy screams between sobs, "What about me an' Mika?"

Without turning round, I shout back, "Now you have a hundred aunts."

"Where're yer gonna go, Jude?" Lucy wails, clearly as terrified for me as for herself.

We never did share deep, dark secrets. Unless she guessed at it, she still knows next to nothing about me, my past, who I was, who I am.

"Who cares?" I shout, deeply hurt and bitterly angry that all of my time and effort has been for naught.

Dazed and confused, I walk slowly. People scramble to get out of my way. I hardly recognize a one of them. They look more out of it than I feel.

Despite the intense pain I feel hollowing me out from the inside; I sense the germination of a seed of power in me, the terrifying energy of when a god walks among mortals.

Lucy's plaintive voice follows to enfold me, causing me to hesitate.

"ME!" she cries, "I care. I love yer, Jude."

I stop and look back at the Togu Na.

Ridiculous for Elders, Lea and Chrystal, both of them on hands and knees, are peering out at me.

Lea shouts to me, "Your Holy Grail is out there, Judith."

"Spare me any more of your metaphysical claptrap!" I shout at her.

Of all of them, despite her past efforts to speak in my defense, I resent that she voted for my termination as guest in residence. I will not forgive her for that. If need be, I am going to fight with each and every one of them that tries to ease my pain.

Next up is Chrystal.

"At least allow a leaving ceremony," she says.

"Must you celebrate damn everything?" I yell at her.

Something is happening. I set out to leave the Togu Na, Taquinta, the whole awful place, and, thanks to Lucy's telling me her sincere truth, I have turned around and begun arguing so that I don't have to leave. Why?

Because I do care. Because... I love her.

My realization is that we do want to be together, Lucy with me and I with her. Of all that is serendipitous in this confused world, she and I tripped over each other and found an instantaneous friendship as deep as a bottomless pit. If I leave, now or ever, I destroy our friendship. Yet, I can't stay here. They, the Elders have "spoken." It's part of their Akashic record for Pete's sake. Most certain of all, for all her own reasons, Lucy is not coming with me, with or without Mika. The lines are drawn.

"May I walk with you?" Maisha asks from a respectful few feet distant.

"Where'd you come from?" I ask amazed at yet another apparition escorting me.

In some magical dream, she begins to walk away from the Togu Na. I end up walking with her to... keep her company.

Several women reach with outstretched hands as if to comfort me. That irritates me something fierce.

I shout at them, "You must've seen someone else thrown out of this Garden of Eden?"

The hands turn lackluster and fold into themselves.

We are beyond the encircling crowd. The road out of the valley is ahead of us. We could change directions and go into the community from here. They're both about equidistant from this point.

Maisha stops.

"We have the clothes you arrived in," she tells me.

"I'm plenty dressed," I say, shaking my bib coveralls. "Call it a fair trade."

We're back in her Money Course. We're talking potentials, but this time it is for real. We're negotiating my possessions. At least we're negotiating. Ariel was a lot less considerate.

"There's your pocketbook with money in it," Maisha informs me. "You'll need money to survive in the outside world. Let me get it for you."

She's really offering in a heartfelt way. She hasn't attempted to make amends. She clearly doesn't believe that is necessary.

"I got here without money," I tell her. "I can make it out of here without money."

For the first time ever, I see confusion in Maisha's eyes. Lucy was right. The Quantum Physics of money is a fancy dream. Maisha has no understanding of what is involved to truly deny the existence of money.

I speak to her in terms I am confident she will appreciate.

"Call it a donation," I say.

She is stunned.

"Are you sure, Judith?" she asks.

"It's other people's money," I tell her. "What goes around comes around."

Though it is not the eye to eye contest I saw when she and I completed the Maori greeting, I know that she and I have just met on a level playing field... and I won.

Maybe, I think to myself, victory in battle requires the victor to adequately compensate the vanquished. That would be novel.

As with my walk with Lea, Maisha is not with me when I look about. I am alone.

I begin to run toward the road. I quickly settle into a long distance pace and am thrilled to feel the wind lift my hair. Out in a field, Didi and Dada are working. They have their backs to me. I am tired of explaining, apologizing, listening to suggestions, being people's fallback position.

I run past them. Besides, how would they know what just transpired minutes ago at the Togu Na? Amazingly, though, they always seem current with the news of events and happenings at the Institution. No, it's not them, it's me. I don't want to have to appreciate anybody, thank them or say goodbye. I merely want to be gone.

That's when I hear the rhythmical banging of shovel on shovel. I raise my right hand with the ring on it into the air as a farewell salutation and they immediately stop banging shovels. We make our peace the way we do. I'm glad I leave them on good terms.

Running takes its toll. By the time I reach the Private Road sign, I am panting to catch my breath. Why am I running? I slow down, then walk, then stop, bent over with my hands braced onto my knees to prop me up. This is ridiculous. No one is chasing me. If they are, what can they want? No, I'm running because... I'm running... away.

That makes some sense. I'm running away. Do I need to run to run away? I can crawl on the ground and call it running away. As I begin to regain control of my breathing, I start to laugh. How nuts is this? How nuts am I?

I don't even need to run away. They, the Elders, asked me to leave. No, that isn't true either. What they did was tell me my guest period was up, over, complete. I took it upon myself to leave, to make some huge emotional event out of what was, in effect, a shopping list of compliments to my time and effort at Taquinta. They didn't fire me, after all. I quit!

There was no contract. There was a commitment to a bunch of principles. There was an implicit agreement that they, the Institution, will provide food, clothing and shelter. They kind of asked, but they never came right out and said, "You ate, now you work." That was a pretty cool deal, really. I mean, they only had the nonsense I told Lea plus Lucy's word to go on. For having a fun time and learning so much, I got off pretty cheaply.

I am Long Stride walking now. It's much easier than running and probably not a whole lot slower. This I know I can do for hours, except, I am hungry.

That emotional jag I took off on in the Togu Na, then the running, what a waste of energy, plus, what a performance. For what? Who did it benefit? Wow, what am I doing? Where am I going?

I hear Maisha's voice resonating in my head from the one time she sat in on Lea's Social Studies Class.

"The Universe has a plan for each of us," Maisha said, "A series of directions. To us simple beings, each change of direction feels like will power, our own mental determination. When we look closely at other people, we can often see the map they arrived with and the schedule they are on. We can typically see others' maps and schedules better than we see our own. It is not unusual for an individual to be completely unaware of what, to others, reads like a billboard.

"The Universe is never wrong. We may feel like trains passing in the night. In actuality, we are weaving the present together in a dance of many participants so that there can be a future. As our neighbors may say it, *Vaije con Dios*, go with God."

When she talked like that, I sat in awe of someone having an understanding of matters that were so complex that I avoided thinking about them until her easy to understand explanation.

There, up ahead, I see the few buildings that comprise the tiny town of Casper. OK, smarty pants, I think to myself. Riddle me this. I have left Taquinta and could have gone in any direction. Yet, here I am, heading to Casper. Did I decide this or did the Universe? Either way, why am I here, headed in the direction that I'm walking?

Before I am able to get into a polemic about the whys and why-nots, hunger pangs remind me that this may be my last chance for a long time to stash some food. I duck down the first alleyway I come to and head for the back of the General Store.

Whatever day of the week this may be, when I arrive at the back of the store, it turns out to be my lucky day. The day old bread stuffs and cakes are amazing. Foraging down I find an old but serviceable plastic bag. There are almost always one or two bags. They last forever, yet, they are so cheap that people use them a couple times and then throw them away.

Alright already, eat while I work. A bite here and there and fill up the bag.

"Hey, you!" the owner yells at me. "Keep out of my trash you... Are you from that women's commune? Have they stopped feeding you? That's enough. Scat! Scram! D'you hear? Next time I see your face round here, I'm calling the sheriff."

He waits till I move off and am clearly leaving, filled bag in hand. I hear him muttering to himself as he steps back into his store.

"I knew it," he says. "How can a bunch of women support themselves without a man in sight? I knew it was too good to last."

His door slams. I heft the bag. I'm good for a couple of days. I eat feverishly while I walk down to the highway. It takes a lot of this food to fill me, unlike the primal raw food. That was so compact and charged with energy. I miss it.

Was this morning's tray a farewell presentation? I'll never know. It certainly was memorable. I miss that food.

Enough!

At the highway, I look for clues to determine my direction. Being in desert country, I decide to stay close to civilization even if all that represents it is federal highway. That narrows my decision making down to two directions. I see a road sign indicating the Sangre de Cristo Mountains. I look to the horizon and there, breaking into the skyline, is a bunch of black, craggily peaks. In the opposite direction is empty horizon. I elect to pursue the detail. I take advantage of the highway overpass to position me on the same side as the mountains. It's a long walk ahead of me, the sun is still climbing to its zenith, and I am already hot and dehydrated.

With odds like those confronting me, I decide to give it up to the Universe.

FOXY LADY

I am hot, exhausted and desperately thirsty. The sun beats down on me in merciless waves. Out in the fields with Dada and Didi, or building the library, even the house, we took regular drink breaks of water and, where possible, spent time in the shade.

The more I reflect on it the more my departure from Taquinta resembles the actions of a self centered, egomaniacal woman. I cringe to the point that I am forced to stop walking as I double over with guilt thinking about the fact that I said nothing that was intimate and personal by way of farewell to Lucy. After all, it was she who brought me to Taquinta defending and protecting me, in her way. When I left, I Just allowed my anger to consume me. No goodbyes, no thank yous. No kisses, no hugs.

I held Mika all of one time right before we anointed him. I never connected with him beyond that brief cuddle. I certainly never disconnected with him, that's for sure.

Then again, my comments to Lea and to Chrystal were uncalled for. I was barely polite and cordial to Maisha. What had any of them done to me? They told me the very first day what will happen.

Did I listen?

No.

Did I ask questions?

No.

I had some fantastic imaginary notion that I would work my way into their favor so they would insist I stay. I never said anything, never gave any verbal indication to anyone that I was even considering staying at Taquinta.

I suppose my departure was the nearest thing I did equivalent to letting anyone know how desperately I wanted to spend the rest of my days at the Institution. Well, buddy, it's way past too late for that now.

And what was that freaky statement by the owner of the store saying Taquinta was falling apart. Weird. I must still represent them because I'm wearing the "uniform." By that standard, any woman in the world wearing similar bib coveralls is a representative of Taquinta, whether she knows about the place or not.

I wake spread eagled on the desert sand, partially shaded by an enormous barrel cactus. I don't know how I got here or how long I've been here. I can hear traffic in bursts as vehicles pass by on the highway, but distantly. I am close to a frontage road. Apart from the rumbling air pressure pulses of passing vehicles it is almost silent.

I dig in to the bag and attack a molding loaf of bread, diligently breaking off the green and black bits and throwing them for the birds. Seems there are few birds as crazy as me wandering loose in the desert. My spit is drying out. The bread needs more moisture than I am able to produce. I quit eating out of exhaustion.

Again, I wake and sit up. The sun is dropping but it is still burning me.

That's what is happening! I'm talking to myself.

It's been so long since I have been alone for any extended period of time, I've forgotten what the sound of my own head is like. It's non-stop chatter. They said doing Kundalini Yoga helps reduce the chatter. Well, Serena put an end to that possibility. Oh, Lucy, Mika, I'm sorry. The Library is a monument to our collective strengths. I still hurt about not having any books to give. Thank goodness Sidney went back to Mexico. She's too wild to handle the Institution. What did Lucy see in her? The money. Everything comes down to money. Me? I have none. Don't need any.

Money is raining down on me. It's splashing on my sun burned face. Coins—silver and copper—splash again. My cracked lips devour it, suck it into my parched mouth, sweet, sweet money, dripping and more splashes.

It's dark. Someone is leaning over me, slipping strong, determined hands under me. Lifting me up, and carrying me. He walks toward headlights of a noisy engine truck. A handsome young man with long, black hair pulled back behind his head, striding to an open door, carefully lowers me onto a front passenger seat, creaking door slams shut.

He walks round the truck smashing through light beams, barrel cactus oozing wet from a small gash high up. He climbs in the driver's side, creaky door slams shut.

"Oh, shit," he says under his breath.

Door creaks open and he stands and reaches across the windshield with its wavy horizontal crack, He removes a plastic bag that lasts forever, ubiquitous, cheap, caught under the windshield wiper. He sits, stuffs the bag under the bench seat, creaking door slams shut, gear jumps, engages. The night world in headlights lurches toward us.

"Am I in heaven?" I ask him.

With a deep, gravelly voice, he speaks, "Only a white person dies of thirst lying by a lake."

It sounds like a metaphor in the form of a reprimand. He reaches behind the seat and pulls forward a plastic one gallon bottle, half full of water sloshing around on the bumpy trail. He drops the bottle on my lap and grabs back hold of the steering wheel.

I open the bottle and drink. I think water is more precious than money. That's what I told the class.

"How much can I drink?" I ask him.

"That all depends," he says leaning forward, staring, as we enter a dust cloud. "If you're gonna die, stop drinking now. If you plan on living, drink what you need."

I drink, drink, drink.

He turns for a moment to watch me. I stop drinking.

"Is something wrong?" I ask him.

He laughs to himself at a joke.

"I was checking to make sure I gave you the water bottle," he says.

I hold the bottle up and squint at the contents refracting in the headlights.

"It looks like water to me," I say.

"Good," he says. "And I guess it tastes like water?"

"To me," I answer.

"You're between Heaven and Hell," he tells me.

"What?"

"You asked if you were in Heaven."

"Oh. So where is between Heaven and Hell, then?"

"You're on the res."

"The res? What's that?"

He turns and looks at me quizzically, surprised. That's when I first see his deeply tanned skin, high cheekbones, and chiseled features. He's Native American.

"The reservation," he explains. "Res-ort living courtesy of the US government."

"You're kidding me, right?" I say.

"Hard to say, anymore," he replies. "Check it out in the morning and get back to me on that."

The truck stops, the dust settles. He gets out. My door won't open from the inside. He pulls it open.

"You OK to walk?" he asks.

"Let me try," I tell him.

I turn round on the seat and slide down to the ground. He steps aside poised to grab hold of me if I appear weak. I was dehydrated. I'm better now. I stumble, catch myself and we walk, with him guiding me. It's a few steps to a house with a light on inside. The door is open. He goes in first and announces me.

"We have company," he declares.

I follow him in. A single, bare light bulb hangs from its wire wrapped twice about a wood beam balanced on opposing walls under the roof. The wire to the bulb is plugged into an uncovered outlet on one wall. The walls were plastered at one time but now are mostly exposed areas of clay blocks loosely mortared together.

The entire house is one room, like the dome, except this room is square. There's a table to one side where two women, seated on folding chairs, stitch a quilt from sections of different fabrics. The younger woman has a baby between her arms as she works. They look over as we enter. The young woman is not pleased to see me; she makes that very clear to me and to my escort. The older woman jumps up immediately and grabs my right arm and guides me to a metal cot bed and has me sit.

I'm surprised how weak I am.

"How do you feel?" she asks.

"I was dehydrated," I tell her.

"You look pale," she tells me. "You will stay here, tonight, and tomorrow we will see how you're doing."

She offers me a gallon water bottle with two fingers of water. I gulp it down.

She takes the bottle away from me and hoists me to my feet. She gets under my left arm and drag walks me out the door, round the corner to an outhouse. I manage myself while she waits for me. We walk back together, slowly, into the house. I aim for the bed and she follows me with a blanket as I lay down.

"What if she dies?" the young woman asks. "What we need is a dead white woman."

"She is strong," the older woman insists. "She wants to live. Tell me what happened, Sky Hawk."

"I was driving along the gully near the frontage road," I hear Sky Hawk relate. "It was dusk and I had my lights on. Some wind sprites were dancing up ahead so I slowed way down. One of them became a big coyote. He saw me and attacked me, leaping at the windshield. I thought he'll break it. When he took off, I got out to look around.

That's when I found her passed out beneath a barrel cactus. I took her for dead. I cut into the cactus and dripped water on her mouth till she came too. Then I brought her home."

"You have a good heart, my son," she comments.

"Let's hope he has a strong enough heart to find food for the extra mouth," the young woman derides him.

"Have you ever gone hungry, Red Wing?" Sky Hawk asks.

"No," Red Wing replies. "But that's because we live here in Sun Path's home."

I struggle to prop myself up onto one elbow.

"If I am a problem," I tell them, "I will leave."

"You bring powerful coyote medicine," says Sky Hawk. "Ignore Red Wing. She fantasizes I need a white woman to satisfy me."

Red Wing flies to her feet holding her baby close.

"You're jealous after I told you that white BIA man took a fancy to me," Red Wing snaps back.

Sun Path grins as she pulls the blanket up over my shoulders.

"They are so young," she tells me. "They still think sex makes for a relationship. They'll learn."

Knowing I am safe for the moment, I close my eyes.

Sunlight streaming through the open door wakes me. I hear the two women outside frame the floating cadences of daily conversation. I can tell how fragile I am when I swing my legs out of bed. I take it easy standing up and walking, step at a time, toward the door.

The sun is really bright and I throw up an arm to protect my eyes. I step unsteadily around the corner and head to the outhouse.

"Good morning," Sun Path calls out to me as I slam the door closed.

When I come back to the house, the two of them are squatting in the shade with their backs to the wall of the house, peeling and chopping vegetables at a furious rate without a board.

Sun Path asks me, "D'you know how to fix vegetables?"

"Good morning," I say. "Yes, I do. Thank you for taking me in."

"You are welcome," Sun Path answers.

"My name is Judith," I tell them. "Judith Fargoe."

Red Wing, her head down, plays with her baby stretched across her lap while she cuts carrots into an enamel bowl. She gives me a sidelong glance.

"What were you doing out in the desert, Judith?" she asks.

I tell her, "I was headed for the mountains."

"Ah," she says. "Then you are a spiritual person."

She irritates me with her know-it-all attitude.

"Are you asking if I attend church?" I demand.

Sun Path gently comments, "That is religion."

That's not gentle enough for me after a day on carbohydrates.

"OK, already," I snap. "So I got lost."

"And you slept," adds Red Wing.

"What does that mean?" I ask, confused.

"When you run till you are out of breath, then Spirit has more room to inhabit you," Sun Path explains.

"Spirit?" I ask. "D'you mean the Holy Ghost?"

"Great Spirit," Sun Path tells me. "Creator."

"Those are all terms for something abstract," I tell them. "I guess at best I'm an agnostic and worst case scenario I'm an atheist."

Sun Path has been carefully assessing me.

"What you are, Judith, is bloated," she tells me. "You are eating food that is bad for you. That is why you are filled with pain and anger. As for Creator, I doubt you have ever personally experienced Great Spirit."

"That's for sure," I easily admit. "Though, sometimes, I let the Universe take charge of my life."

"That is most gracious of you," Red Wing says.

I hear the bite of sarcasm.

"White people have so few rituals," comments Sun Path. "They have little reason to live. That can be extremely frustrating."

"For you?" I ask.

"To me it is sad," Sun Path answers. "White people are frustrated because they have let go of tradition based on Creator. They celebrate holidays. They practice religion once or twice a week. They wander in the desert unable to read the signs put there for all creatures by Creator. They destroy their own home because they are unable to relate to it as being alive."

"Whoa!" I call out. "Wait one minute. I am not "White people," even though I am European in origin. I certainly am not destroying my home."

In response, Sun Path puts down her knife and the white root vegetable she was peeling, stands, and goes over to Sky Hawk's truck. She opens the driver's door, reaches in for something and walks back to where I am standing. She holds out a plastic shopping bag.

"What do you call this?" she asks.

"A bag," I answer. "A plastic shopping bag. There must be millions of them. Surely you have seen them before?"

"You destroy your home, my home, with these bags," she shouts at me. "Do you understand?"

I guess I don't. I shake my head, no.

Sun Path takes the bag in both hands and begins tearing at it. She uses her knife to cut it.

"Do you see?" she asks. "It is impossible to destroy plastic. These bags break into smaller and smaller pieces but never go away. They destroy life by being indestructible. This is Just one way you destroy your home. This planet is your home, Judith. You want to go pillage other places in Space? Hopefully, you will learn to care of this planet before you set foot somewhere else."

Well, I am glad I stopped by here. Seems like time to go. I start to walk away.

"Where are you going?" Sun Path asks.

"Away," I answer. "Away from here."

"That would be easy," Sun Path tells me. "Except Creator has other plans for you."

"Oh?" I gasp, coming to a stop. "Such as?"

"Staying with us to learn some of our ways," she says.

"Creator told this to you, just now, I suppose?" I comment.

"I sent Sky Hawk to look for you, last night, because I saw you were lost in the desert," she answers.

That's a great answer. I was expecting smart but this is above smart.

"You expect me to believe that?" I ask with a laugh.

"Go, Judith," she says. "Leave. You will only come back here. You are free to go whenever you want, but, until you learn why you are here, you will keep coming back. Be easy on yourself. Stay."

"Do I have this stamped on my forehead?" I ask.

"Sort of," Red Wing chimes in.

Yes, I am curious. Everyone seems to know everything about me and I still have it all to learn. Maybe asking direct questions is a short cut.

"What does it say?" I ask.

Sun Path does not hesitate.

"I forgive you," she tells me.

I am expecting to hear something extraordinary; "I forgive you" is not that!

"That's it?" I say, the pitch of my voice going up several notches.

"Yes," Sun Path answers. "You have to forgive everybody."

"Including me," Red Wing chimes in.

My hesitancy, uncertainty, my simple unwillingness to accept what seems so simple, tugs at my craw. Red Wing adding herself in shows me how resistant I truly am. There are other issues.

"You have been generous to me," I say. "But I do need to eat. In lieu of paying you, I can work hard. I can teach you things I know."

"We know all about you, Judith," Sun Path tells me. "Help us finish with these vegetables and we can eat. Believe me, you will earn your keep and we shall benefit greatly from having you here."

"That's all on my forehead?" I ask, still incredulous.

"That was in the fine print," she adds with a laugh.

"Will I learn all this?" I ask.

"You'll learn what you need," says Sun Path. "We will set food on the table and you will eat what you want."

Sounds like Lea's story about Yogi Bhajan and the books people choose to read.

"How do you know all this?" I ask.

Sun Path gives me a hard stare then softens at my sincerely naïve innocence.

"Out here in the wilds?" she jibes. "Without a TV, radio or a computer? We communicate by smoke signals."

My eyes must have been bugging out. They both laugh hysterically. Red Wing struggles to catch her breath so she can speak.

"We listen to the tom toms, late at night!" she blurts out.

That sets them off laughing louder than ever causing the baby to cry.

REFLECTIONS

One of my first acts on the res is to change the way I dress. The clothes people wear there tend to the dark, earth tones and draped. I have not worn a skirt in forever and a large blouse which is all that is immediately available. My Institute issue work boots are just the ticket. It is a matter of matching the code more than blending in which my skin tone and physical features may prevent me from ever doing, especially, if I intend to stay for any duration.

Sun Path takes me for a tour of local homes, and to meet many of her neighbors. Her house is quite a high standard compared to others we visit. It seems to be more of an issue for me more than ever it is for the inhabitants.

She has a clever approach to integrate me since "white people" seem to rank among the least favored races. Sun Path knows where the men are not at home and arranges our visits for those times. The women are not particularly thrilled at the prospect of having a "round eye" on the res, especially a woman. It seems that white women can be viewed as distracting to the men folk.

Sun Path's idea is to let the women meet me, find their comfort level with me and thereby allow them to introduce my presence to the men. If it had been done the other way around, that I meet the men first, the women will make sure I get run off the res in no time flat; unless, that is, I am attached to one man and he vouches for me. Complicated, yes, insurmountable, no.

When it is understood that I have no connection to the Bureau of Indian Affairs or any other agency of the US government, that I am not a missionary, that I potentially am a teacher, but, again, not affiliated with any education agency, plus I live at Sun Path's house, I am given a relatively clean bill of health. They do not trust me, but are less threatened by me, more willing to watch and see how I perform.

My first conscious meeting with Creator is a wholly other happening.

In the midst of this forsaken country of baked hard dirt, mostly scrub for vegetation with soaring high mountains as backdrop in a difficult to reach valley, is a small fast running stream. This is the originating source of fresh water for miles round here. As a result, the valley is largely devoid of green vegetation. Except for a narrow access, the stream is purposely covered over with enormous boulders. If you did not know it was here, you could pass within a few yards and not notice it. The valley location of the stream is a guarded fact known to all on the res but mostly only visited during the performance of sacred ceremonies. The stream feeds an aquifer which supplies most local water needs through a well.

A young woman, White Dove, a peer of Red Wing, helps out at my initiation. She is Fire Keeper in charge of the fire. We spend three days, in our free time from chores, searching for wood—dead, burnable wood—a commodity almost as precious as water.

White Dove requires a lot of wood for her fire set up twenty yards from the stream. She has set aside a large number of special rocks and, with the wood, creates a pyre to heat the rocks. While she diligently lays out the rocks, and,, crafts a wood structure to burn, I assist Sun Path and Red Wing throw blankets over a dome shaped skeleton of woven, willow branches. Set about fifteen feet from the fire, the domed Inipi sits on the dirt surrounding a Hoochka, a six inch deep hole, about three feet in, diameter. The blankets are layered on to the dome to block any sunlight from entering.

Periodically, one or other of them crawls around inside to make sure the structure is light tight. On the side facing the fire, the corners of the blankets are thrown back to create a doorway. We eat our last meal at midday and work well past dusk making the preparations. Red Wing takes off back to the house for a feeding for her baby who is having daddy all to herself, tonight.

When she returns, Sun Path begins the ceremony. When done with men present the women wear full length dresses and the men wear shorts. When only one sex is present, participants have the option of stripping down to their skin. Since I am a student, I do as I am told.

We leave "gifts" to Spirit at an altar close by where the Fire Keeper will be stationed. I leave my ring. Sun Path says if Spirit likes the gift enough it will be gone when ceremony is over. She says nothing has ever been taken that she is aware of but this may be a first.

I tell myself what Ariel told Rachel, "Give it up, girl!"

We three women, Red Wing, White Dove and myself, stand in a small arc by the blazing fire. I assume it is similar for the others. My front is roasting and my back is chilling. One person at a time, Sun Path repeats a blessing for each of us as she smudges us with smoldering sage leaves in the cup of an abalone shell. She incants to each of us she brushes smoke with a feather, from head to toe, side to side, front and back. Complete, she requests White Dove smudge her.

Sun Path enters the Sweat Lodge on all fours, touching her forehead to the dirt at the entrance then crawling in a sun wise direction. Red Wing sends me in next instructing me to imitate Sun Path. The ground is cold and wet inside, the blankets give off a musty smell. I am less than excited to sit on the dirt.

Red Wing crawls in carrying a pair of deer antlers. White Dove's flickering fire is down to a red hot glow. Sun Path instructs me to sit back from the hole in the ground but not to touch the dome's wooden frame.

Right then, using a long handled pitch fork, White Dove picks up a red hot rock from the fire and walks it to the lodge entrance. She diligently lowers the rock onto the deer antlers held by a kneeling Red Wing, inside the lodge doorway. Red Wing places the rock in the hole in the ground. She turns back to the entrance and after a few moments, White Dove is back with another hot rock. They repeat this a couple more times, then, White Dove lowers all the turned up blanket corners.

I am so aware of my physical circumstances. I am naked, which I never do except for a shower or the rare bath. My butt is on cold, wet mud as are my feet. My front is being cooked, again, this time by the glowing rocks, and my back is freezing. The dry heat from the rocks is making my breathing thin.

I look at the other two and, in the slowly waning red glow of the rocks, they both look spaced out as if they're meditating. This is not too bad, after all. I'm not sweating but then we have only just begun. Maybe it's the mood they're creating but I am lulling off to sleep.

The sound of a bird furiously flapping its wings above the rocks and then making a wide circle as it flies out of the sealed roof shakes me alert. There's no way a bird can fly out of here. Judging by the sound, that was an enormous bird. How did it get in here and where is it now?

Sun Path is speaking, praying, in, I guess, her native language. I vaguely see her touch the rocks with a long braided something. The air becomes scented. She sprinkles stuff on the rocks, one at a time, each creating different herbal smells. There's a brief pause and she throws water on the rocks.

In the time it takes for me to hear the splash, my body goes from bone dry skin to sweat pouring off me. I am shocked. The suddenness of the change is so dramatic I am stunned. Now I feel the heat.

My body rebels immediately. I am sucking air through my mouth and my innards feel about ready to explode. It's not a gag reflex. I feel like I am going to lose my bowels, maybe urinate. My hands are futilely wiping sweat from my face. Then I understand the problem. I can feel every nerve ending at once and they all complain they are being cooked. Which way is out of here? Where is the exit?

I sure am not going near those rocks. That leaves sideways but each way is blocked. I am trapped. This was intentional to keep me in here.

Well, I'm ready for you. Remember, I took Agnes down. You guys will be a piece of cake.

When I breathe in through my nose and out through my mouth the heat feels bearable. I am more comfortable. My ass is warm but I can still feel the cold soil. I'm feeling a whole lot better. My back is a river of sweat as is my front. The rocks are dark now even though when I move my right leg toward the pit, I can feel radiated heat.

That's when two huge splashes of water go on the rocks one immediately after the other. I can hear clouds of steam billow into the air. This time my entire body is one massive river of sweat. My nerves race to breaking point. I try to stand and touch the willow branches of the dome with my head. It resists me.

"Sit down, Judith," Sun Path tells me.

I do as I am told because I don't know what else to do with myself.

"This is so hot!" I shout.

"I hear you plenty good without you shouting, Judith," Sun Path tells me.

"Are we done now?" I ask.

"If the heat hurts you, lay your face on Mother Earth to cool you," Sun Path says.

Red Wing tells me, "Pray to the Creator for relief."

I whine, "This is ridiculously hot."

Red Wing tells me, "Pray harder!"

Another cup of water splashes onto the rocks. Then, a drum is struck once. The beat resonates from my stomach outwards. I feel like I am losing control of my mind.

Terrified, I shout, "I want out!"

Sun Path tells me, "It is poisons in your body pushing to leave. Stay, my Sister. This is good for you to know your courage."

I think I must be crazy. We were there at least two hours. Loads more rocks and some beautiful singing of songs the like I have never heard before. We take turns going round the circle talking to Creator about our good and bad deeds, hopes, wishes and prayers for others.

I had a moment when I must have believed because I asked Great

Spirit to take care of Lucy and Mika and it made me cry to be able to publicly ask for help. I threw in an extra that they wait until I get back to them and then we can live together forever after, like in a fairy tale.

Sun Path and Red Wing have no idea who I am talking about but they both break into tears and we all have a good sob. Sun Path throws a ton of water on the rocks for good measure. I bet I sweat off five pounds.

We go out in the order we came in. Red Wing throws back the flaps so Sun Path can leave. We each kiss Mother Earth at the entrance as we give thanks to our ancestors.

Wrapped in a blanket, White Dove sits by the smoldering fire poking it to maintain the glow. When the lodge entrance flap flies back, steam billows out above Sun Path as she crawls out.

"White Dove, my Sister," Sun Path requests. "Please assist the newborns."

White Dove helps Sun Path to her feet. They hug. White Dove helps me to my wobbly feet and hugs me. Naked and cooling fast in the night air, a nice warm hug is perfect. Then it is Red Wing's turn. The three of us Muses walk to the stream and immerse ourselves in the water shouting at the cold.

As we emerge, White Dove has a towel and a blanket for each of us. We huddle by the fire that was built up while we were in the stream. White Dove serves bowls of food and cups of water. Though exhausted, I can feel myself radiate calmness. This is a new me. I like it.

Sun Path is right. My culture has no ceremony that compares. Maybe the nearest I have experienced is the Maori stuff that Aroha was responsible for. Again, the Maoris are first nation people, what we sometimes call aboriginals. We civilized folk are so far removed from our ritual past the best I can remotely associate with are some of the tavern drinking songs dad liked to sing for me when he bounced me on his lap, or chased after mom, singing, to make her blush.

There is so much for me to learn here. I begin to wonder if I will ever leave.

TRADE SHOW

My offer to help devolves down to, first thing in the morning, prepping food for the day. That means a lot of vegetables and, when Sky Hawk has a fruitful hunt, some meat, mostly eaten rare. That works well for me as I seek out the least cooked parts and Sun Path prefers the most cooked.

I let them know that, when possible, I want the organ meats. I often get the liver and heart. It takes a while for me to find out why the kidneys are always missing. It is a tradition in Sky Hawk's family to eat the kidneys raw while field dressing the kill.

After I raise the topic, Sun Path recalls her grandparents' talk about the adrenals. I show them where these tiny organs are "hiding" in fat above the kidneys. I make a short drink with the finely chopped up adrenals which boosts the energy really well.

The first time I make the adrenal drink, we use four of them from two full grown male deer. We split the drink between the four of us. Each of us takes sick. We manage turns at the outhouse and then spend the better part of that day calming down. Everyone notices substantial shifts such as improved sense of smell and vision, particularly. Taste buds take a sizable break that day, though Red Wing's baby, Tree Dancer, is unusually active after breast feeding.

The remainder of every morning until the heat of the sun becomes unbearable, I work Sun Path's garden hoeing, weeding, and planting. Sun Path has strong traditional approaches for maintaining her garden, and we go the rounds about the appropriateness, or, mostly, lack thereof of Biodynamic applications. She resolves the issue by allocating me a section of ground all of my own with which, we agree, I can do whatever I want, but only after I am done working her garden her way.

Finding a cover crop is easy since beans are a staple of the local diet. When I have a couple of feet of growth from the restricted water I am allowed, I lay my first crop down by walking through and snapping the stalks low to the ground. The next day, when it is time for me to work my garden, several of the older women gather in the shade over looking my plot. They hunker down on their haunches and wait for me to begin the entertainment. Since there is little actual gardening to do at this point, I hunker down with them, and, out of deference, wait quietly until spoken to.

One by one they ask about what I am doing, what I intend. It's a struggle to find good translation to and from English until Sun Path comes looking for me. She helps speed up the exchange and, within half an hour, it's like old home week among the gardening set. As a result of my receiving approval for what I am about from the senior women, Sun Path agrees to increase my water allowance. In exchange, I have to teach her each step of my process, as she puts it, "In case you're on to something."

Right.

After the midday meal many people siesta. I sleep so deeply at night in this environment I have energy to spare. I use it to do repairs on the outside of the house with the local clay soil. Sometimes Red Wing joins me. We are slowly healing the rift between us from when I first arrived though she adamantly refuses to allow me to hunt with Sky Hawk. Old ideas are difficult to destroy.

A couple times per week, I collect a few of the young women together to teach them Brazilian Jiu-Jitsu. Red Wing still believes in a short knife as her best means of defense although she practices what I teach her. White Dove is also a good student and faithful to the class. Having others attend regularly enough to really learn anything practical is difficult. So I focus on those who come.

In exchange, White Dove teaches me her family's traditional pattern for quilt making. She keeps referring to the defects and inadequacies of machine sewed quilts while teaching me the advantages, the subtleties of hand stitching. I am not a quick learner of the finer motor movements, so I feel slow. She has the patience of an angel and I do end up with a passable quilt after months of instruction.

My favorite education is the rare times Sun Path takes me on instructional walks in the surrounding desert. She knows the name of every plant and animal. She knows when their seasons begin and end. She knows flowering cycles, many of which occur in the dead of night. She knows what plants may be used, and how, to assist the human body recover from sickness. She explains how the plants divide the territory, for example, why some grow in one spot but not in another.

Her lecturing me about caring for Mother Earth when I first arrived makes a whole lot more sense now that she is guiding me.

Once a month, she tests me by telling me of a plant to locate and giving me a pole to stake in the ground nearby when I find it. This education is important for me in a secondary sense, namely, I am learning how to identify landmarks in a barren landscape, to find my way. She's clever, starting me out with something easy to find and ending with a more unusual one. Her explanation of the process is meant to make me think. She can keep this up all day.

"The pole is a marker for the plant in case you become lost, or you die," she tells me. "That way we can still find the plant whereas you are on your own to find your way home."

She laughs, eyes twinkling. I am not amused.

"Thanks a bunch, Sun Path," I tell her. "That makes me feel wanted."

Her mood changes on a dime.

"It is the same way as your people see Native Americans," Sun Path says. "The res is your pole, the marker you can find it anytime you need to. If the people leave the res or die off, you still know where the res is."

"Why are you talking about dying off?" I ask.

"We are an experiment," she says. "We are the canary in your coal mine."

"What?" I ask.

"When a colorless, odorless poison is present," she explains, "A small bird will die before a large human will necessarily be aware of any danger. What happens to Native Americans on the res is like the canary in a cage. Whatever happens to the res foretells what may befall the country. But someone has to care what happens to the canary. When you are lost, you want someone to find the pole and, hopefully, know to go looking for you."

"Sure," I say.

I feel so Juvenile, inept, when she talks to me that way. She changes topics.

"Do you know why men make all the decisions on the res?" she asks me as we resume our walk.

I shake my head, no. I am focused on collecting sacred objects for my personal medicine bundle.

"Because the women are smart enough to let them," she answers her own question. "Most women are not strong enough to stand up to their men. They need a different way to succeed."

"That makes sense," I tell her.

"Yet, most men are still children at heart," she explains. "They act like grownups until their authority is questioned. Then they revert to demanding and being competitive. Do you think there would ever be wars if women were in charge?"

"I suppose you are right," I say, reflecting on Lysis Strada at Taquinta.

"A smart man tells his woman all his worries at night," Sun Path tells me with a wicked grin. "While the man sleeps, she whispers the answers in his ear and when the man wakes up, he thinks he is inspired."

"Who tells the women what to say?" I ask her.

"A woman who keeps a good home knows everything there is to know," Sun Path explains. "If she is alone, without her women friends and needs to know an answer, Creator whispers in her ear."

"Why does Creator whisper in her ear if the man is the one with the problem?" I ask.

"Men are too busy showing off to listen," she answers. "Finally, when a man becomes too old to hunt, the young men leave him in the kitchen with the women where he listens to us talk. That is how he suddenly grows wise. It has always been so."

I find many of her interpretations of life simplistic, sometimes downright cynical, but often with more than a grain of truth.

"Were you ever married, Sun Path?" I ask.

"Yes," she says, distractedly.

One afternoon, I am supposed to be helping White Dove tan some deer hides but she has left to visit distant family. I return to the house to assist Red Wing finish fixing the outside of the house and to begin on the inside. After an unsuccessful hunt, Sky Hawk comes over to where we are working to complain.

"This house is starting to stand out on the res," he tells us in all seriousness. "My Brothers accuse me of being too uptown for living here, you know?"

I have never seen Red Wing be goaded by him to this degree before. She stops working, removes her knife and demonstrably jabs it into the table top where it stands quivering. She walks past Sky Hawk and out the door. I step over to the doorway to watch what she does.

With muddy hands on her hips, feet spread well apart she yells loud enough to wake Creator from a siesta, "Oh, Lover Boy! Oh, Lover Boy! Where are you, Lover Boy?"

He follows her outside and walking up to her tells her to, "Shush!"

Red Wing gets even louder making sure to wake the entire res.

"Oh, Lover Boy!" she screams. "Where are you, Lover Boy?"

"Stop being so loud," he whispers to her, pushing the air down with his hands. "You'll wake my Brothers."

Her concept for attracting their neighbors works.

Many of the men gather and shout across at Sky Hawk, "C'mon, man. Take charge of your woman. People are trying to sleep, you know, man?"

Seeing she has an audience, she begins a slow, light footed dance around Sky Hawk who is confused by this new woman he has never seen before. She gestures a "Come and get me" with both hands. He makes a weak attempt to lunge at her and she slaps his face lightly as she backs away quickly, encouraging him to come after her.

"Dance like a butterfly," she sings loudly enough for all to hear. "Sting like a bee!"

"Go get her, Sky Hawk," one man calls out.

Other men begin to laugh at him. Sky Hawk grows blind with rage. He starts after Red Wing with a fury.

"OK," he says to her. "That's enough!"

She stops still and takes up her position. By now the women are hovering outside their doors to watch the action as the men jeer and cheer their champion.

BORDERS

Sky Hawk walks right into Red Wing's intention. She grabs him by the collar with both hands, steps around him to one side and lays him over her hip so that he slides to the ground. She lets him down easily.

She steps away from him and waits. Shaken up, he staggers to his feet and dusts himself off. He looks around and his eyes lock in on Sun Path. She shakes her head, no, then turns and walks away. He turns to Red Wing.

"Woman," he addresses her calmly. "You embarrass me in front of my Brothers. I understand your meaning."

Pasting a big grin on his face, he extends an arm and wraps it around her shoulders and makes her turn with him to face the crowd.

Pointing at Red Wing, he shouts to the men, "Now you know why I have only one child. Anyone else feel like a fight? Red Wing is ready for you!"

They all seem to appreciate his joke and turn away laughing and chattering, returning to finish their siesta.

"Tell me," Red Wing asks him, slipping an arm around his waist. "Who do you love?"

They stroll past me into the house, ignoring me. Sky Hawk kicks the door closed with his heel. Maybe he is quietly appreciating me for teaching his wife self defense. Maybe he is demanding a conjugal time-out. Either way, I am not included. I go searching for Sun Path.

That night, there is a serious discussion round the kitchen table.

"There will be a buffalo cull at the National Park," Sky Hawk announces. "I have applied to be one of the hunters. I can earn one animal kill for myself."

"What are your chances of being selected?" Sun Path asks.

"Fifty fifty," he says.

"That's a long drive for a maybe," Red Wing tells him. "What else?"

"The usual," he says. "It would be good to bring in a large harvest ahead of winter. We can make jerky, even sell some."

"Stay practical, Sky Hawk," Sun Path cautions him.

"What about Mexico?" Red Wing asks. "Or Canada?"

"Do you have a passport?" I ask out of curiosity.

Everyone looks at me. I feel I have spoken out of turn.

Sky Hawk eyes me straight.

"These are the lands of my ancestors," he tells me. "Only prisoners need passports."

"But I thought..." I stammer.

"Governments create borders to keep people in so they'll pay taxes," Sun Path tells me. "We are a sovereign people."

"Only on the reservation," I comment. "Right?"

"You have much to learn, my Sister," Sun Path says.

Once again, I lead with my tongue for which I receive a gentle slap on the wrist. They are eternally patient with me.

Next morning, though I rise bright and early, Sky Hawk and his truck are already gone. I decide that saying nothing until told will be the better side of discretion.

Sun Path has a new exciting project for me. She has decided it is time to send me on a Vision Quest. She tells me little directly, but alludes to what will occur.

I am to begin by laying out my medicine bundle every night for the next week. I am to sit in front of it and meditate on every object, cloth, skin, and string, all of it as if it is a single item.

Though they have little meat left, I can tell I am definitely being fattened up.

One afternoon, as I finish teaching my class of Brazilian Jiu-Jitsu to my now eight women regulars, Sun Path tells me, "Come home soon so you can sleep. Tomorrow, you climb the mountain."

That's a double entendre. I will climb the physical mountain that supplies the stream. I will also climb my personal issues which are mountainous in volume. I am ready, willing and terrified. I am about to learn some home truths that any amount of sitting in ceremony in hot rock, steamy heaven is unable to release. That means Vision Quest is going to be tough, really tough.

Next morning, as we walk to the mountain, Sun Path explains, "Creator made Humans last. Many people act as if they own the planet. We are the youngest creation, and the Stars are the oldest. In the Order of Things, the Animals are our older Brothers and Sisters. We have much to learn from them. Make sure to keep your heart open."

Sun Path sets up base camp by the stream. She does one more check of my medicine bundle and supplies.

She tells me, "Be prepared for anything on your Vision Quest. Pray for Great Spirit to guide your dream. I will be waiting for you here."

That's it. No, "You go, girl!," or a supporting hug. She turns her back as if I had interrupted her and now she's resuming her work.

There's the mountain. I begin to climb.

I soon clue in to why we started early. I am about half way up when the sun moves round to shine on me. There are almost no trees and thus no shade. Though I am walking on something resembling a path, I am climbing rapidly. My breathing turns from long deep breaths to more frequent shallow inhalations. With the sun now on me, I feel like I am torturing myself to walk.

"Whatever you do," Sun Path instructed me, "Keep going."

I start telling myself, if others have done this before me then I can do it, too. I decide I do have a slightly competitive streak.

As she directed me, right below the top of the mountain, I find a cliff's edge. The view is magnificent. I can't believe we haven't been here simply as an outing. Maybe it is kept as a sacred space and visiting is not permitted. I catch my breath. My watering eyes begin to clear. Details appear in sharp definition because the air is so fresh and dry. I estimate my view extends ten to twenty miles in about a 270 degree arc.

At the back of the cliff, where the mountain continues up, is a healthy cedar tree. I make note of it in case some predator comes to check me out so I'll have a place to escape.

I am ambitious. If I am going to be up here meditating for four days and nights, I want the best view possible. I lay my blanket on the ground a mere couple of feet back from the center edge of the cliff. I open my bundle and remove my sacred objects, arranging them on the blanket.

I set out bowls of food and water for any visitors then settle myself to sit comfortably. I start by relishing the view. Hard pushed to do so, I give thanks to Creator for availing me of the opportunity to be in such a place and have such a spectacular vista to contemplate. A small internal voice bugs me.

"OK," I say, relenting. "Thank you, Waken Tanka. Aho Mitaquiessen."

I even feel better having done that. I'm uncomfortable thanking the Great Spirit and acknowledging my ancestors, but I really feel liberated once I do it. I acknowledge I don't have to be a believer to say it, but I can tell I do need to say it out loud, with an intentionally strong voice.

I hear a wind rustle the cedar tree. I turn and watch branches sweep and bow.

I resolve to stay looking forward. Sun Path told me I am safe here. I must act as if.

For me to meditate for half an hour is relatively straight forward. I have occasionally done an hour. To accomplish four days and nights straight, I feel as if I've trained to run a marathon by occasionally zipping out of the house to do a hill sprint. I am so not prepared.

"Practice is for sports," Sun Path advised me. "Vision Quest requires dedication and perseverance."

"OK," I said. "I'll give it my best shot."

By mid afternoon, I am ready to quit. By night time, I am questioning my sanity, the whole purpose of Vision Quest and wondering which idiot came up with this idea.

It is a few days to full moon and, once some unexpected clouds pass, the moon sits off to my right shoulder and bathes me in her gentle glow. I cannot ever remember when I Just sat with the moon and simply felt good, hour upon hour.

Beyond the moon hang stars in dangling clusters. Where do they get their light from? Are they suns like the one we have caring for Earth? I don't know my way round the stars. I promise to study the night sky when I descend from this rock.

Did the moon move? It's almost straight ahead. Between my ears so many thoughts chase each other; it's a wonder I can think at all. It is so loud in here, so quiet outside. I am like an orchestra constantly tuning up. Shut up! There, that stops it. No, it didn't. It just moves the sound track to a different section of my brain.

There! It did move—to my left. The moon is lower in the sky. Over to the left the sky looks darker than anywhere else. There's just a shade lighter dark blue. Yes, the horizon shows up as the finest, soft shade of red. The infra red bands circle the Earth. This is the time to send meditations around the globe on non-stop bands of infra red light.

"Hi, Lucy, hi, Mika," I think to myself. "I love you."

That's not a meditation, that's a telegram. Who says what I can send and what I can't? I'm the boss of me. Hello, all this noisy arguing and chatter is now traveling around the world. Oops! Sorry, guys. OK, let's do what they do at Taquinta, the Institutional chant;

Onggggggggggggggggggggggggggggggggggg!

Onnnnnnnnnggggggggggggggggggggggggg!

How beautiful to see sunrise long before people on the ground will.

This is difficult for me because, the more I slow down to be here, more thoughts find their way to be expressed and heard in my head.

It was quiet for a while. I suspect I nodded off for an hour or two.

Here comes the sun! Little darling.

Ugh oh, that looks ominous. Yep, rain. Huh? Did anyone explain to those clouds this is desert, even up here on the mountain? It does not rain like this. Hey! I didn't bring any rain gear. I am soaked. OK, enough already. Eeeeeeeennnnoughhhhhhhhhhh! Stop. STOP! Is anyone listening? I want the rain to stop. Thank you. No, sincerely, thank you. Wow, the sun has mostly dried me in minutes. I am cooking. I will never complain about being too hot in sweat lodge ever again. I promise.

Once afternoon has rolled in, so do mosquitoes; to everything its season. I committed to not kill anything during my quest; not even one single, pesky, buzzing, blood sucking mosquito, or a swarm of them. This is trial by pestilence.

To circumvent focusing on just one issue while it happens, I allow my various parts—skin, innards, brain, nerves, and even sensory perceptions—to discuss quietly among themselves which one of them is getting treated worst and by what. Skin wins, hands down, though my growling Stomach does annoy my Ears' hearing.

Skin has a list of complaints. There is wind, rain, sun and mosquitoes. Brain reminds Skin not to forget cold.

"Well, thanks for the reminder," says Skin in a less than jovial manner.

"Then quit coming to me to complain," says Brain. "You think my job's easy when the operator decides to run on empty. Please!"

The big event of the entire day is a momma and poppa hawk training in a junior novice. The whole show lasts maybe five minutes but it is stand out memorable. The replays are a whole lot better than a TV news station playing over and over their footage of some grisly car accident on the highway. I watch the hunt in process, not the kill. What a difference that makes.

Night is cloudy and cold.; surprisingly, since starry nights are typically colder. Maybe it is the high relative humidity. I probably skip several hours because I wake up close to the edge.

Looking down the sheer drop gives me a start.

Oh, yes, does it ever.

BLUE YONDER

Before I try to stand, I crawl away from the edge. My knees and ankles need a lube job. My wrists and elbows, shoulders and hips also feel locked down. Almost standing fully upright, dizziness takes a turn. As a best option, I take evasive action and sit down versus teetering off balance at the edge of the cliff, again.

My next move is to crawl slowly closer toward the cedar tree, and drag my blanket, and the food and water bowl I put out for guests, further in away from the edge. Despite cropping the vista slightly, I am still able to see one amazing view while increasing my odds considerably for getting out of here alive and in one piece.

I have fleeting glimpses of day three. The perceptual senses either are picking up static electrical interference, or they are malfunctioning. I hang in there because that is the goal. I admit I am one competitive DOB.

Interestingly, I find that in my remaining rarely conscious moments, Creator and/or Great Spirit have begun to play oddly fluctuating roles. They are only present when I invoke them. In other words, they have become my Quantum Physics' energy/matter of existing or not. If I simply recognize something, then it is matter. A rock, for example, in Sweat Lodge lingo is called an Ancient One.

When I give thanks for the Ancient One or rock, I am giving thanks "to" something, i.e., Creator. In this case, the observer dictates whether it is matter or it is energy. When it's a rock it is matter. When it's conceptual, as in an Ancient One, it is energy. Likewise with Creator, giving thanks to Creator I'm talking substantive, or matter. When it's philosophical, such as what is Creator, I'm talking energy.

That passes the time, especially since I am so proud that I understand the concept that I play it over again and again like a stuck record.

That's what the Vision Quest has come down to. Whatever it is that is supposed to happen, does not seem to be happening. I am simply becoming loopier by passing units of time, whatever time is—maybe the interlude between changing matter to energy or vice versa, or the duration between synapses connecting, or light leaving the sun to illuminate the moon for someone looking at the moon through a mirror on earth.

The sky transitions to night, or something resembling night. It's a mid range blue, vibrant—Yves Klein blue. Its intensity is static, from right to left, top to bottom. It surrounds me. If there is a horizon line, it's beyond my peripheral vision. The world is back dropped Blue. I stick out a finger on an extended arm and it ought to pierce the Blue but my finger just hangs there waiting for me to reel it back in. I do because piercing nothing is tiresome work and I have little interest in work right now.

If the Blue will not go, then it is up to me to go. I am too weary to stand up and walk out of here so I just close my eyes. That's interesting. I have completely disappeared but the Blue is still here. Then it occurs to me, I may have disappeared but I am still here, along with the Blue.

"What part of me is here?" I ask myself.

"The "I,"" I answer.

"Where is the "I" when my body is somewhere else?" I ask.

"Here," I say.

"So it is always here, even when I am elsewhere?" I ask.

"Precisely," I tell myself. "But I am loads more fun when "I" am here than when I am all alone."

"You say," I say.

"Only "I" can," I say.

A bright yellow Bird arrives twittering sweetly and hovering, seeking somewhere to settle. I open my eyes and thereby bring back my body. Bird chooses my right foot. It walks back and forth for a moment. As if startled, it flies to my left shoulder. It tweets in my ear and glides, to settle on my left foot. Reluctant to be still, it flies to my right shoulder, barely touching down before it flies away, chirruping about the great adventure it had.

As if viewing myself from behind and above, I watch a Lizard crawl up my back to sit on my head. We both stare straight ahead. Lizard floats up into the air about one foot, hovers, and then evaporates like a popped soap bubble, showering me with dust resembling armor.

Stepping slowly, attentive to noise, sight and smell, a Doe gingerly approaches me from behind, nuzzles the heart place on my back then jerks her head up alarmed, turns and trots off.

A Bear lumbers up on all fours, sits by me, and we lean toward each other while staring straight ahead. After a few minutes, the Bear growls, stands up to tower over me while roaring enough to shake the sky. It drops down to be on all fours, and runs off.

Nothing happens for the longest time. Maybe I sleep. Maybe I wake. When my consciousness gels, me, myself, and I are all present in the Blue. Blue skies, nothing but Blue skies, from now on.

A Cougar drops from the cedar tree and pads over to me. It sniffs me up and down. It eats from the bowl, noisily laps the water, then sits on its hind legs beside me and, out of gratitude, licks my cheek a couple times.

Cougar stands and nudges me gently with its wet nose. Trancelike, I rise up from the cliff with my legs still crossed. I land astride Cougar's back now with my legs down hugging both sides. I lean forward and grasp handfuls of the thick, soft fur of its neck like grasping an opponent's shirt in Jiu-Jitsu. Cougar walks off the cliff into space. The

Blue gradually changes to become an ethereal, metallic Yellow. We fly over golden Plains and snow capped Mountains until we are far from Land over an Ocean. Cougar rolls sideways, and I let go. I fall. Windless, I fall.

A breaching humpback Whale opens its mouth and swallows me. I sit in Easy Pose in Whale's head looking through my closed eyes and seeing out of Whale's mouth.

The Night Sky is filled with crystal clear Stars shimmering above us.

Whale sings a haunting Song to the Stars, combining high and low sounds simultaneously. Though not always "on key," it generates some exquisite Tuva harmonics causing Stars to coalesce into a River of Light that snakes down into the Ocean before us.

Whale swims up the River of Light. Near the top, individual Stars begin to separate out. Each Star becomes a Face of someone I know. The first is Serena. She is truly disembodied, simply her head. No, not even that, just a Face. That startles me. There is that cool look focused on me. Out of desperation, I try talking to her.

I ask, "What do you want from me, Serena?"

"For you to forgive me," she says.

That sounds way too simple.

"Anything else?" I ask.

"That's all," Serena answers.

Still I hesitate. She keeps staring at me, implacable.

I give it up.

"I... I... forgive you," I say

The result blows me away.

That cool presentation dissolves; the hard definitions in her Face soften. Serena begins to cry. I am amazed. That's it? That's it! Was it always this simple?

I wipe my own few tears and the next Star has moved to center stage. It's Doc. No way am I forgiving him for almost a lifetime of misery. Again, his Face is flat, unemotional.

I try wiping my eyes but he is still there. I try blinking my eyes open and shut. He won't go away; he stays and stays and stays.

OK, I tell myself, what is it going to cost you?

I say it out loud, "I forgive you, Dr. Washington."

Doc's flatly 2-dimensional Face immediately springs to life.

"I did the best I knew how," he tells me between sobs as he weeps for joy.

His reaction chokes me up. Who else have I kept at a distance with my "attitude"? I quickly find out.

I said it is a River of Stars. Every Star is someone from my life. One by one, People appear, many of whom I do not recognize.

"I helped your mom with your delivery," says one Woman.

"I forgive you," I say, though I have no idea for what.

"Thank you," she says.

"You're welcome," I tell her.

"You bumped into me while running to catch a bus," a Man says.

"I forgive you," I tell him.

I do?

"Thanks," he says all animated.

I guess I do.

An older Woman says, "I was your substitute teacher for one hour."

"I forgive you," I say.

"Thank you," she says. "You have grown."

"Next!" I insist.

This is hard enough to do without them gushing on.

More and more Stars separate from the River, become flat, lifeless Faces of People and tell me where we "know" each other. I forgive them. They light up become animated. The next one appears.

It seems the faster I move them through, the more there are. The line speeds up faster and faster. After a while I am aware of a change.

"I drive the bus you will ride from Phoenix to Los Angeles," a Man says.

I'm forgiving my future! I'm forgiving people I have yet to meet? There are lots of them.

I try being smarter.

"I forgive you all," I tell the approaching Stars. "Please, all of you, I beg you, forgive me."

That seems to do the trick. Whale swims over the top of the River and, now on the other side; we race back down to the Ocean. I am exhausted. I am exhilarated.

"Home, James," I image to Whale.

Either we think alike or we were already well on our way. A fast approaching shoreline is there, right in front of us. Whale doesn't slow down any and we stall out on almost dry sand. Whale's mouth opens. I step out as an enormous Wave hurls me further up the Beach, then, receding, pulls Whale back into the Ocean.

The sun in my eyes wakes me. I am lying on my side. As I stir myself, I glance over to the food and water. They are untouched. I stand stiffly. Once I can feel my blood pulsing through my joints, I slowly gather up my bundle items and prepare to leave.

I really appreciate that the return trip is downhill. Though I slip and slide a bunch, I know it is more out of excitement at completing the Vision Quest.

The smell of meat cooking on an open fire drives me even faster down the mountain.

"Avalanche!" I shout as I come tumbling and crashing through bushes and out to where Sun Path cooks her hunt over an open fire.

"Right on time for some delicious rabbit," she announces. "How are you?"

"Besides ravenously hungry?" I ask. "Fantastic!"

Sun Path grabs me by my shoulders and stands there checking me out from toe to head.

Smiling joyfully, I add, "Grateful!"

Sun Path smiles. Then she sees how my face is all bitten up.

"Let me treat those mosquito bites," she says.

Sun Path walks to the rippling stream, glistening as it reflects the bright sunlight.

I must be still "in that state" because the reflections become stars. Sun Path transforms to Orion as she scoops the Pleiades 7 Sisters. Then the flash is gone.

Sun Path treats my face with mud.

"As we eat," she says, dropping chunks of rare rabbit onto a plate for me. "Tell me your dream."

Between tearing off chunks of meat and swallowing, I recount what happened on the mountain. When I finish, Sun Path studies me for a while before saying anything.

"Do you have questions?" she eventually asks me.

I am curious to know the meaning of the animals. When we see an unusual creature while out on our walks, she typically tells me about it as part of the Wheel of Life. Each animal represents one stage we must each of us pass through.

"Bird at the beginning," she explains, "Represents the divine. By criss-crossing you like that; it says you are woven into Creator's plan, eternally."

"What about the mosquitoes and the hawks?" I ask her.

"They have meaning," she says, "Right now, let's only talk about your Vision. Then came Lizard, right? I believe it is important that you saw from behind. Lizard begins at your base and crawls up your spine, the very structure of you. He represents much, including renewal. By turning to dust, he is a magician teaching you to change your appearance. His body becomes your armor, your protection."

"Wow!" I say. "Then Deer."

"The female represents the sweetness of your heart," Sun Path tells me. "She touched your heart and thereby created your connection, a bonding, to the whole world."

"Bear," I say proudly.

"Good health and wellness embrace you," she says. "It is impossible to find a stronger protector in this life than Bear."

"Finally," I tell her, "Came Cougar."

"You're forgetting the largest of them all," she says.

"Right, right," I jump up shouting. "Whale! Please forgive me, Whale."

"Let's stay with the order in which they came so you feel their accumulating power," Sun Path tells me. "Cougar focuses on one objective. They follow their heart and have the highest integrity. They are keepers of the peace."

"Now Whale," I say.

"Make sure to absorb all the details of each creature," Sun Path instructs me. "They are all equally important as is every detail of your dream. Remember, your dream is our dream. You dream for everyone, everything: the reservation, the country, and the entire universe. I tell that to you because of what Whale represents.

"They show us that our power is in being harmonious, balanced and giving. It is so important that Whale sang in your presence. You will always remember that song. It unified the sky above and the water below. That song you heard has the power to rearrange the very stars in the sky. Consider how intense that is."

I am humbled by the thought that I am a conduit from Great Spirit.

"You are only able to dream like that because you allowed yourself to be prepared," Sun Path breaks into my thoughts. "We are all special when we allow Great Spirit to guide us. We are also all equal, those who do the dreaming and those who do the listening. Make sure to always remember that."

As we approach the house, Red Wing sees us approaching and runs full pelt at us. She has good news. She stretches her arms out in front. Reaching us, she loops her hands around my neck and throws me into a whirling dance with her, our faces pulled close together.

"I forgive you," she yells at me, her face bright with laughter. "I forgive you, I forgive you, I forgive you."

As she slows down and we can stop, I grasp her arms and look into her eyes with deep seriousness.

"And I forgive you," I tell her.

"I know," she shouts. "Everybody knows. Why do you think we call it Echo Mountain? We heard every detail for four days. We are so proud of you. We love you."

With that she leaps into my arms and hugs me so I cannot breathe. That sure is a change. I notice I am much more serious, stable, grounded. I like the new me.

A few days later, the women from my Brazilian Jiu-Jitsu class organize a get together in White Dove's home. It turns into a Gifting ceremony. White Dove holds up the quilt I made to display it. Several women go right up close and check out my stitch work. They are suitably impressed. They ought to be. If it did not meet White Dove's standard of excellence, she had no qualms about cutting through my stitching and having me do it again until it was perfect. She nudges me in the ribs.

"Who are you gifting with this exquisite quilt?" she asks me.

Well, I'm not thinking of anyone. I had plans to keep it for myself.

I look to her for a clue and she crosses her eyes as if to say, "C'mon, dummy. Give it up, girl!"

I turn to the group of expectant faces and start folding the quilt.

"I never did much sewing beyond replacing buttons," I tell them. "So, when I saw what beautiful work I did with this quilt, I planned to keep it for myself and maybe give the next one away."

The looks of abject horror that I would even consider that idea tells me to speed it up and cut the humor.

"When it was decided I am to stay here, Sun Path graciously gave up her bed for me and has slept on the Mother all this time," I say pointedly at her. "Hopefully, soon, I will learn why I came here and leave your bed for you again. So that you will have a part of me with you in your dreams, please wrap yourself in this quilt."

With that I hand her the folded quilt. She rises to accept it and gives me the longest hug.

As she pulls away, she tells me, "Thank you for your gift. This means a great deal to me. Sadly, I have good news for you, Judith. When you first arrived we told you, you had come to learn forgiveness, to forgive everyone. Well, my Sister, you have done what you came here for and, tomorrow... I sleep in my own bed again... with my new quilt."

The response is mixed. Sun Path's Native American humor raises some smiles and hand clapping. The imminence of my departure hits me like a 2x4 up the side of the head. Here I am settling in and it is time to move, again. As is my wont, I have not given any thought to where I am to go. I do resolve not to do what I did at Taquinta. I am going to show these people due respect and honor their hospitality.

"Now," announces White Dove, "Since you are leaving, Judith, we want our clothes back."

A bunch of women rise to their feet and grab my hands to prevent me from fighting back as they remove the blouse and skirt.

"Then I want my coveralls that I wore when I came here," I insist.

"Negotiate that with Sun Path," White Dove tells me. "Where do you think some of the quilting pieces came from?"

I am stunned. I thought they looked familiar but they were such small pieces I never made the connection. My arms gather about me more and more tightly as I struggle to maintain propriety in just my undergarments.

"Then what am I going to wear?" I ask with a plaintive voice.

With a flourish, White Dove produces a white, brain tanned, leather blouse and skirt with tassels along every seam.

"Try this on," she says. "It may be your size."

Of course, it is precisely my size and designed to fit me perfectly. Though I feel like Annie Oakley in this outfit, I look different and special. I can live with that.

Best of all, the ladies, to a one, all approve. There follows a mighty hug fest.

On the frontage road off the res, we are about to commence our tearful farewells, when along comes Sky Hawk in his truck. Laid out on the bed under wraps is an enormous deer with an absolutely huge rack of horns.

"It's an elk," he tells me. "We have Brothers who raise them."

There is something comforting about knowing my family has meat for the winter.

"I'm glad I made it back in time," Sky Hawk says as he ferrets about and comes up with the heart of his kill and hands it to me carefully wrapped. "My Sister, this is for your journey."

I hug him. I hug White Dove, Red Wing and a final hold of an outstretched hand of Tree Dancer. Finally, the most difficult farewell is with Sun Path.

"My Sister," she tells me as we hold hands at arms' length, "This has been a good year. You are well learned in our ways. Use them to be of service. Be a Lizard warrior, a Cougar guardian of the Mother. May Spirit walk with you."

She and I hug briefly and turn away from each other quickly.

As I set out, I have the sensation that Dr. Michael Kaliban walks with me. He better walk fast. I break into Long Stride.

PRODIGAL

Michael doesn't keep up. I am aware of his stumbling efforts to maintain, but every time I initiate a conversation he says nothing and drops further back. I am left to guess that he is somewhere between there and here.

Most certainly, I am not. I'm a girl on a mission.

The road into Taquinta is worse than I remember it. Wheel ruts seem deeper, with sizable potholes, many of them holding water from a recent rainfall. The space between the ruts is brittle, refusing weeds a chance to grow. The sign at the entrance has had some of the letters crudely painted out.

Now, it reads:

I ATE
RO D

It makes somebody happy to have it like that.

Almost as if, when I ran out of here, I had turned around right away and walked back in, Dada and Didi are at the exact same spot working the field, backs to the road. Upon reflection, that makes sense. It must be about a year to the day.

Their instincts are as good as ever. As I stride along, tassels flying, they spin around as one to stare at me as if seeing an apparition. I watch them sign to each other.

"Who is that on the road?" Didi asks.

Dada answers, "She walks like Judith."

Simultaneously, they concur, "It IS Judith!"

Grabbing up their shovels, they run down to the road ahead of me where, off to the side, rusting, car after car, angled nose down, are stacked symmetrically against each other, roof to transmission. The Twins rhythmically bang on the sides of the cars with their shovels.

Breaking my Long Stride walk, I run to greet them. They are looking good, different. They neither of them wear coveralls. They are clearly in work clothes but more stylish and not identical. Their clothes help distinguish their few physical differences.

As I fly into their waiting arms, I remember to prepare for their bone crushing hugs.

"Ooooh!" I gasp as each hugs me in turn.

My return hug to them must be slight by comparison.

That's when I notice a more recent sign, as yet, not tampered with.

It reads:

TAQUINTA:
SUGAR FREE ZONE

"Good to see you," I sign. "I missed you. I like the new sign. In my honor?"

They grin and shrug ignorance.

They skip, dance and cavort about me as I stride toward the Piazza. Seeing Dada and Didi whirling around me, as we pass them, other women join in. Every last one of them is stand out different, perfect. They come in colors, like a rainbow. I feel like a queen bee in the midst of a swarm when the beehive relocates.

We pass domes, each of them with a satellite dish attached.

Somehow word gets ahead, because, as we arrive at the Piazza, Maisha and Serena, dressed to the nines, are waiting to make formal greeting.

We perform the Maori forehead and nose press. This time, as I part from Maisha, I see where the challenge had been the first time; it was my competitive nature refusing to allow another to lead me. This time I see us as equals, different in the worlds we inhabit, but of a much-ness.

Maisha stands by while Serena and I greet.

Serena comes at me intrigued. She is animated like in my Vision. That first meeting when Lucy and I arrived, I was fearful of Serena. I am no longer intimidated by her. I have found myself. Serena is herself. We neither of us challenge the other. Like old home week, our greeting is long and languorous. We separate, deeply intimate.

"Oh, my!" she tells me. "Have you ever blossomed."

The two of them appear to be in heaven when they make brief eye contact after Serena and I separate.

Maisha faces the chattering hordes that gather excitedly in the Piazza. She raises one hand in the air and a hush falls about the assembly. I note that no one else raises a hand this time.

"One of our own returns," Maisha announces. "When Judith Fargoe first came here, it was on our terms. Today, she returns on her terms. That is truly cause for celebration! We shall dine and party on the Piazza starting 6 o'clock. See you all then."

Serena catches me lightly by the arm to get my attention.

"I will make up a tray for you, right now," she tells me. "Give me about fifteen minutes then check your place in the Commissary."

"My place in the Commissary." It was as if I never left. These are unbelievable emotional hugs being bestowed on me.

I nod my understanding and appreciation as my eyes scan the departing crowd.

When most everyone is gone, there, across the empty Piazza stands a forlorn, blonde haired waif of a cowgirl holding hands with a toddler beside her looking up at her, watching his mom for a clue as to why they are waiting.

I must resemble some fantastic bird as I run across the Piazza, tassels flying, screaming at the top of my lungs, "LUCYYYYYY!"

I swoop Lucy off her feet and, fortunately, Mika and she let go of each other, because I swing her round and round, showering her with kisses as I blubber at her.

"I love you," I tell her. "I missed you. I prayed you are both safe. Did you feel me when I meditated? Oh, Lucy, I came back to see you. Lucy?"

I realize that one person has yet to forgive me. I step back and wait as she and Mika hold hands once more, and she prepares to speak. It takes her a long time to assemble her thoughts.

"I'm less spontaneous these days," she says. "Yer left, Jude. Yer just left."

This is going to be long and painful. If I mess this up, it's over, permanently. I resolve to keep my tongue in check.

Lucy kneels down and straightens Mika's clothes as if performing a meditation, then picks him up in her arms. I see that he is studiously watching both of us in turn.

"Everyone seemed to know what was gonna happen 'cept yer an' me," she says. "We were in some separate world. I liked where we were, but it had ter stop. Did yer have ter leave like that? I waited till today ter hear from yer. Jude? Yer broke my heart. An' what's worse of all, yer pod was empty so Sidney moved in. She's a maniac, Jude! Yer left me ter share the home yer an' me built wi' a lunatic. I cursed yer, Jude. I am amazed at what I knew how to curse yer out, an' I have yet ter learn Arabic."

She stops talking. Tears are streaming down her cheeks. Mika stares at me accusingly. I think the child understood every word said. I am speechless. Maybe we have been apart too long but it felt like Lucy was making a joke at the end about my sticking her with Sidney.

"I need to eat," I tell her. "If you have the time, you'll sit with me while I eat?"

"Have the time?" Lucy yells at me. "Have the time, Jude? Yer stuck wi' us forever. When yer eat, work, sleep an' go ter the bathroom. D'yer understand? Now, are yer gonna hold Mika? Kid's bin waitin' an' waitin' while we yap."

She holds Mika out to me and he puts out two hands for me. I take him in my arms and we look deep into each other's eyes. I jokingly offer a Maori press and he closes his eyes and leans in to me. We touch forehead and nose and I feel as if I am watching a nuclear explosion. The kid downloads data to me at such speed; Maisha's first contact feels as slow as semaphore by comparison.

When we separate, he looks at me as much as to say, "This is just a beginning. Welcome home."

I look over at Lucy. She definitely sees the shock written on my face.

She nods her head as much as to say, "I told yer so!"

At the Commissary, I park them at a table while I go pick up my tray. All I ate on the walk was the elk heart. By now I am ready for some variety.

The orange tray is waiting for me. The meal prepared is identical, down to the last detail, of the very last meal I ate before I left the Institute. That word sounds judgmental. I resolve to drop using it. This meal... the last meal... they're identical. If Serena made this one, then... Serena made my last meal—she made every one of my meals since the "incident." This is insane. It makes no sense to me at all.

I take Serena down and threaten her life, and she turns around to make me some of the best prepared food I have ever eaten? I literally cannot wrap my head round what this means. I race back to my niece and... Mika... and tell them what I just worked out.

Lucy is simply glad to have me back. She can care less about the details.

Mika catches my eye and, I could swear nods his head, as much as to say, "Welcome to the New World Order."

I can barely eat I am in such a state of shock about Serena being the mystery chef.

While I do eat, worker bees frantically decorate the Piazza. I comment to Lucy about how people are dressed. She laughs.

"They are in their work clothes," she says. "Wait'll you see 'em dressed up to party. Then yer'll ask who let the dogs in."

By 6 o'clock, the Piazza is festooned with paper lamps. People are seated at long tables and benches. Others serve food or dance or make music.

At the head table, in a Last Supper tableau, when Mika stops breast feeding, Lucy passes him to me to burp. Once he is in my arms, I feel as if he is in the center of us all, even facing over my shoulder. He is one present kid.

I expect a formal event to start things rolling, but the event is the event. The Elders are scattered among the different tables and having more fun that I can remember seeing before. The atmosphere is very different. I put it down to the clothes. People have been dressed. This is not accidental prêt a porter grab bag coincidence. Someone has gone through Taquinta and fortified everybody's wardrobe with color, fabric and design. Best of all, people wear exactly what "works" on them, all the time—work, leisure and play. Everyone is who they are. The change impacts the Taquinta concept so well—it works!

All around me, I am picking up the same buzz I got from Serena. Everybody is centered and operating optimally. If I were not seeing it in the flesh, I never would have believed it to be possible.

The music switches to Middle Eastern with heavy emphasis on hand drums. A rhythmic chink of castanets, tambourines and tiny metal bells announces a line of belly dancers that winds between the tables.

As they weave and sway past me, one of the dancers leans in to surprise me. It's Sidney. Her mouth makes a wide grin of pleasure at catching me unawares and she dances off with an extra flourish.

The music ends and Maisha stands at her table and raises a hand for quiet.

"This afternoon, the Elders met in the Togu Na to discuss the ongoing issue of naming our Library. We agreed we would like to name it to honor one of its builders, financiers and, since she has returned to us, our own Prodigal Daughter. If she will accept our naming it after her, we intend to call it the Judith Fargoe Library. What do you say, Judith?"

I seem to always be on a different wavelength to Maisha when she makes one of her pronouncements. Until the very end I look around wondering whom she is speaking about. It takes a dig in the ribs from Lucy to help me struggle to my feet and be present.

Mika rouses from dozing on my shoulder and makes it very clear that he wants to move. I assume he wants to go back to his mom so I grasp him and start moving him off my shoulder. He wraps his arms about my neck and clings on. I guess I interpreted him wrongly, too. What he wants is to be held close, up high and facing everybody. His presence commands everyone to look at us.

"Wow!" I say.

That raises some giggles around me.

"Financier?" I ask Lucy in a whisper.

"Yer gave 'em ten grand, auntie," she tells me, loudly.

"Ten thousand... dollars?" I repeat. "I did?"

"That's my auntie for you," she says. "Easy come, easy go."

"You'll have to forgive me," I tell everyone. "I am recently returned... from...."

I remember Sun Path telling me that Vision Quest, Sweat Lodge and some other rituals we engaged in are not always properly understood outside Native American circles, so it is considered smart not to talk about them in public.

"I am recently returned from a trip," I say, "A back country trip. I'm a little spacey. Yeah, well, thank you. That's an amazing recognition; to have a library named after me. I guess I had better go check it out now that it will have my name on it. By the way, do people read books anymore? The last time I visited a working library it was mostly computers and DVDs. Times change. What else do you expect from me?"

Maisha and many of the Elders have walked to where I am, while I speak.

Maisha says, "You appear to consider yourself as ordinary, sometimes less than that, Judith. Take a moment and give us an insight into your core beliefs. I think people will benefit from hearing what makes you tick."

Mika turns his head to watch my reaction to Maisha. I feel like the ventriloquist being manipulated by my dummy. As soon as I begin talking, he looks front.

"As I was about to leave, last time," I say, "Lea encouraged me to seek my Holy Grail. I thought she was referring to a physical object. During my recent trip, much about me has changed, hopefully some of it for the better.

"One thing I did learn is that, for me, the Grail is the courage to live my life in gratitude. With the help of my Sisters, Brothers and Ancestors, I endeavor to stay conscious of what food I feed my body. When I dream, I attempt to dream lucidly so I may be in conscious learning mode. And, I strive for only positive thoughts. With those three tenets is how I choose to live my life. Does that answer your question, Maisha?"

"Oh, yes," she says. "Judith Fargoe, you are truly a woman of whom we can be proud."

Maisha addresses the Assembly. "Sadly, tomorrow, Judith leaves us," she tells everyone.

Mika turns to look at Lucy. I am glad he does because I don't have the heart to. When he bursts into tears, I hand him back to her.

"Yer missin' a fourth tenet, Jude," she tells me, bitterly. "Integrity."

It's like movie night at the Commissary! Women are yelling and screaming at me.

"Judith, stay!" some shout.

"Where'll you go?" ask others.

Hurt to the quick by Lucy's comment, I feel myself project a mask as I face my fans.

"Where Spirit calls me," I tell them.

Maisha signals for quiet.

"To send Judith on her way with strength," she says to the crowd, "We will do a Heart Set in the morning. You are all invited to make it a powerful send off. Right now, please join as we share our blessing with our Daughter."

Maisha and the assembled women close their eyes and rub their hands together.

Maisha leads by saying, "Inhale, exhale, inhale deeply to begin..."

Everyone sings together:

"May the long time Sun shine upon You.
All Love surround You.
And the Pure Light within You,
Guide Your way on!
Guide Your way on!
Guide Your way on!"

There is a long silence broken by Mika's crying in the arms of a depressed Lucy.

Women stand as Chrystal takes me by the hand and leads me to an open space. She waves her hand in wide circles overhead in a come-hither gesture. A crowd swells about us, closing in on us. The women crowd us to form a group hug. Some people hum, some reach out and touch me, stroke me, curl my hair loosely about a finger. It's an intense time. Then it stops.

As the women disperse, Chrystal restrains me. Nearby tables and benches are cleared. Chrystal and I are standing at the entrance of a 1:1 copy of the Chartre's Cathedral Labyrinth which has been painted on the Piazza.

Chrystal explains, "As you enter, clear your thoughts. At the center, make your intention, and, meditate on it as you exit."

Most people have left now. Lucy, teary eyed, holding a quieted Mika, sits by Sidney, still in costume, and several Elders including Lea and Serena. They watch Chrystal and me. Despite my feelings of confusion in reaction to what Lucy said to me, I endeavor to radiate power and confidence as I walk into the Labyrinth.

At the center, I have accumulated enough thoughts. I ask Great Spirit to give my tongue the strength to tell the truth with confidence. Walking out is similar to Vision Quest; I am so spacey when I emerge.

Chrystal follows me out and I turn and give her a hug in thanks.

As we separate, I ask her, "Can we do the leaving ceremony?"

"What do you have in mind?" she asks me. "You know you make it up, like a dream?"

"You sly fox!" I say. "Then, my dream is to leave like, *Lawrence of Arabia*, when they leave the village to cross the desert, and the women ululate."

We walk over to where the others are gathered. Sidney's current friend is snuggling with her.

Lucy, slightly recovered, tells me, "Sidney says you can have her bed for tonight."

"Thank you, Sidney," I tell her.

"Es de nada, Judee," she says.

I am ready to hit the hay. The last few days walking, plus all of today's happenings, has worn me out.

Early next morning, Serena insists on having me beside her as she leads 140 women, each on a mat on the Piazza, sitting in Easy Pose, eyes closed, rubbing their hands together to warm up.

She has us sit on one heel, with the other leg extended forward. Then we switch legs. She has us sit with legs crossed, flexing our backs. With hands together in prayer mode overhead, elbows bent, we do torso twists from side to side. On all fours, we stretch one leg backwards, point the toes while the forehead touches the ground, and return to all fours where we switch legs and repeat the positions. Again on all fours, one foot arches back to touch the arched back of the head, then drop the leg down and head down bringing the knee forward to touch the forehead, then switch legs and repeat the exercise. We sit on our heels with arms outstretched, lean forward to touch the forehead to the ground. We do archer pose with deep knee bend for both legs. Finally, we sit on our heels, palms resting on the knees.

Then comes my favorite part where we rest on our backs with a light blanket for cover and listen while Serena plays a Universal gong.

Women pick up their belongings and head off into their day. Serena holds my hands in hers, looking into my eyes.

She tells me, "The other day, I woke up knowing you had forgiven me."

"As recently as yesterday," I tell her, "You made my tray of food with incredible love and care, the way you did right after I attacked you. Why would you do that?"

"To let you know you are deeply loved," Serena explains. "You attacked me because you felt estranged. Impacting your food was the best way to change you."

"It worked," I say. "Thank you so much."

"Friend?" she asks me.

"Truly a friend, Serena," I tell her.

"Only a best friend will make you perform at the top of your game, however unpleasant that may feel, you know?" she says. "I really hurt when you left."

"You were right to let me go, though," I admit. "Staying here would keep me dependent. My question is, is Taquinta truly self sufficient now, as Maisha intended?"

"Really, it was always my objective for Taquinta," she tells me. "Maisha is sympathetic, but still something of a disbeliever. Your donation gave us breathing room. Thank you for that. Then, out of the blue, money rolled in, in large and small sums."

"I join you to give thanks to the Blue," I answer. "It seems every baby brings its own wealth. Tell me about the absence of uniform and what's with the satellite dishes on every dome."

"A color and design specialist vacationed here soon after you left," Serena tells me. "She suggested that if people were full time dressed to reflect their true self they will work better. We had her assess everyone and design their wardrobe. The change here was so intense, three months ago it felt like we were pushed over the top. We did a mass spoon bend to see if we were of a mind. 98 of 126 flopped over. We opted out of money right there and then.

"Of course, there were detractors. To appease Maisha and a couple other skeptics, we have donors standing by to rescue us. So far so good, we have stayed off the safety net. I truly believe we are on our way.

"As for the satellite dishes, all I can say is, pick your fights. Now, give me five minutes to teach you EFT. Know that the more you practice it, the clearer you will become."

True to her word, Serena leaves five minutes later. Still wrapped in my blanket, I am "Tapping" on one of my issues. Lea stops by with a rolled up, plastic cloth under her arm.

"Judith," she says. "I want to give you a metaphysical claptrap energy gift."

"After insulting you so, Lea," I respond, "How can I refuse such a generous offer?"

Like a carpet salesman, Lea rolls out the canvas on the ground. It's a blue, plastic tarp, about eight feet by twelve, with a Kabalistic *Tree of Life* painted on it. The tree is drawn in a graphic representation with a trunk and three pairs of branches. It has ten points in circles numbered from one to ten marked on it.

Lea has me stand below number one which is the top of the tree and between 2 and 3 which are the first branches down. Using copper divining rods, Lea assesses my dominant Chakra and influencing directions. No surprise that it is four for the heart and that I take more easily than I give. I promise Lea I will change that.

"Make them equal," she says. "Seek balance in all things."

Lea has me remove my ring so that she may pray over it with a pendulum. When Lea returns the ring to me, I react as if shocked by electricity.

She tells me, "Your ring needed clearing from prior owners. Now it is all yours. Your ring and Chakras are aligned. That's all the metaphysical claptrap I have for one day."

After Lea wraps up her tarp, I give her a long hug for the Tree, the Social Sciences, BJJ and her literacy. She stops me.

"I am going to miss you, Judith," she says. "I wish we had a life time to learn about each other. You have been a tonic for me."

Chrystal and Petrina arrive in time to rescue me from drowning in my own tears.

Petrina invites me, "Join us for one last meal before you go."

The three of us head for the Commissary. I drop off my blanket and pad at the office and then we go over to the food line. Serena has been in the kitchen again and has prepared me the most elegant plate of raw meat strips, pads of butter and a glass of green juice with cream.

We take our food to a table and huddle together. It is such a privilege to have my meals prepared for me. I make sure to relish every bite. Who knows when I will be this blessed again?

"It is wonderful to see you so changed for the good," Petrina tells me. "We were deeply concerned for your well being."

"Well," I say. "I feel like I can finally *see*."

"You had to struggle with a lot of demons," Chrystal explains. "To some people your current level of awareness comes easily and early. For most of us, the Veil only gets lifted later in life."

"If at all," Petrina adds.

"How long will this clarity last?" I ask them.

"That's the real blessing," Petrina says. "It remains with you forever."

"What do I do with all this new energy?" I ask.

"Put yourself in overdrive and floor the gas pedal," Chrystal shouts, attracting attention. "Forget the brakes!"

I have never driven anything more powerful than a fixed gear bicycle.

"... What if I crash?" I say with alarm.

"Pick yourself up and floor the gas pedal," Petrina states.

"That's all there is to being alive!" Chrystal says.

"A fast car and a hot rod driver," Petrina adds, with a wink.

The two of them break into hoots of hysterical laughter. I sit and watch them. They look at me and endeavor to sober up.

Petrina says, "Brmm-brmm."

The two of them fold up laughing. It's infectious.

Women all around us start imitating them, "Brmm, brmm."

Soon everybody is laughing hysterically.

All I can do is look at my two Elders and tell them, "You girls are baaad!"

I start to pick up my tray as Chrystal, trembling from laughing, lays a hand on my wrist.

"I'll take care of it," she says. "You go get ready."

"Thanks," I say.

A wall has risen. I will never know how much I was ever really part of this community, but suddenly I know they are distinctly a part of my past.

TRANSITION

The blinds are down at "our" dome as I tiptoe in. Lucy and Mika are cuddled up in their pod.

I go over to them. Mika lays there quietly watching me.

"Lucy?" I say.

She doesn't move. To me she feels depressed. I shake her gently.

"Jude?"

"I'm leaving. I wanted to say goodbye and thank you."

"Why do yer have ter leave? This place is so dull wi'out yer."

"Come with me."

"Where?"

"We'll explore possibilities."

"Stay here."

"There are things I have to do."

"Do them here."

"Come find me when you're ready."

"What a friend yer've turned out ter be. Yer'll head off the map, ag'in. Then how'm I supposed ter find yer?"

"I'll send you a sign. Give me a hug."

Lucy clambers out so she and I can do a Maori press. As we part, eyes tearing up, Lucy slips three bottles of essential oil wrapped in a

Franklin into my jacket pocket.

"Money's useless here, now," she says. "Call it protection."

There's no use arguing with her. I take it in the spirit it is given.

"Thank you," I say.

Mika stretches his hands out to me. I pick him up and give him a long hug.

As I hand him to Lucy, she asks him, "What d'yer have ter say ter Jude here, mister Mika?"

He looks at me as much as to say, I'm not a performing animal.

"Mika love Jude," he says.

I am startled, thrilled, over whelmed.

"Well, I'll be," Lucy says. "What we worked on was, "Bye, Jude." Seems he's got a mind of his own."

"I wonder who supplied that gene," I tell her.

I approach Mika in his mom's arm and plunk a kiss on his cheek. A small hand rubs the spot.

"Jude loves Mika," I tell him.

He turns away and snuggles into his mom.

"And," I tell Lucy, "Jude loves Lucy."

"As much as Lucy loves Jude?" she asks.

We kiss each other on the cheek and I race out of there. Talk about magnetic attraction. I regret not being able to be around to be an active part of Mika's growing up.

Maisha catches up with me as I head for the Piazza.

"Let me walk you quickly through the Library," she says.

I pinch myself to make sure one of us is real. I am.

No longer a construction site, as with our dome, the library is a shock for me to behold as a finished product. Putting in book shelves and filling them with books, having tables to work at and chairs on which to sit and read, it was like Creator breathing life into the child to whom Lucy gave birth the way our crude construction came to life and is now a real, functioning library. I stand in the middle twirling slowly, taking in the details and gasping in admiration.

To slam the point home, Maisha whispers in my ear, "We call it the

Judith Fargoe Library."

My brain does summersaults and pretzel entanglements, simultaneously, as I struggle to contain the emotions and reactions inside my head. I know that anybody looking at me at that instant would see unfurling streamers pop out of my skull while people blow on kazoos. Walking out of there, attempting to retain any semblance of dignity, is purely imaginary.

Maisha escorts me toward the Commissary. Along the way, we encounter, and I receive farewell hugs from, Zichrini and Hazar. My intellectual stork, Lea, blows me a kiss as she hurries by. Lael runs over and hugs me. It's hard for me to place everyone now they are dressed in "their colors." I know them, except, now I know them better.

Sophia and Yen Lu walk with us for a few steps, and then stop to hug me and wish me well. That intrigues me. I feel that by traveling I am immensely flexible but Taquinta has to stay in one place and adapt. Aren't they more in need of my well wishes than am I of theirs?

Chrystal and Petrina are leaving the Commissary as we arrive.

They are still giggly.

In the spirit of our previous conversation, I say, "Brmm-brmm."

They fold with laughter.

Maisha asks me, "What did you say that was so funny?"

"You had to have been there," I tell her.

Desperately trying to be in a sober mood, Chrystal does her imitation of a British military officer saluting with arched back.

"Wishing you good luck and all the best, Captain Lawrence."

I go over and hug her, then Petrina. The distance I felt earlier now has reached a need to handle an emotional break. I kiss them each on the cheek. They separate from me to go about their work.

"You made some extraordinary alliances here, Judith," Maisha tells me. "Unlike anyone else I know."

That knocks me for six.

Serena meets us and presents me with a similar portable ice chest as I had received from Rachel. This one is filled with enough food for two days.

Maisha holds out some cash.

"Here's your 80 bucks," she says.

"For what?" I ask.

Maisha explains, "Change on the 100 Betsy earned and from the candy. The good old days?"

"OK, I will take that," I agree.

Serena makes it clear, she is not coming out with me, and Maisha does the same. I guess this is it. We hug and hold hands looking at each for long, breathless pauses. Then I am on my way.

Off in the distance, as I exit the Commissary, I can hear rhythmic banging. It draws me to it. Until I arrive at the road out by the fields, there are so many women who come up to shake my hand, give me hugs and wish me well all I can do is walk slowly.

When I reach them, Didi and Dada, the source of the banging, drop their shovels and approach me with tearful earnestness. I breathe deeply as I head into the first of two intense hugs. This time they are both of them gentle and sensitive to me. I kiss each in turn on both cheeks. They wave their arms in the air as if conducting.

Along the ridge that runs next to the road, women appear waving silk scarves as they trill. The effect is magical and sears down my spine ending up as tingling in my feet and hands.

I wave to them and the sound grows louder.

I step away from my fans and prepare to Long Stride.

A beat up, green, 4 door sedan rolls along, slowly, beginning to pass me up as it and I diligently negotiate the ruts and potholes. A back window is open. Sidney, in full Drama King fashion, leans way out twirling a flower seductively.

"'Ey, baby face," she calls to me. "Take ride wiz us. Give you real good time; cero worries, cero 'assle, cero dinero. What you say?"

"Bye, Sidney," I tell her. "Without the shadow of a doubt, I'll remember you."

Sidney twists her head to talk to her driver.

"What she says?" she asks.

Her driver tells her, "You are out of luck."

Sidney turns back to face me, now with both hands outstretched reaching for me. Both the car and I are struggling not to misstep on this treacherous road while Sidney manifests her fantasy.

"As you say, Judee, Judee, Judee," she says plaintively sliding back inside the car. "Hasta la vista, senorita!"

As the car gradually pulls ahead of me, I wish them farewell.

"Hasta luego," I shout.

Lurching forward, the car picks up speed and heads down the road.

Sidney, still screeching, "Ai-yai-yaiee! Un que senorita hermosa!" inside the car, fades as women still running along the cliff trill ever louder.

I am unable to repress a smile as I pick up speed Long Stride walking down the road.

The trills thin out.

Alone at last, I feel a sense of freedom unlike anything I have ever felt before.

I stride into Casper, this time proudly walking the streets. I enter the General Store.

The owner barely gives me a glance.

"Howdy," he says. "Let me know if you want help."

"Does the bus stop here?" I ask.

He perks up.

"Going east or west?" he asks.

"Whichever comes first," I respond, as I glance with disinterest at the candy.

"I can get you west," he tells me. "If you pay cash right now, I'll call him off the highway. How far d'you wanna go?"

"Up to one hundred eighty dollars," I answer.

"Must be real bad, huh?" he asks.

"Real good," I tell him.

I drop all my cash on the counter.

"How far will this get me?"

"California, Santa Monica," he says, staring at me. "You remind me of someone. Do I know you?"

"What difference if you do?" I say. "I'm taking it one way. Call the bus so I can get on out of here."

"Yes, ma'am," he says.

He rifles through his tickets wrapped with a rubber band, and pulls one out and hands it to me.

"Make sure the driver sees this. OK?"

"What driver?" I snap. "We're talking like the bus is coming tomorrow. Call the bus!"

He jumps to it. He picks up a Smart phone and works the screen, clumsily, same as I did. It may take till tomorrow before he works out how to place a call.

The speaker rings loud enough to wake the dead. A crackly voice comes on.

"Yello!" the voice says.

"Gerry," the shopkeeper tells the phone. "I got you a ride here in Casper."

"Hold on, folks," the voice cuts in. "Gee, Tony, that were cuttin' it fine. We near missed yer exit. We'll be out front in five. Be ready to go or we're gone."

"You hear, miss?" Tony tells me. "Make sure you got your luggage... ready... you got anything beside that little bag?"

"That's it," I say. "I am leaving in a hurry."

"I tell you what," Tony offers. "Anybody comes asking about you, I'll tell them you went east."

"You're a saint," I tell him as I lean over the counter, grab him by the shirt and, pulling him to me, plunk a kiss on his cheek.

He pulls back stunned, nurturing where I kissed him.

I walk to the door, turn for a moment and tell him, "The last time you saw me was a year ago. You threatened if you saw my face ever again, you'll call the sheriff. Time to get on the phone and make that call."

I walk out as the beat up, green, 4 door sedan cruises by, stops, backs up to parallel park with me. Sidney leans precariously out of the window, twirling the flower.

"Ai yai yaiee!" she calls to me, sweetly. "What say you, Lady? Yes?"

"Yes, Sidney," I tell her. "You're quite the lady. I'm taking the first bus out of here."

A despondent Sidney sighs dramatically.

"Okey-dokey," she says, resigned to the facts. "Ai-yai-yaiee! Andiamo, amiga!"

"Take good care of Lucy," I shout after her. "Bye, Sidney."

A hand pops out of her window briefly and waves an acknowledging flourish.

A bus trundles into town to stop right by me. The front door folds open. I bid farewell to a lifetime and cross the bridge from stationary to motion.

To rephrase Maisha; I came on their terms, but I left on mine.

ON THE ROAD

I had no idea that leaving Lucy... Taquinta... the old me... is going to be so difficult.

Parting is NOT sweet sorrow. It's downright emotionally painful and exhausting.

I find myself churning through memories alternating with attempts to forget, move on, and be present now. Breathing rhythmically helps.

Riding the bus, I sleep erratically, slipping in and out of consciousness. It's as though I do not trust my lucid dreaming ability; that I may default into some prior dream. I don't.

The bus keeps on rolling. Outside, beyond the window, is seamless friendly desert, unlike driving to Taquinta with Lucy when the desert was an unknown, a barren, inhospitable environment. Now, I spot plants, animals and land formations that reveal the desert to me as if reading a book, a thrilling book that I choose to read.

The bus stops in Gallup, releases a few passengers and acquires some additional ones. As he passes driver Gerry, an embarking young boy greets him like an old friend. They Hi 5 each other. The boy strides down the aisle checking out the seats to his right, the side on which I sit, my left as I face Gerry's back. The boy checks who sits on this side seeking a specific seating arrangement. When he reaches me he stops.

"Excuse me, ma'am," he asks, indicating the aisle seat next to me. "Is this seat available?"

"It certainly is," I tell him. "Would you prefer the window seat? We can switch."

He sits, and pushes his travel bag under the seat ahead of him.

"I always sit on an aisle seat," he says, extending his hand. "My name is Xavier."

We shake hands.

"Hi," I say. "I'm Judith. May I ask how old you are, Xavier?"

"I'll be ten in four weeks, ma'am," he says. "I'm going to visit my grandparents."

"Your dad's folks?" I ask.

"My mom's," he corrects me. "I spend a weekend a month plus vacations with them, 'cos, see, like, my mom, you know, she took off, and, like disappeared when I was small and everything. You know?"

"That must hurt lots to talk about it," I say.

"I kind of swallow hard," he says. "I'm good at doing that now."

"I learned how to reduce my pain by doing something called tapping," I tell him. "May I show you what I do?"

The bus pulls out of Gallup and back onto the highway as my new found friend and I work on distancing ourselves from some of our emotional issues.

"So give me a number from one to ten how you feel," I ask him.

"It feels like a one," he says. "I thought I will live with that hurt forever. Thank you."

"You are so very welcome," I say. "Tell me, Xavier, what is there to see along here?"

"By Winslow," he tells me, growing excited, "There's a huge crater."

I watch him become invested in his explanation.

"Millions and millions of years ago," he relates, "This huge rock—at least hundreds of feet across, covered in craters—traveled across Space, and came blazing through the Earth's atmosphere and smashed into us—KERBLOOWEE!—making a crater a half mile deep."

Between his narrative becoming louder and his gestures more and more expansive, Xavier's excitement has several nearby passengers' attention. He grows aware that he has become the main entertainment. Embarrassed, his hands in his lap, he drops his voice to a whisper.

"Astronauts do stuff there before going into Space," he concludes. "My dad's taking me to visit the crater for my birthday."

"How wonderful is that?" I say.

My exhaustion from the past few days is catching up with me. Being next to such charged energy as Xavier brings that awareness home.

"I'm going to nap," I tell him. "I am interested to see the crater. Please wake me when we are near."

"Sure" he acknowledges. "You know you smell real nice."

"Why, thank you," I answer. "It's myrtle oil."

"Are you a cowboy?" he asks.

"Xavier," I say. "I want to nap. I will answer one more question and then I'm taking a time out. Do you understand me on that?"

"Yeah," he says. "You look like Kit Carson. That's why I asked."

"There were a lot of women who opened up the Western Territories," I say. "To name one who may have dressed like me, I think of Annie Oakley. Good nap."

"Good nap, Annie," he says.

I recline my head and close my eyes. Sleep eludes me because I am bothered by the fact that I actively purchased my ticket. OK, so the money was given to me, first by Rachel, I made a loan to Betsy who returned it with 100 percent profit. I did spend twenty dollars at the Casper General Store on candy. That was another break with my goal of being money free. The remaining eighty dollars, along with the one hundred from Lucy, purchased my ticket for the bus.

Am I influencing my free will by using money to direct my physical progress? It seems strange, but I have a hard time accepting myself intentionally impacting my life.

I recall a story told by one visitor to Taquinta. It's a tale of three hungry soldiers returning from the battlefront using their wits to feed themselves with the slim pickings available in a war ravaged village. No money changed hands, yet everyone ate well, especially the villagers.

Compared to those soldiers, my life is gloriously free of such conditions. So what is it that's bugging me about spending money to alter my circumstances? It's no different than, say, dreaming up people to "rescue" me.

Once the money is spent, my back is to the wall, the way I used to operate. I did spend the money. That hurts me. I am so troubled by these thoughts, I writhe in my seat. There must be a reason I did it. Why did I override my intentions? Does that show some inherent weakness in me, in my "system"? It certainly is a lesson, but one without an immediately obvious meaning. It was fine to travel on the ticket Rachel purchased, but not on the one I bought. Though Lucy really shared back her hundred profit. Add the eighty remaining after the candy purchase and it's all earnings; not my money, after all.

Dusk falls in Winslow, AZ. Downtown, a young man stands on a sidewalk as he strums a guitar, stopping briefly to thumb a ride from a flatbed truck driven by a young woman. The flatbed slows. The two of them check each other out. He strums his guitar.

Someone shakes my shoulder vigorously. It's Xavier. He's shaking me awake with one hand while in the other he holds a candy bar.

He takes periodic bites from the sickly sweet smelling bar as he tells me, "Ma'am. Wake up! We're almost at the crater."

It used to be that waking me from a deep sleep was a very unpleasant event for me and, as a result, for the person waking me. I would resist something fierce. I would then project a large amount of anger at the person waking me. Now that I eat healthfully, sleep reasonably and work out, I can slide in and out of sleep with ease and grace. Except, that is, when waking to the smell of candy.

"D'you know eating sugar ages you faster?" I bark.

Xavier hears a wholly other meaning.

"For real?" he asks, his eyes wide with excitement. "How much do I need to eat to look like twelve?"

"Faster, not older," I qualify my answer.

"What's the difference?" he asks, confused.

Now it's my turn to think my logic through.

"Older, mature, is what you were hoping for," I tell him. "Faster here means using up your body."

"Hungh?"

"Imagine you are scheduled to live forty five years."

"Ah huh."

"Then, every time you eat candy, you cut into the total."

"How much?"

"What do you mean, how much?"

"Do I lose a minute or a day? You know? One bar of candy costs me how much... time?"

I find myself studying him. The innocence of the question is both charming and alarming.

"Does it matter?" I ask.

"Sure it does. If ten candy bars equals one minute or one year... "

"You are so young. What happens thirty five years from now seems like forever away. Try thinking about being forty years old, your health has deteriorated and your prospects for living five years in comfort are poor. When you look back and understand that you may be lucky to live one more year because of all the candy you ate when you were ten years old, what would you tell your ten year old self if you could?"

"Is this a trick question?"

"Imagine you are forty years old and sitting where I am talking to you right now. What would you say?"

"How do you know this about sugar?"

"I'm addicted to sugar," I tell him. "I stay away from it to avoid getting sick."

"Is that like allergies?" he asks.

He spots something out the window and jumps up, pointing.

"There!" he shouts.

I turn to the window and look out. We race past signs directing people to the Crater.

Xavier finishes his candy bar and sits down, content. I may not have gained much traction with him regarding eating sugar, but he scored another convert to the meteor crater. I recall Serena's comment, "Pick your fights."

I smile at Xavier.

"You do have a rich imagination," I say.

He smiles at me proudly.

"I have pictures of the meteor crater all over one wall," he says. "I plan on being an astronaut."

"Good for you, Xavier," I say. "You only go where your dreams take you first."

"What's your dream?" he asks.

"To help people," I say without a second's thought.

"You helped me," he says.

"How so?"

"I'm giving up eating any candy."

I'm shocked. I didn't feel I was getting through to him.

"Good for you, Xavier," I tell him.

"Yeah," he says resolutely. "From now on, I'm only going to eat my favorite candy bar."

I perform a mental gulp.

"That's an excellent start," I agree.

We both retreat into our private worlds. He reads a book and I watch my friend, the desert, roll by. The sun sinks behind the horizon ahead of us. Even on this air conditioned bus, I sense the chill of night rising up from the ground below.

I wish I had a way to reach out to the Trinity to thank them for setting me on my path. I amuse myself with the idea that they are sitting up front on the roof of the bus playing a game of cards. It occurs to me that they have stayed close by me every step of my journey since I left them. I wonder if I ever left them.

What if, in some inexplicable way, they have kept up with me?

Though I still suffer twinges of buyer's remorse about spending money on the bus ticket, my expanded aura is already foretelling of great adventures up ahead.

TURN OVER

A cluster of clouds over Phoenix reflect red and pink farewells to the setting sun. The bus trundles into the bus station and gives an exhausted gasp as the doors release, opening for passengers to disembark. Xavier politely enquires if I need help with luggage. When I tell him no, he sets off, stopping by Gerry for a parting Hi 5.

Xavier steps off the bus, stands to the side and turns to wait for me.

"May I give you a friendship hug, Xavier?" I ask him as I step clear of the bus.

He doesn't wait to be asked twice. He hangs on until I shift my weight. When he steps back, I could swear he was beginning to tear up.

"You're special, Xavier," I tell him. "You take good care, now."

Smiling, Xavier turns away and runs to two dour grandparents anxiously scouring the passengers. Their energy picks up when he joins them. He gives me one last wave.

I search out the sign for the Los Angeles bus. There's a sizable line already formed as I arrive. I'm right on time. The doors hiss open and people in the line begin to shuffle forward.

Two people ahead of me, a nervous, stick of a woman, clutching a carpet bag close, concentrates on keeping up with the line. Between us, immediately in front of me in the line, a man reads a magazine as he walks. Someone struggling while boarding the bus causes the line to jerk to a sudden stop. The man ahead of me keeps on reading and walking, until he bumps the woman ahead of him who had stopped when the line did.

She goes down like a house of cards. The man glances over the top of his magazine, mumbles some sort of apology and steps around her as the line goes into motion once more.

The woman sits on the concrete looking extremely fragile, her bag knocked several feet distant from her. When I reach her, I lean over her to talk with her and expand the location by picking up her bag and placing it to protect her exposed side. That way, the people following me in line give us a wide berth.

"The worst is over," I tell her. "Allow healing."

I slowly work my way to be in front of her while maintaining enough of a physical presence to cause people to move around us.

Unfocused eyes rolling, she looks at me crazed.

At one point, I see the man who set this all in motion stop as he is about to board the bus, look back and check out what is happening behind him. Seeing me assist the woman, he starts to board the bus, as the driver struggles against the line to get off and come over to where I am still putting Humpty Dumpty back together.

As he reaches us, the driver asks me, "Is she OK?"

Because I am being a Good Samaritan, I'm supposed to know her condition? I think not.

"Ask her," I tell him.

He bends over her, a hand inching toward her left arm.

"Y'alright, ma'am?" he asks.

The woman's eyes fix on him with a hysterical quality as she answers, "I'll live."

His hand is a mere two inches from her.

He asks, "May I help you?"

He almost has hold, when she violently gesticulates with arms outstretched, fingers fanned, frantically waving about.

"Stay away from me!" she screams shrilly.

The driver jumps back pushing into me so we both have to struggle to keep our balance. I have a flash that I recognize him that evaporates as quickly.

I step toward the woman, leaning forward from the waist, arms outstretched sideways to maintain a no walk territory and remain prepared to help out if needed. The driver retreats to the sanctuary of his seat on the bus.

Silently, like a crumpled marionette rising in a series of awkward, slow motion movements, the woman stands, brushes her cotton frock straight with her hands, and combs her unruly, mousey colored page boy with her fingers before stretching the corners of her sweater, one over the other.

Unwinding her tension, she pouts, then, barely pursing her lips open, she spits out a fine spray. I step out of range in the nick of time.

As they shuffle past, the last people in line now give us an especially wide berth.

I pick up her bag and hand it to her. She gently accepts it from me and shakes her head, nervously, the way a horse might do. She steps past me and boards the bus. Straightening out my soft ice chest's strap over my shoulder, I follow along at a wary distance.

On the bus, a few people in the aisle stow carryon luggage, then take their seats.

I stop alongside the driver as I wait to move forward.

"She OK?" the driver asks me thumbing back toward the woman.

"Why do you keep asking me how she is doing?" I tell him. "Did you ask her?"

He shrugs and looks ahead.

A few steps in front of me, the woman has stopped in front of the man who bumped into her. He is still reading his magazine seemingly oblivious to her. She bends down toward him until her face is a couple feet from his face. He looks up to see her staring at him. At the same time, she puckers her lips and makes a loud buzzing sound.

Startled, the man pulls back as much as his seat will let him before raising his arms to protect his face.

She stands up and, as she steps past him, gives the top of his seat backrest one good thump with a closed fist. He jumps in his seat, terrified, guardedly turning to see if she is preparing another excitement for him.

As the doors hiss closed behind me, the woman stops by a student type sitting on a right side aisle seat with a vacant window seat. She points to the window seat and asks, "Are you saving that for someone?"

"Yes," he says. "Er... Well... a friend."

She checks the aisle both ways. I am the only one left standing.

"Her?" she asks, pointing to me.

Despondently, he shakes his head, no, then reluctantly stands in the aisle to let her take the window seat. She sits, and then holds up her carpet bag.

"Oh," she says with a girlish voice. "I forgot to put this up. Would you mind?"

He takes her bag from her and stows it overhead. As he is about to slide down into his seat, I approach them. I spot a vacant aisle seat back a row across the aisle.

"Would you switch seats?" I ask him pointing to the vacant seat. "I want to ride with her because she fell."

With mounting frustration, he makes the switch.

I sink into the seat next to her letting out a sigh of relief.

Without looking at me directly, she whispers, "We make quite the team, you and I."

I offer her an open hand and she slaps me a lo 5. She whips a paperback out from a sweater pocket, opens it, and holds it close to her face.

I lean toward her and, in my most serious voice, ask, "May I check you out?"

"Are you a doctor?"

"This is an energy scan."

"What do I do?"

"Relax."

Doing the best she can, she puts her open book face down on her lap. With arms straight ahead, hands fanned, rotating rapidly left and right, she sprays spit and her eyelids bat fast.

I cautiously put my left hand, palm out, toward her, as I explain, "I'm checking you for hot spots."

Slowly, her nervous activity reduces as I make passes with my hand over her from her head to her knees.

"I found one hot spot on your elbow," I tell her. "Is that from your tumble?"

She drops her hands instantly and swings on me, irate.

"I was knocked down!" she insists. "It was intentional. The spot you found is from work. I hit my elbow on a door."

"I have some oils we can put on it," I say as I pull out of my pocket the three bottles Lucy gave me. I open each one in turn and have her smell them for the one that most appeals to her. I apply a few drops to her elbow and rub it in. She inhales deeply, relaxing.

Giving me a sideways glance, she asks, "Are you a witch?"

"Ask yourself," I say. "If I were, why would I ride a bus? May I give you a hug?"

She goes rigid as I lean awkwardly over the dividing arm rest and embrace her. She stares straight ahead, tears forming in the corners of her shut tight eyes. I let go and she immediately picks up her book to immerse herself in reading.

"My name is Judith," I tell her.

Without stopping reading, or turning the least toward me, she says, "Hi, Judith. I'm Shirley."

"A pleasure to know you, Shirley," I tell her.

"How can you say that?" she says, still reading. "We've barely met."

"Well," I answer. "You have shown me a lot about yourself."

"Such as?" She puts her book face down on her lap, leans her head back against the seat and stares straight ahead toward the overhead luggage as tears form again.

"That you appear to be physically frail but, in truth, you are strong. You also act as if you are scared but are fearless. You give the impression that you are poor but are rich in sharing with others. And, you are literate in the way you choose your words as you speak."

"Have you been following me?"

"Am I right?"

"I would love to be the person you describe, Judith."

"You think I made this up? Shirley, I watched you. The person I just described is the you I saw."

"What has it been?" she asks turning to look at me with fear filled eyes. "Ten, maybe fifteen, minutes that we have been together. How can you see me unlike anyone else has seen me in forty plus years?"

"Maybe I'm the first to describe you. The others have yet to be asked to describe you."

Cloaked in night, Shirley and I talk well into California. She tells me about her two cats, S'more and Sunshine. She has much to say about her work typing transcripts through the night. I tell her about Taquinta and my year on the res. We each feel like a curiosity to the other because her experiences, which are so alien to me, feel mundane to her and conversely mine to her.

At some point, tiredness sweeps over me. I wake as the bus exits the highway for the Los Angeles Bus Terminal.

For all our discussion, Shirley and I are surprised to find that we are both continuing to Santa Monica.

As we cross the LA Terminal Concourse toward the shuttle stop, a scruffy, mournful boy sidles up to us with a dirty hand held out.

"Spares some change?" he asks us.

"Hi, Albert" Shirley addresses him with a chipper voice.

Albert stops in his tracks, surprised and alarmed at being recognized.

Shirley stops alongside him and talks in low, comforting tones.

"We met the last time I rode the bus," she reminds him.

Albert looks relieved it was nothing serious.

"I members," he says, brightening. "You'ses lady wi' twitchy face an' hand thingy. How yer bins?"

Shirley offers a clenched fist of knuckles to Albert. He happily reciprocates her street hand greeting. The gesture does not veer him off course to his objective.

"Hey," he pitches us both. "I needs some change to buys milk for my sister. Cans yer help?"

"You still peddling that old story?" Shirley taunts him. "Who takes the money, these days?"

Albert subtly gestures toward a doorway. A man standing in the shadows watches us intently.

Shirley dips into her carpet bag and fishes about in her pocketbook. Keeping Albert's back to the man so her actions are not visible to him, she pulls up two single dollar bills and hands them to Albert.

"Put one away," she tells him, "And just show him one."

"It a waste hidin's," he tells her sadly. "Him shakes me down cruel."

Shirley shares a parting hand greeting with him before he runs over to three people. As the two women engage Albert in conversation, the man pulls out a cell phone.

"Meet us at Alameda and Sixth," the man says into the phone.

It's all so quick, and I am adjusting back to city speed, I am not sure what I see.

Shirley attracts my attention as the threesome exit with Albert.

"My step parents abused me," she tells me. "Kids are so special. I always help them out."

Shirley begins twitching. As her hands move up and out, I hug her and gently rub her back until she becomes quiet once more. As we separate out of the hug, she gives me the gentlest of smiles.

"You are such a sweet soul," I tell her.

"Thank you," she says. "You are special, too, you know?"

"I am finding out."

We ride the shuttle in relative silence.

"How close are we to the Pacific?" I ask Shirley as we stand in the almost desolate terminal in Santa Monica preparing to go our separate ways.

"Very," she tells me. "I have a special treat for you. Come meet my precious Saint Monica—matron saint of married women, abuse victims, alcoholics, difficult marriages, disappointing children, victims of adultery... and the list goes on."

Childlike, Shirley grabs my elbow and propels me forward. After a brief, brisk walk, Shirley and I stand before a serene, white sculpture of Saint Monica. What I cannot see yet in the dark is the Pacific Ocean backdrop. While Shirley stares in awe at her saint, I give her a sideways hug. There are no tears, this time, only a serenely peaceful smile.

Then we are off, again. It feels like Shirley is sharing years of solitude with me. Morning creeps up behind us as we run and skip together down to the Santa Monica pier. At the bottom of the hill, she steers me left to a round building. Cupping our hands to block reflections, we peer through windows at motionless, exquisitely painted Carousel horses poised for flight.

We stroll past the shuttered Arcade and stop beneath the giant Ferris wheel hovering silently over Pacific Park.

Further along the pier, fishermen are setting up and casting lines into the still blackness of the glassy Pacific. Both mysterious and silent, the vast mass of water holds a quiet attraction.

My guide sets off quickly leading me as we walk silently to the end of the pier.

"Will we be able to see Asia in the daylight?" I ask.

Shirley checks me out to see if I am serious.

"Apart from the horizon, all you can see are a few islands right off the coast here," she patiently explains. "Asia is further away than New York is in the opposite direction. The Pacific is very big."

The encroaching daylight is beginning to distinguish the horizon line. This ocean is bigger even than the desert. I am impressed.

As we walk back up the hill toward town, the skyline is breaking into light blues between the high rise buildings.

Off in the distance a commotion of vehicles and people activity catches Shirley's attention.

She grabs me by the elbow and steers me toward the bustle.

DAY FIVE

VOICE

It certainly is a bustle. Farm trucks and wagons disgorge flowers, fruits and vegetables while market stalls are being set up for display. I reflect on my joyous times selling produce with Didi and Dada at the market in Santa Fe.

"If you think this is large," Shirley tells me, "You should see the market they have here on Saturdays."

I look forward to that possibility. This is stunningly exciting, made even more so by my guide knowing many of the farmers and merchants by name and they knowing her. Shirley is thrilled to show off her new friend to all the people she knows; another long held mystery revealed.

While Shirley chats with someone, I move on. At one stand, a robustly healthy farmer is putting up fruits and vegetables while instructing his young woman assistant how to display the produce to best advantage. I am drawn to this stand because, unlike all the others, this food radiates energy the same as did Taquinta produce. The farmer sees me checking out his produce.

"We'll be open for business in about half an hour," he tells me.

"It looks like Biodynamic grown," I say.

"You're very observant," he tells me. "Most people can see the difference, they certainly can taste it, but very few know what makes it so."

"I worked on a farm in New Mexico where we grew Biodynamic," I tell him. "We would sell extra at the farmers' market in town."

His assistant has been listening in on our conversation.

She asks me, "Did you ever hear about a women's community out there?"

"Taquinta?" I ask.

She bursts with excitement.

"Yes!" she says. "Taquinta."

"That's where I was," I say.

She becomes totally distracted causing the farmer to rush to catch vegetables sliding for the road.

"Andrea, concentrate," he tells her.

"Sorry, Carl," she tells him, and then turns to me. "Is there any way we can chat later?"

"What's the possibility of my helping out here?" I ask.

"Have you any experience selling produce?" Carl asks.

"Loads," I tell him. "Like I said, we had a stall in the nearby town's open air market."

"Right," he says. "Well, sure. Though I may only be able to pay you with produce."

"That will be perfect," I agree. "I'm Judith. Judith Fargoe."

"Good to meet you, Judith," he says. "I'm Carl and this here is Andrea. I'm going to leave you both in charge while I park the truck."

He drives off and Andrea and I finish up stacking produce and making the display attractive.

When she strolls up, Shirley is surprised to find me hard at work.

Right then, Carl returns.

"You certainly do know markets, Judith," he tells me. "That set up looks great. Shirley? What a nice surprise."

Embarrassed, Shirley waves stiff arms as she sputters through gloriously flushed cheeks. Carl steps over to her and gently grasps Shirley's wrists. Her eyes roll nervously as her hands guide Carl's on an air walk. She has the look of someone wishing they could drill a hole into the ground and disappear. She makes the most of being stuck where she is.

"Judith, this is Carl," she says as she collects herself.

"We've met," I tell her.

Carl has Shirley sit on a crate while he loads a plastic bag with various produce items as a gift for her. Ignoring her protestations, he insists she take it.

Shirley stands with her carpet bag pulling on one arm and the produce loaded bag pulling the other making her look for all the world like Olive Oyl.

"I need to go home and sleep," she announces.

I step between the bags and hug Shirley who closes her eyes as tears form.

She whispers in my ear, "If you need somewhere to stay, tonight, call me. I can put you up on my couch."

"Thank you, Shirley," I say. "Your Carl's a hunk."

"And married. Bye, dear lady."

As Shirley leaves, people swarm into the market. Seeing how at ease I am engaging customers and selling, Carl relaxes. Andrea uses every free moment to pump me for information about what life is like in Taquinta. Unexpectedly, I find myself being an ambassador for the place. Who would have thought it possible?

With a few well placed questions of his own, Carl is quick to recognize I am a ready trained helper for his farm. I know the basics of the Biodynamic farming process, including mixing the preparations, the relationship between animals and produce, plus, I have great rapport with the public. That I know the writings of Rudolf Steiner is icing on the cake.

I find out that, like me, he eats raw food.

At the end of his most successful day ever, an elated Carl is driving his truck past signs for Watsonville with me seated between him and Andrea on the bench seat. For such a long day, we are all three of us incredibly animated. Though he is apologetic about what he has to offer, Carl expects his wife, Lizbet, will work with me to make appropriate accommodations.

Working one quarter section of land, Carl's farm is a few well maintained buildings. He stops the truck by some sheds. We pile out of the truck, stretch, and then begin to unload the empty boxes as Lizbet walks over from the farmhouse.

"Again, Carl," she tells him, clearly frustrated. "You forgot your cell."

"I'm aware," he admits. "Lizbet, this is Judith."

We nod a cursory greeting to each other as Lizbet turns to Andrea.

"Andrea," she says. "Ray fell, this morning. Sounded serious."

"Where is he?" Andrea asks.

"The paramedics checked him out," Lizbet tells her. "I believe he is still at home."

"Carl," Andrea says. "If I take off now, can you manage without me?"

"Please help finish unloading," Carl says. "Let's eat and then you can take off. An hour either way, Ray sounds like he will be fine."

Lizbet nods toward me.

"In future would you give me a heads up?" she asks him.

"Yes," he says. "We were excited. This was my best day yet, thanks to Andrea and Judith."

"Congratulations, Carl," Lizbet says. "I am excited and pleased for you. Finish up quickly so we can get Andrea on the road."

Having flattened most of the boxes at the market, unloading is relatively speedy. As we walk over to the farmhouse, I offer my services to Andrea.

"If you would like, I'm available to go with you. Maybe I can be of help?"

Carl puts two bags of vegetables and fruit inside, by the front door.

"If you stay or go, Judith," he tells me, "These are for you for today's help."

Over dinner, I acknowledge Carl and Lizbet for taking on such a monumental task. Carl tells us that, with a few days each week, doing the kind of volume we did today, he believes the farm will turn a profit by year's end.

"However," he says with seriousness, "That means both of you will be available three days each per week."

By nodding agreement I look like I am a fixture and I only just got here.

"Yes, please come with me, Judith," Andrea asks me. "I have no idea what I have to face when I get there. Your calming presence will be so reassuring."

"My pleasure," I say.

VOICES

Away from Carl's influence, Andrea becomes more of a free spirited exhibitionist. As we ride through the pitch black countryside in her car, she jokes about it, though I have to take her word for it since there is minimal light even from the instrument panel.

"Growing up in the country has its assets," she tells me. "Most women my age from the city would be unable to drive this car 'cos it's a stick shift. Also, I do most of my own maintenance on it, which is simple, since it's a basic four cylinder engine. My friend gave me the car out of embarrassment that if he took money from me for this heap, his friends will pile on him. The reason I am shouting is 'cos of the lack of sound insulation on the roof."

"Are you telling me all this out of embarrassment?" I ask.

"I'm working on a routine for a stand-up comedy night," she says. "It loses some of the humor in translation."

"A lot gets lost," I tell her. "Reminds me of the Brmm, Brmm joke. You had to be there."

"Talking of there," she says. "We are."

We enter a residential neighborhood street and pull in next to a red pick up on the cobbled driveway of a single story California Craftsman house. Even by only a porch light and the car's headlights, it's a stand out property.

The car has barely stopped rolling before Andrea jumps out. She is already inside the front door before her car quits its heaving seizures and the engine dies. I hesitate getting out until the all clear is sounded.

I walk in on an African American woman tending to an Anglo American man lying on a metal cot in the living room of an immaculate, single story house. Andrea kneels next to the man and lovingly holds his hand.

"I'm old and useless, Andrea," Ray says. "How'm I going to manage, now?"

"What were you thinking, Uncle Ray?" Andrea asks him. "On a ladder!"

"Now, honey," the woman gently rebukes Andrea. "Only talks kindly, special as him hurtin's so."

Since Andrea has her back to me, I decide to announce my presence.

"What can I do?" I ask.

The woman looks over to me standing in the doorway. She rises to take better measure of me.

"Why y'aksin's?" she asks me.

If this were a Western movie those would be fightin' words. She was calling me out.

Andrea, lovingly stroking Ray's forehead, turns at the tone of the discussion and introduces us.

"Judith, Sarah is our lifesaver," she says. "Sarah, Judith offered to help."

Sarah totally ignores the introductions.

"When him takes that dive," she tells Andrea, "We has fire trucks an' ev'body here. I'm tellin's yer, chile, them mens was somethin' sets yer eyes on. 'Mm-mm! Thanks Lord, he still whole."

I take the initiative and close the door behind me and approach the center of the action. Having a sizable audience, Ray protrudes a foot from under the blanket. His ankle is swollen. Anything the paramedics had done is no more.

"That bruise needs a cold compress," I blurt out.

"Good luck findin' it in this house," Sarah says.

That was a shift into my court.

"Ice?" I suggest. "A periodic icing will really help."

Sarah shakes her head, no, without taking her eyes off Ray.

"Ah an," she answers. "Like man ter lives this way."

Maybe sensing the equilibrium, Andrea offers the perfect solution.

"Sarah," she asks. "Can Ray stay at your house?"

"Sure, chile," Sarah concedes. "I only gots my gran'chillun wi' me. We gots room for Holy Host an' rooms ter spare."

Unable to curb my tongue in all the excitement, I let fly.

"Is that your pickup on the driveway, Sarah?" I ask.

Politeness be damned, I get a head on glare from two large, beautiful brown eyes.

"While I cans, honey," Sarah tells me, "I walks. Red one? That Ray's. Now, if it cars yer wants, I gots my late Bill's all cross my yard—Lincolns, Caddies. Yer names it."

"Let's settle Ray at your house," I say. "Do we take the cot?"

"I gots rooms; that it," Sarah informs me. "Yer good wi' directin'. Sure knows yer mind."

That was a night to remember. I suggested Andrea to go to the store and pick up some ice to pack around Ray's ankle. It took a while to convince Andrea that I was not able to drive either stick or automatic. Then we determine that Sarah walked because she didn't drive and was embarrassed by having to admit it.

After that it was smooth sailing, particularly, the part where three comparatively slight women raised six feet tall, solidly built Ray to his feet and rolled him to his truck strapped on the refrigerator dolly we found in his garage.

Sarah's house had wood stairs to access her house from the street. The air is probably still blue between the ladies' occasional slip of the tongue acting as backup chorus to Ray's string of epithets as we bounced him backwards up the stairs on the dolly.

Sarah's two story Craftsman house is in total disrepair. A staircase to the second floor leads off the living room. Her furniture is simple and sparse. Andrea sleeps under a blanket on a couch as I assist Sarah reposition Ray on the cot. He is looking much happier.

Next morning, having slept in a formerly recliner chair, I am wide awake when Sarah's grand children—wiry Leticia, 15, energetic Bebe, 14, and feisty Saffron, 13—are up and about, in and out of the kitchen, and watching TV on an old set in the living room.

I lost track of where Sarah slept after we settled Ray. Once the kids are about, she dominates the kitchen, periodically stepping as far as the living room doorway to dictate terms.

"Keeps vollem down on TV," she tells the teens. "We gots us a sick man."

"I thot Ray sleepin' in your room," Saffron asks Sarah with complete innocence.

Of course, there is nothing worth keeping private around children.

"Hush, chile," Sarah bids her. "Yer ready fer school?"

That question distracts Bebe from the upright piano where his is picking out notes in an unusual dance rhythm. He throws out a casual, over the shoulder comment.

"School closed, today, gran," he says as his left hand adds a bass line.

"Where letter from school?" Sarah asks, exhibiting patience and understanding. "Rule is, yer lives here, yer goes school."

Now watching the TV, Bebe yells his frustration, "Why I gotta live wi' an old woman?"

From experience, Bebe knows to expect a reaction from sister Leticia who knows to shoot first and ask questions later. She swings at him, he ducks and she misses.

"Watch yer mouth," she tells him. "We lucky be here."

The instigator of turbulent activity, Saffron, tries a new tack.

"Wake Andrea to ride in the truck."

Curious to see where they are schooled, I offer, "May I walk to school with you?"

Sarah sees resolution at many levels.

"Course!" she shouts from the kitchen.

Bebe shoots daggers at his sisters as if they have set him up. They take the opposite tack and appear delighted to have a new distraction for the tiresome journey.

As we set out, not one of them can give me a simple answer to, "How many blocks is it to school?" So I demonstrate Long Stride walking. The girls work at it. Bebe refuses. Our relatively brief journey takes us from a run down neighborhood to an extremely run down neighborhood. Houses, yards and cars look worse as we draw closer to the school.

Along a particularly desolate street, while Bebe hangs back, I give the girls one final set of instructions.

"Pretend you're heavy like a sack of potatoes," I tell them. "Sink low, swing your legs at the hips. It feels weird, but each step takes you further."

A heavy hand lands on my shoulder.

I am instinctively in motion to take out my assailant, when I hear Bebe's voice say, "This far as you go!"

The hand lifts as I stop still. Bebe runs ahead and turns the corner. The girls shrug and continue to the corner where they turn to wave to me. I wave back, standing still and slow counting to 18. I take measured steps to the corner and peek round. Leticia and Saffron are trying to keep up with Bebe Long Striding toward friends who are laughing and pointing at him as they hang out at the school gate.

Duly impressed, when he reaches them, they slap him playfully making him the center of attention. He leads his group in through the gates as the girls stroll in, having long since given up trying to Long Stride.

I amble slowly towards the school holding back until the bell rings. As the kids make their way to class, I approach the run down building. It feels so sadly derelict. I have a struggle imagining children being inspired to learn under such conditions. My heart aches looking at the disrepair of the schoolyard's acres of continuous blacktop. I recollect seeing Sun Path do a dance in the desert to invite the rain to come nurture the soil to encourage the plants to grow. This schoolyard would offend her. What are they doing to our fair sister?

Seeing no one about, I enter through the gate.

A uniformed security guard steps out of the building doorway with hand raised like a traffic cop.

"This is school property," he calls out to me.

About the same time, a man in a suit approaches from the adjoining parking lot.

"Thanks, Jimmy," he tells the guard.

Clearly intrigued by my buckskin outfit, he asks me, "May I help you?"

"Does the school offer a meals program?" I ask him.

"I take it you are new to the area," he says as we walk toward the building entrance. "How many children do you have?"

"Think of me as a concerned citizen," I tell him.

"That's a new twist," he says. "As the principal, I am grateful if parents attend Parent Teacher meetings."

"I wondered if the school grows its own food to feed the students," I say.

He gestures to the blacktop schoolyard. "We need all the space we can get for exercise programs and playground," he says.

I repeat his gesture toward the schoolyard.

"If this were converted to growing plants with the children nurturing the..."

"Ma'am," he cuts me off. "You're talking matters requiring a Board of Education decision."

He holds the door open for me to enter the building.

"My name is Judith Fargoe," I say. "Would you support such a proposition?"

"Ms. Fargoe," he says politely. "Of late, my opinion on most school matters of consequence is disregarded since I am scheduled to retire in a year."

Right next to the school office are rows of brightly colored, lighted snack and drink dispensing machines. I go over and check the general contents of these glowing, humming, industrialized, food and drink dispensers. I turn to the principal who leans on the counter chatting with a staff person.

"How do you expect children to think clearly on a sugar and gluten diet?" I ask, pointing to the passive market place.

He straightens up, looking preoccupied.

"We receive money back from machine purchases to fund school functions."

"Basically, you are taxing what students eat or drink," I say, "To supplement lack of funding from the school district."

"Times are tough all around," he says.

The loudspeaker system interrupts us.

"Dr. Hyde," a woman's voice requests. "Phone call for Dr. Hyde."

"Please excuse me," he says. "I need to take this call. You can find your way out?"

I put out my hand to shake goodbye. I wish I hadn't. His hand is cold, moist and spongy soft; a principal without principles. I race for the exit.

It does not require much to find my way downtown. I follow a trail of beer cans. Something like half of the storefronts display boarded up doors and windows. Most others are in a sorry condition, peeling paint, damage to the exterior. The only building with any real class and pizzazz is the corner branch of City and Farmers Bank. The few people I encounter on the street avoid eye contact.

One man pan handles me. I ask him how much he has and he shows me a few coins. When I tell him I have no money at all and ask him to share some of his with me, he walks off in a huff.

The driver of a car stands in front of his car with hands on the hot hood while two surly cops frisk him. One cop stares at me, giving me a sexually charged grin. I consider many scenarios playing out, but Serena's voice dominates my thinking: "Pick your fights." This time, I hear the meaning to be, either I set up the fight, or avoid stepping into someone else's need to fight. I walk on by.

Almost to the end of the main drag, I pass an alleyway. Looking down it, I see three kids playing in the dirt. Curious as to why they are not in school, I stroll toward them. I notice that each of them is visibly definable as mentally and/or physically challenged. They are what Sun Path defined as Special Folk, blessed by Great Spirit. They are delighted I want to join them.

Apparently, every day, as I understand matters, being short staffed the school sends the first person available to go look for them. Gaspar, 14, Shoshanna, 12, and Hermione, 16, interpret the system to be playing a game of hide and go seek, so, each day, they play somewhere new. The system has not clued in. That redefines mentally challenged in my book.

They are in raptures over my tassels. When I do my bird dance, they are immediately on their feet and following me. I free form activities; running my hand across a fence and then along the top as I skip down the alley. The three of them giggle and laugh as they imitate my actions. I make a game of it, a flowing dance, and they follow along.

With one exception, all back yards are fenced in. At the only open backyard, we all stand and watch an Asian man in a yard of rock formations designed to look like mountains and streams. The few plants he grows resemble forests in his stone landscape, except for one enormous tree.

Dressed in martial arts clothing, the man performs a ritual at the tree. Palms down, he makes a deep bow to the tree. At the bottom of his motion, he turns his palms up as he rises, lifting his hands overhead. Ignoring us spectators, he repeats his bow many times. The special folk point at him and chatter away. The man ends his ceremony, turns and walks toward us at the edge of his yard. Seeing me, he offers a martial arts salute. I respond with a Jiu-Jitsu salute.

"Greetings," he says. "Jiu-Jitsu?"

He has a distinctly Asian accent. I find myself imitating the style of speaking with clipped sentences.

"Greetings," I say. "Yes, Jiu-Jitsu. Hapkido?"

"Tae Kwan Doh!" he says. "Welcome Song Cho Kim home."

Kim bows deeply only to me.

I do a vague bow and tell him, "Judith Fargoe."

"Kim honored," he says with another bow to me.

Kim stands, and then turns to face the Special Folk. Rolling his eyes back into his head, he raises his arms Zombie like and advances two steps. They scream, genuinely terrified. Backing off, Kim grins at me with wicked delight.

I point to the tree.

"What were you doing at the tree?" I ask.

"Chi Gong," he tells me. "Kim gather energy for visit. What question?"

"My visit?"I ask with total disbelief. "How could you know I was coming?"

"As song say," he tells me, "Kim Seventh Son—know all. Take to sick friend."

He steps into the alley toward me and looks at me, expecting I know what he is talking about. I have not the first idea.

With his hands hanging at his sides, he makes a small gesture with his right hand as if saying, "Let's go!"

I have an intense vision of Ray on his cot and Andrea next to him, crying. That sets me in motion, except I am all turned around and I am unsure of my way home to Sarah's house.

Kim strides over to walk next to me. He gives me confidence so, very soon, I find streets with landmarks I recognize and pick up speed to go home. All the way, Kim chants under his breath and I say nothing so as not to disturb him. I am vaguely aware that the Special Folk are following us, but staying a half block back. I am focused on reaching Ray. The closer we get, the more concerned I am about Ray.

SONG'S SONG

Kim and I are in lock step as we arrive at the stairs to the porch of Sarah's house. We climb the steps two at a time and go straight in through the front door. We walk in on Sarah and Ray in a compromising position. Sarah rises, pretending she was caring for Ray. There appears to be little in this life that fazes Sarah.

She has a wonderful smile for Kim.

"Hey, Kim," she asks. "How's yer doin'?"

"Excellent, always, Mrs. Sarah," he responds cheerily. "Kim see sick patient, please?"

Sarah wags a taunting finger at Kim.

"Long as yer spares us yer tea," she insists.

Dispensing with any further formalities, Kim walks over to the cot and kneels by Ray. Kim places his hands around Ray's ankle and squeezes with all his might making Ray's face turn white as he grits his teeth.

To my way of seeing, this is many times more painful for Ray than even our bouncing him up the stairs, last night. Ray takes it in without making a single sound, not even one blue note. I can't handle it. I turn and go to the door. The Special Folk are standing at the bottom of the stairs looking bewildered how they got here. They light up when they see me. I wave farewell and they imitate me, but go nowhere.

From inside, I hear Kim instruct Ray, "Breathe!"

I do as Kim instructs and feel my whole body relax. The same thing happens to the Special Folk. It's almost as if we were all coming out from under a magic spell.

Unable to make the Special Folk do anything except imitate me, I go back inside the house. Kim is gently massaging Ray's ankle and throwing off the energy collecting on his hands. Sarah is bopping in and out to the kitchen. Ray is as relaxed as can be.

On one of her trips into the living room Sarah asks, "Yer gots any students, Kim?"

"At moment," he tells her, "Teacher wait."

Not particularly understanding their small talk and feeling curious about some of the strange things Kim has told me, I ask, "What is the Seventh Son?"

Sarah glows as she tells Kim, "Kim, when yer all dones fixin' Ray here, plays Judith yer song."

Kim, focused on gleaning the negative energy from Ray's ankle, speaks without looking up, "Be glad."

For the first time since Kim began working on him, Ray speaks, "Me, too!"

"There!" Kim says, releasing Ray and standing.

"Walk careful, tonight, Mr. Ray. Tomorrow, you, Mrs. Sarah dance! Kim give tree energy."

He's joking, right? Ray ought to be in hospital on bed rest. Dance, tomorrow? He can't even tolerate any weight on that foot.

Kim walks over to the funky upright piano that Bebe was picking at earlier this morning. He opens the keyboard, sits on the bench and lets rip with a flat out perfect impression of a Southern musician.

The moment his fingers touch down on the keyboard, I am electrified. Kim plays like an old time, barrelhouse-blues master and sings totally accent free!

To watch and listen, I collapse into the chair I slept in last night.

"In all the ways that a man can be,

There's one alone that is like me.
Look where you will under the big wide sun,
I'm the only one to be a Seventh Son."

Looking over his shoulder at Ray,

"When the sick come to me I heal them well."

Back to watching his hands on the keyboard

"I raise up the dead, free the good from jail.
I talk to trees, read animals' mind,
Bring sound to the deaf, sight to the blind."

Kim turns to face me as he continues,

"In all the ways that a man can be,
There's just the one that be like me.
Search as you must under the big wide sun,
I'm the only one to be a Seventh Son."

Addressing Sarah

"I can tell where people goin', tell where they bin,
Who are their ladies 'n' who are their men.
I help lame folks rise to break into dance."

He turns to Andrea as she enters the front door,

"An' poor kids to realize their wealth in abundance.
In all the ways that a man can be,
If'n you search 'cross ev'ry high sea

Then to me, again,

"Alone among men, under that big wide sun,
I'm the only, yes, the only, Seventh Son to a Seventh Son."

With a flourish, he spins to face the room. Outside the window, the Special Folk clap their hands and laugh. Sarah goes to the door.

"Gets 'long home, all ofs yer!" she yells at them

This time they listen and react appropriately.

For the second time, today, I feel transported. In a flash, Kim the consummate blues piano player singer is gone and the monastic Kim is back.

"You must practice all day long," I say.

He offers a simple explanation.

"Kim home, meditate piano," he tells me matter of factly. "Visit Mrs. Sarah, play piano."

Ray stands awkwardly to show he can, as Kim walks to the door.

"Kim go," he tells the assembly. "Mr. Ray excellent. Wish all people good health."

He bows, turns and exits. Andrea rushes to assist Ray who brushes her aside as he walks to the kitchen, slowly. Sarah steps aside as if Ray walking about was perfectly normal.

"Stays far 'way from Kim's herbs," she cautions me. "Them smells bad. Oo-ee!"

Released from uncle responsibilities, Andrea turns her love and attention to me.

"Kim sure took a liking to you," she says.

The inference is clear as day, but not what I am ready to hear.

"What do you mean?" I demand to know.

Sarah gets all little girl gushy.

"Kim sings to yer like him a angel," she says. "An' him says him waits on a student."

"How's it go?" Andrea taunts me. "When the student is ready, the teacher will appear."

"People says Kim losts his wife an' chile in birth back in Korea," Sarah offers.

What are these two up to? I've been here a half day and they're hitching me up?

Ray comes back from the kitchen chomping down on a huge

sandwich.

"What're you two vixens up to, now?"

He looks over and sees me standing utterly confused. He looks back at Sarah and Andrea and makes the connection.

He tells them, "It's up to her."

"We helpin's her stays in these part," Sarah explains.

"You are match making," Ray insists.

"We keepin's the glue sticky," Sarah tells him as she looks to Andrea. "Now that's a fat!"

I am confronted by people driving me to my destiny versus going under my own steam. Apprehensively, I edge to the door. My step picks up, and I'm on my way.

That is, I'm out the door. Now what? Did I take note of which direction we came from? No. I arrived here with Kim as if in a dream. Maybe it was the chanting. Still, it's my job to stay conscious. OK. I'm having a conversation with myself instead of working the facts. I walk down the steps and assess from which direction we approached the house. Good beginning. I really am on my way.

I set off long striding. I cover two blocks and my directions are falling into place.

As I approach an alley, I am looking straight ahead when Kim leaps out at me uttering the scariest, blood curdling yell. One hand takes control of my right hand and his other hand grabs my throat from front on with a vice grip.

This maniac is going to kill me.

TIME

Instinctively, my left hand goes straight up overhead between Kim and myself. I bend my arm so that it forms a point at the elbow on the descent creating a wedge to prevent Kim from doing any more than grip my throat. By stepping into his stance, I weaken his grip on my throat even more. When I relax my right arm, he seeks a different place to grab me. That split second is all I need to turn and throw him. He slides down my hip as smoothly as Sky Hawk fell to Red Wing. The only difference being that I am going to kill my assailant.

Kim or no Kim, I feel threatened and there is only one end result. With my right hand I have hold of his collar up by his right ear. My left hand slides under my right forearm as I lean in with my full bodyweight behind the lock. I already feel his Adam's apple under my lock that will instantly cut off his ability to breathe and drain his brain of vital oxygen, when... he begins to laugh.

I dare anyone, martial arts Black Belt or whatever, to finish off an opponent giving a good belly laugh. You have to be psychotic to beat that maneuver. He knew that.

I release my choke hold and slide quickly away from him and jump to my feet, prepared to go for the kill at the slightest provocation.

Kim remains lying on the ground, not laughing anymore.

He points to me and says, "*Courage—resistance to fear. Mastery of fear—not absence of fear.* Samuel Clements."

"Mark Twain!" I say. "I show courage?"

Kim lifts his feet high off the ground and flips into standing position.

"Ms. Judith attract, tame tiger."

"I do?" I say. "What tiger are you talking about?"

"Kim teach when student ring bell," he answers.

He bows to me, and then walks off jauntily. I raise my hands out of exasperation as I watch him disappear round a corner. Totally frustrated by this impish character, I plunk myself down to sit on the curb. when the Special Folk arrive.

Grateful for any live body to discuss my predicament with, it doesn't matter what their emotional age level is, so long as they are thinking, feeling human beings.

"What am I to do?" I ask them.

"I always do what makes my heart have joy," Gaspar advises me.

"Really?" I ask.

My heart does feel joy when I'm next to Kim; even if I did want to kill him! He provokes intense emotions.

Decision made; pursue Kim to answer my questions. I stand up.

I smile at them. They smile back.

We're at the beginning, once more. Leastways, it feels like that.

Free, without a care in the world.

Yet, something has changed.

I tell myself, "Out of the mouths of babes."

Alright, I'm lost. After following round the corner Kim turned on, I can go a number of directions. Then what? How would I know which house he's in? If he wants to be my teacher, then he needs to be more upfront with me. My frustration level rises. I have the same sensation like when we were walking to Sarah's house and he was chanting. It feels like someone is prodding me in the back saying, "Faster, faster!"

That's it; he's chanting! I am being trained like a homing pigeon hearing inaudible sound waves. I am being reeled in like a fish that bit down on the hook. It doesn't matter which way I go; my decision making process is not mine right now. I get it and, then again, I don't.

Who was it taught me about free will at Taquinta? I can't remember. I can't remember what happened a year ago? Or is someone blocking my thought processes?

As quickly as I felt the waves override my thoughts, they're gone. My head feels like it has been laundered clean. That is the most amazing feeling. It's like waking as a child on a spring morning, refreshed and raring to go. Turn right here. Why? Because... up ahead, is that a rock garden? Yes! And towering over the house in the back yard is that majestic tree; the one from which Kim gained the energy to heal Ray's foot. I've found it!

This is another street of fenced in, run down homes.

In the middle of the block sits a beautifully maintained house with no fence but dominating the yard is a meandering path of flat rocks resembling a river. By the front door, there's a shelter from which a log is suspended horizontally by two ropes holding it a foot from the largest brass bell I have ever seen. There is only one person who lives in a house as distinctly different as this one.

At the door I search for a doorbell. There isn't one. I step under the shelter and gently push the log. It barely moves. By pulling it back then pushing it forward, pulling back, pushing forward, truly exerting energy, I build momentum until the log strikes the bell. The tone is deep and resonant.

Tired from swinging the post, I let go. Back it comes, then forward, to stop a hair shy of striking the bell a second time. It doesn't need to. The bell is still resonating. The feeling is one of peaceful relaxation.

As I stoop to exit the shelter, I see a pair of bare feet wearing flip flops. Kim stands next to me. He's wearing a butt length Hapi coat tied at the waist. His hair is towel dried mussed. He bows a greeting.

"Ms. Judith," he tells me. "Welcome Kim home."

I don't have the etiquette of all the bowing and formalities of greetings and salutations down, so I feel inept when I nod my head only and respond, "Thank you."

He gestures we go to the slightly open front door.

I raise my hand as I say, "Whoa!"

He looks confused.

"Ms. Judith have problem?" he asks.

"I want to talk first before making any commitments," I say.

"Ms. Judith already state position," he tells me pointing to the bell and the swinging post.

"I rang the bell because that was the only one you have," I tell him.

"Exactly," he says.

"What exactly?" I ask.

"Ms. Judith ring bell?" he asks.

"Yes, I did," I say.

"Kim say teach student when ring bell," Kim says.

"I know what you said," I tell him. "But I want to discuss first."

"Discuss, Ms. Judith knock on door," he says. "Ms. Judith ring bell. Ms. Judith student."

This is way too fuzzy thinking for me. Kim has a logic all his own.

Anyway, how bad can it be? I've already proved I can take him down so there's nothing to worry about. Sarah and Andrea thought this is a great opportunity. Ray didn't say anything adverse. They've clearly all known Kim for years. Be a student. Learn something new. Besides, for a man, he is kind of cute. Absent that thought, immediately!

Kim removes his flip flops outside and, pushing open the front door, steps inside. With another bow and a sweep of the hand, he invites me in. I take off my moccasins and leave them outside, separate from his flip flops. I step into a large, open living room of woven straw mats on finished hardwood floors. A few pieces of low furniture and folding screens define height and depth. This place is sparsely equipped, even for a bachelor.

With another light bow, Kim tells me, "I prepare for your visit."

All this bowing is starting to irritate me because I don't know how to respond appropriately. Then, again, he talks as if he has a future copy of the Akashic Record.

"That's the second time you said you were expecting me," I tell him.

"How'd you know?"

Unfazed, he explains, "Two fact: one, see aura; two, when meditate, see future. Please shower. Much do."

He points to the bathroom. Matter of factly, Kim ushers me along, handing me a towel, a pair of clean, white ankle socks and a bathrobe. This is going way too fast for me. I stop. He looks unperturbed.

"You do this with other women?" I ask.

"Kim teacher," he answers. "Ms. Judith student. Teacher say, student do."

"Yeah, that's all well and good," I challenge him.

"Go," he says.

I go. Why? I don't know, but I go.

From outside, Kim closes the bathroom door. I look about briefly, focusing on a split mirror with my reflection in one pane and the other vacant. Besides the typical stool in its own alcove, there's a wash basin built in to a counter, a glassed in corner shower stall and a good sized bathtub. Everything is spotlessly clean. I take a shower.

Wearing the bathrobe and socks, I emerge from the bathroom. Kim, now dressed in a non descript, cream colored, silk shirt and forest green, silk pants, his hair combed, has arranged the room to accommodate a big mat on the floor.

He points to the mat.

'Please, lie face down," he says. "Open robe front."

This student teacher relationship is back out of control.

As if working with a difficult child, he explains, "Student trust teacher. Open robe, lie on mat. Make comfortable."

Apprehensively, as I go to lie face down on the mat, I gingerly open the robe and spread the sides.

He cautions me, "Breathe steady. Some discomfort."

What is he going to do? How is lying face down—almost naked—an appropriate student teacher relationship? I am contemplating getting up and leaving when he steps onto my back squeezing all the air out of my lungs.

Kim is not simply standing on my back, he's walking about on me like riding a surfboard, working my back muscles. At first I'm resistant, gasping for breath. When I begin to feel the confidence with which he moves about, how he targets specific muscles and how good they feel after being walked on, I finally give it up, relax and breathe.

I'm beginning to zone out, this is so pleasant.

"Deep breathe!" he barks. "Kim fix spine. Next, legs. Much pain."

That's OK, teach. I'm the master of pain. I did sweat lodge. You want to talk pain? Try Vision Quest. You go for it!

Through the robe, he works down my back and onto my buttocks. This is all pleasant. Then I feel his weight shift as one foot comes off me. He's standing with one foot on the mat and the other on the back of one thigh, rolling side to side. I feel proud of how muscled I am. I have extremely low body fat. Now he's working the other thigh. It's not like my back but this is no way painful.

Kim shifts his weight to the foot resting on the mat, and then, with his free foot, he steps onto my calf and presses slightly.

I scream! Do I ever scream?

Hearing such screams, a gentleman would stop. Kim goes for broke. He puts on more weight and aims his heel into the middle of my calf muscle. Excruciating is a mild definition of what I feel. I sweat from my entire body. Then he stops. I catch my breath and gradually calm down.

Then he digs into my other leg full force, no escalation.

I pound the mat. I give in.

He ignores me as he pivots and presses. I feel like I'm about to pass out. Then he stops.

I can't wait to sit up and massage my calves. Kim walks off and returns with a large glass of water.

"Drink," he tells me.

I don't need urging. I chug it down.

That's when I hear him say, "Slow. Chew liquids, drink solids."

Whatever. I slug it back. Then I realize my bathrobe is wide open. Modesty be damned, I hurt. I use my free hand to rearrange my robe while I hold the empty glass out for a refill.

He takes it as he tells me, "Stand slow. Walk."

Sure, pal. You try jumping up and dancing around after someone just dug out your calf muscles. I roll onto my knees and ever so gingerly start to stand. That feels better, making those calf muscles work. They hurt and feel better at the same time.

"64 rocks Sweat Lodge is less painful than what you just did," I tell Kim when he brings me my refill. "Why does that hurt so much?"

"Release emotions," he tells me.

I try chewing the water this go round. It feels strange to do that but I can almost feel my body absorbing it across the mass of me instead of simply going down the tube in my center. I limp around the room and stop periodically to chew more water.

Kim goes to the bathroom and runs a bath.

For somewhere to go, I stop outside the bathroom and lean on the door frame.

"What're you doing?" I ask.

"Make bath ready," he says. "Ms. Judith release much toxin. Wash clean."

The idea holds a lot of appeal. He shuts off the faucets and stands, waiting.

"Please bathe" he says.

"Please leave," I say.

"Kim, teacher," he tells me. "Ms. Judith, student.

"Judith, woman," I say. "Kim, man."

"Ms. Judith trust," he says. "Kim honorable."

I am conflicted. I can feel my whole body aching to submerge in the hot water. Then I try to imagine how my male teacher expects me to strip down and jump in the tub while he stands there watching.

He stands there with a total lack of energy in his face. He is almost bored. I don't know where the thought comes from but I feel challenged to bathe in front of him.

"You're asking for more than trust," I tell him.

He shrugs disinterestedly.

You go, girl. I enter the bathroom, disrobe and step into the hot water. I sit, and then lay down, relaxing my body, all the while my eyes are riveted on Kim who pulls up a chair and sits on it next to me on my right side.

He sits staring off for several minutes as my body heats up and I enter a state of relaxation. Without turning to face me, he tells me what he wants to do.

"Ms. Judith relax," he says. "All travel and fight alter Ms. Judith Chakras. Kim adjust Chakras. Kim touch Ms. Judith private places. Kim honorable. OK?"

All I have to say is, Mr. Kim smooth operator. Do I feel set up? You bet. Has he been respectful? Yes. Has he kept his word? Yes. Do I trust him? Here I am in his bathtub, naked, after he has literally walked all over me. Is that a Yes? YES! Do I give him the all clear to proceed? Gee, why is it all so difficult? Yes.

"OK," I tell him.

"Kim understand Ms. Judith issue," he says, still looking ahead. "Kim tell Ms. Judith relax, go sleep. OK? Kim place one hand, heart Chakra—between breast. Other hand, perineum for while. Move hand to genital, only cover. Move hand to below navel, then heart. Move hand throat, then forehead. Last, crown. When Kim finish, go. Ms. Judith sleep long. Question?"

A stream of questions race through, but nothing I can't deal with myself.

"Let's do this thing," I say.

He instructs me to inhale deeply through my nose, fill my belly, and then exhale through my mouth. We do this in tandem for a while. He rubs his hands together, vigorously, so they are warmed up when he touches me.

Kim is as precise as he was finding exactly which part of what muscle needed what amount of pressure from which direction when he walked on me. Initially, I am terrified, embarrassed, nervous, and even ashamed. I watch Kim. Though he has shifted his position on the chair so he is now facing me, except when placing his hands, he keeps his eyes closed. That gives me a modest amount of relief.

He was right. By the time both his hands finally meet up at my heart Chakra, I am history, off in the land of Nod; not even lucidly. I am out.

I transition from sleeping a deep, energizing sleep to being awake, mellow and peaceful.

Kim is gone. The bath water is the warm side of bearable. I pull myself up and reach for a towel. After I dry off, I slip on a fresh bathrobe and pair of socks. Kim sure covers the bases.

I quietly enter the living room. Kim sits in Lotus Pose with his hands in Prayer Pose as he meditates before a small, low lying altar. As quiet as I am, he snaps to. He stands up and comes over to me checking my eyes as he approaches. He gently takes my hand and guides me to a Futon.

Similar to what I did for Shirley on the bus but much more thoroughly, he performs Pranic Healing of my head and body—front, back and sides. He extends each of my arms and works from shoulder to fingertips. He extends one leg and works down to the toes. All the time he works on me, I watch him as I become more peaceful.

As he completes my other leg, I cup the back of his head with my hand and encourage him with light pressure to turn his face to look at me. He is intently serious, vested in his work.

When both his eyes are looking at me, I smile at him. He smiles back. I pull his head toward me gently, slowly. He looks into my eyes.

"Ms. Judith question Kim?" he asks.

"Ms. Judith feels romantic with Mr. Kim," I say.

"Ms. Judith married?"

"Ms. Judith single," I answer. "Consider relationship with Mr. Kim."

"End teacher student? Now friends?"

"Yes. Trade. Ms. Judith teach Mr. Kim English. Mr. Kim teach Ms. Judith meditation?"

"Kim widow."

"I'm sorry," I say.

"Why?" he responds. "Life."

It's no problem guiding our lips together into gentle touches culminating in a languorous, full kiss.

He gently pulls away and looks at me with the sweetest eyes.

"Kim go store, buy protection."

If ever time stood still for me that was the longest wait. I remove the bathrobe while I wait behind the door.

When Kim walks in through the door, I am so excited to be with him. He swings it open as he enters, stopping to look for where I am. His disappointment at not immediately seeing me is palpable. As he turns to close the door, his joy at discovering me behind the door is the sign I am waiting for. He stands there looking at me. He takes in every detail. If I was checked out during the Pranic Healing, now I am devoured by the eyes of a lover.

He takes me by the hand while he closes the door. We walk slowly to the futon. He is not hiding his excitement at being close to me. He has me sit while he swiftly realigns the room's dynamics by bringing screens close around the futon so we will be in our own secluded area inside the living room. He leaves one narrow gap through which we can see the trunk of the tree in the backyard.

Kim sits cross legged. I sit on his lap, legs around his waist, arms around his neck. There we are together looking into each other's eyes, arms wrapped around each other.

"Woman in charge," he encourages me. "Pull inside."

"What about you?" I ask.

"Kundalini up spine," he says. "Different than ejaculate. Better."

"Did you envision this?"

He smiles, shrugging his shoulders.

"Ms. Judith give Kim son," he tells me.

I feel myself go rigid, tense up.

I hear so many issues when he says that. That old world male dominance destroys my believing we are equals. He wants a son instead of a child, not asking if I even want children, presuming we are already deeply in a relationship. The word "give" symbolizes imbalance. He still refers to me as Ms. Judith; and, he says that during a moment of deep intimacy?

Mind racing, I pull away from him completely.

"You chauvinist bastard!" I shout.

He catches my left hand and holds on as he explains.

"Ms. Judith misunderstand," he tells me. "Future."

We have a lot of talking to do.

Kim offers that we shower together.

I feel a sense of trust has been broken and insist on having the bathroom entirely to myself. He accepts, though I do not feel him to be expressing any remorse, and that aggravates me.

Despite my taking only a quick shower and dressing back into my buckskins, Kim has been busy in the kitchen. When I go looking for him to tell him the bathroom is free, I find him completing an incredible layout of sashimi. Using chopsticks, he picks up a bright, clear sliver of, "Buhri," and holds it up to my mouth. That's when I remember I have eaten very little since early this morning.

Tasting that fatty, tiny morsel in my mouth fires up all my juices. Awkwardly, I pick up a pair of chopsticks and prepare to dive in. Kim playfully slaps my hand down. He picks up a piece of pickled ginger, offers it to my mouth, and I accept. He puts me in charge of all those pieces of freshly sliced raw fish with the instructions that no one can eat until he returns from his shower.

I chew that piece of pickled ginger until all that remains in my mouth is fiber but no flavor. Fortunately, he returns quickly, clean pressed, in a different Hapi coat and we sit down on tatami mats across a low table and feast on sashimi.

"Raw fish tastes so good when it is well cut," I say in praise.

"Sashimi Kim specialty," he explains.

"You have many specialties," I tell him.

Kim smiles at my generalized appreciation of him. Eating is relaxing me after what I reflect has been an arduous day.

"Tell me about the tiger," I ask.

That elicits a playful, sidelong glance. Kim lets me see that before he drops it for a somber looking face. He pauses while he collects his thoughts. For the first time, I begin to understand how difficult it must be for non English speakers to learn the language I take for granted.

"Last year World War II, Kim grandmother, young girl, taken Japan be comfort woman. Escape."

"What is a comfort woman?"

"Jugan Ianfu? Soldier sex slave."

"I am so sorry."

Am I ever? The very concept hurts me deep inside. To know someone who has a family member experience being a sex slave is intolerably hard to bear.

"Grandmother teach, in healthy family, woman request sex. Woman come first."

"That's why you asked me to spell it out."

"Kim ask Ms. Judith. Kim make sure."

"Thank you. Did you lose other family?"

"Big bomb Hiroshima, Nagasaki kill many 1,000 Korean slave worker—lucky. Living, sick."

Again, when I dig through what he just said, I understand despite the complexity of his seemingly twisted logic.

"That would have made me a monster," I say.

He points with his chopsticks in the direction of the backyard.

"Tree fix Kim," he explains. "Kim fix Ms. Judith monster. Forgive—always remember."

"Wow!" is the best I can manage as the enormity of what he must feel.

Yet, how readily he gave himself to forgiveness sinks in to my view of the world.

By comparison, Kim's story makes my little Vision Quest trip up the River of Stars feel like kindergarten for forgivers.

"Why did you come to America?" I ask.

"Kim forgive Japan," he says. "War stop, America make weapons. America Kim tiger. Powerful! Kim job, train Ms. Judith. Ms. Judith job, teach people. People job, pacify tiger."

"Teach people to pacify America?" I exclaim. "Get real. Me? How?"

A_LONE

"Meditate; future visible. One hour each day. Kim teach Ms. Judith."

Having rich protein in my belly, the whole world takes on a different appearance. My anger with Kim dissipates as I grow closer to him appreciating his difficulties to express complex ideas without having control of the nuances of basic English. The evening grows magical with our story telling exchange.

Kim is most intrigued by my adventure at the high school and my encounter with Dr. Hyde. I think of what happened there simply as occurrences.

Next morning, I enter Sarah's house through the permanently unlocked front door. I go directly to the kitchen, where Sarah and Ray sit eating breakfast.

"Good to see you both up and about," I say.

They smile, simultaneously. Ray perks right up.

"I'm energized enough to fix a door," he tells the world.

"An' we gots lot needs fixin'," Sarah points out.

She checks me out as I go to the fridge.

"You sparklin' girl," she remarks. "Kim's teachin's?"

Not much in this world is ever going to pass by Sarah unnoticed. I see little to gain by being evasive.

"I had a delightful evening," I say.

"It show," she cackles, nudging Ray's arm. "In fack, it looks like it weres delicious."

Ray gestures with a hand to one ear.

"Oh, yeah," she continues. "Carl calls, aks if yer'll work, tomorrow."

"Sure," I tell her. "How nice he wants me."

"Special as him pays wi' good food."

"And that you accept it for room and board."

"Yer ain't movin's in wi' Kim?"

"I see Ray's cot is free. May I take it?"

"Sho', girl. I special likes yer wants him chases after yer. Let's fix yers a room u'stairs."

My recent arrival appears to have turned some sleeping arrangements in the small town of Corazon upside down. Ray has moved in with Sarah. Andrea has temporarily taken over Ray's house. Kim has begun work on feminizing his house, particularly the bedroom.

Sarah and I struggle with taking the cot to Saffron's room, and shuffling Saffron in with Leticia. I feel bad that neither girl is party to the decision. Sarah assumes full responsibility, which soothes me only slightly.

The phone rings. Sarah yells down for Ray to answer.

When we finish upstairs, we go to the kitchen for Sarah to refresh her coffee. Ray is still on the phone, chatting away.

"Who yer talkin's to, Ray?" Sarah asks.

"Kim," he tells us.

My heart skips a beat. Sarah looks at me right then and bursts out laughing.

"Yer blushin's like a bride, girl."

I check my hot cheeks with my hand.

"Says you," I tell her.

Ray holds the phone away for a moment and asks us, "Are we free to take a drive with Kim?"

"Sho," Sarah speaks for everyone.

"We'll be over in an hour, Kim," Ray tells him and hangs up.

The conspiracy unravels easily. In our discussion of the previous night, Kim learned that I need to speak to the Board of Education about how children in the district are being fed at the school. After meditating on it, Kim decided that this is an excellent opening to get the ball rolling. He and Ray plotted out the details on the phone, and that's how we two couples end up taking a midday drive to talk to staffers at the school district.

I expected resistance from the staff, but, in fact, they are so bored with the mundane issues that typically come to the Board of Education, they almost go overboard explaining the way things work at a Board meeting.

Sarah, Ray and I sign in as speakers for the upcoming meeting. Apart from showing up that's all there is to it.

On the drive back, as Sarah cuddles up to Ray, and, behind them, Kim and I cuddle on the crew seats, Kim and Ray discuss the fine points of what we may encounter.

Andrea swings by in her tin can limo, early next morning, to pick me up to go help Carl load the truck and go to a market.

She is so thrilled with Ray's almost instant "cure"; she will talk of nothing else.

In Carl's truck I hear what expansion he envisions is ahead for him. He wants Andrea and me to work at the farm as much as we can and then, on market days, help vend. By his calculation for every day each of us adds to working the fields and harvesting he can add an extra day at market. The prospects of reducing, even eliminating his debt load sooner than he had bargained for has him planning and plotting like a demon.

As the three of us unload the truck at the market, Carl excitedly explains his latest acquisition, "I signed a market to do Mondays."

"I'm unavailable this coming Monday," I explain to a crestfallen Carl. "We'll be addressing the Board of Education."

Andrea stops setting up the table to look at me with amazement.

"You've been here how long?" she asks. "Three days, is it?"

As we finish unloading and the first customers approach, I tell Andrea and Carl, "I'm terrified about addressing the Board. This is my first time speaking out."

"You talk to complete strangers all the time," he says.

I barely hear him as I answer question of passersby and sell Carl's produce, while we finish stacking the display. I am having the time of my life. I know that by the size of the grin I'm wearing.

The week passes in no time. I arrange with Kim to spend every day I am not working Carl's farm or a market, studying meditation with him for an hour plus teaching him English for an hour each morning. That turns out to be Sunday. We do slip in an occasional evening of couple time, but I insist on returning to Sarah's every night. He gives me meditation homework and I give him English homework.

Monday morning, Kim comes over to Sarah's and all four of us sit around the kitchen table planning our objectives with the Board of Education and what each person will say. Ray seems to have a good handle on the structure, whereas, Kim's fuzzy logic helps him invert the most complex of ideas to put it in a simple, visual format. Ray calls that process reframing.

Each time he reframes something, Kim raises his right hand like giving forewarning. I see that he is teaching me the technique. Near the end of our discussion, he raises his right hand but says nothing. His left hand gestures for me to fill the void. This stuff is tough for me. He gives me one clue.

"Respond emotion," he tells me.

Then, there we are, just the four of us, sitting near the back of raked row after row of empty seats in the public gallery watching the Board of Education at work.

In the presenter box, one disheveled, balding man, who told the Board his name is Harold Wattiss, addresses the Board of Education. They sit above, facing him, in high back chairs behind one continuous arc of a wood desk.

ID ed by name plate they are: chairperson, Frieda Anders, Alice Blake, John Hyland, Ken Mattingly, and Joseph Flynn. Seated next to

Frieda Anders is the Superintendent of Schools, and behind Frieda Anders are several of the women staffers we met when we signed in, last week.

Everyone is deadly serious.

It is hard to believe, but Harold Wattiss sounds like he is reprimanding the Board of Education!

"Again," he tells them, speaking the way an adult cautions a misbehaving 5 year old. "I have to drag you to court to make you govern properly."

He waves a bunch of folded papers at them until one of the clerks advances, takes them from him and places them on the desk before Frieda Anders who brushes them aside.

"You are hereby served," Wattiss tells them. "I expect I will see your usual sorry excuse for an attorney in court. What is the point of having a Constitution if you refuse to use it? That's rhetorical, Ms. Anders."

Clearly bored by his use of public comment time, she waves him away.

"Your time is up, Wattiss," she says.

"You are too good for us, Ms. Anders," he continues. "You ought to resign and find a job more appropriate for your talents, like dog catcher."

Pulling her mike close to her, she pointedly answers him, "With dogs like you, Wattiss, I got that job, too.

"OK. Next speakers—Judith Fargoe? Sarah Clarke? Ray LeMonde? A veritable crowd. Tell me, did something happen? I'm sure you will... tell me. Sit on the front row and come right on up as each one finishes. Judith Fargoe! You're speaking... now!'

Frieda Anders pushes her mic away and sinks into an involved conversation with the Superintendent of Schools, while Sarah, Ray I file front. Kim calls after us,

"Insist, on record!"

Harold Wattiss is still collecting a wild assortment of documents that he brought with him. I can smell putrid flesh at two yards. He is one very sick puppy.

He exits the box and checks me out as we're about to pass each other. With the incensed glare of the Ancient Mariner, he grabs hold of my upper left arm.

"Be direct or you lose them," he instructs me.

Frieda Anders shouts, "Fargoe, your clock is running."

Harold, spinning round, shouts at her, "The clock starts when she starts speaking."

"Ignore that gadfly," she says. "Let's go."

I adjust the microphone in the presenter box. I lean in to begin and pull back when I hear how loud I come through.

"For the record, Madam President," I say. "Members of the Board of Education, my name is Judith Fargoe, I live..."

"Yes, yes," Frieda Anders barks into her mic. "What've you come to say?"

"As a resident of Corazon," I find myself addressing her though, of all five of them, she's the only one not paying attention, "I am very concerned about conditions at our High School, how students are fed..."

"You're obviously new to government process," Frieda Anders speaks into her mic. "Let me explain a thing or two..."

Luckily for her, we are bound by the code of behavior and separated clearly with good reason by desks and presentation boxes. If she wants to play like this, I can too.

I cut right in, "Madam President, please stop the clock while you speak..."

She is outraged.

"You're telling me how to run a public hearing?" she asks, probably hoping to intimidate me.

Good luck!

The same as in Brazilian Jiu-Jitsu where you let your attacker apply force so you can direct that force to the attacker's downfall, I, intentionally, lower my tone and volume.

"I'm protecting my rights to address you for the time allotted me," I tell her.

From the public seating, Harold Wattiss gleefully yells out, “Hang on tight, Ms. Anders. This time, you got a tiger by the tail!”

With one glance Frieda Anders sees I have captured the attention of her colleagues.

Taking a page out of my playbook, she quietly tells the assembly, “I call this meeting into closed session.”

She smashes the gavel down and starts to rise to leave.

I admit, I am caught off guard. Here I am with the pit bull bitch I had always wished and hoped Serena would be so we could go at each other unimpeded—growling, barking, tearing flesh with our bared teeth, using the nails on both feet and hands, bloodying each other with only one way to victory, the death of the other.

My disappointment at being out maneuvered by such a simple parliamentary device must shine like a lighthouse beacon.

“If you have more to say,” Frieda Anders says as she shuts down all the mics, “You’ll have to wait.”

Like the May Queen, she leads her sheepish followers out of the public room.

Kim told me to rely on my emotional response. Here goes.

“Bad food,” I yell, since I am no longer in a public meeting. “Lousy facilities, prison like conditions. How do you expect children to learn? Get involved now or we’ll settle this up at the election.”

The door slams shut behind them.

Like my Greek Chorus, Harold Wattiss, having found a fellow traveler, yells out, “Death to the Constitution! Long live the Board of Education!”

I turn in the Presenter’s box and appeal to Sarah and Ray for reinforcement. They sit, gob smashed spellbound, staring at me as if I were a god descended from the heavens.

Back in the peanut gallery, Kim gestures one of his favorite meditations, the sound of one hand clapping.

I cannot resist letting fly with one of my more dripping, sarcastic comments.

I ask, "Was it something I said?"

Lit with ecstasy, Harold approaches me.

"Yes, and no." he answers me. "Congratulations on joining the select and growing club of people hated by Frieda Anders."

"Why?" I ask him, "Does she behave so outrageously?"

"Because she can."

"The public accepts this kind of behavior?"

Harold gestures to encompass the almost empty room.

"What public? Those sheeple out there believe her PR machine. Welcome to politics. All the average politician cares about is financing the next election. Harold Wattiss is my name, fair government my game."

I am still in awe of Anders' performance.

"That was unbelievable," I say.

"You want unbelievable?" he asks. "Wait till you follow the money..."

Ringmaster of the three ring political circus, Harold has answers. He knows where all the bodies are buried. He leads us into the imposing County Courthouse for the beginnings of a life viewing the dark side of politics.

He guides us to a dingy basement office window to talk to a clerk.

"This," Harold announces, "Is the secret in plain sight. This is the original 99:1. Here, available to everyone, is the data Frieda Anders is confident you will never seek, and if you do, you'll be unable to convince enough people this is the truth to get them voting for their genuine best interest.

"Hey, Janine, please provide these good folks with copies of Frieda Anders' contributions statements and the Corazon precinct registrations for the last two elections."

Ray pulls his wallet out.

"How much does all this information cost?" he asks.

"Put your money away, citizen," Harold announces grandly. "You have already overpaid with your taxes."

Janine returns with a foot high stack of copied documents and hands it to Ray. Kim looks over to me and gestures a hi 5. I raise my hand to slap his. At the last moment before we make contact, he drops his hand.

"Two persons," he tells me, "One hand clap."

Our first real outing and we've hit political pay dirt. He's thrilled!

I'm still trembling from my encounter with Frieda Anders, but especially from the explosion into existence of the real Judith Fargoe. Now that deserves one hand clapping.

DANCE TO THE MUSIC

The toughest part of working with Harold Wattiss is riding with him in the truck. He is the first reminder I have had of the person I was less than two years earlier.

With the truck windows fully open to air out the truck, we drop off Harold at his apartment building and drive back to Sarah's via Kim's house where we drop off Kim.

As Kim gets out, Sarah reminds him, "'Members, tomorro' night's Block Ca'tain meetin'. Yer pretty lady invited, Kim."

We are all of us delighted with our first exposure to the world of politics. We go up the stairs telling each other our favorite moments.

As we enter the living room, Leticia is sitting watching television.

"Off wi' TV till yer homework done," Sarah insists. "Where Saffron and Bebe? Speak chile."

Reluctantly shutting down the TV, Leticia waves a hand toward upstairs.

"Saffron in my room," Leticia answers, adding, "She not happy, gran."

"Ungh-hungh," Sarah answers. "An' Bebe?"

"Him Krumpin'," Leticia tells her.

Sarah turns on a dime and speeds out the door. Ray looks

perplexed. I take off after Sarah.

Sarah hoofs it. Even Long Striding, it takes me over a block to catch up with the woman.

I have no idea how soon we'll arrive at destination so I am direct with her.

"How can Bebe learn if you're angry?" I ask.

"This fam'ly bus'ness," she snaps.

"Your family has grown, lately," I tell her as we round a corner to an alley.

Half a block ahead, a loose circle of gang kids, some wearing kerchiefs on their heads or dangling from back pockets, each person assuming a more "bad attitude" than the next, is arraigned about a loud musical activity.

The Krumpers are a group of boys of Bebe's age taking turns performing high energy dancing to music from a boom box. As Sarah and I approach, gang members close ranks to block our access. Sarah pushes through as Bebe finishes his routine. Physically pushing Bebe aside, another dancer steps in to strut his stuff. Sarah grabs Bebe by an ear pulling him toward her.

"Get on home, boy," she tells him. "Now!"

Bebe squirms to no avail.

"Leggo," he hisses at Sarah. "Yo' embarrassin' me."

"Better embarrasseds than dead," she shouts steering him toward the re-formed wall of gangsters.

"D'yer see me in a gang?" he pleads. "I Krumpin'."

The gang closes to surround Sarah and Bebe. One of them, Hernando, throws a brotherly arm over Bebe's shoulders.

"We got your back," he says.

I aim for Sarah as I tell them, firmly, "Let them out, guys."

From the other side, moving surprisingly quickly and with agilely, a man wider than he is tall, buffed and tattooed, probably ten years older than the rest of the gang, steps in front of me, sneering at my impertinence.

"Where're you going, bitch?' he asks me.

Still riding on the adrenaline rush from my encounter at the Board of Education, I look him straight in the eye and say, "Through you if I have to."

He is amused by my audacity.

From the other direction, Kim's voice calls out, "Tell him, Ms. Judith."

The gang becomes agitated by so many new unknowns. One of the Krumpers shuts down the boom box. The prevailing silence amplifies what is said.

A gang member announces Kim, "It's the Korean shit kicker!"

Another gang member breaks ranks to confront Kim.

"You messed up my bro," he says.

Kim's response shows my little education is making a difference.

"If like," Kim says, "Kim mess you."

It's far from perfect but it does communicate Kim's intent.

My man steps away from me, telling his troops, "Let'm alone. There'll be another day. We'll be back soon, Bebe."

Sarah bridles and tells the man, "Over your dead body, Mung."

Mung keeps his cool, modeling for the young ones.

"Go home, old lady," he tells Sarah.

Hernando lets go of Bebe.

"See you in school, man," he says to Bebe.

Sarah doesn't waste a moment. She drags Bebe away still holding him by the ear.

I step between them and the gang. I wait for Kim. He calmly walks through the gang, stopping to check out Mung's tattoos.

Kim points out a brightly colored image.

"Zado copy picture reverse," he tells the man.

In awe, Mung asks Kim, "You know Zado?"

"Know work," he responds. "Good artist. San Quentin. Kim mouth shut."

To reinforce my position in the neighborhood pecking order, Kim intentionally wraps an arm around my waist and steers me away.

"Hi, dolly!" he says.

As we close in on Sarah marching Bebe along, having released his ear, I critique Kim's greeting.

"Did you mean, *Hi, doll* or *Hello, Dolly*?" I ask.

"Which prefer?" he asks with his impish grin.

"I guess I'll go for the Kim version," I tell him.

That raises a boyish smile from him.

We catch up with Sarah, and Bebe. I make brief eye contact with Bebe.

"You're a fine dancer, Bebe," I tell him.

Bebe sneers at my praise, but puffs his chest out more.

"I aks yer stops 'couragin' him," Sarah cautions me. "'Special if yer bees family an' all."

"Yes, ma'am," I say.

I ask Kim, "How did you know where to find us?"

"Seventh Son take walk," he says.

"Yeah, right!" I scoff. "Anyway, I'm glad you showed up."

"Now Kim walk pretty lady home," he tells us.

Sarah feigns modest embarrassment.

Flapping a hand toward Kim, she says, "Gets along wi' yer, Kim."

Bebe can't believe his grandmother thought the comment was for her.

"Yo think he were talkin' to yo, gramma?" he tells her.

With her head in the air and a lightness to her step, she rebukes Bebe, "Hush, chile."

Early the next morning, as Carl drives the truck to market, Andrea and I scrutinize documents from the County Courthouse. Following Harold's directions, we read until something stands out.

I ask them, "Whatever is Nantucket Water, LLC?"

"Some East Coast water bottling company," Carl says. "Why?"

"They're the largest contributor to Friends of Anders' last campaign," I tell them.

Andrea asks, "For Board of Education?"

"They must see some political gain," Carl says.

This is the first time I am sufficiently distracted that my heart is not truly in my work, I am so obsessed with questions about Anders' campaign statement. Fortunately, Carl's produce is such a known entity that we are busy without having to try.

Later that afternoon, driving home, I direct Carl to Harold Wattiss' apartment building. We check for him on the tenant's register and troop up to his door. I ring the doorbell. Nothing happens. Andrea sees movement in one of the closed curtains. I make sure I am visible to the spy lens in the door. Harold Wattiss answers by opening the door on the chain.

"Hi, Harold," I greet him. "It's Judith, Judith Fargoe. We met, yesterday, at the Board of Education. I have a question for you about Anders' campaign statement."

"Who is that with you?" he asks.

"Andrea and I work for Carl," I say. "He's a farmer."

He closes the door to release the chain. This time when the door opens he steps outside and checks out Carl and Andrea then looks furtively about the area.

"Come in," he says, pulling each of us by the arm. "Come in!"

Once we are all inside, he quickly shuts the door and locks it.

"I have to be careful, these days," he tells us. "They've tried all kinds of tricks trying to get in here."

We look about. I have never seen anything like it. The entire apartment has newspapers piled up in columns from floor to ceiling, one after another. Imagine putting a folded newspaper flat on the floor and another one on top of that until the stack reaches the ceiling. Then imagine stack after stack until the only pathway through the apartment is one person wide. The place is so full, it is impossible to see where rooms end and hallways begin.

"The place is a bit of a mess," Harold says.

I think to myself: Who could tell?

We follow him into a small open area with a couch and chair with a coffee table between them. The smell that we detected, yesterday, is pervasive here. Carl and Andrea both have hands up covering their noses. I try to act cool.

"Can I fix you some coffee?" Harold asks.

"Thanks, Harold," I say confidently speaking for the others. "We only stopped by to ask a question. We need to get back to the farm while there is still workable daylight."

"As you will," he says.

"Nantucket Water is a major contributor of Anders' last school board campaign," I say.

"And now her primary backer for County Supervisor," he says with glee.

I gather we went right to the issue.

"Why?" I ask him.

"Nantucket already has one vote on the Board of Supervisors," he tells us. "Anders will make two. One more is a majority. That allows in a bottling plant."

"OK," I say. "What's the big deal?"

"What does a bottling plant bottle?" he asks.

"Water?" Andrea asks.

"And where is there water worth bottling here abouts?" Harold asks as he leads us into the logic.

"Our aquifer!" Carl shouts. "That's dirty."

"My friend," Harold is not trying to soothe when he says this. "Democracy requires vigilance; every meeting matters. This has been in the works for four years."

"We have to stop Anders," Andrea states.

"She's a shoo in," Harold says with resignation. "The public has been convinced she's a saint. Wait till she makes Supervisor and sells the water out from beneath them. Wake up time!"

"We merely roll over and play dead?" I ask him.

Harold shrugs his shoulders.

"You know what is really sad?" he asks us. "Though those contributions are a lot of money to us, they are peanuts for the company. Can you believe how cheaply our primary resources are being sold for?"

THE BENDS

We can't get out of Harold's apartment fast enough. Even more than the smell was a feeling of desperation that Harold elicited in each of us about how weak we are, politically.

Andrea posited an intriguing concept.

"Harold has spent so much of his life investigating and fighting issues like this," she tells us. "They are eating him alive, like a cancer. That was what we were smelling."

"All those newspapers," Carl says. "Do you think he read them all?"

"Probably," I say. "I believe he did do us a big favor. He let us find one issue we can all get behind to work on. He sees so many issues; he is unable to separate the trees from the forest. We are spared that because we are fresh. He was goading us, getting us angry enough so that we will do something."

"He sure got me angry," Carl says.

"Now each of us has to channel that anger," I tell him.

When Andrea drops me off at Sarah's, the street is packed with parked cars. One, a low rider, stands out for being perfectly reconditioned.

As I mount the steps to the house carrying the load of paperwork from the Courthouse, a police cruiser races down the street.

Sarah's house looks as if it is party central, except there is no music, singing or loud conversation. That's when I recall Sarah asked me to attend her meeting.

What I walk in on is a Block Captains' meeting. A house full of neighbors, some sit, some stand, many with arms crossed, one crochets and another knits. Sarah's grand kids are there, as are Kim and Ray.

Sarah calls to me as I check out the people in the living room.

"There y'ares," she shouts. "Hey, Jose, ever'one, this here Judith! Bin tellin's 'bout how yer yells at them Board Ed'cation folks. We fin'shin's up."

"Thank you, Sarah," says Jose, seated in "my" chair.

He addresses the assembly. "OK. Any new business?"

Kim gestures to me from across the room pointing at the papers in my hands and then to Jose, the chairperson, at the same time nodding his head, yes.

I jump in hoping I know enough to swim in these new waters.

I ask, "May I address the chair?"

With a scowl on his face, Jose glances at me then checks specific people throughout the room for response. Before he gets that consensus, I go for the gold.

"I apologize for being late to the meeting, but I believe I have information that is relevant to this community," I announce.

"Yesterday, several of us were at the County Courthouse where we received campaign fund data as well as voter registration lists for this town of Corazon. The aquifer this town uses for its fresh water supply is about to be sold out from under this community."

Someone shouts, "That rumor's been perking for years."

I wave the documents for Jose to see.

"This is fact," I call out.

The room buzzes with chatter.

Jose shouts out, "Order!" to no avail.

I raise my right hand in the air. Sarah's grandkids mimic me as does a pretty girl standing by the kitchen doorway. Some of the adults know this routine and, in no time, pockets of silence consume the chatter.

Jose takes advantage.

"In future, please allow the chair to recognize you so we may hold an organized and effective meeting," he says. "OK, then. Now, Judith, remind me which block you represent."

"Jose, Judith my dep'ty," Sarah tells him.

"You have a regular posse of deputies, Sarah," Jose comments.

"Yer hears any problem on my block?" Sarah challenges him.

Someone shouts out, "Yeah, too many deputies!"

"Alright, Judith," Jose tells me. "Keep it short so we can close out this meeting."

I put the stack of papers I'm holding down on the floor by my feet as I wave two sheets for the group to see.

"These are Frieda Anders' election campaign financial declarations from her last run for the Board of Education and her upcoming run for County Supervisor," I tell them. "On both filings, her largest donations come from Nantucket Water, LLC. The company already has one Supervisor's vote to sell the local aquifer. Anders would make two, and then they only need one more to clinch the deal."

"May I see?" Jose asks me.

You could hear a pin drop. All eyes are on Jose as I point out the particulars and he reads. He looks up.

"Those are serious accusations," he tells me. "I am requesting this issue be tabled for one month while the information is verified. This certainly casts a whole other light on the upcoming race for Supervisor. Any other new business? Seeing none, I will entertain a motion to adjourn."

A man in a wheel chair calls out, "So move."

Sarah says, "Second."

Jose requests, "Those in favor."

There are various sounds and noises of assent from around the room.

"Meeting adjourned," Jose declares.

He stands up and turns to face me, holding out the documents I handed him.

"May I keep these?" he asks.

Right then, Kim arrives next to me.

"Make copy, give you," he says taking the papers from Jose.

"You must be Kim's new student," Jose says to me.

"Ms. Judith, Kim lady friend," Kim tells him.

"Oh, excuse me," Jose says. "You are Kim's girlfriend."

With the abiding patience of a saint, Kim points to the pretty girl waiting off in a corner.

"Maria, girl," Kim tells Jose. "Ms. Judith, Kim lady friend."

Who needs perfect when you can have Kim's originality?

Jose excuses himself as Kim steers me over to the man in the wheelchair.

"Ms. Judith Fargoe meet Mr. Charles Whitehorse," Kim says.

"Pleasure to meet you, Judith," Charles says. "Your outfit looks like it was made for you."

"It was," I tell him.

"That must have cost you a pretty penny," he says.

This is becoming a polite interrogation. Kim maybe more interested in my responses than Charles.

"It was a gift," I tell him. "From the lady who made it."

"Were you living on the res at the time?" he asks.

"For a year," I tell him. "How do you know to ask?"

"Your friend is in a Bird Clan," he says. "When you make certain motions you resemble a circling hawk."

"Does anyone round here conduct Ceremony?" I ask.

"They do now," he answers with a smile.

A small group of interested locals gather round us.

"What are some of the issues this community faces?" I ask Charles and the others listening in.

They rattle off a regular laundry list: few local jobs, especially that pay a living wage; how far and expensive it is to travel to find work; kids—keeping them in town after they graduate high school; gangs and the problems they cause; the pending freeway by pass making Corazon even more of a ghost town; and an overall lack of communal amenities.

That last item causes me to flash on a memory of the library in Taquinta.

"Where is a representative from the police department?" I ask.

"He was here," someone says. "Sarah stalled trying to keep him here as long as possible waiting for you, and then he got a call. He left right before you came in."

"Do the police control the gangs?" I ask.

There are some odd glances between several people.

One ventures to say, "I guess it's a question of what you mean by control."

Charles interrupts, "It's an economics issue. Gangs tend to flourish in depressed economies. Police are like coral reefs, the breeding ground between land and sea, the community and crime. Whichever is the stronger, the police respect."

"Where does the City Council stand on crime and the community?" I ask.

"The City what?" someone asks cynically to snorts of derisive laughter.

"They world unto they sells," Sarah says.

"We invite them to our meetings," Charles says. "Someone has yet to show."

"Who is your representative at City Council meetings?" I ask.

"We typically have someone there to monitor," Charles says. "But our people are ignored. It's as if, once the councilors are elected, they decide everything for us."

"Have you run your own candidate?" I ask.

"We did once," Charles says. "Hank Morrisey. Within a few council meetings, Morrisey became part of their culture, like he crossed over..."

"So you gave up trying," I state.

"In a nutshell, yes," Charles admits.

"You were able to elect one of your own and he sold out," I say.

"Yeah," someone says. "It's like the City Council and the Chamber of Commerce versus the people."

I emulate the interrogation technique Howard applied with us earlier.

"Who turns out the most votes?" I ask.

"They do," a voice says.

"Who presents the most candidates?" I ask.

"They do," comes response from several people.

"Who is better organized?" I ask.

"You're right," Charles says. "We sit around worrying about crime in our neighborhoods when we should be electing people who know the problems we told you about at the beginning."

"My take is Corazon can use a central cultural facility—somewhere to party, hold dances—a place to create community cohesion." I say.

"We had one," Charles says. "It burned down."

"Before everyone leaves," I tell them. "Allow me to demonstrate the power of a few determined people."

It's show time. I hope I know what I am doing because I have never done anything like this before.

I ask Leticia to bring some of Sarah's silverware.

I call out, "May I have everyone's attention."

People turn to listen.

"Let's form one big circle," I ask. "Leticia is coming around and giving every person a spoon or a fork. Without using force, check if yours will bend. OK? Now, hold it by the handle, upright. When I say, "Start," everyone yell as loud as you can, "Bend! Bend! BEND!" When you intend it to, your spoon or fork will bend. Ready? Start!"

People check each other out and there is very little coordination and not all of them shout, "Bend! Bend! BEND!"

People laugh from embarrassment. Bebe's fork droops over.

"Mine did it!" he shouts.

People stop laughing and look with utter amazement.

"Twist it, Bebe," I tell him. "Bend the tines. Make a pretzel."

He pushes the tines with no effort and they go in the direction he pushes. Grasping the base of the fork he turns and twists it like it is made of putty.

"Yer wreckin's my silverware," screeches Sarah.

"We'll replace it, Sarah," I call out. "How's about Bebe, folks?"

A few people clap their hands together, applauding, as Bebe proudly walks around the circle letting people touch the fork and see it is as hard as metal again.

"OK, people," I say. "Now that you know the impossible is doable, everybody do this again, except, this time, let's have an objective for the group—a goal. I suggest we all think about building a new community center for the people of Corazon."

Jose drops the spoon he is holding down to his side.

"We know Sarah here thinks of you like you're the Messiah," he says. "But how do you plan to convince a bunch of rational folks like us with gimmicks and bendy toys?"

"You are so right," I tell Jose. "Everyone before we try again, make sure you have a genuine metal fork or spoon. Does anyone have something like what Bebe had? If you do trade it in. Good. Remember, this is like a vote to build a community center, soon. OK? Hold it up. Focus your attention on your piece of silverware. When I say "Start" everyone shout as loud as you can, together, "Bend. Bend. Bend!" Get ready? Start!"

This time there is communal energy when they shout, "Bend! Bend! BEND!"

I look around the group and, at a quick count, I spot nine people gaping at folded spoons or forks in their hands. Startled, Jose holds one.

"OK! Show of hands," I call out. "Who ever thought mind power was this strong?"

People are passing bent silverware around while Sarah looks fit to be tied.

"Folks," I say. "Those of you that bent Sarah's silverware, well done! Take it home as a souvenir and bring our hostess a replacement at least as good as the one you bent. Let me ask those of you that bent a piece, are you prepared to build a community center?"

They don't hesitate. "YES!" they yell.

So as not to lose his crew, Jose steps into the middle of the group waving a crippled spoon.

"Are you prepared to register every person in this town who is eligible to vote?" he demands.

"YES!" they shout.

It's a good beginning.

RUMBLINGS

While people drink coffee by a table of pot luck cheese cubes, crackers and fruit chunks, I head for the kitchen and prep myself the food I eat.

I return bearing a plate of cubed meat and pads of butter with a smear of honey. I go over to the only available seat and plunk down on a couch next to the pretty girl, Maria. With eyes as wide as saucers, she stares at what's on my plate.

"What are you eating?" she asks.

"Meat, butter and honey," I tell her. "Want to try some?"

I hold the plate out to her and she recoils up the back of the couch.

"Ugh!" she screeches. "You need to cook it... at least a little. Yuck!"

Charles rolls toward us in his wheelchair.

"When I hunted with my dad," he tells her, "We ate kidney's fresh from the kill. That was a treat. Heat kills enzymes, you know?"

"The deader the better," Maria replies, evidently at ease with Charles. "Why would you even let that past your lips?"

"I eat raw eggs to heal," I tell her. "I eat raw meat for pure protein. I eat raw dairy to detoxify, juice from raw vegetables to balance my body's acidity; and fats to remove toxins."

"Excuse me..." she interjects. "That is so gross."

Bebe comes over, eyeing Maria.

"I tried it," he tells her. "You swallow fast."

Maria looks at him as if he's crazed. Bebe's interest in Maria bothers Jose. He comes over and blocks Bebe's access.

"May I speak with you," Jose asks me.

As I stand, I place my plate of unfinished food on the couch next to Maria. She squirms away, vaults off the couch and goes over to Leticia.

"I owe you an apology," Jose tells me. "I was out of line."

"Thank you, Jose," I say. "I appreciate you saying that. Question is did we make a believer out of you?"

"Believe in what?" he says. "I saw what I saw, but I could hardly begin to tell you what happened... I mean, why it happened. Do you know?"

"Fantastic magic," I say. "It's all in your mind."

Kim appears.

"Hand energy blocked where spoon narrow," he explains. "Metal hot, weight bend."

"That's a lot of energy," Jose says.

"Kim see man hands fire newspaper," he says. "Kim try."

"Did you ignite the paper?" I ask.

The impish look appears.

"Kim busy read paper," he tells us.

><

Jose doesn't let much time lapse after the meeting. He is at the courthouse the next day verifying the authenticity of the documents I showed him. While he is there, he picks up voter registration papers. He holds an extraordinary meeting by phone that night and, using the Block Captains' list, distributes sets of voter registration signup sheets across town. Where there's a will, there's a way.

Sarah is so thrilled with the replacement silverware people give her; she offers to host a spoon bending party at least once a year.

Meantime, she has a surprise for me. She arranges with Jose to hold a registration leaders get together. She and I go ahead.

Just the other side from downtown is a majestic house and, like almost every building in Corazon, it cries out for care. The owner, who lives there all by herself, is a Pilipino American. Cindy is a long time friend of Sarah's. She gives us a tour of the house interior which is decorated in old world artifacts and furnishings of her island culture. I keep being drawn to the windows and looking out on wide swaths of vacant land.

Out back, close to her house, Cindy maintains a tiny garden plot.

"This is all I can manage, these days," she tells us.

Waving her hand to encompass a huge wasteland of sun baked soil, she tells us that when she and her late husband were raising their family, this was growing vegetables and fruits to support her family and several other Pilipino families.

"What are your plans for this land," I ask, envisioning one of the fields at Taquinta that I worked with Dada and Didi.

"We weres hopin' yer haves us a 'gestion," Sarah tells me.

I come out of my reverie and look closely at the two of them. They are positively bursting with anticipation. I look back at the amount of land. I crouch down and sample some loose soil of the plot Cindy is working. I can see right away how rich it is. I stand.

"Well," I murmur. "With enough help and an opportunity to use Biodynamic techniques, I can imagine forty families being supported, year round."

"That all?" Sarah asks as she digs Cindy in the ribs with her elbow.

"Yeah," I say with a confident nod. "That would be my conservative estimate. Carl would be a better person to give you an exact number."

"Would you be willing to take this on as a project if I give you responsibility for it?" Cindy asks.

"While we wait for the school district to tear up the playground and convert that to growing food?" I muse out loud. "This would be an excellent training garden for the high school kids."

I look at Cindy. She has her right hand out to me.

"Deal?" she asks.

I grasp her hand in mine.

"Deal!" I agree.

"OK," Sarah states as she begins walking. "Nex' projeck!"

The three of us stroll to the lot adjoining the other side of Cindy's house. This is twice the size of the one with Cindy's house, garden and wasteland we just left.

"There were a couple houses like mine here," she explains. "They were vacant when there was a fire—burned them to the ground."

"Wow!" I exclaim. "Another fire?"

"When we heard there were plans to build a three storey apartment complex here," Cindy says, "My husband spent us into debt to buy the land and prevent that kind of development."

I'm torn when I hear this kind of argumentation—housing versus territorial control. I look at this vast area of land, so close to downtown which, ratty as it is, has potential. There probably isn't any amount of land this big so central to the whole town.

"I'm getting old," Cindy laments. "This is too much for me to care for anymore."

"What yer do's wi' this?" Sarah asks me.

I see the twinkle in her eye. She can't get more obvious.

"Do you still own all of it?" I ask Cindy.

"Every inch of dry dirt to past that nearly dead tree back there," she points almost to the horizon. "Can the community make use of it?"

I look at Sarah. She twists her gaze skywards. She's making it my call.

"This would be ideal for something like a... community center," I say hesitatingly. "What would you want in exchange?"

"An invitation to everything that happens here," Cindy says, sticking out her hand again.

"Why are you making deals with me all the time?" I ask. "Who gave me all this power?"

Cindy grabs my hand, shakes it and tells me, "Deal!'

There is no question about it in her mind.

"Do you know whose house you're living in?" Cindy asks.

I point to Sarah.

"Sarah's," I say innocently.

"And do you know who runs this town?" Cindy asks.

"The city council?" I ask.

"That's because Sarah here let's them believe they do," Cindy tells me. "Sarah told me you will be in charge of the school growing vegetables and that you are planning to build a community center. I want them both right next to me so I can walk to them. What else?"

I feel my face assume some dorky features as I take in what Cindy is telling me.

"What else, what?" I ask.

"How do you plan to finance constructing this community center?" Cindy asks.

"With community assistance, I guess," I answer.

"I already told you I'm getting old," Cindy tells me. "Let me show you how to speed things along."

Off the three of us go, walking to the glorious edifice that is City and Farmers Bank. At Cindy's insistence, we are ushered in to the branch manager's fancy office. A handsome man about my age wearing a well cut suit and tie and looking every bit like he could own the bank rises from his chair, steps around his desk and warmly shakes hands with each of us.

"Pleased to meet you," he says with a friendly smile. "My name's John Jackson. I insist you call me John. So, how may I be of assistance to you on this fine day?"

"We've come for a construction loan," Cindy tells him.

"Excellent," John says. "How much are you thinking?"

Cindy and Sarah swivel to look at me.

Let's see: I gave $10,000 of someone else's money to a project completed one year ago in the country with free labor; this is a city project with hopefully donated labor; and, about half as big again.

That amounts to, "Forty thousand dollars," I say confidently.

Cindy and Sarah, dutifully impressed, swivel their attention back to John. A smile he was maintaining droops and becomes a serious look of concern. The pencil with which he was crafting his notes hovers in the air as if awaiting directions.

"Forty thousand?" he asks me.

"Too much?" I ask.

"That's a low ball number," he says.

I can see he is beginning to associate my buckskins and their tassels with back country rube; that I am lacking in the ways of civilized folk.

"Forty thousand might," he says with a studied pause, "Build you a half way decent three car garage... maybe. Four hundred thousand could build you a shell for something that with another several hundred thousand may one day resemble a community center, which is what I understood you plan to create."

"Well, today, we're going to borrow $40,000 to build our center," Cindy tells him. "I am offering the lots adjoining my house as collateral."

"The market is too volatile for me to accept local unimproved land as collateral," he says.

"Are you saying we live in a slum?" Cindy demands.

"Literally, land values are too unstable, ma'am," he says.

"We're all friends here, John," she tells him. "You can call me Cindy."

"Thank you, Cindy," John says. "Please consider a more liquid asset to use as collateral."

"Will a CD work?" she asks. "I have at least one for $50,000."

"That sounds perfect," John says. "We will only charge you two percent above your interest rate. Do you have a business plan so I can see how you anticipate paying on the loan?"

Cindy has clearly had enough. She stands up which makes her a fraction taller than John seated.

"So, John," she tells him. "You plan to quibble over details for a loan of $40,000 which I will be guaranteeing and is a fraction of the monies I have invested with your bank."

"My MBA specialty is construction lending," he tells us.

"In other words," Cindy asks, "You know more about construction costs because you studied it in college?"

"That's one way to describe it," John says. "I also received a lot of experience out in the field."

"Well, John," Cindy winds up. "You spent too much time with the bulls when the ones that knew the answers were the cows."

"Is yer boss here?" Sarah asks.

"I am the boss, as you put it," John says.

"Here?" Sarah asks. "Where's one yer report to?"

"San Francisco," John says.

"And the boss of that one?" asks Cindy.

"New York," John tells us.

"Cut to the chase, John," Cindy says. "Is City and Farmers Bank an American owned bank?"

"That's the name for provincial branches like this one," he says. "This is an international bank with shareholders worldwide."

"Yer kiddin'?" Sarah says. "My Bill banked here his whole life 'cos he thot this a local bank."

"We've been a national bank for decades," John says. "We were bought out six years ago by an international banking consortium."

"Well, John," Cindy tells him. "I appreciate you being direct. Right now, this minute, I am withdrawing every penny that is liquid in my accounts, and putting a stop on all my CDs from rolling over."

He stands, visibly shaken.

"I'll see to it right away," he says.

He goes out the door and arrives back within less than a minute.

"We'd like to oblige you but that will leave us with only enough cash on hand for a few hours," he asks. "Is it possible we close your accounts, tomorrow?"

"John," Cindy says. "This is an international bank. I want all my money, now, in cash, federal reserve notes only. Deal with it. Oh, and John, after I take care of my money, I plan on calling everyone I know who banks here, so, be prepared."

"Is there any way I can offer you an extremely low interest loan for the $40,000," he begs.

"What can you do to compete with the zero interest line of credit I am extending, Judith," Cindy asks him. "Speak up."

He shakes his head, no. Cindy opens her purse and waves him away.

"You just saved me a lot of money," Cindy tells me.

"How's that?" I ask.

"He was attempting to lend me my money I had in his bank, and charge me interest on the loan," Cindy tells me. "My question to you is can you build your dream for $40,000?"

"Hopefully," I tell her, "For a whole lot less."

"Did yer gets yer MBC?" Sarah asks.

"I once built something that I will use as a model," I tell them. "I learned on the job."

"Out in a field?" Cindy asks.

"Middle of the desert," I answer.

"I can see why Sarah is so impressed with you," she tells me. "I took my courage from you so I can close my account. Thank you."

MAKE PEACE

This is a picture for the history books. A tall black woman, a short brown woman, and a white woman imitating a circling hawk, walk down the street together. In each hand, we carry several full, plastic shopping bags filled with cash, documents and jewelry from Cindy's lock boxes.

When we arrive, Ray and Kim are waiting for us at Cindy's vacant lot. Kim is off checking out the dying tree at the back of the lot.

Ray asks, "You been shopping?"

Cindy tells him, "We bought a whole lot of green."

Right then Kim joins us.

"Ms. Cindy," he tells her. "Kim help tree."

"Is it worth the effort?" she asks.

"Tree live," he tells her. "Worth effort. Make tree beautiful."

"I think you are deluding yourself," she says. "Go ahead. Give it your best shot."

"Less puts 'way yer groceries," Sarah says. "Could spoils out here in this sun."

Apparently, Ray and Kim both seem aware of Sarah's plans to take over Cindy's unused land for community projects. When we leave them, they operate their own agendas inspecting and familiarizing themselves with the territory.

Inside her house, Cindy has us put the bags on the dining room table so she can go through it all later and decide how to proceed. Now I am aware that she is probably one of the wealthiest people in town, and how few people are invited inside her house, the difference between how comfortably she lives inside her house versus the run down outer presentation to the neighborhood intrigues me. Her answer to my question about that says a lot.

"If I fix up my house before any one of my neighbors does, I will appear to be better off than they are," she tells me. "Change in a block has to conform to the abilities of those with the least. Otherwise, the less well off neighbor is potentially "afforded off" the block. I grew up believing a good neighborhood is one where the community is diversified, racially and economically."

"How long do you wait before you fix up your house?" I ask.

"Because I can afford to?" she asks in response.

I point to the bags in her dining room indicating wealth and substancc to mc.

"I operate with two rules," she tells me. "The first is: Allow people to spend their money their way. How can I know, from the outside, what are your obligations and commitments?

"The second is: Encourage all the boats to float equally," she says pointing to a couple of neighbors' houses even more in need than hers. "How do you think they are going to react when they live across the street from a thriving community center? Least I'm keeping my fingers crossed that I'm right."

I am reminded of how I felt when I first saw the splendid looking bank on a street of run down store fronts.

When we rejoin the men, Charles has arrived and talks excitedly about manning a card table outside of the Social Services' offices to register people to vote.

He says, "I made up a rhyme to tell people as they went by:

Save our water, save our town.
Register to vote, do it nown!

"I am always amazed at how little people understand of how our social system works," he continues. "Most people I spoke to were unaware that every vote cast counts towards state and county entitlements; and we deserve help as much as the next town.

"As for the aquifer water issue, most everyone had heard some of the story but they were so confused, they told me they'd prefer to abstain than make the wrong decision. To me that means we've got our work cut out to educate folks. The easiest idea to sell is having people request absentee ballots because no one trusts the machines. I'm telling you, registering folks sure is an education about who and what is out there."

Maria and Bebe arrive waving sheaves of completed registrations.

"Look what we got," Maria calls out.

"Well done," I say. "These are high schoolers turning eighteen?"

"Yes," Maria says. "Leticia set up a table outside the school auditorium with a banner saying, IF YOU ARE (ALMOST) EIGHTEEN, REGISTER TO VOTE. I helped before class, so did Bebe. A lot of kids stopped by to chat. Some registered.

"At one point, Dr. Hyde came over to ask what we're doing. I told him we were registering people to vote.

"He got all blustery wanting to know how this was a school activity? I told him, it's for Citizenship, Dr. Hyde. And he stood real tall and looked down his nose at me, and said, "You are too young to be changing the world. Wait till you are older."

"So Leticia, who's all excited about making the squad, tonight, let fly, "When is old enough? Your generation already messed up our future." Kids cheer her and Dr. Hyde looks about him. Then Bebe starts shouting, "We're next. We want the power!" Kids begin chanting, "Power! Power! POWER! POWER!" till Dr. Hyde quiets everybody."

Bebe, picking up the story, performs an amusing take on Dr. Hyde, "He gets all principal like, and tells us, *Power is a huge responsibility.*"

"That's when Bebe does a victory dance," Maria says, evidently smitten by Bebe.

A half block away, carrying papers, Jose walks toward us. As he is about to pass by Hernando, who is clearly watching Maria from a distance, Jose puts his arm round Hernando's shoulders, surprising him.

"C'mon join us," Jose tells him.

Hernando puts on a brave face as he approaches us.

"Hey, everyone," Jose calls out as they approach. "D'you all know Hernando?"

I recognize him immediately from the gang surrounding Bebe the time Sarah and I interrupted the Krumping.

"Hi, Hernando," I say. "How did you do, Jose?"

"Better than I expected," he says. "It's as if people are waiting to receive a personal invitation before they'll register or vote. I went door to door on my block signing up neighbors."

As Jose relates his story, several other Block Captains arrive, each proudly carrying handfuls of signed registration forms.

"Charles, you remember Carlito?" Jose asks.

"The graffiti artist?" Charles says. "He went up for a stretch."

"Apparently, he's been back a while," Jose says. "He was thrilled I knocked on his door.

"Low rider Jose!" he shouts. "What y'up to, man?"

"Registering eligible voters," I tell him.

"When did my vote ever make a difference?" he demands.

"Any time you refuse to use it," I tell him. "C'mon, man. Show you got cajones. Sign. You're lucky you live in this state."

"How's that, hon?" he asks.

"Once you do time in some states," I tell him. "They prevent you from voting ever again. It's a privilege, an honor and a responsibility."

We're talking so long, his eldest, Felipe, comes up behind him.

He shouts at me, "What up, Essee? How old you gotta be do this vote thing?"

"Eighteen before election day," I say.

He pushes his dad to one side.

"Outta my way, old man," he shouts. "It time for new kids on the block. Sign me up!"

Jose is a captivating story teller.

I look for Hernando. Without his gang buddies to back him up, he's lost in this crowd. Then, I see he is trying to avoid being seen by Cindy. Fat chance. She's of the same ilk as Sarah.

Cindy steps up to Hernando and addresses him sternly in a foreign language. He becomes submissive. The change intrigues Maria. Jose uses the opportunity to distract Bebe by having him show Jose their registration results.

After Cindy finishes talking, Hernando walks to the back of her house to a garden shed.

"I apologize for speaking to Hernando in Tagalog," she says to the assembly. "I know his family is having problems right now. I told him, *Your ancestors gave you life, brought you here. You are Pilipino American. Be proud of who you are.*"

Maria watches Hernando return with a shovel. Cindy directs Hernando to a spot in the middle of the double lot. He trudges over and begins work. It's slow digging.

I'm tempted to tell him about soaking the ground but something about the way Cindy addressed Hernando tells me not to interfere. She has purpose in her actions.

Cindy extends her arms in a universal gesture inviting people in.

"After the girls' basketball game, tonight," she announces, "Please invite everyone to a pot luck here to celebrate my donating this land for the community center. Hernando will prepare a traditional Pilipino dish for us."

I give Cindy a long hug. That raises a beatific smile on her face.

Jose collects all of the registration documents.

"We are going to put our heart and soul into registering this town," he tells us. "After that, we are going to really turn out the vote."

At the evening high school girls' basketball game, Kim and I sit behind Ray and Sarah in the bleachers. This is a classic small town cultural experience. As important as the game is, this is family night. It's like the parents are out on a date and bringing the young kids. More amazing to me, everyone is dressed down either in sweats or grubbies.

Reminiscent of movie night at Taquinta, high school basketball is a spectator, vocal participation sport. Within seconds of the start of the game, family and friends of the girl holding the ball are on their feet to scream directions and gesticulate moves. Every player has her own extensive coaching division.

This is a special game for Leticia. As a Junior, tonight is her first time playing for the school in the top league. Sarah confides in me that the team expects to lose so it will be a good experience for Leticia and no one will blame her for the outcome.

Leticia has been instructed over and over to be a team player. She acquits herself admirably. It's a tough game and the Corazon Heartthrobs have to scramble to stay within one point of the visiting team by the start of the second half.

An ancient, tacky, hand numbered score board—over shadowed by a clear, bright sign for City and Farmers Bank—shows the home team down by 1 point at the end of the last quarter. On the sidelines, cheerleaders cavort frantically.

The home team intercepts a pass from the visitors and moves the ball down the court to Leticia who is unmarked. She moves the ball forward, searching for a team mate to pass to. Every parent, every grandparent, every fan and the entire bench are all on their feet screaming one word, in unison—SHOOT!

The visitors are in a daze of disbelief that their defense is so wide open. With one last searching glance for a team mate and one foot inside the zone, Leticia releases the ball into a forward arc. The buzzer screeches for game over as the ball completes its trajectory, teeters on the hoop rim, and drops in as a defender makes a frantic attempt to retain the narrow margin. The ball drops through the net. The home crowd goes berserk.

Grown adults behave like crazed animals. Babies cry, young children stare in disbelief as parents commit far worse behavior than that for which those children had been previously reprimanded.

As Sarah hugs Ray, I lean forward and massage her shoulders. Kim has one hand performing deep muscle rub rotations on my back.

Cheerleaders vault across the court. It's the Heartthrobs' first win in ages.

Something in the town is changing.

Sarah and I go parent by parent to invite them to the potluck party at Cindy's vacant lot. They are thrilled and delighted to have a way to celebrate together. Anyone would think it is Sarah who scored the winning points the way people congratulate her.

Dozens of lit Tiki torches make for a festive atmosphere illuminating Cindy's adjoining lot. Families and neighbors walk or drive up, bringing folding chairs and bearing bowls of food for potluck that they put on long tables set up to one side. As directed by high school kids, they arrange their chairs to form a wide circle on the lot.

People eat, drink and socialize while they watch Hernando, in the center, turn a whole pig roasting over an open fire pit. Periodically, he slices off meat into baking trays which his enthralled gang buddies distribute to add to the food already on the tables.

Using chalk powder, Carl marks off a circle round the outside of the chairs.

One of the side bar entertainments is people looking more closely at what other people wore to the game. It seems that until now everybody at the game looked ahead, and rarely, if ever, sideways. Wives insist husbands stand and slow twirl so the women may mock them, often in an effort to deflect attention from themselves.

I confer with Jose, Sarah and Cindy. Over riding my objections, they insist I be the one to describe the concept to the gathering.

Picking the moment when people are having the most fun talking among themselves, Jose calls for quiet. No such luck. He turns to me out of frustration. I lift one hand high over my head. With great reluctance, he imitates me and individuals in the crowd follow suit. Soon there is a tipping point, a hush descends and people sit and focus on Jose. Before he says a word, he turns and gives me one quick, boyish grin of delight.

"Friends and neighbors," he tells them. "Thank you for coming to a heck of a party at such short notice and giving up your precious TV watching time. I'm confidant most of you know what parcel of land you are on, right now. What you are about to learn is what plans are afoot to do with this land. For about two weeks now, Corazon has had a hawk riding a thermal over Corazon. Some of you have met her, many of you have heard talk about her. Please relax and enjoy what can only be another spell binding evening with Judith Fargoe."

He claps his hands as he turns to face me. He gestures for me to take the floor as he backs into the shadows.

I step forward and all my thoughts about what I am going to say vanish on a passing breeze. I stand where I can see the most people with a slight turn of my head in either direction. The little bit of applause that preceded me ceases. I can recognize a few people, but mostly they are strangers to me.

I have no idea what possesses me to do it, but I drop to my knees, bend my head forward until it is tucked into my chest. With a wide movement, I first swing out my left hand and close the arm about my head then do the same with my right arm until I am tightly bunched up, low to the ground.

Someone in the group utters a one time, piercing cry of a hawk. My arms unfurl as my head looks up and with deep, powerful strokes I pull myself upright and begin circling, tightly at first, growing wider with each turn. Soon I am running, arms out, tassels flying backwards as I make one pass with my right arm outstretched over everybody seated in the circle. The whole event takes less than a minute.

I stop back at the spot where I started, and, arms down at my side look around the circle at everyone. They all sit with eyes riveted on me.

"What about those Corazon Heartthrobs?" I shout.

There's a momentary pause and then the energy I passed out to everyone explodes as people jump to their feet, the girls, forming a kick troupe, line dance and boys hoot and whistle as they kick out their feet and pump the air with their hands.

I raise both fringed sleeves until my hands join overhead. People slowly calm down, regain their seats and quiet descends as I lower my hands to my sides.

"That basketball game, for those of you unable to attend, tonight, was won through thoughtful and caring teamwork. I want everyone to experience one more example of team work before we sink our teeth into the reason we asked you all to be here. Please make sure any loose items like cups, plates, silverware and belongings are either under or behind your chair. Until this is over, and it will be exciting, stay in your seats. That is the safest place. Go for it, Krumpers!"

Bebe and six Krumpers walk over to surround Hernando who continues turning his hog. They take up positions facing the outer circle of chairs. Each dancer picks someone sitting on a chair and points at them as they wait for the music.

Bebe picks Maria. Hernando sees that and points Bebe out to his buddies.

The music starts loud and each Krumper break dances in his own territory. The music ends abruptly. Each dancer takes off running at top speed only to stop an inch, nose to nose, from the face of their target person. Startled, the gathering sucks air before they break into ecstatic applause.

"You may have noticed Carl marking a circle," I explain to everyone. "By attending this event, tonight, you are helping us define the outside wall of a community center we want to build, right here where we are gathered, for the people of Corazon. This can become your home away from home for you and especially your kids. This can be a place to share your cultures—as Cindy is doing, tonight, with help from Hernando. This has the potential, with your involvement and help, to become the heart of Corazon—the center where the people of the town celebrate their diversity and their commonality.

"Now, I want to tell you a story I learned in a land, far, far away."

As I tell the story, I move in and out round the glowing coals that remain of Hernando's fire pit. I'm creating a shadow play.

"Three bedraggled soldiers returning from the battle front cross a barren farming landscape. After days of not eating, they arrive at an impoverished village. At first, the villagers hide behind locked doors knowing, from past experience, that soldiers can be dangerous. The lead soldier sends his two companions to find four large stones

while he sits with his back to a low wall and marks the ground ahead of him with a stick, all the time observing every activity of the villagers.

When his companions return in each hand bearing a smooth stone twice the size of a man's fist, the lead soldier has his companions place the stones to form a tight square on the ground. The three soldiers stand well away from the stones so any villager peeking out is able to see the stones and how large they are.

The soldier shouts,"Come enjoy a bowl of delicious stone soup... If anyone is hungry."

One by one, villagers approach the soldiers. They each arrive carrying an empty bowl and a spoon. They are very disappointed to find only dry stones.

The only person to approach empty handed is a haggard woman, bent double with age.

"You offered us soup," the old woman says between hacking coughs. "All I see is stones that are even drier than my wrinkled skin."

The soldier points his stick at her and nods his head.

"You must be the wise old crone we were told lives here," the soldier says. "You are clearly smarter than all these others who can see the stones as plain as day yet they still arrive with bowl and spoon in hand.

He waves a hand for his companions to follow his example as he leads them to bow before the old woman. This again confuses the villagers who had long thought the woman to have lost any marbles worth keeping.

"We are simple soldiers," he tells the villagers. "Because of our generosity to people along our road home, we were blessed with these four stones. Wherever we can, we share the nutrition inside these rocks. All we need is a big enough pot, water, and a fire to heat the soup. In no time at all, we'll be so full of good food, we will be sitting round spinning yarns, singing our favorite songs and drifting off to sleep, the way it was long ago. Before we start lighting the fire, placing the stones in the pot or pouring in any water, we need permission from grandmother, here, to make the soup."

After years beyond memory of having the villagers kick her as they passed by her, throw sticks, stones and rotting food at her, and generally regard her as the scourge of the village, it is pleasant to be called by the polite term for grandma. It is a delight to have the entire village wait for her to give the OK on any subject, particularly, on whether they should eat.

Because it takes her so long to say yes, guilt begins to consume the villagers. One by one, they line up to take their turn, whispering in her ear how much they regret saying and doing the terrible things they have done to make her life so miserable. Many of them even say that, whether she says to make the soup or not, they foreswear treating her adversely ever again. Then, many of them ask, please say yes. Adding though, of course, we want you to eat before any of those other worthless peasants.

The soldiers stand by, taking no part in the decision. If asked, they answer that they always went with the decision of the village elder.

Had they ever not eaten? The last village before this one.

Are they hungry? Yes, but they feel badly for villagers who only have what they can grow and soldiers are always coming along and stealing everything.

You are soldiers. Do you ever steal? We were tempted but resisted. For that we were gifted the four stones.

By this time, everyone has apologized to the old woman.

"Well," says the soldier, "What is your decision, grandmother?"

Without a moment's hesitation, she says, "We eat!"

All the villagers are relieved she said yes. They rush off to quickly return with a huge pot, loads of wood, and buckets of the freshest water the soldiers have tasted for months.

"Throw in the stones," the villagers urge the soldiers in efforts to get food in their grumbling stomachs.

"These stones are very delicate," the soldier says. "They need to be treated with deep reverence and respect for giving up all the nutrition they do."

Thus, the soldiers have the villagers polish the stones with handfuls of hay until the stones gleam. The soldiers insist on bagging all the hay that was used so they may dispose of it far away from the village so the villagers will be safe from any adverse reactions. They promise they will take turns through the night guarding the hay so it will remain in the bag. First one soldier will lie on the hay, then the next to ensure that it stays in the bag.

"If it were to escape," the soldier tells the villagers, "Chaos worse than war will besiege the village for years, maybe even decades to come."

When the water begins to boil, the soldier takes each stone individually and has the old lady bless it. Then the stone is gently lowered into the cauldron. When all four stones are in, the soldiers ask the villagers to tell them jokes while they wait for the soup to cook.

After an hour of side splitting stories and jokes, with tears streaming down his face, the lead soldier takes his stick and stirs the soup. The villagers are having so much fun, more than they can ever remember; they barely take notice of the soldier.

He borrows a spoon and dips into the soup. Carefully, he blows on the spoon to cool it, and then he slurps a sip. Posing like a chef tasting his finest culinary preparation, he smacks his lips, making all the villagers hungry to share.

"It's unlike me to boast," he says, "But, I have to admit, this is one of the better soups I have made with the stones. Before I share it with you all, because you have entertained us so royally, and, I have to say, I cannot remember laughing so hard, I want this to be the best soup I ever made. Because we have fed so many with these stones in the past, they are not working as well as they did the first few times. If we had a vegetable or two, perhaps a salted hams hock—that will assist the stones. Does anyone feel they can contribute?"

Many of the villagers go home and take the last item they have been storing and, proudly, contribute to the soup. When everything is in the pot and cooked, the soldier serves the old woman first and requests her permission to feed the other villagers. Permission granted, he pours bowl after bowl for each of the villagers. When everybody is full and satisfied, the soldier politely asks permission for him and his fellow soldiers to eat.

The villagers are embarrassed they have not fed their visitors. The villagers insist that the soldiers eat their fill. After they finish eating, with teary eyes, the soldier makes a speech.

"We are deeply touched by your generosity," he tells them. "We have talked among ourselves and decided to gift you our precious stones that have fed us so well for so long. If you are inclined to share the remains of today's repast we will be eternally grateful. We pray your village will continue to prosper."

With that the soldiers leave the village to journey home. They are sent on their way with the cheers of their new found friends, with soup enough for two days march, a bag of hay to sleep on and many new jokes with which to pass the time of day."

Having come to the end of the story, I pause. A few people applaud, others stretch.

"The reason I told you this story is because of something that happened, today," I tell them. "At the Block Captains' meeting, a few nights ago, the possibility of building a community centre for Corazon was discussed. Today, Cindy offered the community of Corazon this land as a site on which to build the center, about the size of the circle Carl drew. Big, right?

"So three of us went to the bank. You know City and Farmers' Bank on Main Street. Give me a show of hands how many of you, like Cindy, bank there."

Many hands go into the air.

"How many of you bank there," I ask, "Because this is a local bank?"

Many hands go up.

"How many of you bank there," I ask, "Because this is a state bank?"

A couple hands go up.

"How many of you bank there," I ask, "Because this is a national bank?"

None are raised.

"If you follow my train of thought," I say. "It will come as a shock to learn, as we did today, that this is merely our own local branch of an international consortium. Basically, that means you put your hard earned money in and they—strangers to Corazon—take it out. That may explain the anomaly of why the bank building looks wonderful and the rest of this town looks like it can use some help.

"The bank has been making Stone Soup with your money," I tell them. "When the bank leaves town, which it can do at a moment's notice, they may even take the stones with them."

While I intend to let this sink in, the response is immediate and irate.

Jose steps back into the circle to stand next to me.

"OK, folks!" he shouts.

The conversation grows louder. He looks at me and, keeping my hand down at my side, I flap it until he gets the message. He raises his hand. Within seconds he has quiet; plus, a group of seething, angry, but silent people.

"I only met Judith a few days ago," he says. "But she rarely asks a question without knowing a good answer. What is the answer, Judith?"

"One answer," I emphasize, "Is to keep the money local."

"How?" Jose asks.

"The idea has been raised of creating a Credit Union," I tell them. "If you maintain due diligence, you will have exactly what you expect to have... and... it will all belong to you."

Raising his hand to capture peoples' attention, Ray stands.

"I got a letter from a realtor who has a buyer for my house," he says. "If I knew for certain where I will live once I sell my home, I will use the sale as seed money for our Credit Union."

"Well, young fella," Sarah calls out as she stands next to Ray and takes his hand in hers. "I'll takes yer... jus' marriage is outs the pichure."

Kim stands up and steps behind Sarah and Ray.

He raises his hands over their heads palms down as he announces, "Mrs. Sarah, Mr. Ray—old souls. Been together many lives. Will again."

"Thanks, Kim," Sarah says. "Who yer callin's old?"

People laugh, applaud and a few briefly gather to congratulate the couple.

A gnarly man stands and addresses the group, pointing to the teenagers.

"My contractor's license is good," he says. "If Ray will bring his carpentry skill, I'll build your center for one dollar. All I ask is, you youngsters crew this and get a trade under you."

"Thank you, Alfredo," Jose says.

"That is incredible!" I say. "If you young people will hook up to be mentored by any of the amazingly talented people here, you will own this town and have good reason to stay to raise your own families here."

"I will be honored to provide straw bale for the construction," Carl states.

"Save that for a hay ride," Jose says. "We're talking about building a community center building."

"I built something that is almost this big using straw bales," I tell Jose. "It's very strong and excellent insulation."

"This I have to see," he says, turning away. "Sarah, if you're taking Ray home, maybe you want to clear a car or two from your yard."

"What yer gots in mind, Jose?" she asks him.

"A 50s fin-tailed Cadillac," he says.

"How yer knows what I got?" she asks him.

People laugh. Jose goes over and gives her a hug.

"Sarah, I know who owns what piece of junk, all over town," he tells her. "That's my business."

"What will we do for plans for the center?" Alfredo asks me.

"I'll draw them up for you to review," I tell him.

I raise my hand for quiet as people begin to move about.

"Folks," I call out. "Before we party, I ask that as many of you as can please attend next Monday's Board of Education meeting. Corazon high school needs help. We want everybody who can to speak to the Board. Let me know your availability. We have signup sheets next to the food tables. Please take a moment and give us your contact information. You may reach me at Sarah's house planning. Enjoy!"

The Krumpers' boom box takes over and some danceable music comes on. The kids take over the area around the smoldering fire pit. Some adults join in, others slow dance in the shadows. It's fun!

A small group of us stay on to clean up. While Jose helps, Maria stretches out on the backseat of his immaculate low rider car, the one I saw outside the Block Captains meeting. When we are all done, Jose offers us a ride, but I take Kim up on his offer to walk me home.

As Kim and I set out, we watch Jose's car, about two blocks away, brake, shut down his car's lights, his reversing lights go on briefly, and then all the car's lights go out.

Already, Kim is pulling me to run after Jose.

With the light from a nearby street light, we can see Jose's car, with all its light out, slowly turn to drive down an alley.

PRELUDE

Kim and I arrive at the alley just as Jose, about five houses in, turns on his headlights. We all see what is happening at the same time.

Kim grabs my wrist and restrains me from moving faster than a steady walk.

"Breathe," he tells me. "Breath control anger."

A flurry of shadowy figures ahead include Bebe being involuntarily jumped in to the gang who are taking turns beating on him. The sudden glare of the high beams stops the action.

The big guy, Mung, shouts, "Santos, shut those lights out!"

Jose gets out of his car, but he's too far away to do anything other than watch as one of the younger gang members uses a brick to smash the passenger side headlight dead.

"Hey, you!" Jose shouts at Santos.

More than protecting his car, though, Jose is in motion on another mission.

People move like leaves caught by a wind sprite. Jose cuts through the activity to grab Bebe and put him behind him as he turns to get out of the maelstrom.

On the driver's side of Jose's car, Kim stops ahead of me, stooping, poised to act. I crouch down behind him and wait. Seemingly from nowhere, Hernando arrives on the passenger side of the car. At the same time, he and I both see a terrified Maria sitting up on the back seat, watching. I hear him whisper to her through open windows.

"Lie on the floor and cover your head," he tells her. "Stay there till your dad returns. Get down. Now!"

"Clive, get that other headlight," Mung yells.

Clive is quickly in place to take a swing at the remaining light. Kim leaps forward to grab the kid's brick holding hand. He squeezes until the brick drops and Clive screams with pain.

With the attention temporarily off of him, Jose drags a bloodied Bebe away from the fray. Still holding Clive's hand in his vice like grip, Kim steers the kid back toward the gang. As Jose and Bebe reach the passenger side of the car, I slip into the shadows on a mission of my own.

Believing that Hernando has stationed himself to protect Maria, Jose does not consider Hernando as anything but a fortunate presence.

"Thanks for protecting Maria, Hernando," he tells him. "Get in the car."

That's when the two boys confront each other in the almost pitch dark. Bebe stares at Hernando with anger and rage. Hernando looks at Bebe, unapologetically. Both know Hernando is playing a double game. Bebe spits blood at Hernando before Jose can steer him onto the front passenger seat and slam the door shut.

"Thanks, Jose," Hernando says. "I'll be OK."

Hernando turns and heads out of the alleyway under the cover of darkness.

By now, Kim has steered his hand held hostage, Clive, into the middle of the gang and is confronting Mung. If anyone approaches too closely to him, Kim squeezes his hostage's hand making him scream with pain.

Imagining a movie mindset showdown, Mung sneers at Kim, "I guess this is it!"

At that moment, I tap Mung on his left shoulder. As I anticipated, he responds by turning to the left thereby putting the bulk of his weight on his left leg. Pulling my right leg up and back, I lean left and release a power kick against the back of Mung's left knee. Off balance, Mung crumbles. As he heads to the ground, I vault across his chest, grabbing his collar and steering him onto his back. The sound as he hits the ground muffles the rush of air bursting out of his lungs.

Taking hold of his collar in a cross grip, I shut down his windpipe with my full body weight on that arm, re position myself, and prepare to smash his face with my fist.

His eyes go from surprise, to confusion, to panic and end on fear with my fist racing at him. His eyes close anticipating the blow.

He opens his eyes to a scenario lit by one headlight.

I am totally astride him, holding him in a cross grip with one hand at his throat, my other hand clenched in a fist, half an inch from his face. Beyond me, the rest of the gang stares at their leader—felled by a woman.

"Kim ready," Kim calls out. "Ms. Judith finish?"

I look Mung in the eye making sure he knows I am in position to cause him serious damage.

"Are we finished?" I ask him.

"We're done," he admits.

Before I give him any slack, I caution him, "Any reprisals and I absolutely will go through you. You understand me?"

Mung, face up to the sky, is performing a full, logic assessment right there. As ruthless as any of his gang may be, with him like this, straddled by a woman who is clearly able and prepared to send him into the hereafter with one well placed blow, he is not providing effective leadership. His gang is powerless in the face of Kim making Clive scream at will. Then, there is Jose lurking about prepared to kill to protect his car. This is game, set and match.

"Yes, ma'am," Mung tells me.

I immediately back off him and stand clear. I extend a hand, offering to help him up. He accepts my offer, but gives me no weight as he stands. We shake hands.

Releasing Clive, Kim strolls over to me, puts an arm around my waist and walks me out of there as Jose slowly backs his car out of the alleyway.

Kim invites me back for the night.

"I would love to," I tell him. "However, I think I am going to be needed to restrain Sarah. Thank you for the invitation."

By the time we get to the house, Sarah's mothering instincts have superseded her anger reactions, she is so grateful to have Bebe safely home.

I ask Kim if his offer still stands.

"Kim accept mind change," he tells me.

"Good," I tell him. "This lady changes her mind a lot."

"Meditate," he answers.

The next morning, Kim and I dress warmly and head out into the backyard. He is concerned that, as much meditating as I am doing, I am not doing enough. I'm beginning to sense that Kim sees the future equivalent to how most people see the past. Though he hasn't said anything directly to that effect, I sense that I am not measuring up to his expectations of me. I feel it as an urgency, more than as a factual or stated concern.

We both assume Easy Pose, fingers in Gyan Mudra, eyes as slits focused on the tip of the nose, concentrating on the breath. Our backs touch the tree trunk. We have done this many times. I draw great comfort from the tree. It acts as a quiet and calming influence over me.

It may only be in my imagination but I slip into long, calm waves of relaxed focus. For the briefest of moments, it's as if I am hallucinating. The small area of contact my back has to the tree explodes with vertical streams of yellow sparking electricity. Like I say, it's a flash. Maybe only half a second in length, it is also timeless in duration.

It reverberates in my memory wanting to dominate my meditation. Having no information from Kim on such possibilities, I push back, resisting letting it become my focus. As in Quantum Physics, the mind of the observer dominates. Soon, I am floating in my expectation of what is meditation.

For me, when I meditate, there is a luxurious place where all I perceive is my brain as a box with my perceptual awareness of me magnifying out to the infinite boundaries of the Universe.

Meditation is like a flexible, three dimensional yoyo between who I am and what I am part of. It works, best of all, when I release expectations and see the box with nothing in it. The yoyo effect becomes a continuous stream from me, as small, to the Universe, as vast, everything. I simply bounce back and forth, until what I am is both small and large plus everything in between, simultaneously.

When I arrive at that point, I know to wait until the yoyo effect stills out. Then me, not I, is able to step in to the box and be both large and small, to dance, cavort, do hand stands for real, like I wanted to do in Rachel's shower. I am in pure, lucid... meditation. I am there and not there, all at once. I am omnipotent, yet nothing.

I single out one thought from the constant stream, the chatter that is my brain, and allow it to float free of gravity like a string of words. It becomes images, transmutes into concepts, and evaporates to nothing.

Like a meteor beginning its flaming path across the night sky, I become aware of a physical body invading my infinity. I feel vulnerable. In the time it takes to think that I am thinking, I race back to consciousness. I am almost there when the tree explodes into a vision of force grasping the deep, thick dark of the ground and hurling it up the trunk like a massive pipeline of electricity to erupt as a Fourth of July fireworks display across the entire sky.

The fleeting image is gone—now only a memory that I grasp for—and I am back in posture. I lust for that image. It is what I hoped meditation will be; not this long eternal empty space... where I am at peace.

As usual, I want the glorious instead of the calm. Yet, by aiming for the calm, I receive intonations of the glorious. Perhaps there is no glorious, just my imagination toying with reality.

Boing! The bell rings.

Reality arrives as a loud, resonating vibration filling all my cells with joyful activity.

Boing! Again.

This time it is aggravating.

Boing! A third time and I reluctantly re-enter myself and wake to the presence of Earth.

Kim is up on his feet as the first strike occurs. By the second, I am vaguely aware of him moving down the side of the house. By the third, I have dragged myself upright to enter the house, put on my slippers and look out the window to see Kim talking with Hernando who is manfully digging his heels into the dirt attempting to halt the striker.

Kim grins at Hernando's efforts.

"Like sneeze—stop," Kim tells him.

Hernando is relieved he is not messing up.

"Thanks, Mr. Kim," he says. "Is Judith here?"

I get a flash of the meteor entering my space. Was that a premonition? Am I seeing the future and not realizing it because I meditate the same as I dream—in metaphors?

"Ms. Judith meditate," Kim explains.

I decide that's enough of letting Kim cover for me and open the door with a blank face, only to light up with a smile when I see Hernando standing there.

"Hi, Hernando," I greet him. "Great roast you did."

"You ate some?" he asks in shock. "Bebe says you eat..."

Enough about his pal, Bebe.

"What I ate was barely heated," I say.

"What if you catch Trichinosis?" he asks.

"A little pork is good," I say. "What's up?"

"I want to be an artist," he blurts out.

Oh! So the gang thing is a way to pass the time until lightening strikes and creativity takes over?

With negative thoughts like that, I am grateful for having learned to think before I speak. I take off my slippers, step outside and close the door. My bare feet ignite on the dirt.

I feel myself unable to diffuse the surge of energy from meditating, experiencing the tree exploding.

I decide to channel my energy.

I go into a free style headstand and begin vertical pushups.

Zichrini would be proud of me. Hernando stares.

"I want to be an artist, too!" I say, as I work out. "Great. So you can teach me."

He tries to imitate me. Kim points to the wall. Hernando moves to the house and struggles to get one foot in the air. He stands up.

"Then why did you volunteer to do drawings for the Community Center?" he asks me.

"I am looking for a teacher," I say. "Here you are. See? It works."

I stand, then point to the ground. Hernando attempts to get his feet in the air. I grab his feet and push him into position against the wall.

"I... I..." he squeaks.

"Pray harder," I instruct him. "Imagine you're at a waterfall. Watch the water drop. Push against the water. Focus!"

Hernando makes a small movement up, then he quits, letting his feet drop. He stands.

"You must be incredibly strong," he tells me.

"Try this," I say.

Standing with my feet shoulder width apart, I raise arms straight out in front, palms down. Keeping eyes front, torso straight, I bend at the knees. As I go down into a squat, my straight arms arc down and back. As I begin to stand up, my elbows bend until I am standing upright and my hands go out front again.

He hesitates. I wave him to join in as Kim, on cue with me, starts on the next round down.

"Hindu Squats," I say.

Hernando tries

"Down, breathe out," Kim says.

After maybe fourteen attempts, Hernando stops to massage his aching thighs.

To accommodate Hernando, Kim and I stop.

"Hindu Push-ups," I tell him.

Kim and I drop into push up position with feet spread wide apart, back arched upward, head tucking chin to chest. We rock forward as far as our arms let us, stomach dropping almost to the ground, head swinging up and back, then reverse.

Hernando tries a few until he collapses face down.

Kim and I stop. We stand and then drop into a backwards arch, feet flat, stomach up, resting on the bridge of the nose, arms crossed over the chest.

Hernando doesn't even try.

After a minute, we both stand. Hernando is pure admiration.

"Do the community a favor," I say to him. "Bring your hoodlum friends to the Board of Education meeting on Monday."

He tries to cover himself.

"They're kids I know from school," he tells us. "That's all."

"Right," I say. "Sure."

He gives me a sidelong smirk.

"For protection?" he asks.

After last night's demonstration? I think not.

"Want to do hill sprints?" I ask him

"I gotta get to school," he answers. "Thank you."

"For what?" I ask.

"Showing me your exercises," he says, seriously. "Inviting me teach you to draw. Friendship."

I get another flash of the meteor, only, this time it is zooming across the mental screen of my frontal lobes.

"You're an amazing person," I tell Hernando earnestly. "You'll see that soon. Let's talk art after Monday's hearing."

I pull him to me and give him a tight, friendship hug, heart to heart. As I let him go, he turns his head away to hide tears that are forming. He runs out of the yard.

I look at Kim. He has a big warm smile, a new smile for me.

"Tree like Ms. Judith," he says, walking off by the side of the house.

I take in what he says as I step toward the bell and striker.

With both my hands resting on the wood striker post, I say to no one in particular, "Ms. Judith like tree."

FORGIVENESS

Jose informs me that people in Corazon have no memory of the community being so active. Between preparations for the upcoming Board of Education hearing—Harold Wattiss recommended we prepare notes for consecutive speakers—the creation of an investigatory committee to form a Credit Union, people drawing their money out of City and Farmers Bank, and the Block Captains spear heading a full out voter registration campaign, the town gives off a new sense of vitality.

People smile and wave to each other when out taking walks early in the morning and late at night, even when driving.

Or as Sarah describes it, "People walks? In this town? Heaven A'mighty, what the world comin's to?"

People find a few moments to chat. There are lots of comments about what can be done to fix up shops and houses. First people dream, from which, change begins.

A sad outcome is that, because of the run on the bank, John Jackson was pulled back to San Francisco and an old timer sent to the Corazon branch in an effort to staunch the flow. The net effect is people in Corazon realize their power and more people than ever remove their funds and other financial instruments from the local branch of City and Farmers' Bank.

On the good side, a neighboring town's Credit Union enters into talks with the Corazon committee, offering to either set up a branch in town or advise on forming an independent Credit Union. The members of the committee decide on a No Comment policy when individuals begin receiving telephone calls from a newspaper reporter friend of Harold.

At the Board of Education hearing, it's like old home week. There is only enough room in the public seating if everyone gets up close and personal. The clerk responsible for signing in speakers to address the board is working furiously to obtain correct information and make sure everyone who wants to, signs in before the cut off when the hearing begins.

Harold, escorting the reporter, arrives at the last minute. Once he spots me, he waves a neighborly greeting and nods approvingly as he assesses the crowd.

Sarah and I arrange for Bebe and his fellow Krumpers to sit on the front row. They wear sweatshirts. One of them has hold of their trusty boom box.

Jose and Ray do final seating, encouraging people to squeeze together that extra inch, to make room for one more on a row. Mung and his gang, along with Hernando, station themselves at the back of the room by the two swinging doors leading out to the hallway. Kim is situated at the very back row in the corner. He meditates until the Board members file in.

Anders is unaware of the crowd until she sits down and glances out. She looks through her notes and the schedule for the meeting, and then pulls her mic close.

"How good to see so many people," she comments.

She turns and gives questioning glances to her impenetrable clerks.

"Is there something on the agenda?" she asks them.

"You betcha!" hollers Harold. "Justice!"

Recognizing that the proceedings are under way, several kids pop up round the room, using the cameras in their mobile phones to record the happenings.

Anders reacts immediately.

"People recording," she calls out while covering her mic with her hand. "You need written permission before you document."

"They're allowed," Harold corrects her. "This is a public hearing. Behave yourself, today. You also have a reporter here."

She ignores him and glancing over her schedule, speaks into her mic.

"Normally, we do our scheduled business first," she says. "But I am sure you all want to go home, so we'll begin with public com ..."

"You got something to hide?" Harold shouts out.

"Start with public comments," Ms. Anders states. "Who is first?"

The clerk speaks into her mic.

"President Anders, we have Judith Fargoe, Sarah Clarke and Ray LeMonde," she reports. "I have a list of 36 speaker requests."

"What?" Anders says, appalled. "That's more than an hour."

"72 minutes plus shuffle time," Harold shouts out in glee. "Or did you get left behind during math?"

"I'm cutting it off at 10 speakers," Anders declares.

"You'll hear them all," Harold yells. "Remember, we're pretending this is a democracy! You've been left alone so long, you forgot."

"Mr. Wattiss," Anders says. "You are making a mockery of this hearing."

"I'm only trying to help," Harold responds. "If you prefer, I'll let you do it all by yourself."

The public laugh as the repartee grows. Anders hammers her gavel.

"Order in the Chamber," she shouts. "If you people behave uncivilly, I'll have the Chamber cleared. Fargoe, you're up."

"Starting pitcher," Harold announces. "Judith Fargoe."

People snicker.

I step into the presentation box and adjust the microphone to address the Board.

"Madame President," I say. "Members of the Board of Education, my name is Judith Fargoe and I reside in Corazon. I have here a list of requests to improve school life for students and staff alike."

I hand copies to the clerk who steps forward to receive them from me and distribute them to the members as I continue.

"I request my notes be entered into the record."

"What the notes say is that to learn to be good citizens, our students need to eat well. Corazon was donated a garden plot to grow vegetables to feed the community. I ask that the school curriculum include time for the students to work the vegetable garden.

"Also, a local farmer asked that the high school spend part of its food funds to purchase from a CSA, Community Sponsored Agriculture. Please permit him to present his food to the Parent Teachers association, and I request you give their determination due accord. Thank you.

"Though you have a list of people signed up to address you, what we prefer instead is that you watch a brief presentation by our young people seated here on the front row. They wish to show you how they feel about school and social issues as well as their view of their future prospects. I ask you to invite their participation."

"NO!" Anders says. "Everything needs scheduling."

"Compared to listening to another 35 speakers?" I ask her.

"My answer is, no," she states. "That is final. Do you have any more to say or we'll move to the next speaker."

The audience is visibly agitated by Anders' arrogance. She makes it obvious that she prefers to shoot herself in both feet than give any appearance she is caving in to my requests.

As vocal rumblings grow, Member Blake speaks into her mic.

"Madame Chair," she says. "I am interested to have these youngsters present."

"Member Blake," Anders rebukes her. "We have a busy schedule ahead of us."

"Precisely, Madame President," Blake responds. "I move that we vote to decide."

Flynn joins the fray.

"Second," he says.

Anders kicks into high gear.

"Discussion?" she snaps. "Hearing none, Clerk, call the roll."

The clerk calls, "Ms. Anders?"

"No."

"Mr. Hyland?"

"Ms. Blake?"

"Yes."

"Mr. Flynn?"

"Yes."

"No."

"Mr. Mattingly?"

"Yes."

There's a moment of silent uncertainty about the count.

Flatly, Anders declares, "The motion carries."

"Members of the Board of Education," I proudly announce. "This ... Is Krumping!"

His face bruised and cut, Bebe plus team jump to their feet. They take off their sweatshirts to reveal T shirts hand inscribed,

"Believe that a few caring people can change the world.
That is all who ever have."
Margaret Mead

Bebe signals, the boom box pumps out a bass driven song, and, in the limited space available, the team let's rip. They are intense, all firing off individually.

Turned on kids in the audience get up to dance in place. The lyrics of the song express deep hostility toward bad school education and its repercussions on the community.

The Board Members, startled at first, get the message.

The videographers have a field day.

Exasperated, Anders picks up a phone and calls out.

As the song ends, the audience claps, hoots and whistles, pumping fists into the air.

Blake applauds enthusiastically. Other members sit shocked. Anders grins like an evil witch.

The entrance doors fly open and three burly, armed, school cops in full uniform arrive.

In a flash, Mung and the gang are on their feet ready to rumble.

Arms spread wide, Jose jumps between the two groups to keep them apart.

As the Krumpers unwind, put on their sweatshirts and give each other brief, congratulatory hugs, member Blake addresses the room.

"Children," she says. "Thank you for such rich expressions. Ms. Fargoe, thank you for bringing this incredible presentation. That was wonderful!

"Thank you, Member Blake and your colleagues," I answer.

Recapturing her dominion, Anders barks at me, "Your time's up, Fargoe."

"Thank you, Ms. Anders, fellow Board Members," I tell them. "I forgive each one of you."

"I'm sure you do," Anders quips.

Escorted by the Krumpers, I head for the exit followed by an excited crowd.

The three cops stand aside, observing.

Everyone from Corazon plus the reporter pile into the hall followed by the three cops. One of them closes the doors to the hearing room. The buzz is wonderful. The reporter lines up the Krumpers on either side of me. They all drop into distinctly individual poses to accentuate their characters. After she takes pictures, I nudge Bebe who looks at me with serious doubt.

'Try it," I tell him. "What d'you have to lose?"

Bebe forces himself to go over to Hernando who immediately braces for trouble. Bebe offers to shake hands. The gang bristles with concern, but they are also aware that Kim and I are present as well as Jose, a bunch of other parents plus three armed cops. A strange hush falls on the entire group. Hernando cautiously shakes hands.

"Hey, man," Bebe tells him, gripping his hand. "I will always remember what yo done to me. I want yo to know, I forgive you."

Hernando stares at Bebe, so dazed; he has to wipe his eyes.

Bebe moves on and repeats the activity with each of the gang members in turn. The adults are amazed at the effect his actions have on these supposed delinquents. The kids and Mung are simply humbled.

Santos and Clive, the two gang members who went after Jose's car headlights, approach Jose.

"Jose? Sir?" Clive says. "I apologize."

"Did your dad tell you to say that?" Jose asks him.

Clive points to Santos, as he replies, "His dad did."

Santos joins his pal.

"I apologize, too," he mumbles.

"OK, I forgive you," Jose tells them. "But... now you have to make it up to me. Ever installed a headlight lamp?"

Both boys shake their head, negative. "Ungh-ungh," they say.

"Well, you're about to," he tells them.

Sheepishly, Mung comes over to me.

"I want you to forgive me," he says of his own accord.

I am duly impressed. I offer to shake hands and he grasps my hand like I'm a lifeline.

"I forgive you," I tell him. "Will you forgive me?"

Now it's his turn to be surprised. "Sure," he stutters. "But what for?"

"It's a while since I got mad with someone," I explain. "I almost did with you."

"Lucky," Kim tells Mung. "Kim fix Ms. Judith bad temper."

"Then thank you, Mr. Kim," Mung says, still grasping my hand.

It's unlike Kim to interrupt, so, I assume, he has good reason to talk over my handshake with Mung.

"Welcome," he tells Mung with a sweet, short bow.

Mung nods his head forward slightly, returning the courtesy Kim offered. I feel the nature of the handshake I am in with Mung change. If that is possible, his grip becomes sweet and friendly.

"I forgive you," he says to me.

We release our handshake.

Kim nods toward the police.

"Forgive cops," he instructs Mung.

"What for?" he replies, as if this is a badge of honor.

"See," Kim tells him. "Take gang."

Even more resistant than Bebe, Mung reluctantly corrals his gang and briefs them. They look at him as if he has truly lost it. They swagger over to the cops whose demeanor stiffens as they instinctively reach for their weapons.

Mung leads off and steps in front of each cop in turn, extends his hand, looks the man in the eye and says, "I forgive you."

The first two stare back at him, coldly. The third one reaches out with his hand, grasps Mung's hand and pulls him into a hug. Now it is Mung's turn to be caught off guard.

As if at a greeting line, the entire gang shuffles past the three cops, one at a time, saying, "I forgive you."

By the end, all three cops end up shaking hands with members of the gang and replying, "I forgive you."

After the whole gang except Hernando passes, the first cop looks to the third cop.

"You ever break rank, again," he cautions him. "I'll..."

The other cop looks back with a dead pan expression on his face.

"... Forgive me?" he asks.

That breaks up any remaining tension as people howl with laughter.

YARD WORK

It is difficult for me to say exactly what happened or the precise order in which matters occurred, but I do like Sarah's description.

"Corazon," she says, "Is like soda somebody shakes real hard an' pops open."

There is no plan. Needs arise, issues are identified, and the townsfolk have enough pent up energy to get their act together and do stuff. Considering how run down the town is, there is a surprising amount of oomph to start small projects such as window cleaning, tending yards and clearing out long left debris.

Once the Corazon Community Credit Union is formally chartered and a board of directors voted in—including, not surprisingly, Ray, Cindy and Jose—larger projects become feasible because actual funding can be discussed and made available.

The biggest project is definitely the community center.

I draw clunky sketches in my attempt to imitate the blueprints from the library at Taquinta. They are sad efforts to show scale, cross sections and inter locking attachments. I would have relented pretty early if it were not for Hernando. He separates out, and organizes my mess of overlapping images and puts each one on its own separate page, marking the pages with letters and numbers. The letters are for the "whole" parts and the numbers are for what we end up referring to as "close ups."

With help from a friend, he redraws them one by one with clean lines and distinct shape and form. We take our sketches to Alfredo who redesigns them again to more closely resemble blue prints. Within less than a month, Hernando and his mysterious friend create working drawings ready to be taken to the county engineer's office for approval.

Interestingly for me, Alfredo firstly makes sure that the drawings are far beyond anything the engineer could fault. Then, when that is done, he intentionally goes through and has Hernando alter three points. One is the thickness of the foundation wall; Alfredo makes it 25 percent narrower than is safe. Another is the connections of trusses at the eves where they attach to the roof; Alfredo reduces the number of bolts. Finally, he doubles up the loading for the headers over doors and windows.

"Now," he tells us, "These drawings are ready for submission."

Due to scheduling conflicts, there is no time for us to discuss the changes ahead of the submission of our construction plans to the county engineer. When they are returned with provisional approval contingent on changes, the requested changes are precisely the three items Alfredo inserted.

Alfredo explains, "The engineer's job is to find fault, otherwise he's merely a rubber stamp. Instead of letting the engineer mess with the plans, we present three blatant problems for the engineer to find and, that way, he leaves the actual design alone."

We subsequently submit our original drawings and the project is approved, with an accompanying note from the engineer requesting notification when the straw bales are being installed so he may observe!

The next phase is the City of Corazon Zoning Committee. This approach is spearheaded by Alfredo and Jose. Jose had sold a prized low rider to Zach, the Chairperson of the Zoning Committee, and it's hoped he will influence a committee known for its dislike of anything different. The final vote is an even split with Zach having the deciding vote. He sends the project forward leaving the ultimate decision to the

City Council. Jose is less than pleased, but everyone agrees the plans did survive another major hurdle.

Fortunately, the council meeting has to be set one week later to accommodate the Public Notice Act requiring a minimum of 72 hours notice. This gives the Block Captains time to organize a gaggle of folks to attend the city chambers for the hearing and generate a long list of speakers that will double the length of the typical weekly meeting.

Word quickly spreads, and the meeting, which rarely draws even a single observer, certainly no reporters, is standing room only.

Jose has transformed himself to become a master lobbyist. He makes a point of button holing each council person to encourage them to vote "for" the community center while reminding them that three of them expect to run for re election at the upcoming election. To the other three council people, Jose gives two years notice for their possible candidacy.

For a political body better known for voting to agree, get along and terminate meetings as early as possible, the meeting is positively electric. Handling an issue where the mayor speaks forcefully against the project and decision making is being viewed publicly is an unusual experience for the council and one for which they lack experience.

Cindy makes an impassioned speech in which she declares she is prepared to donate the community center land to the city for a one dollar per year lease. She offers to pay for the center's construction. All she asks the City of Corazon to do is assume responsibility for the center, its maintenance and insurance liability.

It quickly becomes clear that the Council is split right down the middle similar to the Zoning Committee. In the event of an even split, the deciding vote will rest with the mayor who is well known to dislike Jose and his "kind."

Speaker after speaker presents and it becomes increasingly clear that this is not the night of the community center. Jose speaks with the Block Captains and it is agreed not to let the remaining speakers use their time. They determine that they will definitely run candidates against the three council people up for re election, especially Hank

Morrisey whom they ran as their candidate and now is showing his real colors.

The mayor appreciates the abbreviation of the speakers' list and brings the motion to the floor. Clarification is requested of the details of Cindy's amazingly generous offer. The city attorney presents her comments, basically admitting the deal is unusual but certainly viable. She recommends the motion be voted on with the stipulated condition that Cindy signs an agreement that the attorney's office will draw up, if the council affirms the motion.

The vote much resembles the Board of Education; for, against, for, against, for and for. Out of the blue, Hank Morrisey votes that the city make the deal.

The mayor makes a point of not looking at Morrisey when he declares the city provisionally accepts the deal to assume responsibility for the care and maintenance of the community center, when built.

Celebrating in certain quarters of town runs deep into the night and at least a couple gatherings continue into the wee hours.

Hank Morrisey parties with Jose. He relates a sad story. When no residents attend meetings and few people even speak to him on the street or by phone about issues he can change, it becomes safer and easier to go along to get along. He voted the way he did, tonight, because his people turned out and his vote was finally visible.

"Understand," he says, "For what it may be worth, it is likely both the city council and the chamber of commerce will be watching me like a hawk now that I have broken cover."

He offers to mentor whoever runs against the other two council people up for re election. He cautions that the town has a serious adversary in the mayor; a problem that can be resolved in two years' time. Meanwhile, if the electorate's consciousness is raised, that will grease the path considerably, especially if people make it their obligation to attend the weekly council meetings, even simply as observers. These are hauntingly similar sentiments reminiscent of Harold's statements about the nature of democracy.

Carl has boxed himself in really good. He has committed himself to selling all day at four markets. That puts a greater load on his wife, Lizbet. She originally offered to help out. That offer has transformed in to seven days a week of long hours farming intensively. Even if Andrea and I alternate our days of selling with spending time assisting Lizbet, that does little to accommodate the needs of the farm which demands Carl, full time, as do the markets, but less so. For me it means that Carl needs my help every available moment. That severely cuts in to my availability for projects erupting like a chain of volcanoes across the Corazon landscape.

Not too surprisingly, I am involved less and less in activities as Corazon evolves on the road to becoming a conscious community. As Lea once described it, I am kicked upstairs, relegated to making decisions that are too politically hot, i.e., unpleasant, for those engaged in the day to day action. I almost enjoy being at the farm so that, on the one hand, I am detached from what is happening in town, while, on the other, I am thoroughly grounded for when I am called upon to make the tough decisions.

An example is the occasion Jose calls a secret meeting at Cindy's house. Set for eight on a Monday evening, I am barely able to be there on time after selling at market. Cindy is delighted to see me. She has become my mother and sister all rolled into one.

Alfredo grumbles he doesn't like being at meetings.

"Anyone who knows me," he repeats over and over, maybe in the hope that he can escape, "Knows how I dislike meetings."

Jose arrives after me and has a person with him whom I have not seen round town. The friend has what looks like a large board wrapped in a blanket under his arm. The man is strong, but appears as if he has allowed himself to deteriorate. His eyes are clear and searching as he investigates me, particularly.

It takes Alfredo to blow the man's cover.

"Carlito, you scoundrel," he says. "How the heck are you? It's been a long time."

Cindy shakes hands with him but is not comfortable. He is unfazed and turns to meet me.

Jose introduces us.

"Judith, please meet my long time buddy, Carlito," he says. "Carlito is the artist who now does the finish artwork on my cars."

"Good to meet you, Carlito," I say as we shake hands.

"My pleasure, Judith," he says. "Jose speaks highly of you."

"Thanks, Jose," I say. "Now I do feel set up. Who else is coming?"

"This is it," Jose answers.

"You sure want this to be secret," I say. "Must be super special. What d'you think, Alfredo?"

"Enough that I'm here," Alfredo says with a wink. "Now, you want me to think?"

"Yep," says Jose. "Here's the deal. Carlito has spent the past month on designing a project. He is looking for feedback."

"Why include me?" Cindy says, defensively. "I dislike what Carlito has done to this town with his graffiti."

"Cindy," Jose asks. "Imagine what he can do when he grows up."

Carlito is clearly irritated.

"Just show them, Jose," he says. "Let's get this over with."

Jose stands across from us holding up the covered board which he props up on the table. He carefully removes the cover and we are looking at a cartoon like picture of a ball with flames flowing behind it.

Everyone looks but no one says anything. It's hard to know what it is we are looking at. The more I look, the more familiar the image feels, but I can't say why.

Cindy breaks the silence.

"All I can think is, it's a comet or meteor," she says.

"Exactly!" Carlito says excitedly. "It's a comet crashing into planet Earth."

"Then why do I keep thinking it looks like the community center?" asks Alfredo.

"That's it!" I shout. "I kept thinking there is something fami... Jose! You are not proposing...?"

"You did the drawings Hernando presented for the engineer!" Alfredo says.

"I thought they were unusually fine for him to have drawn," I say. "You're his secret friend."

"I am probably more familiar with this building than all of you," Carlito says. "Except you, Judith."

"What are you proposing, Jose?" Cindy asks.

"Making our community center into a tourist attraction," he says.

"D'you think the city will ever accept this," I say.

"I reviewed the contract," Jose says with a grin. "What they have agreed to accepting is the community center property when construction is complete. Who decides what complete looks like? We do. We're building it."

"They'll have a conniption fit," Cindy says with the slightest of wry smiles.

"Then imagine how they'll react to this," Jose says.

He lays down the meteor painting and proceeds to show a variety of paintings of Corazon with the finished community center as a landing meteor.

"I used the center as meteor as a jumping off point," Carlito explains. "If the whole town accepts the theme and each building is painted as a contribution to the theme, then it will look from the air, or on the ground, as though a meteor crashed into Corazon from outer space."

All I can think about is the time I was meditating that Hernando came to visit. I envisioned a meteor. That was before I ever set pen to paper. Am I truly meditating to envisage the future?

Who cares?

This idea is stunning. What a wild and crazy way to fix up the town and attract outsiders. Carlito is proposing turning the town into a theme park, like Taquinta and its moon domes. That's what an artist does; makes the unimaginable real.

"I'm in," I blurt out.

Jose and Carlito exchange knowing glances and smiles. Someone went fishing and, as usual, I bit.

Cindy asks, "Who pays for this?"

"Can we talk about this step by step?" Jose asks. "First, are you in?"

"Of course," Cindy says. "This will make people wake up to what they have here."

"How do we construct it?" Alfredo asks.

"We need to discuss that but I was thinking it will actually be a combination children's playground and an adjoining skateboard park," Carlito says.

Alfredo nods his head at the possibilities.

Cindy walks around the table and reaches her hands up to Carlito's shoulders.

She tells him, "I apologize for what I said about you. This is the kind of community venture I have dreamed of. With you, Judith, all the talent that is appearing here; I am so glad to be able to make these wonderful ideas happen. If I have any money left by the time I die, be warned, I am taking it with me."

Round about midday on the following Sunday, I rest on the couch in the living room with all the windows open. The air feels still and hot. The only sounds I am aware of are the distant, persistent barking of a neighbor's chained up dog, and the hum of insects and bees about the sweet smelling honeysuckle blooming outside a window.

I am floating in that wonderful space between sleep and day dream. I know for sure I will not be disturbed since Ray took Sarah and the grandkids for a long promised trip to the Bay Area. Kim is out doing rounds doling out his "foul smellin'" teas to people in need.

The ethers begin to tremble. A vibration of the formerly still air forebodes power on the move. Maybe it is those rare jet planes practicing a dog fight. The transition is too slow in evolving to be aircraft. It blossoms as a truck with a huge motor turning onto our street. It rumbles and roars closer, then as it is about to pass the house it turns onto the driveway and stops. That is, it does not move, everything else trembles to the heaving and huffing of this titanic engine. Then comes the clomping of heavy, booted feet on the steps and the pounding of a fist on the frame of the front door.

Reluctantly, I give up hope for a tranquil afternoon. A face next to a hand looks through the opaque glass panel searching for signs of life.

I am not fast enough.

A voice roars out, "SARAH!"

I open the door and a man of vast proportions towers before me.

"I've come to take the cars," he tells me as he turns, clomps down the steps and enters the fire breathing dragon spewing diesel fumes.

Word of the activity spreads quickly on the communication channels not destroyed by the tow truck's voluminous engine exhausting across the surrounding neighborhood airways. Mostly teenage boys arrive in droves to observe, what for them, must be some kind of cultural transition as clunkers leave one backyard for another. The cars will be air sprayed with fairy dust and religiously converted into classic cars.

What else is left for me to do on this beautiful, restful day but to attend this changing of the cars ceremony?

Surprising for his size and the power of his machine, the driver performs feats of agility in the confined space where rotting, formerly majestic, modes of personal transportation are ruthlessly packed away to withstand the seasons in some pack rat created community. As if delicately siphoning off one sardine at a time from a full can, the tow truck, guided by its mammoth human, unflinchingly methodical, takes out one car after another down the alleyway into the street, and off to a nearby neighborhood.

All of this is being thoroughly documented for some historical, unknowable future by scads of ubiquitous camera phones. Otherwise, there is no human quotient to this mechanistic transition.

None, that is, until my special friends turn up. It has been a long time since we ventured out together. They arrive on a gushing river of tears. Their once private playground is being decimated. Gaspar pleads with me to do something. Such an indirect imperative leaves me in my booted upstairs role having to make it up as I go along. Shoshanna clings to me, more like hangs from my arm, wailing and pulling at her hair. Hermione, sadly, seems to be the only one functioning in anything resembling a practical solution. With her arms spread wide, she spins on the driveway as if she alone can impede the progress of the furiously active, fire breathing monster dragging off these powerless prey to feed some future glory.

The tow truck driver well knows obstruction to his work. Probably for everyone he helps, he also takes someone else's precious mode of transportation for lack of adherence to a contract that was easier to pay, back in the day. People lay down in front of these dramatic, upheaval causing changes in their lives. They plead, cajole, arrive with weapons, and the occasional one spins. Hermione is a spinner.

The trucker halts the truck, steps out, and, with the sweet patience I have only previously seen exhibited by Kim, he tells me his only option is to call the cops. His suggestion is, either I do something effective immediately, or he will. His likely accurate guess is that the cops will transfer Hermione to Child Protective Services which will adversely burden someone's possibly already troubled life.

I try talking to her. I am unsuccessful.

I ask Gaspar and Shoshanna what they would do. They do the obvious, they join Hermione. Now we have three spinners on the driveway. The driver throws up his hands. He has patience, but it is limited by the insistent pulse of hands spinning on the clock of time that dominates his world.

"I'm calling the cops!" is his ultimatum.

"Give me one whole minute," I plead.

"One minute," he concedes'.

I join the kids on the driveway and I spin.

"You have to be kidding me?" he yells.

"One minute," I tell him. "You agreed."

Hermione is vaguely aware of us spinning with her. I lead and spin toward the tow truck. Gaspar and Shoshanna follow. Hermione stays in her space. I lead back to her and on past her. It takes one more round before she tags along. We spin together along the driveway to the sidewalk and I lead up to the stairs. I stop spinning and begin tap dancing up and down on the first two steps. Gaspar stops spinning and follows my lead. When Shoshanna joins in I add an additional step. I am no tap dancer, but I do know how to have fun, however discombobulated. Hermione slows to a very slow spin so she can watch us. I slow the dance to match her rhythm. She accepts the invitation. Once she is fully joined, I raise the tempo and include the last two steps.

The tow truck hurtles past, air horns blasting, into the road, with another gift for the yawning gape of Jose's shop.

I remain focused until we are doing a nightmare interpretation of line dancers hoofing, sometimes accidentally together. The laughter that fills the air makes it all worthwhile.

At some point, I stop. My body pleads to lie down, or, at the least, to sit. My understanding is that we are on a different clock now but still time limited. I grab Hermione by the hand and start for the stairs. She grabs Shoshanna's hand and she grabs Gaspar's hand. Like a mother duck, I begin a sideways walk down the steps and along the driveway.

As we arrive where five cars remain, I start to tiptoe, pretending the cars are asleep. With my index finger pressed to my lips, I tread lightly from car to car pretending to inspect each one. Hermione lets go my hand and then Shoshanna's to free herself up to get in touch with cars they have only distantly known.

I pretend to fall in love with a bulky brute of an ancient Chevy. Without missing a beat, Gaspar hits on the fin tailed Caddy, the vehicle that got this whole exodus in motion. I shake my head, no, and imitate rapturous romance with my wreck of choice. Hermione and Shoshanna each pick one of the remaining three.

They are a pushover.

I easily convince them to ride in the backseat of my choice. Then I approach Gaspar and pretend to help dress him in a uniform. He complies, unwittingly. Then I put a pretend cap on him and walk him to the driver's door of the Chevy. He understands he is to chauffeur the two ladies.

He gets in and turns to mimic asking, "Where to?"

They point ahead and he turns front, turns a make believe key in the ignition and off they go, not one moment too soon.

The tow truck comes barreling down the driveway, its roaring mouth displaying gnashing chrome teeth as it arrives for another victim. I literally hurl myself across the hood of the Chevy, playing the broken hearted leading lady, protecting her precious love.

Ignoring me since I have done enough to allow free flow of commerce once more, the driver spins his abominable creature on a proverbial dime, chains his next victim and roars away.

By maintaining this ridiculous silent movie love affair, the kids do their part by remaining in their seats. I repeat my lovelorn performance and another vehicle leaves. Last to go is the Caddy, the crown jewel of the wrecks' yard. Brave heart that he is, Gaspar waves his choice a joyous farewell.

Then, I realize we are not leaving our car unprotected for the ravaging monster.

We remain there till nightfall, waiting for Ray to return with Sarah so she may confirm the breath stopping decision, "The Chevy stays!"

ACTION

Carl's troubles are doubling up. He tries managing the stall all by himself, occasionally hiring locally available day help. With those arrangements, what he runs into is that most of the people he hires are not consistent in their ability to deal with the specialized nature of his produce, which frustrates him endlessly. Carl frustrated is a terrible representative for his farm. Despite himself, or, more correctly, because of the quality of his produce, he consistently sells more each outing.

Though the idea of having me and Andrea assist Lizbet is good in concept, it is not what is truly needed. None of us has Carl's refined sensibilities for determining when to plant how much of which plants. We are all of us basically glorified laborers, mostly good for weeding, picking and packing.

Conversely, my not being able to drive is another stumbling block. I can run the stall fine by myself, paraphrased, as Carl likes to say, tongue in cheek, "If a task requires two men, hire a woman."

However, as he is also quick to point out, it takes two women for me to go anywhere; his reference to the fact that I require Andrea to drive me.

He is more and more resentful that he spends so little time with the soil. I know how that feels. Thus, we go round and round on these same issues. We know there is an answer, probably a very simple answer, but, for now, it eludes us.

Today, market closes early because of a local, heavy downpour of rain, expected to continue late into the afternoon. So Carl has almost an entire day "extra" at the farm. Since he has almost a full load for the next market day, my services are not critical. Carl still fills my two canvas tote bags inscribed, "Re Use Always," and has Andrea drop me home, allowing me to catch up with how Corazon, though dry, but overcast, is doing.

In a sense, Corazon is my farm; though I am not needed anything like the way Carl is at his. That is abundantly evident when I go walk about to check on things. No one is at the house: the kids are off in school; Ray is out on a carpentry job; and, Sarah is with a Residence Assessment group of two other retiree Block Captains evaluating needs of houses where the owners have applied to the Credit Union for a loan to upgrade their property.

Once I track her down, Sarah sends me to visit with Charles at his house.

He has another friend with him who is equally good at math and accounting. I arrive on the tail end of how they spend every morning, developing customized payment plans to assist people in reducing and, eventually, eliminating all credit debt. Both men are quick to tell me how much of a liability it is to survive without debt, and next to impossible with it.

They put their "clients" on a starvation existence of no credit cards and extra repayments. Each "client" also has to attend a debtors' group twice each week, plus, talk a minimum of twice each day, with a debt buddy who will assist them not to put anything additional on credit. As Charles tells it, credit spending is more addictive than narcotics and every bit as emotionally and psychologically depleting; hard won knowledge from his own past experience.

Since I am close to downtown, I take a trip down memory lane. Several store front windows have been cleaned for the first time in a long time. It already makes a noticeable difference both from the outside and particularly from inside.

One store, which still has a boarded up window, is newly open for business. What looks like Carlito's handiwork, the plywood sheet over the window has been elegantly inscribed, "Corazon Community Craft Project." Inside the open, front door, Erika sits on a wooden chair crocheting her celebrated "Buds," cap hats made with combinations of different colored wools. She has a variety of finished prêt a porter samples laid out for display on a trestle table.

At the other end of the store, working in the light admitted through the open back door, Marne sits knitting short neck scarves. She, too, has a trestle table with available product on display. When I enter, the two of them are having an animated conversation across the length of an otherwise barren empty store.

"Hi, Judith," Erika greets me. "Welcome to the project!"

"Hi, Erika, Marne," I say. "Kind of dark in here?"

"We're working a deal with the landlord," Marne says.

She stands up, stretches and walks over to join us.

"We have no money for rent," Erika tells me. "So he gives us the place rent free for one month if we clean up the inside."

"We're making product to sell to repair the window," Marne says. "That's another month's rent."

"And we can earn one more month's rent by painting the inside," says Erika.

"Hopefully, by then, we'll be making enough money to pay rent and have the utilities connected," Marne tells me.

"Meanwhile, we're having fun and sell a couple of items each day," Erika says.

"Very creative," I tell them. "I think you will do very well."

"We're giving it a try!" Marne says.

"Good for you," I say. "I will check back in a week or two."

"You do that," Marne says.

I head toward the City and Farmers' Bank hoping to see other new enterprises en route. I do find one store with the window all clean and polished. A sign inscribed on a plastic sheet is draped across the window that reads, "Welcome to Corazon Cooperative Credit Union."

A hand written notice taped inside the window informs a reader that the Credit Union will be opening soon for walk in traffic, and to watch for announcements.

Just leaving a store, two doors down, Cindy and a couple others are deep in conversation. She is excited to see me and introduces me to two members of the Corazon Chamber of Commerce. Seeing my nervous reaction, she laughs.

"Diane and Eduardo are both highly supportive of our efforts," Cindy tells me. "They agree it's a win-win situation, and they are working to turn around the attitude of the Chamber's Board of Directors."

I shake hands with them both.

"Judith Fargoe," I announce myself.

"A pleasure to meet you," Diane says. "We've been hearing all about you through the Parent Teacher Association. You encouraged the High School to buy vegetables from a local farmer. We wrote to him to set up a meeting for us to try his produce so we can make a recommendation to the Board of Education."

You could have knocked me down with a feather. I had to consciously close my gaping mouth.

"That's wonderful news," I tell her.

Cindy rescues me.

"We're looking at each store, and creating a cost assessment of what it will take to make them operable again," she tells me. "We're going to help jumpstart a few stores and use the loan repayments from them to lend to other stores."

"Basically," Eduardo explains, "We are at the beginning stages of creating an Economic Development Agency."

"That is exciting," Cindy adds.

"How is the center doing?" I ask.

"We're finished here," Cindy tells me. "Let's you and me take a walk over. The kids should be out of school soon."

"A pleasure to meet you, Ms. Fargoe," Diane says.

"Please," I insist. "Call me Judith. It is a pleasure to meet you, Diane, Eduardo."

Cindy and I take off walking, she holding her little finger looped in mine. Rounding a corner, we almost bump into Hernando instructing a group of kids preparing to paint out a mass of graffiti. Before the painters are allowed to start, Hernando supervises one kid holding a phone camera to videotape all the graffiti showing it in location. Then they go through and document, section by section in detail.

"Hi, Hernando, guys," I say.

"Hi, Judith," they call back. "Hi, Cindy."

"What you all up to?" I ask.

"Carlito asked that before we obliterate it," Hernando says with great seriousness, "We document it, so there is some record."

"I for one," Cindy grunts, "Am glad to see it go. I guess he is entitled, though."

"If you step out of your emotional response to its being graffiti," I say to her, "It is amazing the effect they create. I have to tell you, it has grown on me over the years."

"Can you in good conscience call this art?" Cindy asks.

"I can," I say. "What about you guys? Do you consider graffiti to be art?"

"I do," says Hernando. "It's the art of my time. You old people think everything should be the way you know it. That leaves no room for my generation or the ones to follow us. You must have fought your parents and grandparents about what was important for you."

"Gee, Hernando," I admit. "Are you studying philosophy now?"

"Why should I have to?" Hernando argues. "It's obvious."

"Just as you are young," I say. "And we are old."

He blushes.

"I... I..." he stutters.

"That's OK, Hernando," Cindy tells him. "Your turn is coming. You may be surprised how young you feel when you're old. Keep up the good work, guys. We're proud of you caring for the town."

"Really," I add for good measure.

"Having seen so few kids ever participate in town life," Cindy tells me as we take off down the block, "It feels like a revolution what they are doing, today."

I fully understand her when we pass by her house and arrive at the adjacent lot. The ground is staked out with vertical posts, about two feet tall, with their tops color coded. It's more like an industrial site, as enormous construction machines grade and level the dirt. Then I look closely at who is operating the equipment. They're 8th, 9th and 10th graders. They are as comfortable driving these machines as I am preparing food in the kitchen. There are more girls than boys. How wonderful does that feel?

Cindy must be reading my thoughts.

"They're every bit as capable as boys, you know?" she insists.

"I'm just an old fashioned girl," I tell her.

She'll have none of it.

"I'm twice your age," she says. "What does that make me?"

Alfredo blows a whistle. All the machines grind to a halt and the engines shut off.

"Excellent!" Alfredo shouts. "We're ready to dig out the trenches for the foundations. And look who's come to observe. Welcome Cindy, Judith."

He climbs onto the narrow platform of a back hoe, and instructs the young girl how to drive. He has her stop exactly where he wants while he jumps down and has everyone gather round, so he can demonstrate the relationship between the blueprints and the real world. Once everybody understands how they will proceed, he climbs onto the back hoe, has the young driver drop the stabilizer feet down, and has her move the blade out and back several times to familiarize herself with moving the digging bucket.

The back hoe operator begins to dig dirt and drop buckets full in specific heaps. After a while this operator stops and a new person takes over. Everyone operates for long enough to feel confident they know the machine a little better. Alfredo is an empathic teacher.

Progress on the community center is moving right along, at least according to the original plans. It was agreed by the secret meeting participants, not to reveal the final plan until the concreting of the walls to seal the straw bales is under way.

Cindy and I go to her house for tea. Sarah catches up to join us.

I have to say, we spend a lot of the conversation declaring how pleased and excited we are about the remarkable changes happening at lightning speed in the town. From working the markets for Carl, I can offer a critical comparison. Corazon is moving fast next to what other towns are doing. I tell them for me the enthusiasm generated among the populace is palpable.

Sitting there, drinking tea with these two powerful women, I reflect on the mural of "Just Desserts" painted at Taquinta. I resolved to encourage Carlito to create an image for the community center that will immortalize the current power brokers of Corazon.

Leaving Cindy, Sarah and I walk home. As we arrive at the house, Sarah, speechless, grabs my arm. At the top of a fully extended ladder, Ray is repairing the fascia below the roof above the second floor window. Mung stands on the bottom rung to anchor the ladder.

I lay my hand over Sarah's to offer her some calming influence. She walks like one possessed, slowly, with one hand covering her mouth. She is terrified for him. As we draw closer, I call out.

"Hi, Ray," I say.

Acting as if he is standing with both feet on the ground, Ray turns to track the sound.

"Oh, hi, Judith," he says, turning back to the job in hand. "Hi, Sarah. We'll be done here soon."

"Are you safe up there, Ray?" I ask.

He stops work and looks down his nose at me.

"Thanks, Judith," he says. "I need periodic checking in on. You're number four. You're talking to me as if I am some doddery old coot, you know?"

"The good Lord loves an' protex him," Sarah says under her breath.

She turns to Mung, extremely unhappy that he is at, never mind anywhere near, her house.

"What yer doin's here?" she demands.

"I'm Ray's apprentice," he answers proudly.

That answer is almost too pat, even for me.

"Really?" I ask him.

"Hey, I like working wood. OK?" he says with boyish hurt. "This old Craftsman house has good bones."

Right then, a rangy youth walks up the driveway from the backyard. He holds up a right angled metal ruler for Ray to see.

"Zis roove hangle is what ask for, Mr. LeMonde?" he asks.

Ray, looking down, checks the object out.

"Yes, Vladimir," he says. "I'll show you how to use it as soon as I come down."

"What are you doing, Vladimir?" I ask him.

"Em 'prentice wiz Mr. LeMonde," he says.

"Yer lives here 'bout, Valdimir?" Sarah asks.

"Femily moof America," he explains. "I soon school."

Evidently self taught, I compliment him.

"You speak excellent English," I say.

"Sank you," he replies. "Learn from tell vission. Heff nice dey."

And off he goes.

Sarah and I go inside to put away the produce I brought home. Mostly, Sarah does not want to see or hear what happens to Ray.

Exactly one week later, Lizbet, Andrea and I are helping Carl set up two matching tables of fresh produce for an anticipated, large turnout, PTA meeting. Before people arrive, Carl attaches a label to the underside of each table.

Principal Dr. Hyde hosts Board of Education Member Alice Blake, teachers and parents. Everyone congregates around the two long tables loaded with platters of sliced and whole vegetables. Carl explains what we are looking at.

"Both tables," he tells everyone, "Have the same types of vegetables. One has produce from a local supermarket. The manager assured me nothing was more than one week old. He said some of the food comes from overseas. The other table has produce from my farm. I use a technique called Biodynamic that is chemical free. It was all picked yesterday. Please, try both tables and tell me your thoughts. Thank you."

"Carl, you forgot to put out dip," Jose shouts out.

"I did that intentionally so you can taste the natural flavors," Carl says. "What you are eating here are raw vegetables. That means, you are ingesting more healthful benefits from the vegetable. As we cook them, vegetables rapidly lose their food value. Because most vegetables are produced under poor conditions, they taste awful when raw. That's why we cook them, to make them palatable."

Alice Blake takes a break from studiously comparing food on each table.

"Carl," she asks. "The vegetables on this table taste sweet. That other table is what I am used to. Do you add sugar when you grow your food?"

Carl laughs.

"Forgive me," he says. "That is so typical of where our society is now. Even when you grow food conventionally, if you eat vegetables immediately after they are picked they have a natural sweetness. The Biodynamic process for food growth, I believe, intensifies those health giving qualities in each plant. That means there is more natural sweetness in my vegetables to begin with, and that will help preserve them longer. Let's take a show of hands which table has the vegetables that appeal most."

We are not the least bit surprised that Carl's produce was preferred by a substantial majority. Carl peels off the labels from under each table for final proof to determine which produce came from where.

Blake agrees to carry to her colleagues the determination to make Carl the main supplier of fruits and vegetables to the high school. She encourages the PTA to send a formal request to back her up. Blake, also, says she wants Carl to spearhead the garden plot behind Cindy's house. Carl's fortunes are changing. If the school receives the requisite authority, supplying the school would equate to two market days each week, be vastly less demanding and guarantee him a regular check. If the proposal is accepted and the garden project curries favor with the school district, it opens the possibility of Carl teaching a whole generation about healthful eating. Working with curious young minds is always such a delight. Carl goes from the doldrums to riding Cloud 9.

With Alice Blake driving the train, change is scheduled to come quickly to the high school food program, especially with the addition to the curriculum of class time on the patch.

Carl and I plan how we will bring the kids into the process. As a test of our intentions, Bebe's 8th Grade class is sent as the trial run.

An unenthusiastic teacher, Jason, escorts the class to Cindy's arid backyard of baked dirt and one sickly tree. They are greeted by Carl, Cindy, Kim and myself.

Using a block of chalk, while bored kids watch, Carl marks a circle almost to the edges of the yard. Kim, sitting facing the tree with his hands on either side of the trunk, brings in energy. Kids watch him, as does Cindy, until Carl demands everyone's attention.

"See the chalk circle I marked on the ground," Carl calls out. "I want you each to find a spot immediately outside the circle with adequate space away from other people."

Kids jostle each other as they shuffle to comply.

Jason barks at the kids.

"Let's move it, everybody," he insists. "Let's go!"

As usual, the ubiquitous phone cameras record what is happening.

According to our plan, I commence pitching.

"I am so pleased to have you join us," I tell the circle. "As you may know, Cindy, here, has gifted this land for you to farm."

Some of the kids snicker.

"Show of hands," I ask. "Who noticed a change in school meals, this week?"

A few hands go up.

"Tell me what you noticed," I invite them.

"They stopped cooking the veggies," one says.

"They looked real different than regular," says another.

"I thot I were gonna breck my teeth they wes so hard," says yet another. "They wes tasty sweet."

"Very good," I say. "So let me introduce the farmer who grew those vegetables. This is Carl."

I step back and let him take the spotlight as I clap my hands.

Jason steps in from left field.

"Good manners, people," he tells them. "Applaud!"

A few kids make feeble efforts to greet Carl.

"The vegetables you will be eating in school from now on," Carl explains, "Will be coming from my farm, three miles away, and will rarely, if ever, be more than one day old. By comparison, most supermarkets, because they buy in bulk, receive produce from far away to keep their costs down. That usually means your fresh food is, at least, one week old.

"What you will learn here in this project is how to grow the foods you eat to keep you healthy. I employ a farming technique called Biodynamic, created by a talented man, Rudolf Steiner. Biodynamic plants put back more into the soil than they take out.

"Over the years as you work this land, you will create a Garden of Eden.

"Today, we are going to study a few basics. Who knows where is North?"

Those kids we know individually for their striving to prove themselves and how special they are outside of class, in class, seem to compete for who can stand out the least.

Hernando's response to Carl's question is, "Across from South?"

Classmates hoot with laughter prompting Jason to do his teacher thing.

"Quiet!" he yells.

Carl acknowledges Hernando.

"Hernando is right," he says. "So how do we locate where is South?"

"That's where the sun is at noon," Bebe says, bored, pointing. "About there."

"Right," Carl says. "Then where is North?"

Most kids point north. A few smart alecks, acting bored, point in silly directions.

"Some people farm collaborating with an energy called the Diva," says Carl. "This is Mother Earth's "local agent." There's a Diva appointed for each parcel of land, even if it's black topped over or has a skyscraper on it. In case someone wants to work with the soil, the Diva is always available. Let's see if the Diva will talk to us."

"Stand where you are," I tell them. "Close your eyes. Become still inside. Visualize the ground in front of you. Let the Diva tell you how to care for this soil."

Kids are amused by the hocus pocus. They look about to see who closes their eyes. Some giggle.

Apparently, Jason misses the implied intention about being sensitive.

"Do as you're told," he barks. "Close your eyes."

I slow my speech.

"Breathe gently," I tell everyone. "Become conscious of your breath going in and out. Imagine the land."

Carl joins in.

"The Diva has been here as long as the soil we're standing on," he tells them. "All you have to do is listen... from a quiet, internal space."

Kim stops working on the tree and turns to face the kids. Stretching his hands out to the sides, palms facing the kids, he begins a rolling, bass chant. The kids become still.

The period of quietness continues for at least one minute. Bebe breaks the silence.

"The ground needs something," he says.

"What does it need, Bebe?" I ask.

"Looks like dead plants all over," he responds.

"Excellent, Bebe," Carl tells him. "This ground is so old and tired, it requires healing before we plant in it and expect it to work for us. If we cover it with hay and soak it with water for a month or so, we will be able to dig more easily and some needed nutrients will have been added to help grow what we plant. Then we plant legumes, beans, and lay them down to load up the soil with nitrogen. That's what Diva shows us."

"'Fess up, Bebe," Hernando calls him out. "Judith told you."

"My head... like... felt the answer," Bebe says, surprised.

"Now you're hearing voices," Hernando teases him. "Woo-ooooh."

"When you're ready, Hernando," Carl tells him. "You will hear the Diva. Focus on the ground. Feel what is best for it."

"Everyone," I say. "Sit right where you are. Cross your legs. Rest your hands palms up on your knees. On both hands, touch index finger to thumb. Keep the other fingers straight ahead. Sit up straight. Close your eyes. Feel your breath go in and out. Feel the pulse of your heart beating."

This time it doesn't take as long. Hernando begins to grin.

"What just happened?" Carl asks the group.

"Something welcomed me," Hernando calls out. "Weird!"

Several other kids comment.

"Me, too."

"This is freaky!"

"I got a call from an extra terrestrial."

"You lie."

"Me sit."

"Open your eyes, everyone," I call out. "Those of you, who still wonder what occurred, keep coming to this place and be quiet for a minute or so. Sooner or later, you will recognize the Diva."

The kids are on their feet.

Jason talks to Carl.

"You gave them a useful experience," he says. "I think they will remember this afternoon."

"You changed, too," Hernando tells Jason. "When you stop being angry and scared, you're OK."

"From you, Hernando," he replies with an easy smile. "That is praise."

"Wait until they eat what they've grown here," Carl says.

"I have to tell you," Jason says to Carl. "I was extremely skeptical. This feels like a great idea."

Hernando extends his hands, palms up, to Carl and me.

"Give me some skin, guys," he requests.

We slide our hands over his. He strides off as Kim arrives, smiling.

"Begin," he says, "To make circle."

METEOR

People unifying around a common cause—a defined intention—can appear to lose awareness of time. Corazon, to me, resembles a community operating as one. Reflecting back, the details of what lit this fire under everyone are vague and distant. I'll even go so far as to say, they're immaterial. The mere fact that this many of us gather in a cause to make life pleasant and under our control is intoxicating.

Imagine a town of run down houses. Typically, these are homes of scared, isolated individuals and families, spending vast amounts of time aimlessly watching television, movies, computer screens, and video games, believing that community is hundreds, maybe thousands, of "friends" on social media.

Slip a spatula under such a community and flip it over. What may result is another Corazon.

For example, in Corazon every house looks different. The yards, both front and back, are at least spruced up, or, better still, with vegetable gardens producing food enough to feed a household plus some extra with which to barter. Repairs are happening, in many cases done, and a whole new paint job is underway or complete.

The TV, that giant, and, in some cases, gigantic, blue eye of agitated, jerking images, operates occasionally, selectively, consciously. Instead of vacuuming up untold hours of life, it has become a tool for community outreach.

At first it is individuals, and then small groups such as friends and families, blossoming into neighborhood blocks of people agreeing on a program to watch on one screen with raucous, sometimes ribald, verbal assaults on the content.

That quickly spirals into critical commentary of the program content, and, where applicable, the advertising. These gatherings become focus groups, questioning the nature of programming, especially during "family hours." This leads to engaging corporations to discuss the appropriateness of their ads, in particular, during specific programs where children may be in the audience.

The success of the garden of vegetative delights under Carl's care and guidance comes home to roost with many families employing his technology for their home gardens. In several cases, this even expands to sidewalk parkways. One has a sign next to rows of supported, fruit laden tomato plants that reads, "Please help yourself."

It takes almost a year to bring the community center to the point where the divergence from the original drawings is to take place. By that time, Jose, acceding to many requests to have an attorney assess the validity of his claim that the city will have to accept our determination of completed construction, receives a legal opinion that he is correct in his interpretation.

This is all well and good until the City Parents catch wind of the change. The mayor is the first and loudest to decry the idea of the finished product. However, instead of taking the matter to court, Jose appeals to the public. Displeased with years of disagreement as to how the city has been allowed to falter, the newly invigorated citizens of Corazon happily take to the streets on each and every possible occasion to insist that the city continue with the original agreement entered into, leasing the community center from Cindy.

As the media catalog of protests and demonstrations mounts, the mayor finally relents and grasps the power back by personally supporting the cause against his now intransigent council. We believe his political days are numbered. Either that or there will be a group assault on him down at the city forum, come March 15—the Ides of March.

What he did do is unwittingly create a push back. People from far and wide visit Corazon to be in on the ground floor documenting the meteor crashing to Earth.

While they are in town, many purchase combination Meteor Hat and Scarf wearable souvenirs from the Corazon Community Craft Project housed in one of the better decorated store fronts on Main Street. Marne and Erika still dispute who of the two of them had the brainwave of connecting their products, each crediting the other.

One suggestion is that the idea stemmed from an old movie poster for Davy Crockett. Erika says that idea stinks.

There is no farmer in the whole wide world happier than Carl. With what turned out to be a perfect balance of woman power to labor in both his fields and packing houses, he has delegated me to operate at two local markets with assistance from my personal truck chauffeur, Andrea. Meanwhile, Carl spends the bulk of his days working his farm to meet the intense demands of the Corazon High School lunch program. Some of his "spare" time goes into regular meetings with the student elected body to coordinate the health and well being of the up and running large, circular vegetable garden.

Things circular is a new concept for him so he is particularly interested to see how the garden works, also the community center.

I admit it was my idea to make the internal walkways of the garden into a copy of the Chartres labyrinth. Though making the labyrinth appeared to restrict the walkways use for access, when I demonstrated that it was a simple matter of stepping across low lying plant forms, the idea was greeted with enthusiasm. It, too, has now acquired its own tourist community of spiritual folk who walk the paths to experience enlightenment as they inhale the bouquets of herbs. Some smarty pants secretly arranged it so that, as long as a labyrinth walker receives the full intensity of the herbs, he or she will be "on the right path."

Life at Sarah's house is showing signs of mundane ritual. Now that all the dangerous high ladder work is behind him, Ray mopes about looking for some new way to taunt Sarah. The exterior is almost completely primer painted.

Sarah is relieved not to be on the path of the crashing meteor because now she and Mung, who discovered parallel interests in color coordination, have wild plans for making the house a Painted Lady.

One balmy day, Sarah sleeps in a hammock strung between two canopy trees. Her garden flourishes. She has a bountiful vegetable patch and a lawn with surrounding, blooming flower beds.

Ray and Mung work together to hang a new wooden gate for access to the alley.

One car remains; a body shell of a muscle Chevy, on blocks. The wheels and doors are gone, as are all sharp and protruding corners; just seats and steering wheel remain. As trade for Sarah's gift to Jose of the other classic wrecks, he agreed to supervise the education of Santos and Clive in "fixing up" the Chevy. The body is camouflage painted in luridly bright, primary colors infused with iridescent particles so that, for a while around dusk, the car literally glows, multi colored. Taking a ride today, like they do most days, laughing, singing and chattering, are the Special Folk.

I am indulging in my favorite down time activity, eating. I'm in the kitchen enjoying a gentle breeze through the newly replaced window screens. I am having a field day left to myself to watch my mental wheels churn. It's similar to meditation except I permit myself to follow strands instead of just watching them float by. Kim refers to it as self indulgent meditation. It's hard to tell, but I am not sure he totally likes the idea. He says it softens my "edge."

A stranger visits. We know that because the doorbell rings.

"Thanks be," Sarah told Ray. "Now yer gones fixin' it, all kines a strange peoples thinks somebodies lives here."

Sarah stirs in her hammock.

I call to her through an open window, "I'll get it."

I am late to the party. The idea of strangers politely waiting for someone to open the front door is tantalizing to the grandchildren. For them it's a competition of who can be first to comment on whoever waits on the other side of the door.

Saffron throws open the front door as Leticia hurtles down the stairs and I emerge from the kitchen.

From the shadows of the house, I see Shirley, suitcase by her side on the porch and, hanging off of each hand, a travel cage with a cat. Perplexed, Shirley stares at Saffron.

"Who are you?" demands Saffron, staring equally hard back at Shirley. "You look weird."

Still holding on to the door, Saffron rolls her head back to broadcast to the rest of the house as she bellows, "Cat Woman here!"

Leticia reaches the door and pokes her head round. In my mind's eye, I can see Leticia check Shirley out from the top of her hair to the soles of her shoes and shake her head despondently.

"Ungh ungh," she says.

Leticia likes to tell me she does not believe in love at first sight. She feels everybody is a faker, so first impressions are faulty. People have to work hard to win her affections.

Then she lays a gentle hand on mine, looks soulfully, deep into my eyes with her giant brown eyes, and says, "Like you did, Judith."

I make the mistake once, and only once, of thinking she is sincere.

She bounds away from me with a cackle of a laugh and skips around the room, singing, "Another one cowt, another one cowt, another one bite the dust."

As I approach the front door, I can tell that if it were not that she had the cats in travel cases firmly affixed to her dangling arms; Shirley's hands would be up in the air flying every which way. Then the girls would really get a show.

As I enter the frame of the door, Shirley sees me and lights up.

"Shirley!" I scream, making Saffron and Leticia do double takes on me. "Look at you. Which one is S'more and which Sunlight? Come in, come in. I'll bring your suitcase."

I grab Shirley by the shoulders and give a squeeze until her eyes begin to mist up.

"Where are your manners, ladies?" I reproach the girls. "When the Queen of Santa Monica arrives, we welcome her in, help with her luggage and act civilized. Right?"

The two of them look at me weird.

"This here is Saffron," I tell Shirley. "She's our butler in training. And this charmer is Leticia who is our upstairs' maid. Curtsey, ladies."

Totally baffled, the girls hang on each other and giggle as they head to the stairs.

Left alone for a moment, I give Shirley a long, deep, welcoming hug. She talks to me across my shoulder.

"I quit my job," she says. "Sold everything, let go my apartment and here I am. You stepped off a cliff and landed on your feet. Now it's my turn."

I let go of her and step back to give her an admiring look. Of all people, Shirley turns out to be an adventurer first class. I step around her, shut the front door, then loop my arm in hers and drag her with me into the kitchen.

"Leave everything here and follow me," I tell her, taking the cat cases from her hands and putting them in the middle of the living room. "I want you to meet some really neat folks."

By now I have Shirley by the hand as I push the screen door wide letting it slam shut behind us. Fit to be tied, Sarah sits bolt upright, grabbing the hammock sides so she doesn't fall out.

Shirley scrambles after me as I point people out to her and we race toward my objective.

"That's Sarah," I say.

"Hi, Sarah," says Shirley, stumbling past.

"Hi," Sarah says. "Whoever the heck y'ares."

"Back there," I say with a careless wave. "That's Ray and Mung."

I can feel Shirley's step scramble as she attempts to locate the people named on the landscape. As we arrive at the car, I stop and Shirley, still in motion, rubber necking to take in the details, stops before she collides with the car.

"These are the greatest people," I tell her.

Shirley stares for a moment. Shoshanna, in the driver's seat, has hold of the steering wheel. She refuses to listen to Gaspar, seated next to her, beside himself pointing out obstructions in the road as she drives right over them. In the middle of the backseat, Hermione, her hands locked in front of her knees, rocks back and forth thrilled by the controversy.

A smile creeps to Shirley's mouth. She leans in close to Hermione who scarcely takes any notice of her, but pats the seat next to her as invitation to Shirley.

"We're all going to the zoo," Hermione says.

"I'm Shirley," she tells Hermione. "May I come, too?"

Hermione scoots sideways to make more room as Shirley clambers on to the back seat bench.

"Welcome, Shirley," she says. "What can you do?"

Without a moment's hesitation, Shirley sticks her hands out front at arm's length, hands upright, fingers in open fan mode, puckers her lips and blasts a steady spray. Hermione imitates Shirley. Driver and passenger imitate Hermione. They all grin with delight; the group has expanded its membership.

His mouth agape, Ray walks toward the car, amazed. Bedlam has broken loose in Chevyville.

"Hey, Ray," I announce, exuberantly. "It's a cracking party from here on. Shirley's in town!"

Leticia and Saffron burst through the back screen door, letting it slam shut, provoking Sarah back out of her daze, yet again. The girls race across the yard to the car. Ray and Sarah watch, amused.

Kim and I were scheduled to get together tonight. Nothing formal, no classes; we had simply planned to spend time together. I see that I need to devote a substantial amount of time with Shirley, settling her in, orienting her. I call Kim. He listens carefully, like usual.

He listens to my energy more than my words. As I start to slow down, he encapsulates my ramblings with his inimitable cryptic brevity.

"Kim understand," he tells me. "Who Ms. Shirley?"

"She's the reason I am in Corazon," I explain for the umpteenth time.

"Kim reason Ms. Judith in Corazon," he says without emotion.

"Ms. Shirley is the reason I came here," I answer. "Mr. Kim is the reason I stayed."

"Ms. Judith introduce Kim, Ms. Shirley, soon?" he requests.

"Of course," I say. "I appreciate your being so flexible."

"Meditate," Kim tells me.

You'd think I'd know that by now!

Sarah has a friend with a spare cot. When I ask if this area was once a military base because so many households have a cot, people laugh. That's not much of an answer but we found a bed for Shirley to sleep on. Until we make other arrangements, Shirley shares the room I borrowed from Saffron.

Once she and the cats are settled in, I take her for a walk downtown seeing as that is where life in Corazon is happening, these days.

Shirley and I interlock little fingers with each other on adjacent hands. I learned this from Cindy. It seems to increase the levels of communication while speaking more than is usual. It's also a useful tether for someone who rubbernecks as much as Shirley does.

She puts me through my paces about what has changed since I arrived, and why. She is intrigued how well maintained much of the housing is. I explain that this is as a result of a unique policy of the Corazon Cooperative Credit Union.

I give her the pat answers I learned from Ray at the dinner table. I can barely grasp the depths of what I am saying; things like short term, low interest "micro loans" to increase value through maintenance and major repairs of real property. Shirley nods her head approvingly.

"What about collateral to safeguard the loan?" she asks.

I am already perspiring in the sun on this warm day. Shirley is making me sweat.

"It varies," I parrot Ray. "It has to be liquid. Occasionally, the Credit union will take a position on the property title, but never more than second place."

"That's good," Shirley agrees. "What kind of capital margin is the

Credit Union sustaining?"

"I believe 50% minimum," I say, adding, "You better take this up with Ray or Cindy. I am running out of water to paddle in."

Shirley vents a girlish laugh. I see how little I know about her but that we are well met. She will be excellent with our Special Folk, and maybe she can become involved with the Credit Union.

She is agog at how the whole town is pulling itself up by its bootstraps. From a community of extremely high unemployment, the town has turned itself round by creating a hierarchy of defined skill levels for construction and yard work.

With the Credit Union financing the loans, they have encouraged the hiring of local people, plus, developed a catalog inventorying what skills are available.

Using the mentoring system, everyone who wants to is soon training for entry level, and higher work. That simple shift kick starts the economy and makes Corazon a town people from outside begin investigating as a place to live. The initial real estate sales that occur quickly indicate the potential, encouraging more improved maintenance that generates more work for local crafts people and the labor force.

I tell Shirley of the conversation with Kim earlier on. She glows when I tell her I only came to Corazon because of her. We are both surprised when we work out that we maybe knew each other for fourteen hours total before she went home and I left for Corazon. I begin to understand that, with such a tenuous link as that beginning, forming so intense a bond, we are soul sisters, and very special.

Seeing the business district through Shirley's eyes, I recognize what changes have been wrought. It is magnificent!

Fewer shops are boarded up. Many glass windows sparkle. Woodwork is either painted or primed.

Accompanied by two girls, an elegantly dressed woman steps out of a luxury SUV and enters the decked out Corazon Community Craft Project. Shirley and I follow them in. Even I am amazed. The store is the same one I first saw Erika and Marne start out. Now, there are teens serving the clientele, crafts are elegantly displayed and many new products are available as more people in town, and the surrounding area, find there is a market for their hobbies. Front and center, the two girls make a beeline, are the Meteor bud and scarf combinations.

Shirley is impressed. She tugs on my arm in advance of a confidence.

"I am saving my money until I have a regular adequate income," she tells me.

"Is that what you thought I am doing?" I answer. "I'm showing off the town. That's all."

"Good," she says, giving my arm a friendly squeeze.

We walk past a couple more stores to "freeXchange." The large front window has hand painted ads all over the glass. This is a store front in early transition. Inside, racks of clothes sit on a painted concrete floor. Display items are pinned to walls. There's an electronics section with dated items. There's furniture. I hold up clothes to check them against Shirley's face and hair.

"You may want to do this with Sarah, sometime," I say. "She has a wonderful eye for color and design."

"I'd love to," Shirley says. "If everything is free, how do they make any money?"

"People volunteer their time," I say. "Shoppers bring equal or better than what they leave with. You can take a blouse and a skirt plus shoes equal to what you're wearing. There's a box for Free Will Offering. People are generous because what they "buy" is free. It works."

"What a neat idea," Shirley agrees.

"Let me take you to dit Union," I say.

"OK," she says. "Is everything, alright, Judith?"

"I am so thrilled to have you here, Shirley," I say.

We intertwine the little fingers of adjoining hands and leave the freeXchange and go down the street to the Credit Union. We meet up with Cindy who has stopped in to check on how the co op is faring. I have her meet Shirley. There is only one teller, Magda, who works part time. Cindy introduces us. Cindy schedules an interview with Shirley as a possible clerk and we head on out. Shirley is delighted her integration into Corazon is working so smoothly.

"You did the same for me," I tell her. "It was a long time ago, but you left only when I was safely in Carl's hands. Remember?"

"I guess," she says.

As we exit on to the sidewalk, the two girls, proudly wearing new Meteor buds and scarves, leave the craft store followed by the woman.

Driving slowly down the street, a police cruiser passes. The passenger cop leans out his window.

He calls out, "Hey, Judith. Looking good!"

Shirley looks at me aghast.

"The local cops acknowledge you?" she asks.

"Sure," I tell her. "We've reduced their work load. They receive the same pay. They're happier and crime is down. What can I say?"

"Outside of Corazon," she asks, "Does anybody know what is happening here?"

"The media has written us up all the way to San Francisco," I say. "Radio and TV news have covered us. Corazon is happening."

"You did all this in two years?" she gasps.

"I reflected back need," I say. "Local people did the work. When the debt load is totally eliminated, this town will rock. Taquinta Economics 101—Abundance is in the mind of the beholder."

As we walk past the City and Farmers' Bank, it is nothing tangible, but to me, it lacks the vitality it once had. Shirley seems unaware of it. She doesn't give it a second look.

I take Shirley to visit Cindy's yard. The planted circle is green with growing and fruiting plants. The tree is beginning to come back. The Community Center is built and the streaks of fire are ready for finishing. The playground is marked off and the skateboard park is mostly dug out and waiting for the concrete to be poured. For me, the place is already on fire.

"How often do those... breaks... happen, Judith?" Shirley asks me.

"What happens?" I ask. "Breaks?

DAY SIX

CAKE WALK

Time flies when you're having fun.

Corazon has unified into a community operating as one. People gather for all manner of social events at The Meteor—how they now refer to the community center. Folks seem to lose awareness of time in The Meteor. That so many of us gather there regularly makes life a sweet pleasure. Whatever lit this fire under everyone was worth it.

When Shirley and Kim meet, they get along well. Kim jokes that I have been working so hard that once Shirley arrived, I began to relax. Along the way, he feels I lost one or two pieces of the puzzle. We all three of us go out looking for them without success. It would help if Kim were more specific about what it is we are looking for.

I am unusually tired that night. Kim asks Shirley to sit by me while I lie down and he goes outside to meditate with the tree. I probably sleep through it all. She is such a gentle soul. When I wake, she is sitting in exactly the same place, with the same light smile, and her hands still in her lap. Out of the corners of my eyes, I see Kim's hands doing slow rotations alongside my temples, about one inch away. At the same time, he breathes long, deep, slow breaths into the top of my head.

"What are you doing?" I ask him.

"Prepare Ms. Judith meditate with tree," he says sweetly.

Shirley leaves to go home. I worry how she will find her way, but she does fine. She's not only an adventurer, she's smart, too.

Kim carries me out and props me up with my back to the tree. Though it is night time, he wants me to meditate, even briefly.

I am not in the mood. However, to appease Kim and knowing he never does anything without good reason, I comply.

I cannot remember anything to compare with that night. When I ask him about it, Kim swears I was there for no more than five minutes. It feels like days.

Almost from the moment Kim steps away from me after propping me up, I feel swallowed in a flowing river of mud, the color of dark umber. Normally, I am not comfortable with the sensation of being under water. The mud is different. Somehow I am able to breathe. I remember staying under the surface for an extremely long time but feeling totally at peace when Kim swims toward me, into me.

I am enormous, the size of a Thanksgiving Day Parade balloon. Kim is tiny, darting about, searching. He periodically surfaces for air, sometimes putting small, shiny metal objects on the banks as if he is collecting them. Meanwhile, I float slowly along, stalling, as if waiting for him to catch up to perform yet another search through me.

Kim must have carried me in. My next memory is of waking to sunlight streaming in to his living room where I am stretched out on cushions and covered with blankets. Kim sits at back of my head, his hands alternately rotating by my temples.

That was exactly one year ago. There have been no more episodes, and no more treatments. I am conscious of Shirley being protectively extra conscious the way I imagine how a sister may be, though nothing is ever said.

The Meteor is finished as are the playground and the skate park with its perpetual clack and rattle of kids dreamily riding concrete waves and performing devil may care antics along metal hand rails or hardwood planks.

One day, The Meteor's two huge sliding doors are open as dressed up townspeople file in. Tension released from face and posture, kids dressed in Sunday best escort adults to rows of folding chairs set up to face the open doors. While they sit and wait, many contemplate the round vegetable garden in the distance, awash in colorful plants. A majestic sign announces the garden as, PERELANDRA USA, WEST.

To kick off the proceedings, the now calm, collected Shirley holding a microphone steps out front to address everyone.

"Thank you all for attending, this afternoon," Shirley says. "Please join me to recognize County Supervisor Alice Blake."

The audience applauds as Blake stands and waves. She sits back down beside Charles in his wheelchair. Phone cameras record.

"Please join me to recognize our new mayor, Jose, and city council members," she says.

The crowd gives an especially loud and raucous recognition to Jose who is surprisingly reserved and quietly appreciative of his supporters. The City Council all stand and wave back. Four of them are still also Block Captains. Three of them are women.

"I want to personally thank Judith for recognizing my skills as a teacher," Shirley continues. "Without that, I may never have had the privilege of working with such terrific kids. Please, put your hands together as the Corazon Dance Troupe presents, WOW!"

The Special Folk, now numbering seven kids, dressed as sylphs, parade in as an awkward, jostling line. What was fun in rehearsal assumes some conscious liabilities of awareness at being in public. There is pushing and pulling, a couple of collapses in tears, one temper tantrum, and one simple refusal to budge. Each re/action is handled in calm and loving fashion by Shirley.

Soon, they are all standing, relatively side by side, facing an eager and expectant audience. Shirley, off to one side but angled to be visible to each of her students, raises her hands on outstretched arms, presses them out front, fingers in fan mode at right angles to her arms, mouth puckered up ready. Each kid happily imitates, and, watching Shirley nod her head three times, she slowly begins to flap her hands and spray, as do the kids.

Though they are in no danger, front row audience members stiffen, and then laugh at their own foolish temerity. Tensions released, the music starts and, for about one minute each of dancing to familiar themes, the kids do their own free expression to a medley comprising Stravinsky's, "The Rite of Spring," Copland's, "Fanfare for the Common Man," and, Strauss' "Thus Spake Zarathustra."

Off to one side, her eyes weeping tears of joy, Cindy grasps my hands in hers.

"I have lived here 43 years," she tells me. "I have seen the area go through all manner of change. But this—I've never seen community here before. Bless you."

"Thank you," I say. "There's a quote I like by Marianne Williamson:

Our deepest fear is that we are powerful beyond measure.
It is our light, more than our darkness that frightens us.".

"I am so glad to share your light," Cindy says as she draws me into a hug.

Many of the audience stand to applaud, moved by the kids' willingness to be seen so publicly and for being so comfortable in their bodies.

Shirley directs the kids to bow and then, pretending to be the Pied Piper, leads the kids to the back of the auditorium.

Supervisor Blake steps forward to address the audience.

Still applauding the kids, she begins by saying, "I wish I had the fearlessness those children displayed performing for us now. What a wonderful environment you have created... for them to feel safe enough to put on such a... a magical... show.

"As politicians, we tend to believe we know what the public needs, what is best for a community. The town of Corazon opened my heart and the hearts of my colleagues to the fact that it is the people who know, and it is we politicians who need to do the peoples' bidding.

"As a result of you expressing your desires: the highway by pass is sign posted to direct travelers to visit your town, especially this incredible Meteor; and, I believe you will be pleased to know, the bottling plant project is dead... In the water!"

The news breaks over the assembly and explodes with people jumping to their feet with excitement, screaming their delight, hugging each other.

Blake waits at the mic, smiling quietly as the community experiences one more political victory.

"Well done," she tells everyone. "However, I put you on notice to remain eternally vigilant.

"OK. My colleagues at the Board of Supervisors asked me to make the following presentation."

She waves to me to come join her at the mic.

"Judith," she tells me as I approach. "This quote from Dr. Harman describes you well:

Prophetic is seeing what is possible.
Creativity is making the prophetic happen."

She holds up an ornate, gold framed document with colorful, florid first letters followed by calligraphy. As I stand next to her, she passes the frame to me.

"On behalf of the Board of Supervisors," she announces, "I present you our Certificate of Recognition signed by all of the Supervisors in recognition of what you have done to make this community what it is today."

"Thank you," I say.

I take it from her with both hands. I look at it, but it's a blur before my wet eyes. I turn it face out and, holding it above my head, gesture with a sweep of one hand to the assembled people of Corazon that this is as much theirs as it is mine. Jose leads a standing ovation as everyone rises.

After a short while, Blake tries to shush the crowd. Jose helps out by raising one hand and within moments a joyful crowd are seated and mostly hushed.

"Thanks, Jose," Blake tells him. "Judith, as my personal gift to you, I signed a copy of this most memorable photo."

With an arm about my shoulders, she pulls me close while she shows off a framed photo of the Krumpers at the Board of Education under a headline, KIDS TEACH BOARD OF EDUCATION.

I take it from her, allow a few moments for the transfer to be documented by our growing body of photographers, and then give her a big hug. As we separate, I tuck the certificate and the photo under one arm and start to head away from the limelight. She grabs my free hand and reels me back to the mic.

"Where are you headed, young lady?" she asks me, raising a titter of laughs from the audience. "I am just getting up steam. Remember, under this friendly exterior, I am a politician. And one thing most politicians like to do is to be seen and, especially, heard telling others how great they are."

This is a cue to the audience and they settle back on their chairs as Blake sets the stage for her next act. Pulling herself to her full height, she struts about in front of the mic, all the while holding my hand.

I search for Kim and he catches my eye. He raises both hands over his heart and flutters them like butterfly wings. That's our code for, "Come from the heart." I pump my conscious energy from my heart into the hand holding Supervisor Alice Blake's hand.

I can see the transfer take hold as she smiles to begin her story.

"Why do I love this town?" she asks the audience. "When I ran for this position of County Supervisor, the machine vote count had me losing. It was the absentee write in ballots from Corazon that gave me a substantial lead. I owe my election to you folks. By an unprecedented turn out, you pushed me over the top to win. So many of you participated in that election, the same one as revolutionized your City Council and mayor's race, the whole world sat up and took notice. In fact, from Sacramento to Washington, D.C., politicians want to know Corazon's secret."

She gives a slight nod in my direction and people smile, a few applaud.

"Very soon," Blake continues. "The United States Senate will hold subcommittee hearings on voting in this country. Because the turnout in Corazon was so far ahead of anywhere else in the country, we were invited to send someone to address the hearing. Do we have a volunteer?"

Blake takes my hand she is holding and thrusts it into the air.

"Judith Fargoe!" she shouts. "That's good, because these hotel accommodations in D.C. have your name on them. So does this airplane ticket. And, to show you how much we love you, it's a round trip ticket."

Strobes flash as Blake hands me the travel documents. I am overwhelmed. I can barely register what she is telling me. To me, the whole idea feels like a mistake. If it were left up to me, I'd send Harold Wattiss. He understands the system. Me, I'm a bit player who can raise emotions high enough to get the proverbial ball rolling.

Out of the corner of my eye, I catch a glimpse of Kim bowing deeply to me and offering his Tae Kwon Do salute. I am swept up in a sea of exhilarated people. Blake and I manage to shake hands as the audience gives another standing ovation.

An approaching, heart stopping, rumbling noise followed by loud, car horns blaring causes people to leave The Meteor to see what is happening outside.

Jose is first out the doors to wave a greeting to a parade of Low Riders as they strut their stuff while they circle the block. Some of the cars are Sarah's junkers now beautifully refinished. The lead car, paint gleaming in the sunshine, is the fin tailed Cadillac.

Jose dashes to the road to hold open the rear passenger door of the Caddy. Dressed like a queen, Maria steps out to be escorted toward the community by a proud Jose. As the cars park, dressed to kill gang kids, including Mung and Hernando, fall into line forming Maria's entourage.

It is as if Jose has been waiting his whole life for this moment.

"Ladies and gentlemen," he proudly announces. "It's my great honor to present to you my daughter, Maria, who turned 15. In keeping with a tradition of my people, Maria is recognized as a queen on this her Quinceanera."

People applaud, and, moments later, a Mariachi band strikes up, inspiring everyone to become involved.

Tables loaded down with food are carried out from The Meteor and set up in the now copious shade of the once sickly tree.

Jose leads Maria to the concrete dance floor and slow dances Maria in a circle so everyone may see her close up. When the song ends, Jose waits for the next to begin. Bebe steps up to request a dance with Maria. Reluctantly, Jose relinquishes control of his most grown up daughter.

While they eat, many people clap in time with the music, many others dance.

Kim, Shirley, Sarah and Ray rescue me from Alice Blake. We settle near the tree.

Cindy comes over to join us.

"I was always hoping to have people make use of these lots," she tells us. "This is beyond my wildest dreams. And this tree... is a miracle!"

"Kim has a thing with trees," I say. "A most unusual talent."

HEART TO HART

Thus commences a series of nightly meetings to prime me for my exposure to the Senate subcommittee. The principal people assisting are Kim, Shirley, Charles and Cindy. When they are available, Sarah, Ray, Carl, Lizbet, Jose and, occasionally, Carlito participate.

I suggest Harold Wattiss. The one time we meet with him, he is like a different person. We never found out what was going on, but something occurred that upset him. His comments at that meeting were harsh and unforgiving. I am sad not to be able to include him. It's like seeing a trusted adult display a fatal flaw. But as a group we determine to let him well enough alone.

We review hour upon hour of archived C SPAN footage. We discuss all manner of positions. One notable factor that stands out, introspectively, is that, everyone in this community is either an immigrant or descendant of recent immigrants. The term "recent" is inserted to appease Charles who feels his ancestors could lay claim to some thirty thousand years of life on one or both American continents compared to one to five generations for the rest of us. He and Jose are still in negotiations.

We research every last detail about each member of the Senate subcommittee including published statements, voting records and campaign donor lists. We are as thorough doing our homework as is possible to be via the internet.

As the last of our peace council meetings ends, Kim comments in an aside, "All hinge introduction."

Whether he means mine or someone else's, like with Blake, is for me to find out.

I am loaned a mobile phone with voice command GPS capability. Apparently, so long as it is charged, the phone always knows where I am and how to get me to where I ask to go. I am being propelled into the technological present by necessity similarly to how I was when Lucy was preparing to deliver baby Mika.

The night before I leave, Kim insists I spend two hours meditating against the tree, getting grounded. My brain is still processing the mountain of new data I ingested plus my own nervousness about flying which I settle with three rounds of EFT.

That is the toughest meditation ever. For the entire two hour period, what I receive is tree. There are no fancy dreams, no exhilarating psychedelic trips. All I get from the tree is... tree.

I can swear sometimes it feels as if Kim and the tree are in cahoots. How can I go from wildly ecstatic to the pedantically mundane? It is the same tree when all is said and done.

I confront Kim on the topic.

"First meditate tree, tree," he says.

"OK," I say. "But I was learning to meditate back then."

"Learn, today," he says with a shrug as he walks away.

I'm back to basics. Maybe I plateau ed. Maybe, after all, I did lose my "edge" as Kim calls it. He never did lead me to expect anything; meditation is meditation. The rare treats were just that, rare. I need to meditate on what it is the "I" wants when I meditate.

Suddenly, I leave. I leave behind my precious community with hugs and tears, lots of well wishing, handshakes and waves goodbye.

I fly in a plane. I land at Reagan International Airport. A mechanical woman's voice directs me to a subway. The lady in my GPS knows where I am and what is up ahead. I exit at DuPont Circle towing my carry on suitcase and walk to my hotel.

As I ride the elevator to my room, I get an amazing twinge that I am a stooge. I have been set up. Alice Blake has pre arranged my life in D.C. for me to slot in, do my thing and slot out. Inside the Meteor was a gradual softening up process to have me conform to other people's projection of how they want the world to appear. I'll be on camera stating platitudes that say, to no one in particular but to everyone who needs to know, all is well with the world. Here I am to prove it.

Wow! That whole train of thought is freaky.

I freshen up, call the Junior Senator for California, Senator Chris Franco's office and slowly make my way down the "emergency" stairs to the lobby. Within minutes, a bright, freshly scrubbed, sparklingly intelligent youth, attired in suit and tie checks with the front desk and rushes towards me.

"Judith?" he asks. "Judith Fargoe?"

I rise slowly, with dignity, and extend my hand. He shakes my hand hurriedly and moves for the front doors.

"I'm Jonathan," he explains as we stride along the sidewalk. "We've got the smallest window for you to meet with Senator Franco."

He steps into the road and flags down a cab. He all but throws me in and chatters at breakneck speed distracting me from looking out at where we are and what we're passing. The cab pulls up some distance from any one building and, again, we're off to the races.

We weave between concrete traffic control posts and into a white building. Especially on the fly and with buildings being so close to one another, it's hard to get a sense of the architecture. Inside, we go, through the metal detection and right past the inscription to Senator Phillip Hart.

I interrupt Jonathan's soliloquy on how important it is that I came to be a witness and how proud Franco is to have a constituent make such incredible changes.

"Can we take a picture of me below the inscription to Senator Hart?" I ask.

"The what?" he asks.

"That," I say, pointing, as we move quickly past it.

"Amazing," he says. "I never noticed it before."

"If you are unaware of it," I say, "That's because it is pretty well hidden by all the security apparatus."

"Later," he says, almost pushing me into an elevator.

"Do you have any electronic presentation, DVD, video, anything I should set up?"

"We discussed that, as a community, and we decided we want people to visit Corazon," I say.

"Absolutely!" he agrees. "Here!"

And I am thrust out as the elevator door opens.

"Left!" he says. "This is us."

Hello, California—in a bottle.

He slows to a brisk stride, slips past me and opens both doors, and stands aside.

I step into a painted, soft, pinkish tan cloud. As if on cue, some frantically busy staffers stop what they are doing, rise from their desks and applaud me.

Throwing on his suit coat, Senator Franco emerges from his inner office, hand snapping up to greet me.

"Judith Fargoe," he says, breathlessly. "I hear amazing things about you from Supervisor Blake. It's an honor; an absolute honor."

"Thank you, Senator Franco," I say. "I appreciate your arranging for me to address the Sub Committee. It's exciting to be here."

He and I shake hands as he passes by me.

"I shall personally introduce you at tomorrow's hearing," he informs me. "Right now, I'm expected for a vote. Jonathan's like a son to me. He will do a great job."

And he's gone. The men staffers are already seated back at their stations, working their computers, or on the phone. Several of the younger women are still standing though checking the work on their desks as they, too, begin to sit.

There are a series of vacuous smiles, almost saying, "Well? That's it!"

I turn to Jonathan who is beginning to hop from one foot to the other.

"You must have taken out from your schedule to bring me here," I say.

"I have a map," he says unfolding a city street map.

He leans across a desk and picks up a marker pen.

He circles, "We're here," and, again, "Your hotel is here. If you like to walk," line along Constitution Avenue, "It's an exciting area. Then there is Pennsylvania Avenue," another line, "My favorite is the Mall with all the..."

"Museums," I say. "Thanks. What time, tomorrow?"

"They start at nine," he replies. "They're pretty punctual."

"I can be here at, say, quarter of?" I ask.

In my peripheral vision I note a woman gesturing.

"Eight thirty," he starts. "Make it quarter after. Eight will be great."

"OK, then," I say to him. "Eight it is, bright eyed and bushy tailed, notes at the ready. I'll find my own way out since I know you have international trade agreements and such to deal with. Till tomorrow!"

Downstairs, in the entrance lobby none of the security people look available to help, so I hold my phone at arm's length and snap myself in front of the inscription. I check if I got a good picture. I did. I captured the wording:

"A man of incorruptible integrity and personal courage
strengthened by inner grace and outer gentleness …
He advanced the cause of human justice,
promoted the welfare of the common man
and improved the quality of life …
His humility and ethics earned him his place as the conscience of..."

And there's my grin in place of "the Senate."

I turn on my navigator and say, "Lincoln Memorial."

My lady is ready, and humble, in an instant. She gives me her undivided attention late into the evening.

Tonight, I eat alone.

My mind drifts to Kim meditating at the tree. I send him a mental message of me being grounded. I receive a strong image back of the tree.

Bless this food, thems as growed it, thems as harvested it, thems as prepared it and thems as eat it.

NIGHT OF THE SOUL

For the first time in a very long time, I sleep poorly. I wake several times during the night and have a difficult time going back to sleep. I wake up at five to seven, groggy and stiff.

So that I can shower, I skip exercising. I know that isn't wise, but I'm cutting corners.

I take a sip of green drink and my stomach revolts.

Once dressed, I hurry down the stairs and, realizing I left the phone in the room, thus, no GPS, I decide to depend on the map Jonathan gave me. I insist on walking. I take wrong turns, go the wrong way on boulevards and arrive at the Hart Building security check, only to find out I have silverware from the hotel in my pockets.

To get around that issue, I organize an impromptu spoon bending with two of the security personnel. I give them respectively the fork and the spoon and I work the knife. Mine is the only one to bend. Since I have no choice, I leave all three items with them along with instructions to keep trying until they make it work.

Up in the California Suite, everyone is freaking out. They have been trying to reach me.

"Thank Heavens you're here!"

"Let's go!"

From watching the C SPAN tapes, I know these hearings are rarely punctual, so I refuse to join in the panic mind set. These folks definitely could use meditation to make their lives less stressful.

We enter the hearing chamber and the C SPAN cameras are rolling, the full committee is seated, and Franco is making some kind of deal with subcommittee chairman, Abe Davis. I check out the name plates and everyone is present: John Gordon, Tom Neil, Aloysius Seeds, and, Jackie Poll.

Davis points me out to Franco, who gives me an if looks can kill stare. I shrug it off. I didn't volunteer for this gig.

"Another fifteen seconds, Ms. Fargoe," Davis snarls into his mic as he points to a clock showing nine minutes after nine, "And we would have been out of here. We would have, as we like to think of ourselves, been History."

Jonathan sets me up at the witness table then disappears.

I smile at Davis who gestures at me to, "Get on with it."

"Are you going to introduce this hearing, Mr. Chairman?" I ask into my mic.

"I gaveled this hearing open ten minutes ago," he tells me.

I look over to Franco. He offered to introduce me, yesterday. Is he reneging now?

Reluctantly, he approaches a mic off to one side.

"Mr. Chairman, subcommittee members and good friends," he says. "I am told Ms. Fargoe is one of my constituents. She has a few comments to offer you. Thank you."

Wow! Is he snippy? For an organization that struggles with funding for the railroads, never mind having the trains run on time, they're complaining when a constituent is a few minutes late. I flew across America for this?

"Ms. Fargoe?" Davis asks. "That was your cue."

"Thank you, Mr. Chairman," I commence. "Good morning, Sena..."

"Just the facts," Davis interrupts me. "We all have other hearings to attend."

You want the facts. I'll give you the facts. I decide, in light of their behavior, to skip all the prepared material and provide them with some hard news, off notes.

"There are at least two versions to the story," I tell the subcommittee and the C SPAN cameras. "The pretty one is about motivation and desire overcoming hardship by striving for an ideal. That's the one where we wear clothes, speak to each other in polite platitudes and walk away calling each other a hypocrite under our breath. I call that the charade.

"Then there is the version that arrives in the middle of the night when we feel alone, vulnerable and insecure. This is the one where we are naked, displeased with our bodies and how we look. Where we recall each and every transgression we have committed. Where we use remorse and regret as weapons against ourselves. Where fear of the other, something more powerful and dangerous, rides in on us, refusing to let us sleep, forcing us to stuff food in our mouths only to regurgitate it, urinate and defecate without a bathroom to do it in, to be even remotely civilized.

"This is where we tear our own flesh, drink our own blood and feel the fat accretions we are no longer able to remove by willpower or dieting.

"That's about the time when our faces are dashed against the fabric of society by unknown hands, over and over, until our eyes are pressed tight against the woof and the weft such that the textile disappears. Society and social order cease to exist.

"We're loose in the wilds, one predator against many. It's a place of constant danger—kill or be killed. This is where the niceties are all gone. Where politeness is simply a moment's stalling tactic, a delay, before we're torn to shreds, dying from such unbelievable pain, we pass out; only to wake and find out that it is worse than the last time we were conscious.

"Voting? You want to know about encouraging people to vote. How do you teach wild animals to represent themselves, to make clear logical decisions? You are so remote, detached, absent from the daily life of most citizens, the only way you can begin to reach them is to fight each other in a periodic circus of rude, abbreviated, mean spirited accusations. A few people vote. The majority of the few that do vote dictate the outcome for everyone, voters and non voters alike, and that's how come you are here. We're damned if we do vote. We're equally damned if we abstain.

"You're walled up in this exclusive club making ludicrous niceties to each other, simulating politely while, all the time, you're plotting and scheming how to snatch power to enhance your campaign contributors and, thereby, your own future in or out of office.

"You sell your values and principles to the highest bidder and use the money to delude the few voting masses of how honorable are your intentions.

"It's a chimera, an illusion, a deceit... by conceited people.

"You are only powerful while we, the public, remain distracted. When we focus on the fact that the clothes you wear only hide your true bestiality, when we see you gorge yourselves and then throw up, have your sordid affairs in vain efforts to exert real power, you are like our worst nightmare.

"Then we have to decide whether to vote for you or some facsimile with other useless opinions only intended for the short run of an election cycle.

"You contrive to have us believe in money, money that loses value daily, to pay down debts even you have difficulty wrapping your heads around. Money is useless. As the numbers increase the value diminishes. We act with it because everyone else does, but, in truth, we do not buy the belief you feed us that money has value, is protected.

"The only money there is, is some chaotic delusion. Money is out of your control more now than ever before, if you ever did have any. It's a belief system fraught with engineered highs and lows, overproduction, underproduction, pluses and minuses, all of them manipulations by unseen others trying to capture chunks of the illusion.

"When we finally, collectively, turn our backs on your money belief system, you will go away, disappear. What you need to prop you up will be gone, made meaningless.

"We, the People, are real, tangible. We will remain. We will survive without money because we have purpose. Life is purpose. Government has minimal purpose unless it can be fabricated like so much cotton candy on television and in the social media. Once we bite into it, it turns back into being distorted lumps of overheated sugar.

"Money is controlled by a little person with a powerful microphone. Once the dress up you have us invested in is demolished, there will only be soulless greedy people without any proper value to society.

"Vote? With our lives? Go to war? With our lives? Die for God and country? For what? Some freedom that you so easily take away with your arbitrary laws. Be good or we'll lock you away, strip you of your vote, deny your family another food provider, and abuse your children so they quickly become criminals, more fodder for a system out of control.

"It may be a different charade, but it, too, is a charade all the same."

I stop.

I look around; dead silence. No one moves.

I stand up and walk toward the committee. They have the flat look of photographs.

As I approach I see that they are photos mounted on boards, propped up.

I am alone.

The lights dim.

WHAT'S THE DIFF?

Jonathan politely ushers me to my seat at the Hearing Room Witness Table below the dais.

Almost immediately, the C SPAN cameras swing into action as, at precisely nine o'clock, Senators Abe Davis, John Gordon, Tom Neil, Aloysius Seeds, and, Jackie Poll file in, like so many ships of state.

Dressed in suits to make them look authoritative, it's evident the men are masking unhealthy bodies. I think to myself, if that is how politicians take care of their own bodies, they've got a nerve telling women how to care for their reproductive systems.

I hear my mind going into judgmental mode and quickly pivot my thoughts away so that I am present and open as the senators take their seats.

Senator Davis gavels the hearing to order.

"I call this Senate Subcommittee Hearing on Voting in America to order," he states. "At this time, I invite my good friend from California, Senator Franco, to introduce our next witness."

Off to one side, Senator Franco speaks into a microphone.

"Thank you, Mr. Chairman," he says. "Fellow Senators, friends, it is my privilege to present a constituent from Corazon, California. Until her involvement, Corazon was in dire economic straits. I believe this witness will provide insight into higher voter participation. It is my honor to introduce, Judith Fargoe."

According to Kim's ideas, there I have it. What stands out from Franco's intro of me is the transition from dire economic straits to higher voter participation. I hear him define the issue of increasing voter activity as being directly tied to enhancing economic standing. Community wide, is that all boats floating equally causes a higher turnout, versus, restricting the economy by using austerity reduces voter participation?

"I thank my friend for his warm introduction," Davis pronounces. "I welcome you to these hearings, Ms. Fargoe. For the record, please state your name."

"Thank you, Mr. Chairman," I begin. "Good morning, Senators. My name is Judith Fargoe."

From our training tapes, following instructions precisely expands the likelihood of discussion ensuing. The chairperson appreciates immediate witness confirmation of who is in charge.

Davis invites me, "Please present your address."

"Senators," I read from my notes, "I appreciate this opportunity to address you with my comments about voting. Bear with me please as I present some background.

"About four years ago, when I arrived in Corazon, it was a town with little industry, mostly run down houses and storefronts and surrounded by farms, many of them vast enterprises operated by industrial machines. That process of mechanization had transitioned the town from an agrarian based community of farm workers to one of occasionally employed residents inhabiting a bedroom community. As a result, the residents were unable to sustain the heartbeat of the town, its commercial district.

"In addition, over the years, fire had destroyed many key community centered buildings.

"Most residents had to travel far from the town if they were fortunate enough to find work. Exhausted by struggling to survive, the majority of townsfolk lacked a sense of self worth. This translated into disinterest in being a community. Only a few charismatic Block Captains were active in politics, and that comprised largely of crime prevention. The local City Council had turned itself into a boys' club focused on protecting the few remaining commercial concerns in town and keeping the roads and sewers operational.

"That all changed when it was learned one candidate for County Supervisor was in cahoots with a corporation seeking a sweetheart deal to sell off water from the local aquifer. Because the aquifer was deep seated, it had been minimally impacted by chemical runoff from the surrounding area monoculture industrial farming practices. This is what made the aquifer attractive to the drinking water bottling company.

"Educating the townspeople about a potential for further economic damage to the locale and its few neighboring small farms by the possibility of having their water privatized galvanized interest in the election.

"At a Block Captains' meeting, it was agreed that one priority was to create an active community center. Land for the center was donated by a community member who also underwrote most of the construction materials costs.

"That same person also donated additional land nearby for a vegetable garden conditioned on the local school district making working there part of the high school students' academic curriculum.

"When the community approached the only bank in town to ask for a loan to cover construction costs for the community center—a loan for which the land donor was willing to act as guarantor—the bank balked at the financing. When the community heard this and, that what they had assumed was a local bank was, in fact, a particle of an international financial consortium, they initiated a run on the bank, eventually forcing it to close its doors. Much of the removed funds went into the creation of a local Credit Union operated by community members who aggressively financed restoration of buildings, both residential and commercial, and thereby generated a local, labor pool of skilled craftspeople. By especially focusing on the more manageable micro loan for property repairs and restoration, the Credit Union enhanced a rapid increase in real estate values across the town, plus greatly reducing local unemployment.

"The school bought fresh produce from a local farmer who uses Biodynamic techniques. These foods greatly improved the children's mental acuity. The noticeable change encouraged the students to grow their own produce using Biodynamic technology on the donated land. Their garden became so impressive; those same gardening practices were taken up by the public citywide.

"Each aspect—the aquifer, the community center, the Credit Union and the vegetable garden—interacted with the others to engage the populace. As community formed, people also grew aware of the power voting would provide them. Registering voters became an obsession, a social activity where residents got to know their neighbors better. Because of a pervasive distrust of computerized voting machines and as a result of their socializing, almost every vote cast in Corazon was by absentee ballot.

"I think it fair to say that, that first election was issue driven at many different levels. Three Board of Education members were voted in, three County Supervisors were elected, and two City Council seats were won by Block Captains. At the election two years later, the community made additional adjustments installing one of their own as Mayor and electing enough women for them to comprise half the City Council.

"Working that initial window of concern for the local water supply stimulated the community's awareness of other pressing needs. That led to community improvements spearheaded by hands on management by elected representatives.

"For example, the people fostered intense community pride when they took back control of their money via the formation of the Credit Union. Additionally, substantial growth in community well being was achieved by a concerted, cooperative effort to eliminate all residents' debt, starting with credit cards.

"Encouraging high school kids to apprentice to mentors as a means to fix up the town was fundamental to the upsurge in local community consciousness.

"Giving kids hands on control of growing many of the vegetables eaten at school and at home established an enthusiasm for the area that will hopefully last for generations. Here's an appropriate quote from Daniel Webster:

When tillage begins, other Arts follow.
The farmers, therefore, are the founders of human civilization.

"Furthermore, understanding that one person in need unbalances the whole community, individuals were encouraged to meet with neighborhood committees to express their specific needs and to have their issues addressed.

"Recognizing that, at core, every individual wants to be an energized, creative participant in society; then Corazon represents a microcosm of the world's people by thinking globally, acting locally.

"To do this, the community took two decisive steps: to be stewards of area water, and, to care for their neighbors.

"It took time. Then, again, all Life is, is time—how we use it, and what we do with it."

I take a breather to check that I have the panel's full attention; so far so good.

"Clearly," I tell the panel, "The people of Corazon voted with the expectation that their elected representatives will respond to them. However, by the time we reach the level of County Supervisor, most local concerns are submerged by broader county issues. So Corazon is lucky to be represented by Supervisor Alice Blake who has a soft spot for our community. By the level of State Representative and Senator, we're shading on a map. From the viewpoint of our Congressional delegation, we are close to nonexistent.

"With all due respect to our Junior Senator Chris Franco, the only reason we are even remotely part of his consciousness now is that there may be a few new pockets to tap when he comes to town for a photo op in front of The Meteor."

Franco waves and gives me a big smile. Am I hosting a Franco Roast?

"Immediately post Revolution, America was what?" I continue. "One quarter, maybe one third, of the land mass it is now? Certainly the population was miniscule by comparison with today's numbers. The Founding Fathers designed their community to be run by elected representatives. It was tough for those officials but they were effective because many decisions were made while socializing. Of course, the only people to vote back then were men who owned land and wealth, so the chain of command was pretty direct and they and their elected representatives had many of the same issues in common.

"That was then. Now we have a vast country with many times increase in population. The wealthy male voter waters have been expanded by giving the vote to women and everyone else of age who is a citizen.

"As you can see, the people of Corazon, leastways the participating electorate, made short shrift of any representative selling off the community chest. Would that the nation followed that simple example?

"Let me close with some suggestions for how to encourage people to vote. For one, support more women to run for public office at least until there is a representative female male balance throughout the political hierarchy. For another, give the electorate a cast iron guarantee that they control their communities instead of corporations. It's my own belief that elections will simply be replaced by a massive dawning of consciousness.

"Thank you, Senators."

"Thank you, Ma'am," Davis tells me. "Senator Gordon."

"Good morning, Ms. Fargoe," Gordon says. "You do have strong opinions. Let's discuss the one initial election that had a huge voter turnout. What I understand you to say is that without centrally vital issues, those kinds of numbers are unlikely to repeat."

There is something about being questioned on the Hill. It's similar to playing a strong tennis rally with a superior opponent. I can feel my timing, my choice of words and their order all turn up several notches of poignancy.

"Senator Gordon," I say, "After igniting the initial fire of awareness, what was done was to enable and encourage home ownership. It's a known fact that homeowners take a more active role in elections. Why else do banks foreclose on peoples' homes and then demolish much of that housing stock other than to reduce participation in elections? It makes terrible business sense in the short run, but it does skew the political balance.

"By providing opportunity for more people to own their own home, an increased investment as to who is elected sustains high voter turnout."

"What other changes do you believe can boost voter turnout?" he asks.

"There are always the obvious," I say. "Move elections to the weekend. Instead of winner take all, develop proportional representation.

"It's my understanding that the radio and TV airwaves belong to the people. If elections were reduced to twelve weeks of public campaigning, having all speeches and debates broadcast in their entirety will assist voters to make more educated decisions.

"I would limit total contribution per donor to any one campaign to a low maximum amount.

"Eliminate all paid lobbyists' access to both elected and appointed government.

"Bar any elected official from ever working for any company directly affected by a vote that official made while in office.

"Definitely stop the rotating door of corporate officers becoming government administrators because that, for sure, corrupts the public interest.

"I come from a world in which women are empowered, are comfortable with leadership roles. Politics is the art of compromise. Women know plenty about compromise. That gives them a head start in politics.

"The time has surely come for women to assume a proportionally greater role in public office. If a particular office needs a woman candidate, in the space on a ballot for a write in, voters can enter the name of a responsible woman, or, at least, write in *Jane Doe*.

"I'd like to see you gerrymander gender lines if women voted only for women candidates."

"Gerrymandering would be more of a House of Representatives' issue," Gordon says. "Though this may be a simplistic model, for the Senate to reflect something comparable, perhaps it would be one woman Senator and one man Senator representing each state."

"Thank you, Senator," I say. "That certainly would be a good start."

"I read somewhere," he resumes, "That you encouraged children to be active in the election process. Is that so?"

"Probably what you read, Senator Gordon," I say, "Is that there was an intense voter registration drive at the Corazon high school by middle school students."

"I take it you were good with that?" he asks.

"Sure," I say. "Most kids are aching to be adults. I say let them feel the weight of responsibility as early as possible."

"If I were to ask you at what age people can start to vote," Gordon lobs me a soft ball. "What age would you suggest?"

I know to swing and hit that one out of the park.

"Kids deserve to vote," I say, leaning into the mic, "By the age that logical thinking kicks in. That is age eight."

Senator Gordon fumbles with his notes as Senator Neil, next to him, short of exploding, flips out.

Neil looks to Davis and asks, "Recognition from the chair."

It's a familiar dance routine on the C SPAN tapes.

Davis looks to Gordon and asks, "Senator Gordon?"

Gordon smiles knowingly.

"I release the balance of my time to my friend," he says.

"Senator Neil," Davis says.

"I thank my good friend for relinquishing me the balance of his time," Neil graciously says to Senator Gordon.

Turning to me, his voice acquires a sickeningly sweet, demeaning tone.

"Miss Fargoe," he asks me, "Can you imagine the chaos that will result if we did as you say and gave children the vote?"

I am so tempted to engage him in battle. I am armed to the teeth with barbed comments. Try these, Neil.

"Who of you actively advocates for children's rights?" or,

"If it's good for business to keep kids deprived of representation, who in their right mind would let kids vote?" and,

"What we have now is a model of perfection from which kids should learn?"

Kim warned me if I engage a Senator in battle, I might as well commit *seppuku*, Hara Kiri, and just fall on my sword and get it over with. Then I recall what Serena did for me when I felt so antagonistic towards her; kind of how Senator Neil may currently be thinking about me. It's time to make a meal fit for a king.

"You know, Senator Neil," I say as demurely as I can manage. "I was more thinking that kids under 18 without a vote are unrepresented. I believe that exercising their opinions via voting would be so liberating for them. I mean, they do comprise such a substantial part of the economy. Right?"

Neil takes a hard right.

"You are originally from Detroit?"

"Yes, I am, Senator," I say.

"You lived in New York City before you visited Cuba?" he asks.

Wow! It can't be the Army-McCarthy hearings redux. Neil isn't old enough.

"New York City, yes," I say. "I have yet to voyage out from beyond the confines of the lower 48 states, Senator."

"Then where did you come up with those wild ideas, Miss Fargoe?" he asks.

"You think, Senator?" I gasp. "I thought my "ideas" are common sense simple."

"Somebody taught you," he berates me, wagging a finger at me. "These are complex ideas..."

"I have been hanging with a bunch of immigrants," I offer, to spare him making any regrettable, defamatory accusations, my being a woman and all. "They do see the world differently. That's for sure, Senator Neil."

Senator Seeds seeks the floor by flagging Davis with his pencil.

"Mr. Chairman?" he calls out.

"If Senator Neil is complete," Davis says. "The chair recognizes Senator Seeds."

"Ms. Fargoe," Seeds says, "You referenced that the community's starting a Credit Union was a factor in voting. Why do you think that is important?"

"Being member owned, Senator Seeds," I say, "A Credit Union shares its profits with its membership. National slash international banks suck capital out of community banks from deposits, loans and especially credit cards. Conversely, Credit Unions are specifically geared to foster local growth. That, I contend, encourages home ownership which, in turn, fosters more active community participation and that, surely, ties in to voting."

"I believe you are correct there," he says. "Are you a member of the Credit Union's board of directors?"

"I was invited to join, Senator," I say. "I declined. Also, I refuse to buy shares in the Credit Union."

"Really?" he says. "I find that incredible. You registered 90 percent of the electorate and turned out 81 percent of them to vote, yet you refuse to support the local Credit Union which seems to be your idea?"

"You give me undeserved responsibility, Senator," I tell him. "In both voter registration and turn out, local people did the footwork. As far as the Credit Union goes, I was present when the idea was posited."

"You're too modest," he says. "By half."

"Senator," I tell him. "The town was about to receive a death blow if the bottling plant came in to use up the aquifer water. The citizenry used voting as a tool, wielding it as a weapon, to protect themselves, unlike other people in past times."

"What other people are you referring to?" he asks.

"Those people who educated us about many of the principles incorporated into our Constitution," I say. "Those people who gave us the idea of three branches of federal government. Those people who suffered perhaps the worst genocide in recorded history, descendants of whom, to this day, have the love to cradle all of us in their hearts."

"Of course," he says sardonically. "The Indians."

"Native Americans, yes, sir," I say, "This nation's first people. I live by much of the basic philosophy common to most indigenous peoples of the world because it treats every person as holy and holds Mother Earth in highest regard.

"By contrast, in its current incarnation, this country thrives on policing the world... with wars on drugs, immigration and terror, to name only a few. As a result, many people in the world have lost respect for the stature with which our nation was held for so many years. This country changed its tune from, "The Yanks are Coming," to, "Shock and Awe"; from chocolate bars and bubblegum carrying Dough Boys to videogame characters in Kevlar suits. Some people even regard us as bullies the way we use unmanned drones to spy and execute.

"In turn, our government learned to distrust people who question its policies, such that now those people, and also we citizens, are all potential suspects till proven innocent, if we can even go to trial. How do people pursue happiness under such constraints?"

As Seeds backs into his chair with an air of resignation, Davis pulls his mic close.

"This Committee has been extremely tolerant of your remarks, Ms. Fargoe," he instructs me. "Your comments have been inflammatory more than once. I ask you to stay on the topic for which this Committee was created; voting."

"Certainly, Senator Davis," I say. "At the time of the 2010 U.S. Census, this nation had a population of 310 million people of whom 54 million are children. About 10 million of those kids live in poverty and many more are food insecure. This is my question to you as a panel; if you were one of these children and you had the vote, would you believe it is in your interest to vote for any of the current crop of politicians?"

Neil takes the bait.

His response isn't perfect by any stretch of the imagination, but it contains makings of a concession.

"With minor changes to the Child Labor Laws," Neil suggests. "They can work and earn money to buy food. Maybe then we can look into teen voting rights."

Unable to judge where the seams of tolerance are located, I press on.

"Millions of people in this, the wealthiest country in the world," I state, "Still live how many people did in Corazon four years ago—desperate for food to eat, unable to afford adequate heat, or, worst of all, homeless. Instead of being statistics; they are flesh and blood like you. They believe that they depend on you; that, you, as their elected representatives, have the power to affect their lives. When they come to the realization, like Granny D did, that their votes are an exercise in power and they decide to take back control of their republic; that will be a game changer. Then it may be you who will become the statistic.

"Consider that, of the US population, 51 percent are women. In 2012's national election, 53 percent of people who voted were women; six whole percentage points more than men. Is that reflected among our elected representatives? At best right now it's one woman to every four men. Proportionately, as a gender group, women should be the majority in Congress and the Judiciary.

"I am sure we are lucky if the number of women serving on this committee represents anywhere near the proportion of women elected to Congress; which may begin to explain why it is so difficult to have Plan B."

Senator Poll waves a hand for Senator Davis' attention.

"Senator Poll?" he asks.

"Good morning, Ms. Fargoe," she says. "My staff scoured Corazon voter registration rolls and we were unable to find your name. Did you vote, Ms. Fargoe?"

I can hear where she is going. These are dangerous waters and, at the same time, also an opportunity to bend some minds.

"It was the local peoples' issue, Senator," I tell her.

She stares at me over her glasses.

"For you to wreak the changes you effected in Corazon," she says, "And yet to stand aside at such a critical juncture makes you a conundrum."

"You're assuming the current practice of voting is a valid system," I say.

"I am," she says. "However, judging by some of your comments here, today, you seem to think otherwise, despite Corazon's clear and outstanding success with voting."

I know that what I am about to say matches most peoples' conception of extreme thought. Insofar as it digresses enough from the norm, it may even make me appear to be deranged.

Before anyone makes a rush to judgment, I hope for two things: First they will hear me out; second they will give themselves a chance to think my idea through since, over the centuries, what once was thought absurd now sits in the center as acceptable; a classical example being that the Earth spins around the Sun. OK, here goes nothing.

"Senator," I tell her. "There are at least two planes of existence. You call yours Reality. I call mine Dream Time. To you, yours is palpable. Mine operates by Lucid Dreaming. If you are new to this idea, it may sound farfetched. Yet, there are people who know such truths to be self evident. They take heart I speak these truths.

"Your Reality is, in fact, so insecure and tentative, you often feel the need to go to war to defend it. In fictional terms, that equates you with the Dark Side.

"We who dream, we Dreamers, are the fictional equivalent of the Federation—absent the war machines. We come in peace. That time is fast arriving!"

Senator Davis speaks for his colleagues who, judging by their glazed over eyes, have clearly lost the thread of logic I weave.

"Can we expect extra terrestrials to be landing any time soon?" he asks. "Is this Close Encounters with Your Kind?"

Bless her heart; Senator Poll wants to give me the floor, even if my ideas are from somewhere far, far away.

"Mr. Chairman," she asks. "If I may be allowed to complete the balance of my time..."

Davis waves for her to continue while, at the same time, he looks to Senator Seeds for camaraderie to find in me a laughing stock.

I decide to play out my metaphor.

Indicating Poll and myself, I say, "Senator Poll, what if we women are the ETs men have been waiting for?"

She rolls her eyes at me, clearly hoping for recognizable logic, not more of the same.

"There have always been two worlds," I continue. "We humans are simple. We demand a black and white answer. Some call it Heaven and Hell, others the Garden of Eden and Whatever, dark energy versus light, Black Holes and White Dwarves or just Them versus Us.

"Our choice of words has often led us to perceive an issue as a conflict requiring a sensed need to rush to join one side or another. Yet, when we tune into our Gut mind, we inherently know that when the time is right, *que sera, sera*—what will be, will be.

"In one of the world's variety of Good Books, there are regular references to Dreams. One tells of a man who tore down the walls of Jericho. Another describes a man with a many colored coat who, though sold into slavery, through the power of dreams rose to be advisor to a Pharaoh. Yet, another awoke from a dream that led him to cast the money changers out of his Father's house of worship.

"History repeatedly tells of Dreamers and their remarkable exploits. One group of descendents from religious refugees assembled to create a Constitution that formed the foundation of the United States of America.

"Right now, worldwide, there are Dreamers taking to the streets by the tens and hundreds of thousands. The best way they can describe what they want is to call for change—rapid, massive change.

"These crowds operate with a seeming lack of coherent, uniformly agreed upon argumentation. They encourage each individual to see the change he or she wants without limiting themselves to conform to a one policy fits all. They trust their fellow humans and expect that their trust will be reciprocated. They move collectively similar to birds flocking in flight performing murmuration.

"Change is the constant. We have valiantly tried one or two lines of thought to the intentional exclusion of others. The world's people are finished with doing things that way. We are fast moving to simultaneous, multiple streams of thought.

"You have to admit that the crowds on the street—each person demonstrating a different need, yet walking in the same direction—are remarkable.

"People are called. They are compelled to act, to respond. Each is right. They're alright!"

Poll tells me, "When I leave D.C. and am completed meeting with my constituents, there's a library I go to when I can. It is named after you, Ms. Fargoe. That you bring your sensibilities here, into this lion's den, appears to be easy for you to do. I commend you for your courage."

"Thank you, Senator," I say. "I find it remarkable that I am here with you in these opulent surroundings. At the same time, I am so displeased with much of what you all are doing. I do understand now what is meant by the Washington bubble."

This feels like I'm revisiting my nightmare from last night. I am talking away but no one is making a move to cut me off. It's as if they are all hypnotized. While I can, I want to fill these chambers with thoughts that may hopefully take seed and grow.

"It's as if it is permanently Sunday afternoon here," I tell the panel. "It's raining outside so you stay in and play board games. You are so detached from reality; you are in a fantasy. You invent cures for a failing economy such as austerity. It matters little to you if your answer is right or wrong because you float above the fray.

"The people of Corazon made a concerted effort to eliminate every debt owed by anyone in the community. That was hard to do and often extremely painful. For their troubles, though, they have a beautiful town of which they are rightly proud."

Like Sleeping Beauty struggling to wake from a deep sleep, Davis asks, "Your point being, Ms. Fargoe?"

"My point, Senator Davis," I tell him, "Is that in the last thirteen years, Congress and the Administration have spent an unbelievable fortune, incurring a debt in excess of $17 trillion. By my calculation, it would take all 310 million people, each child, woman and man contributing fifty four thousand dollars apiece to pay down this debt."

"That is a lot of money," Davis concurs.

"It is, Senator," I say. "And I would tell the people to ignore ever paying it."

"Now," he quips, "After everything you have said here, today, that comes as a real shock."

"The people," I tell him, "Already have all you want them to have. Paying off the national debt will leave the same politicians, give or take a few, who created this mess. The only people to benefit will be the ultra rich and the banks that help finance your election campaigns. You are most of you either indebted to the ultra rich or one of them.

"This once great nation is sliding into feudalism as fast as you dare let it go without rocking the boat to alert the peasants to their impending servitude."

Neil has had enough.

"We were warned about you," he tells me in all sincerity.

I ignore him and go after Seeds and Davis.

"The public sweats to pay down debt," I tell the panel. "And, because you are spending other peoples' money, you demonstrate few qualms about being profligate."

"Ma'am," Davis groans at me. "Please exercise restraint. In fact, I'm ready to call recess. Are there any closing questions or comments?"

He checks in with his colleagues on either side. Seeds moves close to his mic.

"Frankly, Ms. Fargoe," he tells me. "Listening to some of the ideas you have expressed here, today, I am amazed you achieved what you did."

"As I have said, Senator," I reiterate. "Others led. I merely reflected their strengths. I am an agent of change, a catalyst, if you will; a cheerleader."

"Tell us, briefly," he asks, "What motivated you to embark on this path?"

"Senator," I say. "A Third world country would be embarrassed to have a high school that looks like the one in Corazon. If we were in a Third world war zone, there would be Department of Defense monies, US taxpayers' money, to pay a contractor to build a new high school. As it is, Corazon is merely one more bunch of tax payers.

"The USA has been permanently at war somewhere in the world since the Spanish American war of 1898. Meanwhile, this country's people have suffered sizable fluctuations in the economy, extended periods of high unemployment, are gouged by overpriced healthcare, and struggle to improve themselves utilizing dubious standards of public education.

"Who has been in charge? Mostly men. It's time for them to step aside and let women try their hand. There certainly is plenty of room for improvement."

If I am from another planet, I am beginning to think Neil is from an alternate universe.

He looks to Davis as he declares, "I propose sending scientists to Corazon to check out what's in that water they are protecting."

As if waking from torpor, Davis seeks completion.

"Senator Gordon?" he asks. "Senator Poll?"

Senator Poll waves off the opportunity.

Senator Gordon approaches his mic.

"I am concerned, Ms. Fargoe," he says, "That we may be, as you suggest, a peoples divided. If this great country is to prosper, we need innovative thinking to move forward. That will be a bite, but I believe we do need to take it. I thank you for your information and wish you God's speed, ma'am."

"Thank you, Senator," I say to him.

"Ms. Fargoe?" Senator Davis asks me. "A few closing words?"

I cannot imagine what comes over the man, but I surely won't waste a good opportunity when one is provided.

"I thank you, Senator Davis," I say genteelly, "And your Committee. I acknowledge each of you for your willingness, today, to open yourself to think differently than you are accustomed to do. I honor each of you for rising to that challenge.

"It may come as a surprise to you but there are many people like me around the world. We adhere to a paradigm of humans living in harmony with the Gaia. To define ourselves, some use the term homo sapiens-sapiens, others Cultural Creatives or Evolutionaries. If you insist on a name, I go back to the beginning and call us Dreamers.

"Permit me to conclude with a story:

A person dies and meets with Creator to decide where to spend eternity. The Creator offers two options.

They arrive at a door and Creator says, "On the other side of this door is Hell."

They enter a room where thousands of people sit around an enormous pot filled with succulently smelling stew. Each person holds a spoon but the handle is so long it's impossible for people to bring the bowl of the spoon to their mouths. Everyone is desperately famished. The moans of suffering people are terrible to hear.

They leave and approach another door.

The Creator announces, "On the other side of this door is Heaven"

They enter a room that is identical to the first room—thousands of people sit around an enormous pot filled with succulently smelling stew. Each person holds a spoon with an extremely long handle. In this room, everyone is well nourished, happy and smiling.

Deeply confused, the person asks, "Everything is exactly the same, yet here the people are filled with joy. What is going on?"

Creator explains, "In this room, the people feed each other.""

I look at my rapt audience. I am beginning to wonder if I should take this show on the road.

"This Universe of plenty has more than enough to go round," I say. "How did we end up with a select few persons determining who benefits and who goes without? All of what is on this planet belongs to Mother Earth. We will pay a terrible price if we continue to ignore the coming changes.

"For the joy you will find when you do, I hope you will join us.

"I thank you for giving my thoughts opportunity to be voiced.

"And, because you do know what you do, I forgive you."

Senator Davis stares at me perplexed.

"Excuse you?" he says to me.

I offer a coquettish smile and shrug my shoulders.

Raising himself up, he assumes full control.

"On behalf of my colleagues and myself," he says to me. "I thank you, Ms. Fargoe. Any other business?"

Like a traffic cop, he looks both ways to his colleagues.

He announces, "I hereby declare this portion of these hearings closed."

SMOKE SIGNALS

I later learn that what they did is almost unprecedented; Senators Poll and Franco took me to lunch. I found out that Poll strong armed Franco into attending, but that he did succumb easily.

Surrounded by Native American crafts, beside floor to ceiling windows with parkland views of the Mall, I sit across a table from the Senators as we share a large platter of assorted, delectable foods. We are in the expansive Mitsitam Native Foods Café of the National Museum of the American Indian. It's a spiritual contradiction for me that any life be displayed for others to observe, but the museum does help educate about the complex world of some very special people.

Franco presents himself as an example.

"Thanks for suggesting this museum," he says biting into a maize morsel. "I have been promising myself to visit here, forever. You've broken the ice."

Poll sits there eating with us and beaming at me. It's flattering but embarrassing. It's my guess that Franco and the other Senators missed her reference to the library at Taquinta.

As he takes another bite, Franco comments, "Your address, today, made me think back to when I first brought a case before the Supreme Court. I only wish I could have had your confidence, Judith."

"Thank you, Senator," I say. "To change the topic, if I may. I just worked out that, today, I celebrate my sixth anniversary of when I last ate out of a dumpster."

Apparently this was further off topic than they were expecting.

"Judith?" Jackie Poll exclaims.

With a chunk of food bitten off in his mouth, Chris Franco almost chokes.

"For real?" he gurgles.

"Most people live to eat," I tell them. "Once I learned to set my intentions to accomplish what I dream of doing, I ate to live."

"You ate..." Franco squeaks.

"... Out of a dumpster?" stutters Poll.

"I was indigent," I explain, "Destitute. I was sick with hypoglycemia, Candida.

"Since I can dream lucidly, I had three storybook characters from my childhood reading take me off the streets. Life has been really good since."

Franco stares at me wide eyed and slack jawed. Poll grasps both of my hands in hers as she leans her elbows on the table.

"Judith," she tells me. "This is such an honor. Now I understand why Maisha is so proud of her prodigal daughter."

No sooner said, they are called away to the floor of the Senate for a roll call vote. That is unfortunate because they left me with the bulk of the food. Not prepared to waste it, I invite some passing college kids to join me. We have fun.

><

Arriving back in Corazon, Washington quickly resembles a busy night of dreaming. There are memorable highlights, but those quickly blend together into restructured crazy pattern storylines. Not to worry, as Ray and Sarah drive me home from San Francisco's airport, along with Kim and Shirley, my greeting committee tell me their favorite moments of my televised performance. Ray proudly announces he has recorded the entire event for posterity.

There go my opportunities to embellish on the facts!

It is gratifying to return to my family after so large a venture. Interestingly, it seems to have been larger for them that it was for me. Shirley makes sure I catch up on my diet by prepping my meals and taking care of my laundry. Kim is anxious to have me meditate at the tree with him; that's a first!

Later that night, I check in with Carl. He tells me next time not to stay away so long. Apparently, Andrea is so well trained by me; she got along fine without me. Meantime, he suggests I take one more day to get my life back on track and recover from jet lag. The former is welcome but the latter is unnecessary as I drank copious amounts of water to offset dehydration from being in the pressurized plane.

Early next morning, I walk over to Kim's house.

As dawn breaks, I have a strange feeling, almost like a premonition. As familiar as the streets and houses feel to me, I have the sense of seeing them for the first time... as if it may be my last.

When I get to his house, Kim has been meditating already for a long time, maybe all night. There's that state he's in of being perfectly balanced while connected to something else, something distant. He's here, present in his consciousness, but he's also definitely hooked by more than a thin silver thread to something undeniably powerful. I expect sparks to fly as we approach to hug. I feel nothing of the kind. He's warmer, softer and more accepting than ever. He's also eloquently abbreviated.

"Kim miss you, Ms. Judith," he says during the hug.

That is such an expression of affection for him. It's his first time saying anything that personal to me. He is letting me know how he feels about me—with words.

"I love you," I tell him. "Thank you for the image of the tree while I was away."

"You welcome," he says.

My cup floweth over. For the very first time, he is speaking to me, not about me.

After digesting these emotional ecstasies, I tell him about my experience walking over to his house. You would think I'd know his answer by now.

We spend an hour with our backs to the tree. I swear it feels like Kim is running touchdown sprints back and forth across the Cosmos. That's when I realize he is revealing himself to me while he meditates.

I ignore my Earth mind's desire to look and see whether he is physically next to me by telling my inquiring mind there is no place else he can be right now. When I float back from those thoughts and rise up into my meditation, again, everything is changed. I can no longer discern the difference between the tree and the Universe. They are one enormous, fast flowing river of energy. Kim has become a brightly shining, distant star, a beacon calling to me silently.

The river of energy is the rock pattern Kim designed as his garden. The worldly version has his house in the middle. The garden isn't a landscape at all. It's a physical representation of the Universe.

There is no transition. One moment I am deep in Space, the next, I am in Washington on Capitol Hill, contemplating my brief time presenting to the Senate subcommittee. I have an increasing sense of satisfaction with my Senate performance. I was unaware, before meditating, of being dissatisfied. That's why I meditate; to flush out those deep, dark secrets so I can be free and whole.

Later in the day, I sit in sweat lodge ceremony with Charles. This is the debriefing I really looked forward to. This is for my soul, not my mind. I feel the tension ease out of my body as I sweat to the pounding of the drum. I find my own spirit return, strengthened. Having voyaged to the land of the lost, I am now returned and reinvigorated.

Charles has a beautiful voice and the two of us sing traditional songs, despite the wailing of emergency vehicle sirens in the outside world. On their account, I ask Charles to sing for the loss to the community. He is a wonderful connection to Spirit. We smoke several rounds of pipe, and remain in ceremony for a very long time. Charles understands my spiritual needs and willingly stays my course.

He leads us out of the lodge, similarly to the way he led us in.

At the doorway, he throws back the flap and calls out, "My Brother, prepare to receive the newborns."

As Charles leans forward to touch his forehead to the Mother, one last time, I glimpse our fire keeper, Hernando, put down a wood flute he is whittling by the smoldering fire some distance off. He grabs a couple towels and hurries to us.

A bedraggled Charles drags himself out, and Hernando covers Charles' head and shoulders with a towel, and then helps him up into his wheelchair.

I crawl around the Hoochka, the Sun, toward the Inipi entrance, all the time bearing Charles' prayer pipe. With both hands supporting it, respectfully, I hand it to Hernando to hold while I thank the Mother. Once standing, I receive the pipe back and hand it to Charles. As I accept the towel from Hernando, Charles takes the pipe apart and wraps it before stowing it in his medicine bag.

After a few minutes, our body temperatures have dropped to be closer to normal. We cast off our towels and allow Hernando to spray us thoroughly with the garden hose. For me this is a most precious ritual, to rinse in the aquifer water we all helped save.

Hernando brings us each a fresh towel to pat down with. In the late afternoon sun, our skimpy clothing for the ceremony dries off quickly. I wrap Charles in a blanket and another one for myself, and we sit up close to observe the dying embers of the life warming fire. Hernando returns with a bowl of food for each of us. Charles and I eat slowly, at first. It's been a long ceremony.

After an extended silence, I look up and understand that Hernando is following strict instructions from Charles. Why did Charles choose Hernando? He is a most unlikely candidate to be a fire keeper, to my mind. Then I flash on Cindy's party to announce giving the land for The Meteor. It was Hernando who dug the pit and managed the roasting of the pig. He was the fire keeper then, as he is now. That's why Charles had waited so long to perform ceremony with me after promising it when we first met. It took this long to train Hernando to make such an event possible. This is my spiritual journey and they are along to make it everything I want it to be. Such a gift has been given to me.

"Charles," I say. "I can only imagine I was brought here for your wisdom."

"And you for ours," he answers. "Spirit shares with all of us according to our skills. Is that right, my Brother?"

"Yes, my Brother," Hernando says, understanding he has passed a most important test.

Charles gives me space by deflecting the conversation.

"How is your flute coming along?" he asks Hernando.

Hernando holds it out for us to see. Charles has hidden nothing from his student.

"Show and tell," I say to Hernando. "Let's hear you play."

Hernando self consciously puts the flute to his lips. He is aware that he is being tested. He gives up his ego and creates haunting whistles of birds and flowing winds all magically appearing through the combination of his breath and fingers.

I put my bowl of food down on my lap and I rest with my eyes closed, dreaming of other trees of the same wood as the flute bending to the wind, grasses rippling like reflective currents.

Somewhere in that space everything disappears

silence

There's a rushing, clattering sound... lights flashing...

silence

As Hernando finishes playing, I see Charles checking me out.

"Are you OK?" he asks.

"I was being... transported... by the music," I tell them. "Thank you, Hernando. I am so impressed with how you have matured."

"You told me," he says. "I listened."

"And you studied," I say. "School is all around you. It never stops teaching so long as you are a willing student. Take our Brother Charles here. His body has seen many years but his mind is as agile now as it was the day he was born. We all of us have choice. It's simply a matter of what we do with it."

"Thank you, my Sister," Charles tells me. "I wish you Great Spirit's continued love and care on your journey."

He wheels his chair over to me and we hug. I feel his heart beat, his inhalation and exhalation. I sense tears streaming down his face. I realize we may be experiencing his journey to Great Spirit. I wait till he begins to release me before I let go.

At that moment, Shirley bursts into the yard, eyes rolling wildly.

"Come quickly, Judith!" she says. "There's been a fire. Kim's house burned to the ground."

I should be freaked out, but I am so calmed from the ceremony, I simply stand up, drop off the blanket and return the bowl to Hernando. Charles offers me a loving smile.

"All is as it should be," he tells me. "All is good."

I slide skin with Hernando.

Shirley grabs my hand and begins urgently pulling me toward the gate.

"You see the leaves on the trees in the forest," Charles calls after me. "You are a Chosen One!"

Shirley drags me by the hand down the alleyway and then we stumble along a sidewalk. Finally understanding she has my undivided, she lets go. We begin to long stride in tandem. Being individuated is much more efficient.

"We heard sirens during Ceremony," I say as we turn the corner to behold a scene of destruction.

An exhausted fire crew is finishing cleaning up, stowing equipment on trucks. On lookers are drifting away.

Arriving at the front yard, we can see that the house is almost entirely gone. It is possible to look across the front yard, its rock rivers polluted with burnt debris, over the charred remains of the house to the backyard tree, slightly singed, standing resolutely over the backyard river of rocks. The Universe is united, as Kim contemplated it, as it was in our last meditation.

"I hear the fire department believes it was arson," Shirley tells me nervously.

I am separating out of a reverie that I am dreaming what I am looking at. The anxiety in Shirley's voice brings me to ask the obvious question.

"What about Kim?" I ask her. "Is he OK?"

She looks at me as if I am supposed to know some big, dark secret.

"Seems he's disappeared," is all she says.

Now panic catches up with me. As my Earth mind takes charge, I become utterly distraught. I step onto the rock river toward the remains of the house, checking round. I pretend to swing the striker post at the bell. It's not there. A metal bell doesn't burn. There are no remains of the shelter or the thick post. Something doesn't... no, it does add up. I hear Charles' words to me.

"All is as it should be. All is good."

"Have you been home, yet?" I ask Shirley.

She shakes her head.

"I was teaching the kids when I heard it was Kim's house," she tells me. "I came right here. I talked to the Captain. She's the one told me they suspect arson. I recalled you were scheduled to be with Charles so I came got you."

"Let's go to the house," I say. "Maybe they heard word and know what's happening."

We set out walking in the direction of Sarah's house. Shirley grabs me by the wrist and spins me to face her.

"What do you mean by "know what's happening"?" she asks.

"Exactly that," I say.

"Well, I smell a rat," she tells me, pointedly. "How convenient is it that you are pulling an all-nighter with witnesses?"

"You read too many crime novels," I tell her. "I admit some things need more explanation before I jump to any conclusions."

Gradually relaxing, Shirley and I chatter as we stride to Sarah's beautifully finished, painted Lady. It was worth waiting to be last house on the block to be finished. Sarah ends up with one of two jewels in town; her house and Cindy's. I make a mental note to keep an eye on these wily, old ladies.

A white convertible sits on the driveway. Corazon is not a town for flashy cars, unless they are Low Riders. This is a car from a wholly other world. Sarah has visitors.

As we arrive at the house, a boy sits on the steps to the verandah pushing a one foot long piece of unfinished 2 by 4 like it's a car. He's happily in a world of his own making. He glances toward us as we reach the steps. I can't stop my mouth.

"Mika?" I ask.

He nods his head.

"Ungh-ungh," he says, returning to play make believe car.

"Where's your mom?" I ask.

Mika gestures toward the house.

"I'm Judith," I tell him.

"And she's Shirley," he says without looking up.

"Did someone... tell you?" Shirley asks, confused.

"Jude did," he says.

"When?" Shirley asks.

"She and I go way back," Mika says proudly.

"Are you telepathic, Mika?" I ask him.

"I'm all kinds," he says matter of fact. "Mom came to you for help."

"Did she ask for help at Taquinta?" I ask.

"I used them all up," he tells us. "It's kind of like we're looking for fresh meat."

"So eloquently stated," Shirley remarks.

"Hey," he comes back at her. "I mostly hung with adults. I speak my mind. That's all."

"Definitely your momma's boy," I comment out loud.

I turn to Shirley.

"Come meet Lucy," I say.

I ask Mika, "You coming, too?"

"Sure," he says, parking his wood car. "They're about as finished as they can be."

All three of us head for the door. I cannot resist giving Mika a quick hug and a squeeze. He's compliant, that combination of enjoying being loved and not wanting to display affection. It's definitely a male thing.

I hold back at the door, when it occurs to me I am running round town dressed in T shirt and shorts after almost 24 hours in lodge. All I have done for cleanup is to be hosed off. My hair is matted, and I know I smell of sweat lodge.

Eager for news about Kim and curious to learn who is the mother of this extraordinary child, Shirley charges in through the front door.

I hear Sarah playing host.

"This here's Shirley," she announces. "That Lucy."

Waves of tension from expectation and anticipation roar at me through the open door. Tired of waiting for me to enter, Mika cuts ahead and goes in.

Again the waves of energy rise, subsiding more quickly and transforming into loving pleasure. She's a good momma.

I hear their relationship.

"She'll be right in, mom," Mika tells Lucy.

"Thanks, honey," she says, appreciating his concern for her.

He offers protection for that gentle fragility Lucy feels obliged to safeguard with her wildly, over the top displays of bravura. All she has to do now is worry about how her birthed child is doing. That's a big leap for her. I can't wait to see what that looks like.

I finally quit struggling to make myself presentable and enter.

Again, I am aware of seeing the living room as if for the first time. As with the exterior, it is exquisitely finished, though the furniture is still all the same.

Lucy vaults from her seat and pulls me into a long Maori hug. This time, there are sparks. Two channels of energy go at, over, under, and round each other in a frantic search for satisfaction. We both want to know how the other is doing, how we are, what has happened, how we've changed and how we've grown in the interim. We have enough charge between us to power the annual electrical needs for the entire Bay Area.

We are both abundantly conscious that Lucy is still relatively powered by frenetic energy. She has acquired and mastered some tools. Up against what Kim has trained into me, I am a vast, still lake which she plows into like a—crashing meteor. I receive her without judgment. We come together in peace, unbelievably glad to have reunited with one another.

When we part foreheads, eyes searching for last details like a final sweep of the floor, we stay holding each other by the shoulders exploring the physical.

"Yer lookin' great, Jude," Lucy tells me, smiling.

She wrinkles her nose.

"Ceremony?" she asks.

I pull away from her, admiring how fresh and young she still looks.

"I need to shower," I tell her. "Mika? Wow!"

Heading for the stairs, I catch a glance of a brave faced, dejected Shirley. She knows she is no competition to vie with Lucy for my attention.

Mika sits between Bebe and Maria demonstrating on his laptop. They strain to keep up with what he is explaining.

I catch a concerned look on Lucy's face. I give her the thumbs up as I point to Mika. Lucy struggles to reflect back pride. It's hard won.

Sarah's backyard is festooned with round, white, hanging, oriental paper lamps. Wrapped in each other's arms, Sarah and Ray sit on a sofa. Shirley, Lucy and I sit in big, stuffed chairs. Maria and Bebe sit on a swing bench in the shadows. Asleep, Mika lies across my lap and in my arms.

"He feels the same, only bigger," I tell Lucy. "I can feel his personality, you know?"

Almost as a cautionary warning, Lucy tells me, "He still listens, even in his sleep."

Shirley has listened quietly all evening. She can't contain her concerns, anymore.

"He's a child, Lucy," she tells her. "Does he get enough sleep?"

"He's all energy," Lucy tells us. "Taquinta was great. They totally gave him the run of the place. If he got out of line, everyone was empowered to curb him over-steppin' bounds of acceptable reason. He had a ball. Everyone took turns teachin' him anythin' an' everythin'. He has talents we're unable to teach him how to use. In the end, though, final responsibility always fell to me. I'm so tired, Jude."

"Did you hold council?" I ask.

"For sure," Lucy tells me. "Everyone agreed I had to do somethin'. They was beginnin' to be more like arguments then discussin'.

"'Bout week ago, we were in the middle of a real knock down session when Sidney showed up, all excited babblin' a mile a minute. La mujer joven hermosa, Judee, está en la TV! Sabemos donde ella vive—Corazón, California!

"Usted habla español mucho bueno," Shirley tells her. "She does. She has an almost flawless accent."

"Thanks," says Lucy. "Maisha's like freakin' out sayin', Sidney, slow down. What's that about Judith? Is that our Judith? And Sidney is sayin', Judee on tele-vizion. She live in California, in place call 'Eart.

"We spent hours searchin' for Heart. A day later Maisha got a sweet note from Senator Jackie Poll about yer. The council determined I bring Mika to yer for a while."

"Why me?" I ask.

Mika stirs.

Without opening his eyes, he speaks, "You are a Chosen One."

"That's what Charles said, today," I tell everyone because of the coincidence.

Mika continues, "We leave, tomorrow."

This is becoming too unreal even for me. I raise one hand off of Mika and wave to Lucy to come take him. She holds up a hand, palm facing me as if to stop traffic.

"I just got through 'splainin'!" she states. "I'm done bein' the last resort."

"If Kim were here," I tell her pointing to Mika. "He'd be perfect. Do we take him literally?"

"Thin's go smooth when you do," she says. "Buckin' him can be a real pain."

I find myself reflecting back to that final conversation with Charles when he told me, "You see the leaves on the trees in the forest." There sure is no forest here. Then I look at Mika on my lap. He has that audacious smile of someone being caught out doing something naughty but thrilled with the result. I am becoming his ventriloquist's dummy.

"I feel complete with Corazon," I announce. "Perhaps leaving is for the best."

"Yes," Mika says. "Travel light, travel further."

Shirley giggles. Mika is a whole other educational need about which she knows next to nothing.

Sarah sits speechless. Ray gives her a side on hug; they cling to each other.

Speaking of deep friendships, this is the dénouement I would prefer not to have to deal with.

"I want to go with you," Shirley declares.

My ventriloquist has the perfect answer.

"You'd leave the kids, now?" I ask.

I reach out a hand to comfort a saddened Shirley. Unable to restrain herself, she looks at Lucy with what I can only define as an admission of surrender. I am proud of her for doing that.

Inside, I deeply feel her hurt as I watch tears roll down her cheeks

DAY SEVEN

ON THE ROAD AGAIN

Even at such short notice, about the entire town turns out for my send off.

Lucy and Mika ride up front in her white, top down convertible as we cruise slowly along Main Street. Like a parade queen, I perch on the center, back seat arm rest waving to the townspeople lining the sidewalks.

Mika joins the ubiquitous Smart phone camera club to document The Meteor when we pass by it.

Intuitively understanding this may be the last time, it is heart wrenchingly saddening for me to see all those salient faces: Special Folk, Charles, Hernando and Cindy, Vladimir, Dr. Hyde, Supervisor Blake, Andrea, Jose, Maria and Bebe, Lizbet on one side of Carl, Shirley on the other, Sarah and Ray, Leticia and Saffron, Mung and the former gang kids.

Jose organized for a squad of Low Riders to drive toward us horns blaring as they pass on either side of Lucy's car, each performing a variation of motion specialties including front end rising and lowering, rolls to both sides and hops.

Lucy drives on the highway with the roof up. From the front passenger seat, I turn to her.

"What amazes me," I tell her, "Is that of all the people, Sidney is the one watching C SPAN."

Lucy gives me a serious glance.

"For all her whacky behavior," she says, "She is a well brought up young lady. She keeps up with business."

"On C SPAN?" I ask.

"Sure," she says. "Politics is the sport of the elite; sports are the politics of the public."

I passively observe passing mile markers while I meditate on that nugget.

For the longest time, Mika has been in the back quietly working on his laptop.

"So Mika," I ask him, "Where're we going?"

"Headwaters of the Missouri River," he tells me without missing a beat.

"Montana!" Lucy calls out. "He's been workin' on this for a while. Well, I'll be."

"Any special reason?" I ask.

"Right now," Mika says, "The headwaters' energy is scattered. You are to lead prayers there—prayers of Love, Thanks and Respect to Water. Your prayers will change the water at its source. That will change the river, which, in turn, will change the country. You are Change Bearer. As America grows healthy, so can the world."

That's a mouthful for anyone, never mind a five year old. I turn to Lucy to ask. She beats me to it.

"Yer think he's kiddin' yer?" she says. "Mister Mika, tell Jude who we're gonna visit."

I hope she will forgive me, but my worst fear is that Sidney is waiting at the end of this road trip.

Mika says not a word. He is obviously waiting for me to clear my mind before he speaks. I vacate and go empty.

"Song Cho Kim," Mika tells me.

I stare at Mika, dumbfounded. The possibility that he is pulling a cruel joke is not realistic. How does he know of Kim? How does he know where Kim is located?

"How do you know about Kim?" I ask.

"Kim yer beau, Jude?" Lucy inquires with a whole lot of probing waiting on the back end.

Rankled, I tell her, "I'd like an answer from Mika, first."

"Sure, Jude," she says. "We're barely half way thru Cali-for-nai-ey. Kick back an' relax, girlfriend. We're together fer a long ride. 'Sides, Mika's unable to hide the truth. Much as 'times I wish he would."

I turn back to face Mika.

"So tell me," I ask.

He places his laptop on the seat beside him and turns his sea green eyes fully in my direction.

"Mom wanted to know where you are, right?" he says. "So I opened a channel seeking contacts in or near Corazon, California."

"On the internet," I say. "Social media?"

"That's for amateurs," he says.

"See what I mean?" says Lucy. "Blunt as a hammer an' twice as effective. That's my boy."

"Well, then," I ask. "How?"

"Meditalepathy," he says. "That's what I call it. I meditate on what I want and beam it out there. Kim was meditating and we made contact. He said you were beginning to learn how to do it."

"He did, did he?" I ask. "How?"

This ought to separate the men from the boys.

"You asked to be grounded while in Washington, D.C." he tells me. "Kim sent you an image of a tree right back."

"Whatever happened to secrets?" I ask recoiling in shock.

"Oh, yes," he says. "Compared to who reads your private internet activity."

"I thought the meditation was private," I say, very hurt.

"It is," Mika tells me. "Kim told me to tell you this, so you will accept other things he may want you to know."

"Why does he send through you?" I ask. "When he can send to me directly?"

“Because I am a stronger medium,” Mika says. “It’s a question of efficiency.”

“OK?” asks Lucy.

“I guess,” I say.

“You’re hurt,” Mika says. "Understand that it’s only business.”

“Sure,” I say. “Let me tap on it. That will help.”

“Yer right,” says Lucy. “An’ when yer done doin’ EFT, yer can tell me all ‘bout yer Mister Kim. I want yer ter spill the beans.”

“What about young ears?” I ask her.

“Yer know the women at Taquinta,” she says. “They can hang real loose an’ he heard thin’s as would shock a sailor. Yer gonna tell Auntie Lucy ev’ry last, juicy morsel.”

Who knows why, but I do. I tell Lucy things that still shock me. And how time flies. As a result, she tells me about Mika’s dad. Every so often, Mika butts in and corrects statements and plot points. Not only has he heard it all before, but, during his meditations, he has talked to people familiar with the situation in which Lucy, nee Betsy, found herself. She takes it all in good sport. Frankly, I would be embarrassed to have the world know some of what transpired, never mind my five year old. Lucy sees no problem with Mika knowing every last detail.

“He’s mature fer his age,” she says, “Because we talk ter him honestly. He holds what he wants an’ lets the rest go. That’s fine wi’ me.”

At one point, Lucy is driving, concentrating on the road as we ride through some incredible canyons. Mika is busy on his computer.

I decide to run a test. I hold up my hand with my Chromate Sapphire ring facing me. All around my hand is the incredible canyon. I send it to Kim. As I finish sending it, I receive a vision of a clear glass dipping into a stream and the water being poured over what could only be a brass bell. I turn my hand sideways and send an image of one hand clapping. I instantly receive an image back of his opposite hand also clapping.

What is the sound of two hands clapping? Love.

I turn around to see if Mika got any of the transmissions.

Without looking up from his computer to acknowledge that he knows I am looking at him, he says, "Kim sends his love."

"Thank you, Mika," I tell him. "Please send my love to Kim."

"OK," he says. "Message sent... gratefully received."

"Thank you," I say.

"You're welcome," he replies.

The entire dialogue, three way really, is conducted with Mika engrossed in his laptop.

As if confirming her beliefs, Lucy pats my knee and says, "See?"

I don't, but I do let it rest. I don't wish to go down in history as trying to prove, beyond all reasonable doubt, that Mika does, in fact, intercept all transmissions. Let's face it, I don't know whether Kim is even in Mika's league.

I can see the headline, now—FAMILY HELD HOSTAGE BY TELELPATHIC 5 YEAR OLD.

Finally, reason starts to kick in. Other than reading our thoughts, how is Mika holding us hostage? I decide to do like Lucy, allow him access to all information and also give him the benefit of the doubt.

Then, it dawns on me: how do I even know which of all this is my own thoughts?

Really time to let go!

Despite my repeated mental questioning asking an un verbalized, "Are you absolutely certain?" Mika turned out to be better than my telephone GPS lady.

Mika coordinates with Kim for directions and we end up in a remote section of the mountains in Montana by a pristine, running stream in densely wooded country, miles from civilization, with Kim.

For the first time ever, though in plain view of Lucy and Mika, Kim abandons his oriental reserve and sweeps me up off my feet in a swirling hug as he spins and dances with me.

Or as Lucy says, "I think he likes yer."

We live in a cozy log cabin. It's pretty intimate, but I don't care anymore.

As Kim put it to me that first day, pointing to Mika, "You give me son."

I am speechless. My head takes off like a rocket while I struggle to put all the pieces together. I have to stop myself. So what?

Kim's thoughts are in my head, too.

"Indeed!" he communicates.

He and "our son" are perfectly matched. Lucy is thrilled. There is now a male influence for her son from a grounded, well balanced man, who plays electronic keyboard—"Pick up on way"—and happily teaches all of us anything that he knows.

Lucy and I covered our ground work of close proximity living when we built our dome house.

The cabin is off the grid with combined solar and wind charging embedded batteries plus geothermal exchange for heating and A/C. While he waited for us to join him, Kim prepped a garden for me to plant. He also dug out a cache in which to store our food, similar to local Native American custom, to take us through the winter.

Our respective duties are delineated, and, surprisingly, acceptable to all. Lucy is in charge of the house and shares food prep with Kim and Mika. I tend the garden, growing food and, each day, pray for the water. When not helping with food prep, Kim and Mika play; they hunt, fish, meditate, play the keyboard, commune with Spirit and do repairs and construction.

To strengthen Mika, Kim has him push the striker for the bell. It may take a year or two before Mika is strong enough to ring the bell.

Two days after we arrive, right before all of us, except Lucy, are due to rise to meditate, the bell is struck once, firmly. Kim is in bed with me. Lucy, for sure, is asleep. Mika sits on the side of his bed having a good stretch.

"Someone is here," I whisper to Kim.

He smiles.

"Son call teacher," he says.

I look. Mika is getting dressed.

"Mika is inside," I say.

"Mind stronger than body," Kim tells me.

I check one more time. Mika has that audacious smile he showed me while he lay in my lap out in Sarah's backyard when we established who is the ventriloquist and who is the dummy.

Ten times each day, at regular intervals, I kneel on a rug with the Hopi pattern of a circle divided in four by two lines. In each quadrant is a circle. I draw water in a glass from the stream and place the filled glass on a crude, wooden altar. I cup my hands around the glass without touching it.

I stay that way until my palms can feel the warmth of the energy bouncing back and forth between my hands, usually within a few moments to a minute or so. I keep the prayer simple so my intention is clear.

"I offer my Love, my Thanks and my Respect to the water," I say out loud.

When I offer Love, I feel that from my heart. When I offer Thanks, I feel that from my belly. When I offer Respect, I feel that from my head.

I typically wait a minute or so after praying to transfer as much of my energy as possible into the glass of water. Then, I pick up the glass and gently empty it back into the stream.

As I release it, I imagine the energized water tumbling and spreading to mix and mingle with the surrounding water, passing along my offerings as the stream merges with other streams to find the Missouri River and on to join the Mississippi River. All that wide, deep body of water is changed in energy, one glass at a time, to impact all the water.

Each time I visit the stream I offer my blessings with five glassfuls of water. That's my choice.

I like to think there are other people blessing the waters of the world, respecting a commodity that is constant, and used to flush every living organism, bring life to the one legged plants which in turn give life to the creepy crawlies, the winged, the four legged and the two legged, over and over, every day without fail.

My blessing is tiny by comparison to the work done by water.

I love to see my ring stone flash in the sunlight. It reminds me of how far I have come and strengthens my resolve as I bless the water. Such an honor is mine to give part of my day to something most of us tend to take for granted.

About once every two days, now:

silence

There's a rushing, clattering sound... lights flashing...

silence

Each time, the noise is incrementally louder and the lights that much brighter.

When the occurrences begin to happen daily, I relent and tell Kim. He calls a family council.

He is very loving when he tells me I am beyond his care or that of Mika.

"The two of you, together?" I ask.

He shakes his head.

"Reason, here," he explains, "Make peaceful for you. End of line."

He did this all for me; hooked me back up with my soul sister, Lucy, and her Indigo child, in this, the most luxurious retreat imaginable. He and I, together in love, are here to give back to Life in the gentlest way possible.

"What happens when I go?" I ask.

He indicates the four of us.

"All go," he says.

I look at Lucy, barely in her mid 20s and Mika, only 5 years old.

"Do they have to?" I ask.

"You go, we go," he says. "Dreamer wake up, dream over. That life."

"Is that OK with you guys?" I ask Lucy and Mika.

Mika becomes silent, very still.

Lucy waxes philosophical.

"We are here 'cause of yer," she tells me. "When yer go, we have to go. We are yet."

For the first time, I don't want to be lucid so I can cut them free. Why should I dictate to such lovely people when they will come and go?

"*Because we are you,*" Mika talks inside my head. "*As you change, your dreams change. Where you are now is your perfection of Dream/Life. This is as good as...*"

silence

There's a rushing, clattering sound... lights flashing...

I wait for the next silence, but it doesn't come.

People are approaching me, talking.

I hear voices that I recognize.

My eyes are tight shut.

I hear the people stop right by me.

"This job requires confidence," Michael says. "People you meet in this line of work expect you to know the answers. Take this one."

"This... Woman?" Rachel asks.

"What is she?" Michael says. "She's a bottom feeder, scourge of the city, an embarrassment to her family, a drag on society, a complete and utter nobody. People like this are so much trouble. Good riddance, I say. She would never have amounted to anything. What a wretch. Go ahead prod her with your nightstick. Make sure she's dead."

"Get real!" Rachel squeals. "Me? How?"

I hear that familiar "pop" sound of someone operating a Smart phone.

"Send paramedics to meet us at Bleecker Street," Michael says. "A single. My guess? Diabetic heart failure."

There's a cup in my right hand. Judging by the weight, it's about half full.

I feel gross. My clothes feel sticky. Something is resting on my lap. My left hand index finger is in something gooey. Is it a donut? My elbows roll over full plastic bags as the train races along.

The way these two people talk leads me to think they're transit cops.

"Go on," Michael says. "Prod her."

"We'll back you up," says Ariel.

They're here! All three of them are here. We're starting over!

"Do I say anything?" Rachel asks.

I can literally feel Michael grin as Ariel answers with a coarse cackle of a laugh.

"Lady," Ariel says to me. "Are you dead?"

"What if she's deaf?" Rachel asks.

"Oh, yeah," Michael says. "Then you shout, Hey! *It's Time to Wake Up*!"

The train brakes sharply, causing Rachel to lose her balance. She falls forwards and, with her nightstick, prods me hard in the upper left arm. I fall to the floor, giving out a long slow gasp.

DAY EIGHT

POSTSCRIPT

JUDITH FARGOE: DEAD AT AGE 12

WIRESERVICE, Detroit, MI—Pre teen, Judith Fargoc, 12, who was seriously injured in a highway accident seven days ago, died today in the ICU at Pointe General Hospital, Detroit, MI.

Present at the moment of Judith's demise were hospital physicians and nursing staff plus Mika Auchin, 5, and his mother, Betsy Auchin, 24.

The center of a worldwide controversy followed by tens of millions of people, Mika is the source of the blog which, he claims, was dictated to him by Judith Fargoe using telepathy from her hospital bed.

Judith was orphaned, last week, in a car accident when her father mistakenly drove the family car down an off ramp onto an oncoming heavily trafficked highway. Driving in the wrong direction in the passing lane, their car was struck head on by a truck.

George Fargoe, 38, and Ethel Fargoe, 35, Judith's parents, were instantly killed by the collision's impact.

Judith, who was riding behind her parents on the car's backseat, suffered a concussion as well as massive contusions to her body, according to a hospital news release.

By twitching the finger wearing a child's ring, Judith reflected sunlight that attracted attending fire department personnel's attention to her. That led to her rescue from the wrecked car.

At the same time as Judith Fargoe was being transported by ambulance to Pointe General Hospital, mother and son Auchin were traveling east on that highway from their home in Montana making their way to visit her parents in Virginia.

Mika claims that, as the ambulance carrying Judith Fargoe to Pointe General Hospital passed by them, he received the equivalent of a telepathic SOS from Judith Fargoe. Mika requested his mother follow the ambulance.

In what a hospital spokesperson described as "a series of bizarre circumstances," Mika rapidly convinced attending ER physicians that he was in full communications with the comatose patient, Judith Fargoe. In a briefly worded statement to the media, the hospital said that Mika described "with uncanny detail" where Judith was in the hospital and "other matters" that led the hospital administration to agree to his proposed blog to tell the world what Judith "requested to dictate to him."

Judith's dictation was recorded by Mika repeating her telepathic words into voice recognition software on his laptop. Betsy edited her son's transcription and then sent out the results as a daily blog.

Up until the moment of Judith's death, Mika and Betsy Auchin were not allowed to visit Judith Fargoe. For the past week, Mika and his mother occupied a private hospital suite, paid for by Ms. Auchin's parents.

The blog resulted in a remarkable story for a 12 year old.

It is conjectured that the story comprises Judith's imaginings how life may be for her if she survived to age 33.

Within two days of going online, the blog went viral around the world, read daily by millions of people.

A day of mourning has been requested by populaces of several countries in recognition of Judith Fargoe's passing.

Here, in the USA, politicians are also becoming involved. Senator Jackie Poll (D DE) added an amendment to the Highway Bill, currently making its way through the Senate, for rumble strips to be installed on all federal highway off ramps as an additional warning device. Capitol Hill media has nicknamed this the Judith Fargoe Amendment.

Caught up in a tight race to retain her seat, Senator Poll's leading competitor, Rep. Jerome Mitchell (R DE), accused Poll of emotional grandstanding using an accident victim to aid her political career. Poll called Mitchell's accusation, "sour grapes."

Betsy Auchin's parents, Al and Babs Auchin, a retired couple, have arranged to reimburse the hospital for Judith Fargoe's care as well as to pay all funeral expenses.

The Auchin family invites those members of the public wishing to honor Judith Fargoe to donate to their favorite charity in her name.

—30—

The End

><

COMING SOON!

><

Volume Two of the *Dreamers Trilogy*

I
AM
MIKA:
Loss of Innocence

><

www.DreamersTrilogy.com

ADDITIONAL STORY RESOURCES

WEB SITES

www.schwartzreport.net	Trending current information
www. calearth.org	Taquinta houses
www.mattfurey.com/index.htm	Combat conditioning - fitness

MOVIES

Joseph Campbell: Mythos

American Experience: Eleanor Roosevelt

ISHI, the Last Yahi

Queen of the Sun

BOOKS

Sugar Blues by William Duffy

GENERAL TOPICS

Dowsing Tree of Life Togu Na Kabbalah Tarot Lysistrata Meditation Fohat OWS Water Birth Quantum Physics Remote Viewing Crystals Credit Union Telepathy Feudal Shamanic Journey EFT Taxes Spoon Bending Biodynamic Water Wars Cargo Cult Tantric Lucid Dreaming Vision Quest Community Candida Money Dream Time Akashic Record Tuva

CHECK the front of the book for STORY RESOURCES

ABOUT THE AUTHOR

Emanuel Culman, at age 26, arrived in North America from England where he was a rock n roll singer/musician, photographer and Arts Lab Director. He has written on theater, travel and politics for national newspapers and co-art directed a feature film. While owning an art gallery, he took two of his artists as Artistas Convidads (invited artists) to the '86 Sao Paulo Bienal. He hosted and co-produced a television series, *Changes*, and, currently owns a movie theater. Emanuel lives with his wife in North Dakota.

Made in the USA
Charleston, SC
06 June 2014